Praise for Sandra Byrd

"Sandra Byrd's novels draw me in, hol[...]
I even realize it, I am changed in my o[...]
the story she has written. *Heirlooms* is [...]
connects and weaves change and hope into your heart."

ANNIE F. DOWNS, *New York Times* bestselling author of *That Sounds Fun*

"With the enchanting Puget Sound as a backdrop, Sandra Byrd deftly explores the meaning of family, the great power of love, and the intrinsic worth of each one of us. Here is a compelling story that underscores why we treasure the past and value its echoes. I loved it!"

SUSAN MEISSNER, bestselling author of *The Nature of Fragile Things*

"Byrd's riveting intergenerational story of mystery, culture, romance, and hope demonstrates God's hand in families and his expert care for each aspect of their lives. As a Korean American, I connected to the Korean cultural details and characters."

TINA CHO, author of *The Ocean Calls: A Haenyeo Mermaid Story*

"*Heirlooms* is one of those beautifully written novels that you'll want to savor with a mug of hot tea, relishing the gardens on Whidbey Island and every morsel of wisdom passed down through the generations. Sandra Byrd's past and present-day characters are full of heart and courage as secrets slowly unfold and friendships are restored. Like the sweetness of *son-mat* in her story, *Heirlooms* was crafted with great care and creativity in Sandra's hands. An absolute delight to read!"

MELANIE DOBSON, award-winning author of *The Winter Rose* and *Catching the Wind*

"A poignant exploration of the ties that bind us through family and friendship, *Heirlooms* has it all—secrets, romance, mystery, recipes, a lovely island setting, and far more. At its heart, this unique, well-researched novel is about the legacy we leave moment by moment, day by day, heirlooms that are both timeless and beautiful, if we are willing to embrace the best of the life we've been given and gift others along the way."

LAURA FRANTZ, Christy Award–winning author of *A Heart Adrift*

"*Heirlooms* is the kind of story that begs readers to linger. I loved the attention to detail in the historical story line and felt fully transported to Helen and Eunhee's world, and the modern-day story was equal parts intrigue and charm. From secrets uncovered to relationships gently explored, the richness and depth in this story is meant to be savored. Sandra Byrd delivers a poignant, beautiful read!"

MELISSA TAGG, *USA Today* bestselling, Christy Award–winning author

"Thoughtful, poignant, and so sharply written you can smell the sun-warmed strawberries, *Heirlooms* honors friendships that transcend culture and family bonds that transcend time. Sandra Byrd's memorable characters remind us that we are forged by the lives of generations past and called to plant seeds of hope for the future."

STEPHANIE LANDSEM, author of *In a Far-Off Land*

HEIRLOOMS

a novel

HEIRLOOMS

Sandra Byrd

Tyndale House Publishers
Carol Stream, Illinois

Visit Tyndale online at tyndale.com.

Visit Sandra Byrd's website at sandrabyrd.com.

Tyndale and Tyndale's quill logo are registered trademarks of Tyndale House Ministries.

Heirlooms

Cover designed by Faceout Studios, Jeff Miller

Edited by Sarah Mason Rische

Published in association with the literary agency of Browne & Miller Literary Associates, LLC, 52 Village Place, Hinsdale, IL 60521

For information about special discounts for bulk purchases, please contact Tyndale House Publishers at csresponse@tyndale.com, or call 1-855-277-9400.

Library of Congress Cataloging-in-Publication Data

A catalog record for this book is available from the Library of Congress.

ISBN 978-1-4964-2687-1 (HC)
ISBN 978-1-4964-2688-8 (SC)

Printed in the United States of America

28	27	26	25	24	23	22
7	6	5	4	3	2	1

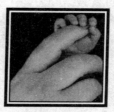

For Mirabelle

Mimi's little French plum. I love you.

Helen

CHAPTER ONE

March 1958

Helen Devries carefully removed her nurse's cap, fluffing her platinum back-combed bouffant, crackling the Aqua Net lacquering it in place. On the television in the back of the living room, Elvis offered a flirty smile and almost wink as he was measured for his uniform.

"You're in the Army now, young man. Good for you. I hope serving your country won't take your life." She turned up the volume against the evening's emptiness just before the phone startled awake, eclipsing the low hum of the TV.

She was rarely invited to the party line.

Two short rings and one long requested Johanna Jansen, the Dutch woman on the farm behind hers. Four short bursts summoned the old man with the chickens whose cackles sounded like giggles or moans. Three short, one long reached out to her supervisor, Captain Adams, and his icy wife.

Two long rings, three short.

Helen hesitantly moved toward the phone. It sat upon a small table next to the window overlooking the unused canning shed, set in a field sleepy with wet weeds splayed against the ground like closed eyelashes. Licorice rope phone lines stretched toward the farmhouse. Four birds convened on the line, silhouetted by the outdoor lights she'd had installed for safety.

Two long rings, three short.

One bird cocked his head and looked directly at her. *Are you going to answer?*

Helen reached for the receiver. "Hello?"

"Hello. Is this Mrs. Helen Devries?" a lady's voice queried, her tone undergirded by strain and slightly nasal, as if spoken by someone who'd been crying. "The wife of Lieutenant Bob Devries?"

"Yes, this is Mrs. Helen Devries."

"I am sorry to bother you at this hour. I am Choi Eunhee. Wife of Chief James Roy."

Helen shuffled through her memories. "Hello, Mrs. Roy. Am I right to think that your husband served with my husband?"

"Yes. In South Korea, where I am from and where we married. My husband told me that he served many years with your husband and that if I were ever in trouble, I should contact him, as he would help me."

Helen's fatigue lifted and the sound of the news in the background faded. "Are you in trouble?"

"Yes."

Helen steadied herself. "I'm honored that Chief Roy thinks so highly of my husband. But my husband can't help you. He was killed two years ago."

"My husband is also dead." Silence bled into the white space of the moment, and then she continued, "They whisper that I helped kill him. That I might help kill them, too."

A gasp wheezed across the party line. Helen lit a cigarette to calm herself. After inhaling and then resting it on a hammered silver ashtray, she said, "Our phones out here are all on party lines. There is the possibility that others are listening."

"Ah. I see." Distress colored Mrs. Roy's voice.

A moment elapsed before Helen spoke again. "How can I help?" Bob would want her to help the wife of his old friend and comrade.

"Could we speak in private?"

Helen nudged the cigarette and a long pencil of ash fell freely into the tray before she put the hotter, shortened smoke to her lips. She could certainly offer advice, comfort, and occasional companionship as the widow made her way through the system. Maybe Helen would invite her for coffee and to chat once in a while until Mrs. Roy left the base for good, as most widows did.

Unless Choi Eunhee was detained, of course, for involvement in her husband's death.

"Yes, we can do that. I'll help however I can." Even as she said it, Helen sensed she'd committed to something far deeper than coffee and companionship.

Mrs. Roy told her where she was currently living—on base, in a tiny compound with other enlisted personnel and their wives with little privacy and no car—so they agreed Helen would pick her up the next day and bring her to her home.

After Mrs. Roy hung up, Helen stayed on the line for a moment, listening. A baby cried. A rough male voice barked, "Foreigners!" followed by an abrupt click. A third line was set down gently, as if to deceive.

As Helen set the heavy receiver atop the black rotary dial and looked out the window, the last bird lifted from the licorice line and flew into the night.

* * *

The morning kettle sang, and when Helen added water to the Folger's in her mug, the crystals dissolved into the magic black water that would power her through her shift.

Locking up, she headed for Bob's car.

It's not Bob's car, she reminded herself. *It's your car now. Your house. Your land.*

On the way to work, she passed the complaining chickens and the old man tending to them with a bucket of food scraps. He looked up but didn't wave.

Twenty minutes later, Helen was in Oak Harbor, pulling through security and parking just outside the hospital that served the Navy. Truly, except for small maternity "hospitals" run by owner-nurses and midwives, there was little medical care on the entire island, and she knew she was lucky to have her job. She couldn't bring herself to work at the maternity hospitals, nurturing women about to have the beautiful babies Helen longed for. *Empty womb, yearning heart.*

Once parked, Helen grabbed her purse and made sure her nurse's cap and pin were straight. As she headed toward the building, someone got out of a parked car near her. "Mrs. Devries?"

Helen turned. Oh, dear, it was the boss's wife. "Hello, Mrs. Adams. I'm surprised to see you here. Visiting the captain?" Even as she asked, Helen knew it was not very likely. Mrs. Adams only showed up to meddle.

"Oh, you know. I like to make sure things stay straight and true." Mrs. Adams's dark hair was fashionably styled to look like Elizabeth Taylor's, but her eyes were brown, not violet blue, and rimmed with dull shadows. "Keeping busy?"

Helen resisted the urge to look at her wristwatch. She was going to be late. "Yes, of course. The hospital takes much of my time."

"I'm sure." Mrs. Adams smiled tightly. "You must have friends over for coffee or luncheons as well. Or after work."

Was she fishing for an invitation?

Helen shook her head. "Not often."

Mrs. Adams's face grew firm, and her pancake makeup

creased but did not relax when her smile fled. "This is a Navy town—and a Navy hospital—and we must remain within naval protocol. Officers' wives don't fraternize."

Three short, one long was the Adams's ring code, not two long, three short. But etiquette was apparently for those beneath her, and eavesdropping was okay. Mrs. Adams had heard Helen invite Chief Roy's wife—an enlisted man's wife—to her home.

As Helen nodded curtly, Mrs. Adams reached into her patent handbag, withdrew a poodle key chain, and then drove away. Apparently the only purpose of this trip had been to ambush Helen.

Helen bustled in the hospital corridors as the lone civilian nurse at Naval Air Station Whidbey Island, caring for Naval personnel and their dependents in a way no one had been able to do for her husband as he met his icy death. Broken bones and bandages. Between Helen, the physicians she helped, the Navy nurse, and the corpsmen who worked with them, there were busy days but filled with care, camaraderie, and mutual respect.

After her shift, Helen started the lido-green Buick Skylark, its top as smooth and white as a bald eagle, and drove to pick up Mrs. Roy. Sure enough, she stood outside in the rain, the only Asian lady in sight. Her face looked drawn and tired, confused, as Helen's had been in the months after Bob's death.

"Mrs. Roy?" She rolled down the window. "I'm Mrs. Devries." She reached across the bench and opened the door from the inside. "Please call me Helen."

The woman settled herself on the bench, and Helen started the car.

"Please call me Eunhee," the woman said.

"Not Choi Eunhee?"

"Choi is my surname, and Eunhee is my first name. In Korea women do not, traditionally, take their husbands' surnames. When Korean women marry American men, they follow the American custom. So here I will be known as Mrs. Roy, though I feel like Choi Eunhee still."

"Eunhee it is. We'll be at my home in a few minutes. You can tell me your story, and we can find a way to help you."

They remained awkwardly silent for the remaining ten minutes' drive. When they pulled up, Eunhee said, "What a nice house! And a nice garden—well . . ." She glanced at the bramble and bush and tumble and weeds. The roses on the arbor struggled to emerge from clouds of dead foliage hanging on from years past. "Could be someday, anyway."

Helen laughed out loud. "Yes, it needs some work. I don't know how to garden. I'd planned to learn with Bob—Lieutenant Devries—but then . . ."

Eunhee patted the back of Helen's hand. "I understand. I understand, like most people do not."

In that instant, they became friends.

They walked through the kitchen and into the living room. "Please," Helen encouraged. "Make yourself comfortable in any chair and then tell me what happened."

"We have been here for about eight months," Eunhee said. "Coming from the base in Korea. My husband shared many stories of your husband and what a good man he is. Was. And said if I needed help, I should ask him. I did know that your husband—I am very sorry—died in a training accident." She looked at Helen with compassion through tired eyes. "But when trouble arrived, I had no one else to call."

Helen leaned forward reassuringly. "What trouble?"

"My husband, Chief James Roy, died."

Helen nodded and let her continue.

"He died of the flu in the field hospital on base," she continued. "I buried him at Sunnyside Cemetery three days later."

There had been a huge, but waning, outbreak of the Asian flu on base. The sick were isolated in field hospitals three stories high because of their sheer number and to protect them from transmitting the virus to others, though it had quickly spread, and several men had died. "I'm terribly sorry to hear of this loss, but how can people blame you . . . say you helped to kill him?"

Eunhee shrugged. "I am Korean. This flu is called the Asian flu. So when people get sick, they blame Asian persons. I am not sick. I have not been to Korea for eight months. But still, they whisper and point and speak rudely, accusing me."

Helen reached out and cupped Eunhee's hand. "I am very sorry. You have lost your husband, and now you are told you are to blame by awful, ill-informed people."

She nodded. "I am supposed to have thirty days more to move off of base after my husband's death, but the people at my housing want me to leave now so they do not catch it from me. I have looked for apartments to stay in until I can return to my home—Korea—but there is nothing. This is why I have called you. Can you help me find an apartment until I can return to my parents in a month or two?"

"Have you called any apartments in Oak Harbor?"

"Yes, as many as I can. I do not have a car and cannot drive anyway, so I took the bus and then walked. I thought maybe you might know someone who could help."

"Have you asked the chaplain?"

"He says he cannot help me."

He says. Eunhee was too polite to say it aloud, but she clearly did not believe that he was willing to help.

"May I use your bathroom?" Eunhee smiled through her fatigue.

"Oh yes!" Helen showed her the way and then returned to the living room. How could she help? Did she know anyone to contact? Not really. She'd been out of touch with the military while finishing up nursing school, and it was, after all, only Bob's hero's death status and his passing friendship with Captain Adams that had allowed Helen to get her job on base.

She suddenly realized that nearly ten minutes had gone by, but Eunhee had not returned. She got up and headed toward the bathroom but found her, instead, admiring the sewing machine in the teal bedroom.

"You sew?" Eunhee asked.

Helen laughed. "No, my mother wanted me to, but I was

never very good. I can sew up a wound if required, though. Do you sew?"

"Oh yes," Eunhee said. She swayed a little, and her face looked pale.

Feverish . . . flu? Helen could hardly touch her forehead to check. "Here, sit down on the bed," she said, nurse kicking in. She, of anyone, knew the strain a new widow felt, and she had not been accused of contributing to Bob's death. "Let me make a sandwich for you, and I'll bring it in." A few minutes later, she brought a tuna sandwich into the room. Eunhee stood but once again swayed a bit.

"No need to stand up. Just eat it right here." Helen patted the bed. "My husband spoke fondly of your husband. He admired him and counted him as a friend. He told me Chief always had a song for the day, and the entire crew would sing it on the plane during the long hours of surveillance."

At that, Eunhee smiled. "He was always singing. Even Elvis. I noticed you have his records in the living room."

"I do." Helen smiled back.

"He sang a song at our wedding. We met at a Christian mixer in Korea—I was working on base as a translator. We both loved music, and he was so funny and not afraid to show his emotions or tell me that he loved me. He told me I was smarter than he was, and I could do anything. So I tried to! And then—well, 'Que Será, Será,'" she said. "That was the year Doris Day sang it." She looked sad again. "'The future's not ours to see'—just God's. Between duty and illness, we did not have much time together before James died."

Hmm. If God saw the future, it seemed problematic that he didn't head off some of the troubles at the pass. Helen tried to focus on something more positive. "I admire that you are fluent in two languages."

"Three. Japanese as well, and I have a degree from the Ewha Womans University." Eunhee smoothly changed the topic. "How did you meet the lieutenant?"

"We met at a mixer when he was stationed in Virginia and I was in nursing school. When I told them I planned to leave school before finishing, to marry him and follow him to his duty stations, my parents grew furious." *My father tried to hit me again, but I left before he could,* she thought but didn't say. "They told me to leave their home, and so we eloped immediately. Years later, when he died, they told me I'd made my bed," Helen said, smoothing the covers on the bed between them, "and now I'd need to lie in it." She smoothed the bed once more, comforted by the feeling of the fabric under her fingers, though the coverlet was already completely flat. "So now I make my own beds in my own home, and no one can tell me to leave."

"I see. They were angry you left your schooling?"

"Partly. Mostly Mother was angry that I wasn't going to be around any longer to help her around the house while she spent time with her girlfriends, her charity events, or her evenings out. She'd always relied on me to help—and I always did." *And to be the receptacle for my father's temper so she wouldn't have to.*

"After we were posted to Whidbey, I fell in love a second

time, with this homey farmhouse and its neglected victory garden. Bob said yes to buying it because we planned to return to Whidbey Island after his final years in the Navy." Helen caught sight of his picture on the mantel and looked into eyes that could no longer look back at her. "We didn't know his final year was already close at hand."

Helen saw that her new friend's face looked heavy and tired. Maybe she'd just ask her to spend the night. And then Helen thought . . . why not? Maybe she'd just like to stay here.

Mrs. Adams's sharp warning against fraternization buzzed across Helen's mind.

Helen wasn't married to an active-duty officer anymore, but she worked at a Naval hospital at the goodwill and plea-sure of Mrs. Adams's husband, the hospital CO, a Navy regs man through and through. In the short time until Eunhee, an enlisted man's wife, could get back home to Korea, no one needed to be made aware of this "fraternization" between the ranks.

Looking at Eunhee's wan face, Helen realized another risk—bringing the flu into the hospital. Was Eunhee sick? If so, Helen could catch it and share it with her patients. A wave of fear came over her but she let it roll through her and then out. There was no indication Eunhee was ill, and she was not going to fall into the trap of the woman's other accusers. "Would you like to stay with me?" Helen asked.

"Oh, I did not bring a travel case or toothbrush. Although that is very kind."

"I don't just mean tonight. I mean until you can complete your arrangements to return to Korea in a month or two."

Eunhee stood up. "Oh. I see. That was not my intention when I asked you for help. I'm very sorry if you thought so."

Helen patted the bed next to her. "I know that wasn't your intention. You'll be safe here. And it's as much for me as for you. I'm lonely. Besides, someone has to use that sewing machine."

Eunhee closed her eyes for a moment. Was she sleeping? Praying? If she was praying, it would be helpful to pray that neither she nor Helen caught the flu and that Mrs. Adams minded her own business.

"Yes," Eunhee said. "I would be very thankful to stay with you for a short while. And I can teach you how to garden."

CHAPTER TWO

The Navy had agreed to ship any of Eunhee's belongings back to Korea, but she told them she'd store them until her travel arrangements were completed.

She just didn't say she'd be storing them at Helen's house.

Once on the base, Helen lifted every box and suitcase into the trunk herself, tired already after a long week at work. Eunhee did not offer any resistance and climbed into the car. As they passed the hospital, Helen crossed her fingers that Mrs. Adams was not making busybody rounds and wouldn't see them out and about.

They drove first to Oak Harbor, where Eunhee sent an

airmail letter to her mother to ask about living accommodations when she returned home.

"Will your mother receive the letter easily?"

"Oh yes. Korea is still poor and disorganized from the years and years of war and all that was taken from us, but the mail does get through to the main post office. Umma—Mother— usually answers within one day, but it takes at least a week to get here. She has not yet answered my last letter, sent after my husband died. Maybe the postal service lost it?"

"Hopefully this one will get through." Helen put her signal on and made a left-hand turn. "Our mailman is very efficient, delivering to our rural route box each afternoon. Do you have other family?"

"My father was an important man, but now he is not, and he has not been well. My mother sews for the little money she brings in. I have the small survivor's benefits from James's death, not so much since he died of sickness and not in duty, but I will send half to them until I get there. Once I return, I can give it all to them. My brother, very sadly, died in the war. Sons are important in Korea, but a mother always wants a daughter, too."

A pang twinged Helen's heart. She'd so wanted a daughter. Ever since she was a small girl, her dolls had always been her "daughters," and when she'd had to leave them at her parents' home, her consolation had been that she'd have her own daughter someday. Bob had wanted a little girl, too, and she'd dreamed of the day when he'd return home from a duty station or a flight for her to announce with great joy that their baby was on the way. After his death, she'd realized she could finish nursing school, free from the time restraints mothers had. It wasn't a silver lining so much as an agreement with a statement she'd once read. *"He picked up the lemons that Fate had sent him and started a lemonade-stand."*

"It is much the same here," Helen said. "I am sure your mother will be thrilled to see you, then, when you return."

Eunhee didn't answer. Helen didn't press.

When they arrived back at Helen's home, Eunhee took her shoes off at the door. Helen brought the boxes into the small room next to the teal bedroom and then brought Eunhee's suitcase into the teal room. "I thought you might like the room with the sewing machine?"

Eunhee smiled. "Yes, please. That is very thoughtful of you."

"It overlooks the garden. Such that it is." Helen grinned.

"I noticed all of the rooms in the back look at the garden," Eunhee said. "So hopeful. But there is much to do. I can help you start before I return home. It would be enjoyable."

"I would like that," Helen said. "But first, lunch." Helen usually picked up something from the commissary for herself or ate TV dinners, but she could scramble eggs.

"Join me at the table?" she called through the living room toward Eunhee's room when the food was ready.

Eunhee joined her, and her eyebrows rose. "I have never had egg balls before. I look forward to trying something new."

"You mean scrambled eggs?"

"No, I have had scrambled eggs, just not where they were

19

scrambled into small balls. So pretty. And I like it when toast already has a hole in the middle so it tears easily."

She pursed her lips as if to hold back a smile, and Helen did too.

"The rain stopped," Helen said when they'd finished. "Would you like to walk in the garden?"

"Yes, that would be wonderful!" They walked out the back door, and as they did, a score of goldfinches fluttered from the lilac bush just outside the mud porch.

"I love birds," Helen said. "Especially goldfinches, with their pretty yellow feathers and black wings and caps. They've been my closest friends since Bob died. I see them every day—they wait for me to open the door, and then they flutter to the feeders to make sure I've done my job. They swoop and soar and fly around and even travel south for the winter but return. They remind me of Bob. He often flew away, but he always came back to the same soft nest." She caught her breath and looked at the birds to stop a tear from spilling down her cheek. *I miss you, Bob.*

Eunhee reached out and touched one of the rosebushes struggling up the gate, its leaves spotted and brown. "Lieutenant Bob died a hero's death," she said. "James would have been very sad, had he realized, to have died an ordinary death."

Helen twisted one of the branches so that it caught a wire in the gate, training it, wanting to think of something to comfort Eunhee. The military certainly did put a high value on a hero's death. "Isn't it more important to live a hero's life than to die a hero's death?"

Eunhee smiled. "Yes, it is. And he did."

"I'd like to live a hero's life," Helen said.

"I'd like to live a hero's life too," Eunhee agreed. "I am not sure what two women like us could do to be heroes, though."

Helen nodded. "Someday that opportunity may come to us. Will we be ready and willing, like our husbands were?"

"I hope so. But today, here we are, eating egg balls and getting dirty in the garden, instead. Not a very heroic life." Helen laughed with her. Eunhee glanced at the roses. "Perhaps this week we can clean up the garden some and also see what you would like to plant?"

"How about some lettuce? I like garden salads. Vegetables are very practical, and this is a victory garden, used to provide for meals. Maybe berries."

"Birds like berries," Eunhee said. "How about flowers? Finches love sunflowers. We have them in Korea."

"Definitely berries then!" Helen linked her arm through her friend's, and they returned to the house. "And sunflowers. I don't find flowers useful, but I love anything sunny!"

Hours later, Helen pulled two TV dinners from the oven and placed them on the coffee table in front of the console. "Dinner's ready!"

Eunhee looked down at the dinners. "I have not eaten a meal in an aluminum tray. Is this like prepared meals for away duty in the military?"

"Kind of." A small ice rink of gravy teetered like a lopsided hat atop Eunhee's portion of turkey. "Oh! It needs more time in the oven. I'll be right back."

Once Helen returned with the meals, fully heated, Eunhee ate slowly, smiling between each bite of turkey, corn bread, and buttered peas. Helen reached over to take their trays and noticed Eunhee's was largely uneaten. "Don't you like TV dinners?"

"They could use a few spices," Eunhee admitted.

Helen's heart sank. "I wanted to offer a comfortable, soft nest to you, my new friend."

Eunhee smiled and looked her straight in the eye. "Perfect cooking does not make a good friend or a soft nest. A soft heart makes for a soft nest, and love and honest talk make good friends."

But Helen truly wanted to learn to cook. Asking for assistance with anything had led to sharply sarcastic rebukes from her mother, so Helen had chosen independence. She prided herself on it. Helen bit her lip and bit back her pride. "I think I need help. Do you know how to cook? And if so, would you help me to learn?"

"I can cook, and I can help you to learn."

Helen smiled. "Thank you. I look forward to expanding my repertoire beyond egg balls."

They laughed until they had happy tears and then Eunhee went into her bedroom. Helen pulled out the uniforms she'd washed the night before to starch them, propping herself on the ironing board in between pieces to keep awake.

At least she'd have Sunday to rest before heading back to long shifts on Monday. The thought of clearing the garden wearied her. Just as she turned Lawrence Welk on, the phone shrilled.

Who called at this hour? Probably for the teenage girl who lived in the house with the windmills.

Two long, three short. Two long, three short.

Helen set the iron down on the board before picking up the receiver. "Hello?"

"Hello, Helen Devries?"

"Yes."

"This is Johanna Jansen. Your back neighbor across the acreage."

Helen had met her once when they'd first moved in. She'd brought bulbs to plant—Dutch bulbs, as Bob had been Dutch, and so was Mrs. Jansen and many of the non-Navy island residents. Helen, however, was not Dutch. "How can I help, Mrs. Jansen?"

"I'd like to come and visit you and your friend tomorrow. Just after church? Would that be suitable?"

Mrs. Jansen knew Eunhee was there and disclosed that on the party line. "I don't attend church, Mrs. Jansen, but noon should be fine to visit *me*."

"Wonderful. I will see you then. Make coffee, but nothing else."

Well, that was demanding. Mrs. Jansen clicked off and Helen set down the receiver and went to tell Eunhee they'd have a visitor the next day, but she heard her softly snoring, left her be, and went to bed herself.

Hours later, a guttural noise startled Helen awake. She tiptoed to the top of the stairs, hoping the floorboards wouldn't creak. Light seeped through the cracks at the sides and bottom of the bathroom door. Eunhee was in there.

Vomiting.

*   *   *

Helen came downstairs the next morning and found Eunhee sitting at the table, drinking an unusually fragrant tea from one of Helen's mugs. "Would you like some?"

"Yes, that would be lovely. I've only ever had Lipton tea."

"You will enjoy this." Eunhee set the kettle to singing again and then poured water over loose tea leaves. "As soon as it's the right color, I strain it with this." She held up a piece of cheesecloth. "You can have sugar in it if you want, but it's better without."

"Without is just fine." Helen told her about Mrs. Jansen's call as she took a solid coffee cup in hand. When sipped, the tea presented many flavors, soft and then strong, a note of citrus and then a bitter taste like the birchbark twigs she once chewed as a girl on a dare. "It's delicious!"

Eunhee smiled. "I'll make a list of things we can get from the store, and we can start cooking lessons this week."

Helen studied her face and held her gaze. "Are you sure you're up to it?"

Eunhee averted her eyes, but before she did, Helen caught a look, the look of someone hiding something. "Yes, certainly.

Now, if you do not mind, as it is Sunday, I will read my Bible until our guest arrives?" She held the book in her hand.

"Yes, yes, of course. Is that—is that in Korean?"

Eunhee nodded.

"May I see it?"

Eunhee held it open for her. "Quite different from your Bible, I am sure."

"Yours is beautiful. I don't have a Bible."

Those eyebrows again—raised and then quickly restrained.

Helen set about tidying the house and then took a little walk outside. Daffodil buds emerged from the soil in the path leading to the walkway and around the greenhouse, the only thing currently blooming. The bulbs Mrs. Jansen had brought by years earlier.

Helen hurried into the house at eleven thirty, left her shoes in the mud porch as Eunhee did, and headed into the bathroom. She slicked bright-red color over her lips, then spoke to the mirror to ensure none had stuck to her teeth. "When you feel the desire to conquer . . . then let your lips be savagely red, warmly moist, tenderly soft." Well, that's what the ad promised, anyway. If it was good enough for Elizabeth Taylor, it was good enough for Helen Devries. Perhaps she'd be an equal match to her confident neighbor.

In the kitchen, Eunhee put out the kettle and three mugs. Helen took out the instant coffee. At noon exactly, a car pulled into the driveway.

Footsteps on the porch announced an arrival. "Knock,

and it shall be opened unto you!" sang out a voice from beyond the door. "But I can't knock!"

Eunhee smiled and sang back, "Ask, and it shall be given to you."

"Then I will ask! Can you open the door?" Mrs. Jansen called. "My hands are full!"

Helen pulled open the door. Mrs. Jansen looked down at Helen's stocking feet and the shoes on the porch and slid off her loafers. "As you said you do not attend church, I am surprised that you know that Bible verse."

"I don't," Helen replied. "Mrs. Roy answered you."

The two of them walked into the kitchen, Mrs. Jansen carrying a large platter filled with something that certainly included fragrant cinnamon. Whatever it was, it hid beneath a large, clean dish towel.

As she came into the kitchen, Eunhee bowed slightly. "I am pleased to meet you. I am Choi Eunhee. Please call me Eunhee."

Mrs. Jansen awkwardly bowed back and then smiled. "Please call me Johanna."

She set her platter on the table and then lifted the towel from it. "My famous Cinn Rolls. I only bring them to special guests."

"'Sin' rolls?" Eunhee asked. "As in, I must confess and repent?"

Johanna laughed, and Helen joined her. "By the size of those," Helen said, "I would guess Sin Rolls might be the proper name, but I think she meant cinnamon rolls."

"Oh, I see." Eunhee joined the laughter and winked. "I would have had one anyway."

Helen brought out three small plates on which she settled the puffy wonders, a platter for the butter Johanna had brought, and some forks and knives to bring them into manageable bites.

"Welcome to the neighborhood," Johanna said. She unfurled a bit of the roll, placed a pat of butter on it, and then bit off that section. "This is how you do it."

They followed her lead. "This butter is delicious!" Helen said. "I have never tasted better."

"From our cows," Johanna said. "My husband doesn't believe in corporal punishment, so when our boys get in trouble, they churn, churn, churn until their arms ache. I needn't tell you we always have plenty of butter." Her eyes sparkled. "That's why my rolls don't need frosting. Never ever use frosting." She shivered.

Helen nodded her agreement. "How did you know Eunhee was here?"

"The party line, of course," Johanna brazenly admitted. "When you told her to be ready on Saturday at noon, after she'd told you she was in trouble in the earlier call, I guessed she was coming to stay for a while. I'm a good guesser."

"Apparently the chicken man was also listening in." Helen took another bite of her roll.

"The chicken man?"

"The old man up the street with the big chicken coops, who hasn't liked 'foreigners' since the war."

"Mr. Beeksma. Yes, he listens to all calls. Nothing else to do."

"And my supervisor's wife."

"Ah, that's not good. Do you speak a second language?"

"What . . . ? No, why?" Helen answered.

"Pity. I always speak Dutch on the line, limiting who will understand my conversations or at least the gossipy bits." She turned to Eunhee. "You should speak Korean on the party line."

Eunhee smiled. "I would—if I knew anyone here who spoke Korean." She took another bite and washed it down with tea. "These Cinn Rolls are wonderful."

Maybe Helen could learn to make them. "Would you share the recipe with me?" she asked.

"Oh . . . ," Johanna began. "I don't exactly have a recipe. I learned to mix and roll them at my mother's elbow, and I just do what she did."

"That is how I learned to cook too," Eunhee exclaimed.

Helen felt her face fall. Her mother mixed drinks, not rolls.

Johanna must have noticed and looked at Helen with kindness. "I see the daffodils I gave you and your husband some years back line the drive. I was sorry to hear about your husband's death. It was in the paper, of course."

Helen swallowed her resentment. "I missed hearing from anyone in the neighborhood when he died. Perhaps because I am not Dutch. The Navy I expected to ignore me, but I'd hoped . . . neighbors . . ."

Johanna didn't lie. "I'm sorry to say I was overwhelmed,

and then it clean slipped my mind. I apologize. Do you forgive me?"

Eunhee tried to hide a smile. *Honest talk makes friends,* she'd said.

"Certainly. I'm so glad to see that the bulbs you gave me have multiplied!"

"Like my many sons," Johanna teased. "But truly, I always plant bulbs, not only because they're Dutch, but because you do the work once, and it rewards you for years. Those and everbearing plants." She set a pretty, closed bag on the table near Eunhee. "When I heard you were a Navy widow, I figured you didn't have much. Let me tell you a story."

Both Eunhee and Helen sat rapt, eating rolls.

"When the Dutch first came to Whidbey Island, they had very little to their names. Some of them came from Michigan and some from Alberta. Later, they prospered. When the circuit preacher came to visit, he would collect clothing from us to take to other Dutch Reformed folks back in Alberta. Some of them immigrated here, and when they arrived, we were there to meet them. Imagine the surprise when many of them were wearing our clothes—the ones that had been collected. It became a tradition, then, to give someone new something that belongs to you."

She turned to Helen. "The bulbs I gave you, I dug out of my garden."

Helen's heart squeezed in guilt over her earlier indignation about being ignored at Bob's death. It wasn't like they had known each other well. "Thank you," she said softly.

Johanna turned back to Eunhee and opened the bag and took out an apron. "This is one of my best aprons. Stand up! I'll try it on you."

Eunhee stood, and Johanna wrapped it around her. It was a beautiful cream-colored apron with sprays of roses on it. Johanna's eyes narrowed, and she wrinkled her nose.

"Does it not look good?" Eunhee asked.

"No, no, it's lovely," Johanna said. They had another cup of coffee and then Johanna rested the towel over the remaining rolls. "Keep these, and I'll get the plate later."

"Thank you," Helen said. "That is most generous."

"The rolls will multiply, too, but not in the same way as the daffodils!" Johanna patted her ample stomach.

"We will bring something delicious to you soon," Eunhee promised.

Helen fixed her smile. It might be delicious if Eunhee made it. Johanna would not be impressed by holey toast, Bible reading or not!

Johanna slipped on her shoes, and they said their good-byes.

Fifteen minutes later, as Eunhee and Helen did the dishes, another knock came at the door. "Knock, and it shall be opened to you," Johanna sang again. "Ask, and you shall receive."

Eunhee looked at Helen and Helen back at her. Then Helen opened the door, and Johanna stepped in and handed another apron to Eunhee, cream with pink-and-garnet flowers scattered across and a ruby tulip trim. "You'll be needing a larger size soon. This is roomier."

This time Helen's eyebrows leaped in surprise.

Johanna smiled as she headed toward the door. "I've had seven sons and I'm a good guesser." She winked at Helen.

Eunhee headed into the living room. Helen joined her. "Is it true?"

Eunhee nodded. "Yes. I wasn't certain until recently. I thought perhaps the stress of James's illness and then his death had delayed my monthlies. I think the baby will be born in September." A tear slid down her cheek. "James will never know his child here on earth."

Helen sat close to her friend, wanting to comfort her but also in need of comfort herself as that yearning wrenched deep inside her again. Eunhee would have the blessing of a baby by which to remember her husband. Helen would not. "I'm so sorry about James not being here to meet his child. But perhaps this is also something hopeful? New life after a death."

"Yes, that is true."

"I didn't recognize the signs—though I did begin to wonder when you were unwell in the bathroom last night. I was going to come down with a damp cloth, but then I figured you'd prefer your privacy."

Eunhee smiled. "You're right, but I'm sorry you heard. That must have been unpleasant."

"I'm a nurse," Helen replied. "It did not bother me at

all, except for concern for you. Unlike Johanna, I'm not a mother. But I am a nurse, and I can take good care of you. After work tomorrow, I'll buy groceries from your list and start to cook good food for you. I don't get much mail, but I'll stop by and check every day after work from now on. You'll hear something from home soon."

CHAPTER THREE

"Hello, Nurse." In the far bed by the window, a young boy greeted Helen in a gravelly, faint voice.

"Hello, young man. How are you feeling without those troublesome tonsils? I'm happy to see you awake."

"A bit better, I suppose. Can I go home now?"

Helen shook her head. "Maybe in a day or two. I don't think you'll want to leave today, though." She smiled. "Let me take your temperature, your blood pressure, and look down your throat to see if it's healing all right. If everything looks good, I have a surprise for you. One made by an eleven-year-old boy."

Frank sat up a little, his blue gown falling open at the neck. "An eleven-year-old boy? You mean, like me?"

Helen nodded. "Like you."

His temperature was up, but only slightly, and down from the day before when his tonsils had been removed. Blood pressure looked good, and pink began to bloom on his cheeks. "Everything looks great. I'll tell the doctor, and he'll be in soon to see you. Your mother will be here to visit just after dinner. I've heard you're not eating."

"They keep giving me cornflakes and other crispy food. It hurts."

"That's to help scrape away any tissue or blood left in your throat."

"It hurts." He crossed his arms. "I won't eat it."

Helen lowered her voice. "If I order pudding and mashed potatoes, which will not be difficult to swallow, will you promise to eat it all?"

He uncrossed his arms. "I promise, Nurse!"

Helen let her stethoscope fall back to her chest and then reached back to the surgical tray. "Ta-da! I hope you like orange flavor!" She bent down and whispered conspiratorially, "I thought about giving you cherry and that we might have a secret laugh when the doctor comes to visit you and sees your throat and mouth all red. Like blood. I'd be relieved of my duties for that, so I had to change to orange, despite the fun we might have had!"

Frank laughed for a moment before stopping, due to

pain, she knew. But he smiled. "That's a good joke, Nurse. I'll tell you tomorrow what he thinks."

"An eleven-year-old boy invented Popsicles, so I knew it would be just the right thing for you, and it will make your throat feel good, too. I'll tell the night nurse to bring another one to you. You get well so you can go home and invent things."

"I will," Frank said. "My dad will be back from sea duty in two months, and I'll think of something to invent before he gets home. Then we'll have a whole year of shore duty when he can be home to help my mom and me."

Helen ruffled his hair and checked her watch. Time to debrief the nurse who would take the three-to-eleven shift and go home. She yawned once and then again. As she did, Captain Adams came around the corner.

"Hello, Helen."

She was instantly awake.

"Hello, Captain Adams."

"You look tired," he said, "Pretty as ever, but tired."

In the few months she'd worked there, he had been friendly to her, she'd thought because he'd known Bob. But he had never used her first name or commented on her appearance. "Long but successful day, sir," she replied.

"If you need your hours lightened a little, let me know." He winked. "I'll see what I can do. I don't assign them, but I am the boss."

Helen nodded, and as she did, she saw, over his shoulder,

Mrs. Adams round the corridor and come into view. Helen inclined her head politely and the captain turned around.

"Hello, dear," he said. His wife smiled but not happily. "Please complete the paperwork before you leave for the day, Nurse. That will be all. Dismissed." He turned his back and walked toward his wife.

Helen frowned. That was odd. And uncomfortable.

She debriefed the nurse and corpsmen on the next shift and then headed to her car. Once inside, she tied her scarf around her head and left the roof down to enjoy the beautiful April afternoon. She slowed as she drew close to the rural, country-road mailbox that serviced their neighborhood. She reached her hand in and withdrew the bounty: a Sears catalog, a card from the Avon representative. And then—a thin letter, onionskin, written in English. *Mrs. Choi Eunhee, c/o Helen Devries, Rural Route One, Box Twenty-Four, Coupeville, WA, USA.* Return address? *Mrs. Park Ji-Woo, Republic of Korea.*

Helen flew the rest of the way home on high spirits and a heavy accelerator foot. Once parked, she left the grocery sack in the car and ran toward the house. "Eunhee! Your mother. There is a letter from your mother!"

Eunhee came racing out from her bedroom. "Really? Thank you!"

Helen handed it over and then went to the car to unload the groceries. When she came back inside, Eunhee had disappeared. Helen had expected to find her in the living room, reading, but she was not there.

The door to the teal bedroom was closed, and Helen heard some muffled sounds. Crying? Crying. Perhaps her mother was unwell, or her father had died? Eunhee had mentioned that he was frail. Helen knocked lightly on the door, but there was no response.

Helen pulled herself together, put away the groceries, prepared a large garden salad, and put the chicken in the oven to roast—one of Eunhee's first lessons to her.

An hour later, as Helen pulled the chicken out to cool, Eunhee emerged from her room.

"Is something wrong?" Helen asked.

Eunhee nodded and then lightly shook the letter. Helen watched the beautiful Korean characters dance on the page. "Umma says there is still not enough good food that is easy to find in Korea, not without a Navy husband to help, like when James was there with me. She also thinks there is no good medical care for me right now, not like here. She thinks it is much better to have the baby in the United States."

"So . . . she doesn't want you to come home?" She caught herself, hoping she hadn't hurt Eunhee with a harsh tone. "I suppose that is not much different than my mother not wanting me to live in her home."

Eunhee sat at the table as Helen made tea. "Kind of, but also different," Eunhee said. "Just for a little while. Because the baby is a Navy dependent, medical care will be taken care of here."

"Yes, certainly. Without a doubt," Helen affirmed. "I can

help with that. And your monthly survivor's pension will be in soon."

"I must send half to them. There is no food for a mother expecting a baby, but also not enough for elderly people like them." She looked up. "I have James's small life insurance, though. Now that there is no rush, we can find an apartment for the baby and me. The insurance will be enough for that."

Helen nodded slowly, sensing her friend had more to say.

"I think . . . I think they are ashamed to tell their friends that the daughter who is successful in America is not so successful anymore."

"But you are . . . ," Helen said.

Eunhee shook her head.

Helen stood and walked to the window overlooking the garden. It was mid-April, and the flu was no longer a threat to the base. No one but Mrs. Adams had raised concern that a former officer's wife shared her home with a former enlisted man's wife, not to Helen's knowledge anyway. Eunhee's baby would be born in September and could likely travel by October or November, the end of the year at the latest.

Eunhee's baby. A baby would be born in this house but not be Helen's. "I have an idea," she said.

Eunhee shook her head.

"I'll be right back," Helen insisted.

She headed up the stairs to the attic and gazed upon the brand-new bassinet stored near her hope chest. She knelt and stroked the soft, silk interior. As she did, the desire for her own child leaped to life. "I would have loved to have your child, Bob," she said. "But it was not meant to be for us. Maybe because you were away so often. Maybe because you were going to die, and I'd be left here with the child. I would have missed you but would have loved that child for both of us. Like Eunhee will do."

She could put the unused bassinet, bought on a whim during a month when her period had been late, to good use. There was a child who could sleep soundly on this soft silk. She'd ask Eunhee to stay.

On the floor next to the bassinet was the box holding the exquisite tea service Helen's grandmother had given her when she'd married. Her grandmother had passed away soon after, and Helen had never enjoyed tea in the set.

Maybe . . . maybe her mother had softened some. Maybe she'd like to come for a visit and see the house. There were two other bedrooms. Surely she'd be proud of Helen's job, though she couldn't make the graduation ceremony. Helen would write to her. She would share the bassinet with Eunhee. But the tea set would wait for Helen and her mother to begin again.

Helen went back downstairs to offer the use of the bassinet to Eunhee before presenting it to her, in case she had plans to buy her own, but Eunhee had already returned to her bedroom.

They were good friends now. She'd likely known that Helen was going to offer her home in place of the apartment and had left before she could ask. Pride, perhaps.

Independence. Grief over not being able to return home. Helen was intimately familiar with all three.

No more insisting. Helen could wait and let her friend ask when she was ready.

* * *

Days passed with the women enjoying one another's company, though neither discussed the future. Eunhee sewed during the day when Helen was at work, making lovely drapes for the living room. She was also busy sewing something for her baby.

One evening, as she taught Helen how to cook, Eunhee took the small red pepper flakes they'd found at the grocery store and pounded them into a paste that resembled the pepper paste she used at home, *gochujang*. "It's not really the same," Eunhee said, nose wrinkling. "But I'm lucky. Usually, when a woman gets married, she must make recipes taste like her new mother-in-law's, so the food tastes the same for her new husband. Because James was not Korean, I keep making them like my *umma*. Her food is delicious. But I do not have the right ingredients."

"There's a store in Seattle, Uwajimaya, that sells Asian food and spices. Do you want to go on my next day off?" They'd not left the island since Eunhee had come to stay with her.

"Yes, I would love to go. Do they sell *gim*—seaweed?" Eunhee asked. "I need that for the baby. Seaweed soup is very healthy. I will teach you how to make it."

Helen kept a straight face. Spicy roast might be okay, but seaweed soup? Still . . . if the baby needed it. "We can get that right here on the island. There's a beach down by Langley that has lovely seaweed to harvest as much as you like. I've heard from the corpsmen at work who clam and crab. Do you want me to find out?"

"Yes!" Eunhee's eyes sparkled for the first time in weeks.

A few mornings later, they set out for the beach. Helen wore beige slacks and a pair of loafers. They took a bucket, a rake, and a couple of large towels to dry themselves off. Eunhee donned a straw hat and gave a second one to Helen.

"Johanna says good friends give things that belong to them," she said. "This is your new hat, good friend."

Helen's heart swelled and then she looked in the mirror. Stylish. "Thank you!"

They slid into the Skylark, top down, and when the wind was about to blow off their hats, they tucked them on the floor near Eunhee.

"I wish I could drive," Eunhee said. "Someday I will learn."

They made their way to the beach, and as the tide was out, they first laid out their towels and sat on them near the shoreline. The chilly weather meant they had the beach to themselves.

"I miss the water," Eunhee said. "I have always lived near water."

"You live on an island," Helen teased.

"Yes, but I don't visit often. I am always at the farmhouse, where we can see it, but we do not go there."

True. Helen hadn't thought of that. She'd taken Eunhee to visit her husband's grave once and they went to the store together on occasion. But otherwise, Helen was so busy trying to keep up at work or catch up on sleep, she hadn't taken her anywhere.

"I like the beach, too," Helen said. "Let's come more often." She slid on her big, green, cat-eye Ray-Ban sunglasses. "Let me do the work as the tide is coming in. You sit here and enjoy the sun for a moment."

Eunhee nodded, happy in the sand. "You just rake the green part, the leafy portions, and leave the stalky parts behind. Put them into the bucket and I'll wash them for us at home before I make our soup."

Helen headed toward the sea. The water was more gray than blue, reflecting the partially cloudy sky. Shells with peck holes littered her path—the seagulls had certainly eaten their fill. She raked up a bit of the kelp. As she did, it stirred the sand, lifting the scent of the sea into the air.

Why didn't they go to the beach more often? The farmhouse had a magnificent view of the sea, just across the street, and there was a lovely stretch of gray sand: no seaweed there but plenty of places to walk.

Just ahead, Helen spied a brighter, bigger, lusher patch of seaweed closer to the water's edge. If a little was good, then certainly a lot would be better. She raked a huge portion into the large, flat bucket they'd brought. Could you dry it and—?

Her left leg fell through the sand and was instantly swallowed by cold, wet earth, thigh-high. "Oh no!"

"Helen!" Eunhee cried out, stood up, and came closer.

"It's quicksand!" Helen's right leg slid through the sand, too, ingested by the earth faster than she could have imagined possible.

Helen threw the filled bucket and rake in front of her. If she pressed on the sand with her hands, would they, too, sink in? She was well and truly sucked into the earth. Behind her, the water lapped progressively closer and the seagulls cawed tauntingly. The world seemed surreal, and Helen was simultaneously paralyzed by anxiety and shocked into a peaceful numbness.

This is how death took you, Bob. Drowning. I've seen it over and over in my nightmares. Were you anxious? Did you call out? Were you peaceful? I hope so. I hope you are now. Cool water lapped at her.

Eunhee's shrill voice brought her back. "Slip out of your shoes and take off your pants," she yelled.

"Pants? Take off my slacks?"

"Take them off," Eunhee insisted. "The sand will grip the fabric, and then you can slip your legs out. But hurry. There is not much time!"

Yes. That was sensible. Helen reached down and unbuttoned the trousers and wriggled her way out of them as the wet sand clung to the fabric. When she did, she was able to push and lift herself forward.

"Don't walk!" Eunhee said. "The same thing will happen. Crawl on your knees, keeping your weight equal."

Helen got on her knees and began crawling out, dragging

the prized bucket of seaweed, though leaving the rake to the tide.

As she did, she scrambled over dangerous territory, onto the dry ground, and into the arms of her friend. They clung to each other for a moment, and then Eunhee handed a towel to Helen. "You should wrap this around your legs. Soon Mrs. Adams will drive by with her Kodak camera and report you to the Navy command."

At that, they laughed until they cried.

"How did you know what to do?" Helen asked.

"Korea is famous for our mudflats, which are very much like this kind of sand," Eunhee said. "Even children know of people who get trapped there and then how they get out."

"I am so glad," Helen said. "I wouldn't have known to get out on my knees."

"I get out of the worst problems on my knees," Eunhee said, a twinkle in her eye.

"What do you mean?"

She put her hands together as if to indicate prayer.

Helen shivered, and Eunhee helped her to her feet. "We must go back now. I will make some nourishing soup to warm you."

"Seaweed soup?"

"Of course!" Arm in arm, with the bucket of seaweed, they headed to the Buick.

Helen kept the towel wrapped around her. "If you're going to pray, you should pray that the police do not pull me over, half-naked." They giggled and shivered all the way home.

Eunhee made the soup while Helen took a hot bath. After putting on new clothes, Helen drank a bowl of the warm liquid.

"Do you like it?"

"It's interesting and pretty," Helen said.

"Interesting and pretty like egg balls?" Eunhee teased.

Helen laughed. "Yes. Exactly. But warm!"

After lunch, Helen said, "The truth is, I never learned to cook after Bob died because I had no one to cook for. I didn't bring the garden to life because I did not want to do it without him. But today I realized how very much I still want to live. I will not let grief swallow me alive. I want to feel alive again."

Eunhee set down her mug. "Yes, this is true. I, too, cannot be swallowed up in grief. Thank you for sharing that with me." They chatted for a while, and then Eunhee went back into her bedroom to sew.

Helen looked out at the garden. The skies had cleared, literally and figuratively. It was not too late to plant. To start. She'd head out to the farmers' co-op in Oak Harbor and pick up the strawberry runners one of the Navy nurses had mentioned. She would wrestle victory out of the garden and life.

The late-afternoon sun shone on her as she walked the garden store's aisle. There was only one country store in town that stocked tools, bib overalls, paint, and some bedding plants.

"Can I help you?" A pleasant-looking woman with a ready smile approached her.

"I'd like some strawberry runners, please," Helen said. She looked around her at the wonderland of green and buds. "And some leaf lettuce."

"What kind of strawberries?"

Helen smiled sheepishly. "I don't know much about gardening. Are there strawberry plants that fruit longer than others? That birds like?"

The lady laughed. "I'm going to give you some blackberry canes for the birds—just don't let them take over your land. The bees will visit them and pollinate your other plants, too. As for the strawberries, how about everbearing? Plant once, harvest at least twice."

"Yes, yes," Helen replied. That appealed to her practical sensibilities. The woman helped her understand what she'd need to do to keep the slugs away—salt or, if her husband was a beer-drinking man, a small bowl of beer set next to the berry plants in which the slugs would dive and drown. Not having a beer-drinking man around, Helen settled for the salt cure.

"I'd like some rose food," she added. "And—" she spied some gardening gloves—"two sets of those—both size small."

The proprietress snagged two sets of green gloves. "Would you like some flowers?"

Impractical, but perhaps Eunhee—and the birds—would enjoy them. Flowers signified hope. Helen nodded. "I don't know much about what to plant, but could you help me find some of the ones that bloom every year?"

"Perennials."

"Yes, then, some of those. Not too many to start with."

She laughed. "They become an addiction. You'll be back once you master these. You might want to look into buying the *Better Homes and Gardens, Garden Book* at Masten Variety Store, across the street. Lots of tips and tricks."

"Thank you. I'll consider that." Helen packed her goods into the car and got back on the road. Would Eunhee be happy to see the plants? Even if she were not, Helen would plant them. There was quite a lot of cleanup to do first, but she'd only clear and plant one of the fifteen acres to start with. That couldn't be too difficult, could it?

She pulled into the drive and then took the boxes out and put them near the potting shed. She looked at it clearly for the first time since they'd bought the house. It was wood and glass and beautiful and bright—or would be once the windows were washed. Someday, maybe, she'd build a big, beautiful greenhouse, if she could justify it.

The gate squeaked, and Eunhee joined her. "Oh! Strawberries!"

"Do the plants look good? The farmers' co-op lady said I would have some in the summer and then through autumn."

"Delicious!" Eunhee said. "And you bought such pretty flowers. I will show you how to plant them. Just up to their crowns and then water deeply."

"She also said to find the *Better Homes and Gardens, Garden Book*, too, for ideas on gardening."

"Yes—we will find that at the variety store," Eunhee affirmed. She held a small cloth bag. "I would like to go to the store you mentioned, in Seattle, to buy Asian ingredients. But I have a favor to ask."

A long silence went by. Helen waited this time.

Finally Eunhee asked the question Helen had been hoping to hear. "May I stay with you until the baby is born? I will understand if it is too much trouble. I will help to pay for things with my survivor's benefit."

"I was hoping you would. I would like nothing more!" Of course, Helen would let Eunhee pay, but then when she returned to her home in Korea, she would give her all of that money back. Helen's savings and Bob's life insurance had been spent on tuition to finish her degree and live on while studying. But Helen had a good job now and would not need Eunhee's money. Eunhee and the baby would.

Eunhee opened her bag and withdrew brown paper packets tied with twine. When she opened them, they revealed seeds. "I brought these from Korea. I'd thought that this summer I would plant them in a small patch that James and I would have. Korean plants in an American home. Best of both worlds, just like for me. These seeds are from my mother's plants. Can we plant them?"

"They will have the best corner in the garden."

"I can eat the produce this summer, and then, when I return to Korea, you will have some, too, to make sure your aluminum dinners have good spice." She grinned.

Helen grinned back. "No more aluminum dinners!"

"Together," Eunhee said, "we can bring life to this dead garden."

Helen reached to the side and picked a small bouquet of sunny-faced daffodils. "And that will bring life to us. We won't let grief bury us alive. We must live—for ourselves, for this baby, and for all the babies to come."

Cassidy

CHAPTER FOUR

Late March

The hospice nurse stepped back as I leaned over the bed and kissed Gran's cheek. She fluttered in and out of a morphine-tinted twilight, paper-thin and wan like the moths in her evening garden, and then looked at me, working for clarity. "Who are you?"

"Cassidy," I said softly. "I raced to get here." I placed the small bouquet of daffodils I'd picked on the way into the house in the porcelain vase on her bedside table.

"Oh yes, my sweet Cassidy." Fully awake now, a tear trickled down her left cheek.

I lifted a bit of the soft sheet draped around her to dab the corners of her eyes. "I'm sorry I wasn't here sooner. I thought we had months left."

"So did we," the nurse said. "I'll be right outside if you need me." She closed the door behind her.

Gran stroked my hand. "You are my only, my everything. You were to your mom, too. . . . Your mom. So many years ago. But just like yesterday."

"Sixteen years, nine months." My heart clenched as that bedside scene flashed through my mind. I'd been a bewildered twelve-year-old girl, squeezing my dad's left hand and my bedbound mom's right, Gran on the other side of her, a paper-doll chain soon to be snipped apart.

Gran turned her head and caught a glimpse of the daffodil posy. "Sunshine from my garden. Sunshine is all a garden really needs, you know. It's all a life needs, too, which is why mine bloomed. I have you. You are my sunshine." She turned back to me. "The garden, the house, the evergreens, they are ours. *Yours* . . . I did what I had to do to keep them for you."

Did what she had to do to keep them? Had she been struggling? She'd said nothing about it.

No matter. "I've got this," I promised.

"I know you do. I've given you a head start." She nodded. "I'm so tired." Gran sighed and closed her eyes but kept talking. "It's in the paperwork. I'm passing the baton now. Or trowel, as it may be." A faint smile tickled her lips.

"I see your trowel and raise you a spade," I teased back to lift her spirits, then kissed her hand lightly.

She dozed off, quick breaths followed by a small series

of choking snores. The nurse quickly opened the door and stepped in. She took Gran's blood pressure. "Her breathing is irregular, blood pressure low, and her mind cloudy because of the pain medication. I've seen it many times. She waited for you. It won't be long now. Maybe within the hour."

Within the hour? My heart pumped and skipped; then dizziness swarmed me. I steadied myself and propped a pillow behind Gran's head so she could breathe more easily. We wouldn't have days together before she passed. But we'd had twenty-eight years together, and nothing could take that away. Gran's beautiful silver hair had thinned to unruly tufts sprouting on her pink scalp. Her skin was dry and her rose-dotted nightgown a size too big, though it hadn't been the last time I'd seen her.

She was the most beautiful woman I knew.

The nurse gently touched Gran's shoulder and spoke before leaving the room. "You wanted me to remind you about having the friend help your granddaughter pack up."

Gran's eyes opened again. "Oh. I'd almost forgotten. How could I?" She focused intently. "Grace must help you pack the attic. Don't put it off. Time is of the essence."

My eyebrows rose at the odd request and its even stranger deathbed timing. "Grace help me pack up the attic?" Maybe her mind was still murky.

"Yes. Promise me. Before you return to California." She looked at me, focused and clear. "I must insist."

Gran never insisted on anything.

"Please," she whispered.

She never pleaded, either.

If I said I'd do it, would that make her feel she could let go? I wasn't ready to lose her. But if this were one thing she wanted from me to die in peace, I would give it to her. Unreservedly. "Of course. I love you. I would do anything for you."

"And I for you, my lovely one. I'm leaving, but not leaving. I'll still be here, all around you, and so will your mom—you'll see us in every tree, flower, room. In here." She tapped my heart before taking my hand.

It was time. I captured one last mind's-eye image of her here with me, though I had a thousand in my heart and head to review whenever I wanted. "It's okay to go now," I told her softly.

Her grip relaxed and her breathing slowed, but there was no more snoring, just a measured slipping away. Outside the bedroom window, in the distance, the tops of her beloved pine trees swayed as if waving goodbye. Nearer to the window, her favorite apple tree budded. Birds perched on nearly every branch, peering into Gran's window until, almost as one, they sang and lifted their wings.

Gran exhaled and flew toward the light.

* * *

I held the funeral at the small church Gran had attended for as long as I'd been alive. *"Now faith is the assurance of what we hope for and the certainty of what we do not see"* was the passage I'd asked her pastor to speak on, the same one Gran had chosen when Mom died. All her life Gran reached for hope, wanting to rest in it, but work was a better-known friend, more easily controlled and quantifiable. If she failed, she could blame herself and not God. I ran my hand down the top of the smooth cherrywood casket. *I'll hope for both of us.*

The church was packed with folks and flowers. The bouquets weren't ungainly, professionally composed arrangements sent via an 800 number or Google search. No, they were local beauties freshly dug from gardens or roughly snipped with office scissors from the edges of lawns and then tied with household string. Little bundles of grape hyacinth with plump purple cones jostled alongside bone-china magnolia blossoms plucked from low branches, looking every bit like the pink teacups I'd treasured as a girl. Best of all were the dozens of daffodils—narcissus—named for the Greek god so beautiful he fell in love with his own reflection. Gran, not overly fond of flowers, did love those that had a sentimental meaning, and daffodils had reminded her of her dear friend Johanna. I laid one on top of the casket before taking my seat.

The whole Kim family had come—almost. They sat with me. "Are you doing okay?" Mrs. Kim asked as she hugged me.

"I am." My voice wavered and I steadied it by looking away. *Make it through the day with your emotions intact; then you can cry alone at home, later.*

Mrs. Kim looked beside and behind me. "Is your father here?"

I shook my head. "They can't make it at this time."

"Oh." She patted my hand lovingly.

I'd hoped, of course, that Dad would come. Before Mom died, he and Gran had really liked each other. After she died, he'd never returned to Whidbey, and Gran finally took their wedding picture off the living room wall.

In the end, Dad and Mary Alice, my stepmother, hadn't been able to make it from the East Coast in time for the funeral. Mary Alice always made sure they couldn't attend anything related to my mother.

They sent a card.

Mr. Kim and Grace's brothers stood nearby, but her *halaboji*, her grandpa, was in a skilled nursing facility. "I am sure my father is very sorry to miss this," Mr. Kim said. "He has the deepest respect for your grandmother and is glad they spoke recently."

"Thank you, Mr. Kim. I hope he is well soon."

I leaned over and whispered in Grace's ear. "I need to talk with you right away. Maybe after the service?"

"Of course," she whispered. Her new round, light-blue tinted glasses were impossibly chic.

I squeezed her hand, and she didn't let go of mine.

"Helen taught me how to garden," one of Gran's friends eulogized. "Mostly vegetables, of course, including those prizewinning cucumbers. I'm guessing there are many people here today whose lawns and salad bowls would be empty or sickly without her generosity." She looked directly at me. "I hope you'll revive that beautiful garden."

I nodded. Someday. The garden slept for now. Like it or not, I'd be back in California long before planting season was in full swing because that was where my immediate future lay. But the land would wait for me, for the season of life when I could come back and claim it like the prize that it was and make my life here with a family of my own.

The woman descended from the pulpit and walked toward me, giving me a sticky old-lady kiss, floury face powder gathering in the doughy folds of her sweet face.

After the service, I stood at the door and shook hands with people as they filtered out of the church. When the last person left, Grace asked, "What did you want to talk about?"

"Gran wanted you to help me pack up the attic," I said. "It's really odd, but she insisted and insisted we start soon. Do you have time? Like right away?"

Mrs. Kim's ears perked in front of the medium-length hair tucked behind them.

"Sure," Grace said as she ducked her head.

Is she blushing?

She hid behind those blue lenses, and when she turned away from me, her mother blinked and dropped her gaze, too.

When the last car started up, I got into my old Mustang and followed the hearse. An hour later, after Gran was interred, Mrs. Kim asked, "Would you like to come to our house tonight?"

"No thank you. I'm okay. I want to be at home every day I can until I have to return to my job." I wished I were staying for the whole summer like I had when I was a girl, eating Popsicles till they dripped sticky rainbows on my tanned arms.

"Okay, dear Cassidy," Mrs. Kim said. "You are welcome at any time."

"Call you later," Grace whispered in my ear as she hugged me before leaving with her family.

I drove home, kicked off my shoes in the mud porch, and went inside. It was so . . . quiet.

An undertow of grief threatened to pull me down. I changed, slipped on my mud boots, and headed toward the garden, where I always felt better.

The land still had good bones and had been put to bed properly the past autumn, but nothing had been planted. A few persistent perennials and the trees held firm, though. The roses of Sharon budded. The peonies had begun to spread their branches. I ran my hand lightly over their tops. The peonies meant everything.

I'd always preferred flowers to vegetables, for their sentimental value. After all, people don't order baskets of brussels sprouts delivered for Valentine's Day, nor do brides carry bouquets of asparagus down the aisle. I'd presented my first bouquet—dandelions, milk dripping from their just-snatched stems—to my mom. She'd cared for it, and me, as if it were the rarest, prettiest treasure. I learned that if I blew on a spent blossom, the fluff would carry my wishes far and wide, so I puffed myself into light-headedness until Gran told me to stop seeding the garden with mischief.

Gran's eyes had twinkled as she chided me. "Mary, Mary, quite contrary, how does your garden grow?" As a contrary teenager, I'd rebelled against the many required hours in the produce gardens. But Gran had taught me to tend those vegetables and herbs, and without that, Pamela wouldn't have hired me. Gran also gave me land for the flowers, which made me not so contrary after all.

I shook myself from the happy memories and gave those peonies a big drink of water before heading to the greenhouse, with its unwashed windows, passing three or four empty bird feeders along the way. I wasn't planning to fill them because I'd be leaving soon. The birds needed a reliable source of provision. I did, too. They'd have to move on, like I had.

What did we have here? Inside the greenhouse, pots filled with moist soil and lots of strawberry runners squatted on the ground. Whom had Gran hired to start the berries? I'd put a gentle stop to it. No one would be around to care for them.

After trudging back to the plots where the dahlia tubers would have been planted in a month or two, I yanked weeds and threw them to the side. A song played in my thoughts, one Gran and I used to sing together as we worked the garden in our summers together. *"This land is your land, this land is my land."* I reached into the soil, letting it run through my fingers.

All soil smells different from other soils. More mineral,

less chalk, heavy with plant mulch that smells of a garbage disposal or coffee grounds or of animals and their tang, which feeds the soil that feeds the plants that feed us. This mud, this dirt, this smell of home. After Mom died, I'd had to live in New Jersey with Dad and Mary Alice nine months out of the year, quietly holed up in my room to avoid confrontation because anything I said or did seemed to push her buttons. Dad told me how thankful he was that I did whatever it took to keep the peace and how much he loved me for it, love I was not going to risk losing. But he'd always encouraged me to spend summers with Gran. I figured he knew she was my only escape, though he'd never say as much because that would mean pulling the thread which would unravel our uneasy peace. But Whidbey and this house . . . this was my home. My safe space, where I could be myself.

Yes, Gran. This land was made for you and me.

"Hey, you," called a familiar voice.

I fell forward, nearly planting my face in the ground at the sound of the voice. Nick?

It had been so long and yet like time hadn't passed at all. He held himself with a little more assurance and smiled with a bit more depth. Even from a distance, I could see that.

He walked carefully through the garden, avoiding dirtying his leather oxfords and perfectly pleated cuffs. It was funny and genuinely Nick.

"Hey." By exercising total self-control, I kept myself from looking at my dirty nails and my muddy boots. I brushed back strands of hair from my tugged-out ponytail.

He stopped when he reached me and stood so close. "I hope I didn't shock you."

Shields up. "To be honest, I am shocked. I thought you lived in Texas."

"I did. And then I moved back to Whidbey," he said. "Not too long ago."

Tears brewed in my chest. Why? This was the most casual conversation. Just 100 percent totally unexpected.

"I wanted to come to Gran's funeral," he said. "I saw the posting on the Whidbey Community Facebook page. But I didn't want to startle you or be a distraction."

I relaxed a little. "Thanks. That was thoughtful."

He pulled his hand from around his back. In it was my favorite gardening hat, the straw one that had *Hello, Sunshine*, printed on the brim. "You accidentally left this in my car a . . . while ago."

Oh, that had been no accident. I'd purposely left it in his car when we broke up, riding shotgun to remind him of me. Of us. I took it back and put it on my head, touched, really, that he'd kept it.

He traced the word *Sunshine* on the rim. "Hi ho, sunshine," he said softly, and at that, my tears broke through. He reached out instinctively and took me into his arms as the tears coursed down my cheeks. "Hey, I'm sorry. I didn't mean to make you sad. I just wanted you to know that there is still somebody around who remembers how Gran called out to you."

I nodded and a couple minutes later stepped out of his

embrace, pulling myself back together. "I know. It's okay. I'd made it through this hard day without crying, keeping my cool for Gran's funeral. Then that phrase popped the bubble and let it all out."

"Uh, I'm really sorry about Gran. I wanted to tell you in person. I wasn't sure how long you'd be here."

"It's all good." I stepped back another foot or two. "I'll be here for about two weeks."

"I'm glad to see you in the garden. I hear you're gardening professionally in California."

"Not yet," I said. "I'm still serving tables at the five-star inn to pay the bills, but I've been interning for their head culinary gardener, and they've hinted I'll be promoted this spring."

His eyebrows rose. "So you're focusing on vegetables?"

I smiled wryly. "I know, I know. I do get to work with nasturtiums and pansies once in a while, and flowering herbs because they're garnishes. But the money is with food, not flowers."

"I see. They're lucky to have you," he said.

I'd become increasingly concerned that they did not feel that way about me. "How about you? Why are you back?"

"My company closed about a year after I got there."

"I'm sorry," I said. "I didn't know."

He nodded. "It's okay. One of our big clients asked if I'd like to work their account remotely. My parents are always traveling since my sisters' kids live in Oregon and Montana, so I moved home to Whidbey, for the short-term, anyway.

I'm also working on a marketing start-up. I'm doing better than before I left."

So you wouldn't have had to leave home, and me, at all, I thought but didn't say, because why? There was no going back in time.

We walked to and under the arbor where the Peace roses, untended for perhaps the first time in my life, tangled in on themselves. They'd get black spot if I didn't clear some space for air circulation. "Maybe we both needed some room to breathe. And I needed to find my way."

"Did you find it?" he asked. "I want that for you."

He always knew how to get right to my heart. "I think so. I hope so."

It started to rain. I didn't invite him in, and it didn't seem like he was expecting it.

He lightly tapped my straw hat. "I'm sorry I made you cry. I never want to do that."

"You didn't. I'm kind of glad you were here when the dam broke."

He smiled. "Me too. And I'm glad you got the hat back."

"I have good memories of you saying, 'Hello, sunshine,' to tease Gran that you were tweaking her phrase."

"She didn't mind, did she?"

"Nope. She liked you for it. She was a military woman. Couldn't abide wishy-washy men."

An awkward silence passed. "Okay if I still say it?" he asked. "Hello, sunshine?"

Why not? It wasn't like I'd see him often. "Sure."

He smiled and looked at his watch. "I'd better go. I'm meeting someone on the mainland."

Cue the moment when he would have kissed me good-bye. Before.

"Have a good meeting," I said, and he said he would. On the way to his car, he turned around. I was still looking at him, and he smiled and waved. I waved back before going inside.

Half an hour later, he texted. **How about dinner in a few days? I've got to drive some things to Oregon for my mom, but I'll be back soon.**

No, no, no. I didn't want to open an emotional door I wasn't willing to walk through. But was he even asking for a door to be opened? Or just that the one we'd slammed might be shut quietly and with maturity? I owed him that. He'd been kind to me today when I needed a friend. **Okay,** I texted back.

Great! I'll text in a couple of days so we can find a good time and day. Mussels at Tony's?

Sure.

Looking forward to it.

I headed into the kitchen and warmed up one of the meals a neighbor had dropped off. Then I headed to the purple bedroom. I lay on top of the bed in the room that had been mine every summer when I stayed at Gran's, rubbing my hand over the puffy nubs to soothe myself like I had when I was a girl, and closed my eyes.

Drip. Drip. Drip.

The sound definitely came from above the ceiling.

I got up, walked to the attic stairway, pulled it down, and clicked on the light before walking up the stairs. Sure enough. There was a leak in one corner. Alarmingly, the roof sagged slightly, plump with water retention.

I had zero experience with roof issues. I'd get a quote on a repair.

I looked around at unopened boxes, garment bags, and of course, the hope chest. Something looked different about it . . . Oh! It had always been locked with a heavy, old-school padlock, but not anymore. I smiled, remembering my stoic, practical, beloved grandmother. Once Gran had been hurt, she locked up her hopes where they could do no more damage to her or to anyone she loved.

I stepped toward the chest. But Gran had asked me to wait for Grace, and I would. I stepped back, clicked off the attic light, and headed down to the living room. A few minutes later Grace's face appeared on my phone's screen, and I answered her FaceTime call.

"Hey. Sorry it took me so long. We stopped and visited my *halaboji* on the way home."

"How's he doing?" I asked.

She shrugged and answered a bit too brightly. "Seems good to me! So what's this about me helping you in the attic?"

I settled deep into the recliner. "I dunno. I think there's something Gran felt would make me emotional and she ran out of time to sort it with me. Did she seem okay when you saw her a few weeks ago?"

She nodded. "Yep. Sick, but not, you know, so bad that I thought it was close to her passing. I would have told you." In the background, her brothers chatted, and the TV volume rose.

"I know. I think it just got bad fast. I feel terrible that I wasn't here sooner. Gran made me promise that you'd help me and that I'd do it before I go back to California, and I'm leaving soon. I know work is always crazy for you, Mademoiselle Success, but maybe you can come for a few days?"

Her face froze.

"Are you okay?" I asked.

"Let me go to my room. Hold on."

Once in her room, she closed the door but still spoke softly. "Hey. I didn't want to overwhelm you while stuff was going on with your gran. So here's the deal. I failed the bar exam last month."

I sat up straight. "You what? You've never failed anything."

"I guess I can cross that off my bucket list," she said wryly.

"Your parents?"

"Don't know. Can't know. They didn't know I was taking the February exam, so I can keep the failure a secret. I told them I'm taking the exam at the end of July—which is true. I have to pass that one. Results are due back no later than Labor Day."

Grace could keep a secret. She'd make a good lawyer. She had a great poker face and never had to lie to keep it. "Your boss knows, though, right?"

"Yes. He knows 'cause he was expecting to promote me.

I'm working as a legal researcher—for now—since I'm still unlicensed. After this project is done, I'm taking an unpaid leave of absence to study. If I pass, I keep my job and move forward in the firm to a great career path. If I don't, I won't have a job, as the next round of graduates will be offered the research positions till they pass the bar. It's the only career ladder up." Grace sighed, then continued, "To be honest, I'm not even sure I want to be a lawyer anymore."

"I totally get that. I'm on a shaky ladder up, too, even though I'm not sure I'm even climbing to the right place."

She nodded. "I think that's why I have a hard time studying. Do I really want to spend the rest of my life helping people get out of trouble? DUIs? Divorces? Real estate deals gone bad?"

"I'm guessing that's a rhetorical question. But the plan was for you to be a lawyer, right?"

"Right. My parents' plan, anyway. I have no interest in being a doctor or an engineer." She tilted her head. "Well, I think I might like to be a lawyer, but I don't know. I really don't. I feel like I have no control over my life."

"Maybe you have more choices than you're willing to acknowledge. You just might not like them. No way you can do your own thing?"

"I might have to if I don't pass the next exam." She sighed again. "I can't face the shame of failing a second time. I don't want to disappoint my family. They have great hopes for me. They're so proud of me. You know? I just need to buckle down and study. It's hard to do with all my brothers and their activity at the house. Plus my mom will be checking in on my study progress every hour, and that's stressful."

"So your parents will know you're not working?"

"I'll tell them that after this huge project, my boss is giving me a couple of months' leave of absence to study and then I'll head back to the firm. I just won't mention what will happen in September if I don't pass. Because I must. And I'm still living at home, so yeah, they'll know."

I looked around me. "I'm living at home, too, at the moment."

"But you also have an apartment in Cali," she said. "Speaking of Cali, what are you going to do?"

"Go back," I said. "To the place I get a paycheck deposited every two weeks."

"What are you going to do with the house? The land?" she asked. "I mean, for good."

I sank back in the recliner. "I don't know. It's all happened so fast I haven't even had a chance to process it. Maybe I'll rent it out so someone is here keeping an eye on the place until I come back and make a go of things in a couple of years. Build up a healthy nest egg, then see what I could do about growing flowers. But back to you." I looked around Gran's cozy house. "What if you live here for the summer? It's quiet and no one will check in on you while you study."

She dropped her phone and picked it up again. "At Gran's house?"

"At *my* house! And why not? It'll be empty, and I'll feel

better knowing someone is on the property. It's very cozy, and no one will bug you. Gran would have approved."

She nodded thoughtfully. "Yeah. She knew I failed the bar exam."

I nearly dropped *my* phone. "She did?"

"Yep. I found out shortly before I went to check on her for you. I was distraught over failing and felt like I had no drive, no purpose, and she could tell. She was so good. She prayed with me and told me she knew I could pass the one this summer. She encouraged me that I could do anything because she knew from whom I came. My *halmoni*—that's what she meant."

Grace looked up. "It would be perfect, wouldn't it? I mean, my mom heard you say that Gran wanted me to come and help you with the house. Which is true, so it's not like I'm lying. I'll just tell her I am going to stay on for the summer as a kind of . . . housekeeper."

"Right. You and the forest animals cleaning the house, Cinderella," I teased. "I'll teach you to garden and you can take care of that while I'm gone."

Alarm crossed her face.

"I'm kidding! I know you don't garden. *Mi casa es su casa.* Every day of the week. If your mom buys this story, you're in. And then I won't need to pack anything up until the end of the summer except—" I hated to pressure her—"the attic, because Gran said soon."

"Thank you so much. I'll be there in a week-ish, before

you need to go back to Cali, and we can do the attic. I'll be there in case it makes you sad."

And it might. Grace had stayed with me after Mom died, too. "It'll be like the extended sleepovers we had when we were younger. Meals. I'll make some."

"Movies. I'll pick them," she said. "We'll talk about boys. Well, men, now."

I held my breath. She read my face.

"Cass? No holding out."

"I'm having dinner with Nick. It's just an evening to sign off in a friendly manner since our breakup didn't ever really feel resolved."

"Uh-huh. You need me. I'm moving in next week."

* * *

For the next couple of days, I puttered in my garden and brought my morning coffee out to the picnic table where I'd eaten lunch almost all of my childhood summers. I binge-read the books Gran had saved, one after another, with hot chocolate and mini marshmallows, heavy on the marshmallows. I fed treats to the cats who had taken up residence in the barn and thanked them for mousing. I wore Gran's house slippers and rubbed her Vicks VapoRub on my sore elbows a couple of times, because the menthol scent reminded me of her.

The house was more carefully preserved than anything Gran had ever picked and canned from her victory garden. Returning to Cali for a few years would let me build the financial base I'd need to maximize my farm's potential and help me keep it intact for all of us. For my mom, who grew up here harvesting apples with Gramps. For my daughter, whose name I already knew would be Quinn—my last name—like my name was my mom's maiden name, and my mom's name was Gran's.

Four generations, mother to daughter to daughter to daughter. I would keep the land and its legacy for all of us.

CHAPTER FIVE

The next morning, as I dusted the teal bedroom, I looked out the window onto the garden and a movement caught my eye. Was that a man?

Definitely. An old man, bent with age, leaving my property, closing the gate behind him.

I slipped into my mud boots and headed outside to see what he'd been up to.

Once in the garden I spied little runners now planted in the strawberry field—rows and rows and rows of them. And they'd been watered in. I walked over to the reeled hose and held my hand under it. Cold water spattered my palm. Someone had just been using it.

I'd heard of garden fairies, but not ones that looked like seventy-five-year-old men.

As I headed back into the house, my phone buzzed. I pulled it from my pocket and read the text from Nick.

Still on for tonight?

Yes.

Do you want me to pick you up, or do you want to meet me there?

Hmm. **I'll meet you there.** I'd be driving myself from now on, literally and figuratively.

Okay. I just didn't want you to go back to the house alone late at night, he texted back.

I'm used to it. I live alone. Well, not for long. Don't worry. What time?

The dots came and then went, and there was a blank where the text should have been. Finally he said, **Seven?**

Seven. See you then.

A few hours later, I put on a denim dress with yellow turned-up cuffs that reflected the color of my hair. Mom had always called it dandelion—Gran's and her blonde with a twist of brightness from my redheaded dad. I wrapped a leather belt around my waist and pulled on some brown knee boots to match. If the suit made the man, then the dress made the woman. Made her confident, anyway. Would our conversations be awkward? Was Nick going to mention the breakup? I hoped not. Better to just let bygones be bygones.

I hopped into my Mustang and headed toward our favorite hangout.

When I arrived at Tony's, Nick was already at the corner table, the one we'd hung out at after work. *Our table.* We'd met as servers at Tony's a few summers back. At the end, I'd thought things had been serious. No, they had been serious. Then Nick had gone on to a successful career.

Me? I was still a waitress. Just not at Tony's.

As I walked toward him, he stood until I took my seat. I looked out at the water. "I miss home. The water is moody, sometimes gray and sometimes blue, sometimes green. Sometimes the sky is sunny, sometimes misty. In California, it's always sunny. On the outside, anyway."

"Are you happy there?"

"I will be once I'm full-time gardening and not waitressing." The bread basket arrived, and we ordered mussels and beer.

"Culinary gardening?"

I smiled. "It sounds good on paper and on LinkedIn. Eventually I can network with people who design and tend flower farms. I hope."

"Good, useful plan."

"Down-to-earth," I said with a grin.

"Punny." He smiled back, but when he spoke, his voice was reserved. "So you're moving in with someone from Cali?"

"No." I shook my head. "From here."

"Here?" He set down his beer. "Is it someone I know?"

I kept a serious face. "Yes, of course. You know everyone around here, don't you?"

"Who is he?" His voice grew a little gruff.

I set down my own beer and laughed. "Grace is moving into the farmhouse for the summer."

He ran his hands through his thick, dark hair—like his mom's, a nod to their Greek heritage—and blushed under his five-o'clock shadow. "Oh. I see."

I grinned. He was jealous. "You thought I was moving in with a guy? Instead of a roommate?"

"I mean, no . . . I should have known it was a roommate. Stupid. Right? I didn't think that was something you'd do, but . . ." He hung his head. "Not even sure why I went there."

He wasn't going to admit it would have bothered him, so he'd blurted. In some small way, it made me happy to know he cared.

"So Grace is moving to Whidbey? But you're leaving?" He looked confused.

"She has to study for the bar exam. She's coming to house-sit—because it's quieter—and to help me pack up Gran's stuff." I stopped for a minute before continuing. "Gran made me promise that I wouldn't pack the attic without Grace and that I'd do it soon."

He sipped his beer. "Why do you think she asked you to do that?"

"I think I'm going to find something in there that she was worried will freak me out or make me sad and didn't want me to be alone when I find it. I arrived too late for her to do it with me, and her mind was fogged by morphine, so she wanted someone to be with me. That's my guess, anyway."

Nick nodded. "I'd agree. Call me if you need anything.

I'm happy to help." He pried open a mussel shell and popped the plump, salty morsel into his mouth.

I set aside a shell that remained firmly closed. "What happened with your company?"

"They promised me the sun and the moon, but the sun and moon were quickly eclipsed by bankruptcy. Thankfully one of their big clients in Boston took me on full-time, and like I mentioned, I'm also working my new start-up. Digital marketing, both for them and for me."

"I'm sorry about the bankruptcy," I said. "I know how much that job meant to you. But you always have so many great ideas that I'm not surprised you have two successful jobs going at once. Just sorry it didn't work out for you." *For us.*

He ate a couple of bites. "Can I be real?"

I buckled my emotional seat belt. "Sure."

"When it all collapsed, I felt super selfish and foolish. I left everything important for my dream job. Only the dream job was a complete nightmare. I needed to be a bit more practical. And now I am."

"I understand," I said. "That's why I'm culinary gardening. Practical."

"Down-to-earth," he punned back.

"Exactly. Gran always talked about thinking more of 'we' than of 'me,' so if I focus on what I can do for my boss, that will help her see what she can do for me."

Nick nodded and gestured for another order of mussels. "Hopefully. I guess using that same idea, I recently figured out I'd been spending too much time making decisions that mostly benefited me, and I needed to flip that a bit. But if you spend too much time on 'we' and none on 'me,' you just turn into a codependent. Someone else is running your life because you're afraid to make them unhappy, even if it's hurting you. It's a balance. I'm learning."

I forced open a shell and looked at the meat. He'd just described what actually went on between me and my boss, Pamela. She was running my life and I didn't want to make her unhappy. But since when did Nick talk like that? Codependent? I mean, the concept was solid, and he did seem like he had matured a lot since we broke up, but wow. "That's a great insight," I kind of fumbled out. "I need to think about that for myself."

"Thanks," he said. "The woman I'm seeing shared it with me. She's really wise and understanding."

The woman he was seeing. Like—seeing?

"I'm glad that if you're seeing someone, she's wise and understanding." I tried to be big about it.

"She's amazing," he said. He set his beer down. "I'm 'seeing' a therapist, Cassidy. Want to figure out what I've been doing wrong." He smiled at my misunderstanding, as I'd done with his.

"Touché," I acknowledged and laughed.

"Your laugh is so pretty. I'd rather make you laugh than cry any day of the week."

"You didn't make me cry the day of Gran's funeral," I said.

"I didn't mean just then." He looked at me intently, and I didn't look away.

We paid the bill and he walked me to the waterfront. The moonlight on the water shivered.

"Here." Nick stretched his coat around me. I slipped my arms into the sleeves, and as I did, his scent rose from the brown wool. It was too big for me but summoned memories of being wrapped in his embrace.

"I need to remember to start bringing a jacket or a sweater. Never do in California," I said.

"So you're going back?"

I nodded. "My job is there. Going to get stuff settled here and then head back." We looked at the water, not at each other.

"When I said I left everything important," he said, "I meant everyone important. You. I'm sorry I wasn't more mature. I was chasing a job, and my drive told me that the window to succeed was closing, that if I didn't grab it and hold it, it would be gone forever. I know I said I wasn't ready to commit to you. But the job is gone—and now you are too. I think I committed to the wrong thing. I needed to slow down. But all I could see was the hustle and I moved too fast."

I looked directly at him. His eyes showed he spoke truthfully. "You didn't tell me any of this in the past couple of years."

"Before I deactivated my account for a while, I saw on social media that you were dating someone else. You'd told me, when we broke up, that you weren't willing to do a long-distance relationship. I didn't want to interfere with your life if you were happy. So now I just want to say I'm sorry. I should have said it earlier. I had some growing up to do."

I inhaled. *You just came to say goodbye to him, right? So why don't you just say goodbye?* "It's good," I said. "I'm not dating him anymore."

"I didn't know that," he said.

"But in the end, it all worked out as it should have between you and me." *Right?*

He walked me to my car, and I shrugged off his coat. "Here."

"No," he said. "Keep it. Then I'll have to come back and get it."

"No thank you," I said gently as I handed it back to him.

He nodded and took the coat. "Can I stop by before you go back? Take you out again?"

I thought for a long minute. "I've missed our friendship."

He flinched. "Okay, I get it. I'm still here—as a friend—if you need anything."

It was dark when I arrived at home, but by the light of the moon I saw that more strawberry runners had been planted. Nick's concern about me being alone rang in my memory. I hurried into the house and locked the door.

* * *

A couple of days later, there he was again. The elderly gardening gnome. I pulled on my mud boots and went to greet him.

I slowed down so I wouldn't startle the old guy. He

stooped over the mounds, propped on a kneeling stool. Ah. I knew who he was! I hadn't recognized him from the back with his hat on. "Mr. Beeksma?" Despite being some years younger, Dirk Beeksma had been a faithful friend to Gran forever, since she'd helped him and his grandpa when he was a boy. His chicken farm was just down the road. I'd have to let him know that we didn't need strawberries or anything planted this year.

He unbent and looked up at me. "Miss Cassidy. How are you doing, young lady?"

"I'm okay, Mr. Beeksma," I said. "But . . . what are you doing?"

He looked at me as if I'd lost my mind. "Planting strawberries? Have you been away so long you've forgotten?"

I grinned. "Of course not. I mean, why?"

He stood and walked toward me, taking his cap off his head and swishing away a cloud of gnats before putting it back on. "Taxes."

April showers began to pelt, so we moved into the greenhouse for cover. It had once been a small potting shed with few windows, but Gran had eventually built a big, beautiful building around the original structure. It smelled of stems and roots, and the humidity made my skin dewy. I'd missed that and a hundred other things in dry Cali.

"Taxes." His voice snapped me back to reality. "They will crush you if I don't help plant and sell these this year."

I smiled. "You don't need to worry. Gran paid the taxes

in advance. Even though I haven't sorted all her paperwork yet, I did look that up."

He nodded. "Yep. Helen paid ag taxes." He set his hat on one of the wooden potting benches. "But if you don't sell some produce this year, all of her taxes, retroactive seven years and then going forward, are going to be taxed at the regular rate, not the agricultural rate, and maybe with interest and penalties. You'll be stuck with a tax bill as thick as one of the old trees in Oak Harbor, and money doesn't grow on them. You got that kind of cash?"

My body grew cold. "No." I sat down on the stool. "I don't understand."

He sat down next to me. Thin webs laced the greenhouse's four corners, and a few tiny spiders stopped spinning, eavesdropping instead.

"Your first order of business is to raise enough income from the property to keep your land taxed as agricultural land. It was how your gran filed, and it's the best way. Keeps taxes down on big properties like this one." His arm swept out as if to encompass the land. "Five acres of evergreens. Five or so acres for the house and the gardens. Acres of orchards—but they haven't been tended for a bit, so not a lot to sell—and some of farmland on the other side of the barn. To keep that exemption, you have to earn at least a hundred dollars from each acre of land, every year, five years out of seven. That's making fifteen hundred dollars this year from the property. Your gran was not able to work the honesty stand or sell enough at the farmers' markets for the last two years."

"Two years . . . since I left." Ah. That must have been the struggle she'd mentioned. She'd said nothing of that. Told me I was free to fly the nest when I scored the gardening internship. In fact, when I'd resisted, she'd insisted. And so I flew. We both knew I'd fly home someday. Someday was today. I was here to take care of it now.

Mr. Beeksma shrugged. "She did everything she could do to hold on to this place—upkeep, pipes, ground, taxes. Was all she had left, really, and her roots grew deep. I was a young boy on my grandfather's chicken farm when she and her first husband bought it, and I remember how much she loved it through the years. She just couldn't keep on top of it all. It's clear now that you don't have but this year to catch up."

I looked at the strawberry runners. "The strawberries aren't going to make fifteen hundred dollars this year."

"Nope. But they're a start."

I stood and looked through the dusty windows toward the land adjacent to the barn, where Gran had grown a huge veg patch in years past. I'd always wanted to extend the flower beds there. Now that the land was bare, I could do so. "Flowers could bring in money at the honesty stand at the edge of the property. But I'll have to head back to California soon."

"Flowers aren't going to grow 'soon,'" he said.

Yeah. "Do you know of anyone who could help tend a few while I'm gone if I plant some before I go?"

He rubbed his jawline. "Well, I, uh . . . could."

I shook my head. "Maybe someone who doesn't have as many . . . responsibilities?"

"You mean, who isn't old."

I pursed my lips into a smile. "It's sweet of you to offer, though."

He tilted his head back and took off his cap. "There's Annika, Marty's girl. She's helping me a few hours each week, and I know she's looking for more. She's going to college this fall and needs a bit of money. Don't know that she has experience with flowers, but she grew up on a farm, and she's young."

I had to be back to work in a week, tops. There was money in that shared savings account. Not a lot, but enough to invest in keeping our taxes down by planting and selling something and paying someone to tend it, because there was no way I would have the money to pay ten thousand dollars in back taxes and increased new taxes next year. If that happened, the land would have to be sold. I needed to do something now.

"Ask Annika to come see me. Right away."

* * *

"This is pretty." Grace brought her suitcases into the teal bedroom.

"You can put your laptop and stuff in the little yellow room next door—it'll be a good office for you."

"Thank you," she said. "You think of everything."

"I want you to nail the bar exam. You can, 100 percent."

"I hope so!" Grace hung her purse on the doorknob and ran her hand along the newly dusted Singer. "Cute vintage sewing machine."

I arched my eyebrows. "Do you sew?"

She grinned. "As you know, I have limited household skills."

We sat on the bed side by side, and I explained the tax situation to her.

"That's huge. Did you know about this?"

"Nope, one of Gran's friends explained it to me. I think once Gran started the pain meds, things kind of slipped away. The garden is clear but empty, except for the few perennials that pushed through neglect. I'm going to plant a few starts."

"A few?" Her look told me how well she knew me. "Wouldn't food sell better and faster? Herbs, tomatoes, lettuces, and stuff like that? Farmers' market kinds of things?"

"It probably would, but if I'm going to hire someone to help, I can't expect her to run to the farmers' market every week, and the booths for this year are likely spoken for—we had to do that months in advance in summers past. The honesty stand is right on the property, and flowers are easy to cut and bundle each morning. People can pay with apps and . . ." I couldn't hold back my enthusiasm. "I would like the garden to be filled with Gran's plants. Really *our* plants because I was the one who planted most of the flowers. I was so crushed when we had to take those gardens down and thought I'd never see those varieties, those plants I worked so hard on, ever again. And now I will."

Grace raised a skeptical eyebrow. "How can you find plants that came from your own garden so fast?"

"At Gran's funeral, a lot of people told me how she'd shared cuts and starts with so many people. So I hopped onto the Whidbey Island Community Facebook page and posted a request. I also called some of the old-timers around here. One of Mom's really good friends is coming by later today with some of the plants people offered. That should be enough to start with and pay those taxes. Best news? I won't have to grow everything from seed—which means I can get all this into the ground before I head back to Cali."

"I love it," Grace said. "You have great ideas!"

You know what? I think I do!

"I wish I could help with the plants," she continued, "but I assume you want them to live."

I laughed. "Yes, and you are here to study."

* * *

About an hour later, a truck pulled up to the gate that met the acreage's street side. My mom's friend Brenda parked and then called to me. "Yoo-hoo!" She waved her hand in the air. "Bring a wagon."

A wagon? I hustled to the back of the fenced acre and pulled the rusted red wagon I used to transport pots and such. The wheels squeaked in protest as I headed to the gate, where Brenda waited. Her truck bed was filled with plants. I mean, *filled* with plants. Many, many wagonloads. There were a few tomato starts jailed in cages, and those prize-winning cucumber runners streamed over pots' edges, but mostly loads and loads of glorious flowers.

"Hi, hon, howya doing?" Brenda asked.

"Hi, Brenda. Thank you so much for doing all this."

"Oh, this is just one truckload. I knew exactly who had starts and slips and seeds from your family's garden. I've gathered as many as I could so you'd have a variety, and there are more to come. It was such a shame when Helen put the garden down for good. Everyone I know is so excited you're going to resurrect it. And, Mary, Mary, quite contrary, I know who nurtured most of these flowers. You!"

My heart burst with affection and joy as I surveyed the sea of black garden pots filled with green plants, mostly stubs and shrubs but some of which were blossoming already, promising a good growing season. Most had pieces of tape on the side, indicating the plant's variety.

"You remember what all of these are, right?" Brenda asked hesitantly as she started loading some onto the wagon.

"Oh yes," I said. "Of course. We—" I indicated the plants before me—"grew up together. I know just where to put them so they'll flourish." I bent to look at the haul. "Chocolate cosmos," I murmured as a mother would to a child who'd returned home. "And my beautiful mint. They go well together." I brushed my hand against a lacy Queen Anne, so often thought of as a weed but a delicate flourish in any bouquet. Red and orange poppies, phlox, and lilies. This was a week for reunions! I emptied that load and filled the wagon up twice more, setting the pots on the ground near one another.

Brenda carried over one large pot, set it down, and then ran her hand over one of the plants. "Helen's beautiful blue nigella was the local envy and did well in other gardens, but try as they might, no one but you, not even Helen, could coax those reluctant blue poppies from the ground." She handed a packet of seeds to me. "Work your magic." She continued her inventory. "Bachelor's buttons and, well, you'll know them all. The seed envelopes are marked and if you get them into the greenhouse now for seedling starts, you'll have what you need soon. Just call me if you have any questions. If you have time to call. I think you're going to be a sunup, sundown, farmer's-tan kind of girl with all of this."

I stepped back and, now out of the cloud of bliss, looked realistically at the challenge before me. And this was only one truckload. "I hope to have someone helping me this summer after I return to California. I have someone in mind. Would it be okay if she got in touch if she has questions?"

"Returning to California?" She let the wagon handle drop to the ground. "You're not staying? Then why in the world are you planting now?"

I leaned on my spade. "I want to bring the original garden back. This all happened really fast, and I'm trying to figure out a workable plan. First job, I know, is to make fifteen hundred dollars in sales to keep the ag tax exemption by selling flowers at the honesty stand."

"Oh." She wiped her hands on the sides of her jeans, but the undersides of her nails were still dirty, the badge of the informal "sorority" of gardeners. "Honey. Trust me. That's not going to be possible. Not with just flowers at the stand. Lots of competition these days, lots of flower stands, not as many buyers. People are selling their land, and the ones who are snapping up houses for occasional vacation rentals, they don't usually buy flowers."

Brenda looked down the road toward the Wilson property, which had been developed into houses a couple of years earlier. "I'd count on maybe five hundred, tops, for the flowers. Maybe more like two hundred."

I repositioned my straw hat. My face must have revealed my dismay.

Brenda stepped toward the wagonload protectively. "I hate to seem stingy, but I think the people who donated these would be pretty put off if they thought they may not be well taken care of. Everyone robbed their gardens for the very best to help repopulate your and Helen's garden."

Well, if they were robbing their lands of the best, they'd also kept plenty and, after all, they'd been gifts from us to start with. I swiped the sweat stinging my eyes. I could understand them not wanting to see prized plants left to die, though. I felt sad when I saw anything dying on the vine, literally, due to neglect. As of that exact moment, I didn't even know if I'd have help. "So . . . do you not want me to keep them?"

"Are you staying?" Brenda asked softly. She was caught in the middle too. She'd been the go-between and plant shuttler.

Was I? I mean, could I, even? "I need a few days to think about it," I said.

She reached out and gave me a big hug. "I hope you choose to—I don't look forward to returning these." She smiled. "And maybe, maybe people wouldn't want them back if you go back to California. But good summer help is hard to come by." She nodded toward the plants we'd already unloaded. "Don't let those die or hire anyone that can't take care of them. That wouldn't be the legacy you'd want to leave."

What *was* the legacy I wanted to leave? More important than a far-off legacy, what life did I want to live now? I wiped my hands on the garden rag looped through my jeans before hugging her back. "Thank you, Brenda. This means so much to me, but I'm not sure what I'll do yet. I have big plans for this place—later, when I have a nest egg to do it right. Now? I'd have to start small if I can start at all."

"'Do not despise these small beginnings,'" she said, "'for the Lord rejoices to see the work begin.'"

"Bible quote?" I asked.

"You betcha. I'll keep the plants watered until you let me know what you decide." As she drove away with the bulk of the plants still in her bed, I stood like a conductor before a small floral symphony, instruments poised, ready to begin. A harmony of starts, seeds, slips. By the time I added these to our peonies, roses, and roses of Sharon, we'd definitely have enough for bouquets. There was no way I could have purchased the heirloom plants represented here, not from my family's stock, which was so important to me.

But how was I going to earn enough money to keep that tax exemption? And then if I stayed on Whidbey, how could I pay my bills if I quit the almost-not-quite-yet-if-ever dream job?

Maybe I just recognize reality, quit with the sentimentality, and sell the land like the Wilsons did. Head back to California with money in the bank and keep the dream job.

Was it the dream job? Sure, if the dream was a steady paycheck and a great LinkedIn profile.

I looked at the view across the street from the farm. Mountains in the distance, breathtaking water view. When Gran and Bob bought this property, it had been a beautiful backwater home and a run-down victory garden. Now it was a beautiful, water view farm with parcel potential to developers, which was why the Wilsons had sold their land.

But this . . . I bent and scooped some soil. *These.* I held a five-gallon pot—a generous gift—on my hip like a mother held a baby. They were my legacy. My roots. My real dream. I'd promised to keep it for all of us.

So first things first—how to earn the ag tax money. I stood among the pots and thought, *Who would know how to help me make money on the land? Fast.*

Nick. The marketing genius. He'd said to let him know if I needed anything.

I pulled my phone from my back pocket. **Want to come for**

dinner with Grace and me tomorrow? I need a friend. And some marketing advice.

I'll be there, he replied. **What should I bring?**

Your Superman cape.

CHAPTER SIX

So. What to make for dinner? I opened the pantry and tugged the string to click on the light. Something fun and friendly, to repay Nick and Grace for brainstorming with me.

On the shelves to the right were the cookbooks. Oddly, face out on the first shelf, Gran's old red- and white-checked *Better Homes and Gardens New Cook Book* offered itself. I hadn't seen it in years and years. Not since Mom died, I realized. Gran must have made sure that it was pulled out and waiting for me. I took it and my coffee outside to the picnic table and sat down before opening the book.

Months after Mom died, Dad had taken a new job and moved us clear across the country. He'd met Mary Alice at that new job, and she cleaned all of my mom's stuff out of our house within weeks of their wedding. I'd tucked away my anger then because, well, where was I going to go? I had thought that Dad had been as crushed as I was when my mom's breast cancer went from diagnosis to death so quickly. We'd dealt with the pain differently, though. He remarried quickly and was happy to give away everything that provoked memories of Mom so he wouldn't feel the pain. I wanted to wrap myself in everything Mom had touched, worn, or held. Her pink blouse still hung in my closet.

Gran's way of dealing with pain had been to contain it. Out of sight, out of mind, but never far from her heart, I knew, because I knew her well. Her first husband's uniforms remained locked in a case in the attic. She talked about my gramps and my mom, of course, but only with me, because we'd shared them. She never talked of her own parents and shut down that conversation if it arose. I'd seen her wipe away a tear as she did.

I opened the cookbook. It was ring-bound and divided into sections by topic: meal planning, casseroles—did anyone use that word anymore?—outdoor cooking, pastries and pies. There were envelopes clipped into the binder, too, filled with clippings Gran or Mom had cut from the paper, and recipe cards with tips and ideas in friends' handwriting. One envelope had *Helen* scrawled across it. In it, I found a picture of Gran in a faux-fur coat in the sixties, standing in front of her Skylark with a pot in one hand and a long wooden spoon in the other. I smiled.

Also inside were favorite recipes, yellowed paper on which Gran had either written her own recipes or glued on a clipping, and lots of notes. *Don't let this curdle by adding the citrus first. Ben loved this, but Lauri left it completely uneaten. Try with ground beef next time. They should retitle this from "Chicken Divan" to "Chicken Divine!" "Mince Meat" from Etta. Simmer a long time and then can.* All of her recipe titles were in quotation marks. So cute. So Gran. She'd placed pages from her other cookbooks in her section, too. *Meat is money—take care of it.* Truth. Then, *Men like meat.*

I paged through her old red- and white-checked friend, looking for something delicious to serve. I flipped to the meat section and found some she'd tabbed: Swiss Steak and Mushrooms. Liver Loaf. I shuddered. Anyway, I didn't want to make a romantic dinner, so—no meat. As I turned the pages, the scent of lemon thyme lifted from the pages and I closed my eyes for a moment, breathing in the memory. Gran's hands had always smelled of garden herbs.

I opened another envelope clipped into the binder in the bread section and found the original Cinn Roll recipe card. Gran had never used a recipe to make them that I could remember, but she must have at one time, 'cause here it was. They were the best weekend breakfast. I would make that one, for sure, but I didn't need the card because she'd already taught me the recipe.

Gran and I had cooked together every summer. She'd make grown-up meals mostly from our gardens, and though I didn't always love vegetables, I did love eating together what the two of us had grown under her tender care. When I was old enough, I'd made kid food like grilled cheese and lots of burgers for my parents and grandparents, hovering over the grill on a step stool with Gran right next to me. I'd loved cooking with and for her—it's what families did. When I was a teen, I moved on to more challenging dishes for a while, but when I went back to Dad's house in New Jersey and then to college and Cali, I'd stopped cooking.

No one to cook for then. But now?

Next came an envelope clipped into the cookbook titled *Lauri*. Tucked inside was a photo of my teenage mom, so sweet sixteen in her cheer outfit by a bake sale table filled with cakes, hand pies, and her to-die-for brownies. I dragged my finger along the photo, wanting to touch something Mom had touched. I pulled out a few of her recipes and also looked for ones she'd tabbed with an *L* on them. Next to Deluxe Eggs Benedict, Mom had written, *Sauté mushrooms, dice, and then add fresh thyme and sherry before serving.* My hand hovered. *Mom. Mama. Mommy. I miss you.* The pain dulled but never went away. The hole shrank but never closed.

Mom's next recipe was vegetable pizzas on the grill. That I could do! I remembered her making them, and they held such good memories. I could use the sourdough recipe I'd been tweaking since I'd been home instead of the tortillas she suggested, but maybe changing up Mom's and Gran's recipes would be like erasing a part of them. I couldn't bear to lose any part of either of them. Sticking with tortillas.

Tucked in Mom's envelope was a picture of the two of us in the garden, holding up tomatoes for eyes and curling our upper lips to keep our fresh tarragon mustaches in place. *Cass loves tomatoes, and so do I!* Mom had written next to a smiley face.

I pulled out another large recipe card. *Save for Cassidy later. "Honeymoon Salad." Lettuce alone, without dressing.* ☺☺

Oh, Mom. I smiled. *You are the best.*

Chocolate Chiffon Cake with confetti sprinkles. *Cassidy's favorite. Lots of sprinkles. I told her if she didn't tone down the Cass sass, next year it would be pineapple upside-down cake.*

I hated pineapple.

Next to that recipe was another envelope, clipped into the notebook's binder, too. I reached into the envelope and pulled out pictures of my tenth birthday.

The whole scene replayed in my mind. Mom sang "Happy Birthday" to me a dozen times until I was annoyed and told her so.

What I wouldn't give to hear her voice singing.

Chocolate blotches and fingerprints polka-dotted the page. Her fingertips. Mine. I touched them gently. Some confetti sprinkles fell out of the envelope, and I put one in my mouth. It was stale, but I knew her hand had put them into the envelope, so I savored it until it dissolved and allowed a few tears to salt the morning.

I looked at the book again. I saw a Cassidy envelope clipped into the cookbook—empty.

Not for long.

I'd start by writing out that recipe for my sourdough—fermented with the wild yeast that came from my own land, my mom's land, Gran's land. Gran had placed this book face out for me to find. To take. To own.

I'd own it.

* * *

Later that afternoon, I made a salad of soft butter lettuce, peppery baby arugula, torn mint, and basil. Three individual flasks of vinaigrette waited to be swirled. Grace spread a pretty white cloth on the table and set some of our white dishes at each of three places. White dishes let the food shine, I'd learned at the inn, just like putting white flowers in a bouquet made the other colors pop. In the center of the table was the farmhouse pitcher, empty. I headed to the orchard to clip blossoms to fill it.

Nick pulled in and walked to meet me in the orchard. "Hey," he said. "I see the grill is going. Steaks?" He looked so hopeful.

"Vegetarian pizza. I hope that's okay?" He liked meat, but Grace was not a big meat eater. He liked pizza, so I'd been hoping to please them both—and capture a bit of my mom—with this recipe.

His face registered the smallest flicker of disappointment. "It's totally fine," he said. "Good for my girlish figure." He pretended to vamp, and I laughed. "What are you doing out here?" he asked.

"Cutting branches for the vase on the table."

"Branches?"

I nodded. "Till we have more blooming in the garden." I glanced in the direction of the garden where the pots, still unplanted, waited. Maybe for a return trip in Brenda's truck.

I plucked an apple blossom, chiffon pink and smelling faintly of the fruit it would one day bear. "Did you know an apple is said to have started the Trojan War?"

"Uh, no, that's not information I've come across," Nick teased.

"Well, the fable is that a goddess had a tantrum and threw a golden apple into a wedding she wasn't invited to attend. First, though, she'd written on it *For the most beautiful*, to see which person would have enough pride to pick it up. Zeus told Paris of Troy, 'Pick which of the beautiful women clamoring for this forbidden apple is the fairest of them all.' Paris picked Aphrodite, and the chaos that ensued started the Trojan War."

"Seems to me like women wreak a fair amount of damage with apples. Eve, Snow White, Aphrodite. Maybe you should grow pears."

I laughed. "I do. Those trees just haven't been tended for a while." I turned back to the apple branches. "I'm the nerd reading up on stuff like this when everyone else is on a date or partnering wine flights." I snipped more branches and gathered them into a bouquet. "The floral meaning of apple blossoms is, 'I prefer you to all others.'"

I looked up and he held my gaze for a moment, until I

turned away. I hadn't meant for it to sound like I was saying that to him! "We'd better get the pizza going," I said in a rush, and we walked together to the house. As we did, I pointed out the pots and told him about my idea to get all of Gran's and my plants back.

"Genius!" he said with real admiration, and I basked in it. He high-fived me, and I high-fived him back.

Over dinner, I explained the tax situation to him while Grace nodded. "So," I said, "there's no way I'm going to make enough with selling the strawberries and stand flowers. Not this year, anyway. I knew you guys would have some ideas."

Nick pulled out his phone and then jotted in his Notes app. A few minutes later, he texted an invite to the note to both of us.

Business Ideas
1. Website (home page, Nick makes) and social media (marketing, Cassidy sets up)
2. Flowers—bouquets at honesty stand. Brenda told Cassidy this would be hard to make a lot of money on.
3. Berry baskets at honesty stand. How much can this reasonably make?
4. Floral salts. Someone on the island is harvesting salt from Penn Cove. Partner?
5. Weekly salad Community Supported Agriculture boxes. (Love this idea! Really popular now, could do on the fly.)

"Okay," he said. "I just looked up some stats. Whidbey has seventy thousand full-time residents now, many high-end consumers, and many summer visitors and second homes. You could do full-on CSA boxes next year, but I don't think you have time to sign people up for that this year. Lots of cool CSA programs on the island now."

"I don't know. Since this is small-scale and I don't have to make a lot, I'd rather think of something I can do with flowers. Maybe that would give me a rationale to keep the ones Brenda brought."

Nick leaned in for the kill. "Didn't you tell me Brenda said there was no way to make a living with the flowers? And you yourself told me that the money is in the food, not the flowers."

I leaned back in my chair. "Right, but I'm not an inn trying to make a big cash flow."

Grace's face lit. "I love the CSA idea." She turned toward Nick. "I told Cassidy I think food is the best idea too. Move on it!"

Nick pressed on. "I'm thinking of a website and then social media promos. Maybe reaching out to friends. You need to start right away. I'll draft a plan."

It didn't quite feel right to me, but Team A-plus was probably right, and I had asked them to brainstorm with me and bring ideas. "All right. I don't really want to focus on vegetables. But there's a time to be practical, too, so CSAs it'll be. I have no idea how I'll get those delivered even if I can hire someone to help me tend the plants . . ." Brenda was going to have to return the flowers, but the tax exemption would be saved.

Nick scooted his chair closer to mine. "I'm really happy you're going to do it this way. I'll be here all summer, so I can help with the CSA pickups if you get it all organized. You won't need many, just enough to pay the taxes. Maybe you can think of something to make them different."

"Yes, for sure. I could include wrapped bouquets with floral quotes or something with each of them." Except who was going to harvest and wrap them?

"Still getting those flowers in," Grace teased.

"A couple of small CSA subscriptions should get you over the hump," Nick said. "That's all you need. Like, maybe ten. But there's no time to waste. I should start working on this tonight."

Wow. That quickly? "Okay," I agreed. It was wise. Practical. "I'll get an extension on my leave of absence, get this all set up, and then fly back to Cali. Thank you for this."

"It's what friends do," he said.

Friends. Me and Grace. Me and Nick. He was honoring my request to keep our relationship at that level, and that showed me a lot about the man he'd become.

"Thank you," I said. "I can't lose our land. I can't let them down."

He knew *them* was Gran and my mom. "I know. You won't."

As Nick put his jacket on, I wrapped the apple blossom branches and handed them to him. He raised his eyebrows.

He remembered their meaning. *I prefer you to all others.* I frustrated myself by sending mixed messages, but they were coming, mixed, from my heart. As soon as I held them out, I wished I could undo it, to stop from hurting him, from hurting myself. But I couldn't very well grab the bouquet again. "For . . . your mom," I said. "Tell her I said hello." *Argh.* Sending something for his mom was a mixed message, too.

"I will," he said. He didn't call me out. Maybe he had mixed-up feelings of his own.

* * *

The next morning, I went into the greenhouse and looked around. Everything was organized and ready for me to take charge. I'd buy baby lettuce starts and other greens that very day. Some Early Girl tomato plants, some heirloom radishes, and blue-skinned potatoes for variety. Those cukes would be great with a little vinegar and sea salt.

I walked to the pots of flowers, lined up in neat rows, waiting patiently for me to rehome them. "Sorry I can't keep you, guys," I whispered. I'd call Brenda and tell her I couldn't, in good conscience, take all the flowers but hoped she'd let me keep a few.

I needed to get everything in line for the CSA boxes for the summer season, hire Annika, and calmly process whatever surprise lay in wait in the attic. I'd call my boss and ask for an utterly reasonable short leave extension, given the circumstances and the work I'd done for her for free, and then we'd uncover Gran's treasure in the attic. I was ready for both.

"Hey, Cassidy!" my boss said as she answered the phone.

"Hey, Pamela. How are things going?"

"Great. We're gearing up for the season. Marcelle is looking forward to your help in the garden. Back next week?"

I swallowed and took the tiniest moment to shore up my courage.

She bulldozed right over the silence. "You're not asking for more time off, are you?"

"We ran into some complications," I said. "I need a little more time. Maybe a month?"

She sighed dramatically. "I'm sorry; there will be nothing for you to come back to in a month. I've given you every opportunity here, and this is how you repay me?"

Every opportunity to work for free, with no firm date for my promised better job. What did I want with my life? To be an unpaid intern? What did I want as a legacy? I wanted to be the master gardener of fields and fields of flowers. Someday. "Things will be okay for another month. Jacki can help. The garden is in perfect shape right now. It was before I left."

"It was in perfect shape before you came to work for me."

I winced. It was true, though. Did I have the makings of a master gardener, or would I remain a botanical manicurist? I glanced at Brenda's bounty and grew desperate to free those straggling, struggling plants from their confining pots and repatriate them—and maybe myself, too.

Faith, hope, and love. I didn't struggle with faith or love. I hadn't thought so, but maybe like Gran, I struggled with hope. Maybe it was time to take the padlock off my own hopes.

"Are you going to be here next week?" Pamela pressed.

I looked out over my property. I wanted to keep those plants—Gran's plants, Mom's plants, my plants. They needed me. The inn did not. I turned to view the sweet peas beginning their steady climb up the supporting nets alongside the barn. *Leap and the net will appear,* I'd once read.

"No," I said. "I won't be back next week."

"Then I'm terminating you." Her voice was cold. "I'll direct deposit your final check."

"I'm sorry that's your decision," I replied, and I was. I hated disappointing people. "I appreciate the things I've learned and relationships made."

"Right." Her voice was snide, and then it warmed a little. "Good luck. We will miss you."

Mmm-hmm.

I clicked off. And then surprisingly I felt a surge of joy. For a broke girl, I was unreasonably lighthearted. Leaving that job to tend to my inheritance—my land—was the right thing to do. "Woo-hoo!" I shouted, startling a confusion of yellow warblers into flight. I bent to pet my plants. "I'm home to stay! And so are you!"

Grace came running out of the house. "Are you okay?"

"I told my boss I needed a bit more time and was terminated."

"What? You've never been terminated from anything!"

I smiled wryly. "Bucket list, I guess." I ran my hand through my hair. "My head is spinning with everything that has happened since Gran died . . . but I want to stay home. For good. Pamela fired me, but she freed me."

Grace put her arm around my shoulder. "Okay, free girl, how are you going to earn a living? Because life isn't free."

"I'll get the CSA boxes to cover the tax exemption, which is job one. I was a waitress in California, trying to make ends meet for someone else's garden. I can be a waitress here, working for my own garden until I figure out how I can make a living from my land, which is job two, but I can tackle that when the exemption is covered. I'll see if Tony will take me back as a waitress. A job is a job and I'm good with that."

"I'm so happy for you," Grace said, and as she did, music sounded from her phone along with a voice singing, *"I'm a sucker for you."*

"Whaaaat? Is that Justin calling? I thought you were trying to keep him on the down low from your parents!"

She grinned. "Yeah. I silence it at home."

"Don't you think they'd like him?"

"If my mom knew, she'd get right on setting up my marriage."

"So she'd . . . approve?" I arched my brows.

"Yes and yes. I met him at church. He's Korean American. Although what truly matters is that he's the right man for me. I think he is."

"The right man!" I stopped. "Have I been so busy with my own stuff that I haven't made time for you?"

She smiled. "Gran just died. You have a lot on your mind. You're always there for me, and now that we'll be together all summer, we can share even more. We're still like this." She held up her hand with the first and second fingers entwined.

I held up my right hand with the first two fingers entwined, back. "We are. When can I meet him?"

"Soon. My mother threatened to find a suitable husband for me if I don't find one on my own before I'm twenty-nine, so the clock is ticking. Speaking of my mom, she wants you to come for dinner soon. I think she feels bad she hasn't had you over already."

"That's sweet," I said. "Let's find a time soon."

Grace nodded. "Let me head back into the house and save my work. And then—since you've got things settled and you're staying, we'll head to the attic. Ready to face what we might find?"

Was I? Still riding the high from the toe-to-toe with Pamela, I was. "Ready."

* * *

Half an hour later, we headed up the attic stairs. Once we were in the attic with the light on, we looked around.

Grace pointed at a tin box. "What's that?"

I opened it and showed her. Hairy. Bony. Scrawny. Creepy.

"Eeewww!" She jumped back.

"It's dead," I teased. "Gran used to keep me out of the attic by telling me that there were bats up here. She didn't want to lie, so she put a dead bat from one of the barns into this tin." I heard it again. *Drip. Drip. Drip.* But from a different corner of the attic this time. "Oh, great. It's leaking again."

Grace followed my gaze. "Yeah. Better call that repair guy."

I rubbed my fingers together to indicate money.

She pointed at some boxes. "What are those?"

"Uniforms from Gran's first husband and some from my gramps, too." Pain contained. "The keys are probably in her filing cabinet."

In one corner was a jumble of toys and lamps and a stack of blankets. In another corner hung a huge plastic bag that held Gran's old nurse's uniform, cap, and the pin she'd earned when she'd become a nurse so long ago. There was a stack of posters from the years we'd volunteered at the Special Olympics and signed T-shirts from the Island Shakespeare Festivals. Shoved way back against a far wall was a pretty white box. I lifted the lid and saw carefully wrapped teacups and saucers.

"How about this?" I turned at Grace's voice. She put her hand on Gran's hope chest and read the note taped to the top. "'Don't open. Fragile. Likely to break.'"

I put the lid back on the tea set and went to Grace's side. "Gran's hope chest. I wasn't allowed to open it. It was always locked."

"It's not now," she said.

I nodded. "Yeah. I think this is what she was talking about when she said to pack the attic together."

I carefully undid the fraying leather straps and pushed back the lid. It smelled of herbs. Little mesh bags of dried rosemary and thyme nestled in the corners of the chest, protecting against pests and keeping the contents fresh-smelling too.

The most fragile items were on top. I lifted out a tissue-wrapped garment. "My mom's wedding veil. I'm so glad she kept it here, or it would have been pitched during Mary Alice's Great Clean Out." I lifted a baby gown next. "My mom cut up her wedding dress to make a dedication gown for me." I held it close. Would I have a daughter someday?

"So your mom was a seamstress? Like my *halmoni*? She'd always wanted to teach me to sew, but I didn't want to. She told me that was okay. I should focus on school anyway."

"None of us sewed," I said. "Mom must have had some-one do it for her. Maybe your *halmoni*! Our sewing machine came with the house, and I just think Gran didn't have the heart to part with it even though no one used it."

Next came my baby blanket and a few photos of Gramps. My parents' wedding picture—so that's where she'd hidden it. Another picture, black-and-white but hand-colored. "Look! It's our grandmothers!"

Grace took one corner and we held it together. "Ooo-eee, my *halmoni* was a looker in that twisty updo. Oh, my goodness. She's got a sassy swish of red in it. I would never have guessed!"

Gran's hair sported a cool teal swirl.

"And look here—a picture of them together with their aprons on." Eunhee's apron was a pretty cream with garnet-and-pink flowers on it, trimmed in ruby. Gran wore a blue apron, dotted with peach and baby-blue flowers and trimmed in navy blue, of course.

I lifted another package, wrapped in tissue paper. Gran had layered the items in the box from lightest on top to heavier as we went down, as this package was a bit weightier. On the top was a picture of Gran. With a baby. A baby that looked . . . Korean?

"Is that another picture of them?" Grace asked.

I handed the picture to her.

"Your gran and a Korean baby?" Her face reflected confusion.

I kept unwrapping the tissue paper and discovered the tiniest little pink silk baby gown perfectly stitched with rose of Sharon blossoms and some embroidered words. "Are those words Korean?"

"Yes. It's a *hanbok*," Grace said. "A baby's *hanbok*."

"*Hanbok?*"

"Formal Korean dress for important celebrations. Like a baby's first birthday or one hundred days ceremony or weddings and such. My mom wore one when she got married."

I handed the *hanbok* to her. "Can you read the words?"

She squinted at it. "No. This is old-school Korean, called *hanja*. Most of my friends and I who were born here in America were not taught *hanja* but rather the more contemporary Korean language, *Hangeul*. Let me ask one of my older friends who was born in Korea." She snapped a picture of it and sent it via text. Grace looked up at me slowly. "Could your gran have married a Korean man before she married your grandpa? And had a baby?"

I shook my head. "She was married to Bob and then to Gramps. I saw all the paperwork. I've started sorting through her desk and filing cabinets."

"Well, who is this baby then?"

I swallowed hard and handed another photo to Grace of her *halmoni*, Eunhee, swathed in a long fabric cloth swaddling a baby to her. Grace's *halmoni* was kissing the baby's head. The attachment between them was clear and far different from the photo of Gran and the baby. This was a mother and her child. The back was dated 1958. Of anyone in the world, Grace was the one I wanted least to hurt. In a lot of ways, she was the only family I had left. But I needed to be honest. "Maybe this is your grandmother's baby," I said.

Grace set down the picture and the *hanbok*. "My *halmoni* was not married before she married my *halaboji*. And just before she died in 2011, they celebrated their fiftieth wedding anniversary, so they were married in 1961." Her voice and hand shook.

"Did your *halmoni* embroider?" I asked.

Grace's face paled. "Yes." She traced the stitches with her fingers.

"Does this look like other things she's embroidered?"

She nodded and stood up. "I'm sorry. I think I need to take

a break." She put the *hanbok* and photos back into the chest and then closed the lid before rushing down the attic stairs.

Pain contained.

My heart ached. We both knew that we'd opened not a hope chest but Pandora's box. Neither of us had been prepared for it, but I knew, in my head and heart, that this was what Gran had wanted us to find.

I headed back down the stairs and knocked on the door to her bedroom. "Hey. Can I come in?"

"Sure." Her voice was flat.

I opened the door. Grace sat cross-legged on her bed.

"You okay?" I asked.

"Not really." She showed me her phone screen. Her friend had responded to her text. **Mi-Ja. That means "beautiful child."**

I sat down next to her. "We don't know how this is going to turn out."

She looked up. "Do you think this is why your gran wanted me to sort stuff with you? Not something for you to find, but for me to find?"

I nodded. "I do."

"What does it all mean? Do you think that baby is my grandmother's? From before she was married, and someone no one has ever breathed a word about? I'd think it was maybe a picture of my dad or something—but the date is way too early."

"It could be her baby. I don't know. Possibly. Probably."

"If it's true, and she kept it a secret to her death, wouldn't she have wanted that secret to remain hidden? Why would your gran leave this for me to find? I mean, it was incredibly shameful to have had a baby out of wedlock in those years. Do you think . . . do you think this baby was adopted or something and has lived nearby all of these years without us knowing? That would be a total shock to my family. My grandfather!"

"I don't know. I know Gran would never hurt you, who she felt was like a second granddaughter, or your *halmoni*, who was her best friend. Maybe Gran felt your *halmoni* would want you to meet and know her child?"

Grace nodded. "Then why wouldn't my grandmother have told me? I feel like maybe your gran didn't want to die with the secret, but maybe my *halmoni* wanted her to."

"I don't know. I don't understand. Gran made sure we'd find it together so you'd have me to lean on. You're a good researcher," I told her. "You can figure this out."

"But should I?" she whispered. "I don't have any idea what to do, and I don't have any headspace to do it. My bar exam! This could not have come at a worse time."

"Maybe Gran didn't tell you everything so you could decide for yourself whether to pursue this or not. You don't have to, you know."

She shrugged, uncertainty written on her face. "And I might not."

"I'm here to support you with whatever you want to do. Want me to pray with you?" I asked.

She nodded, and we did, and I hugged her and gave her some space.

As I headed to town to talk to Tony about hiring me back, I thought about that pretty *hanbok*, stitched with roses of Sharon, which had been so important to Grace's grandmother. I could have sworn I'd seen the characters on that baby's *hanbok* someplace. Maybe I was wrong. I didn't read the language, after all.

No. I'd seen them. But where?

Helen

CHAPTER SEVEN

May 1958

They cleared a tiny bit of the garden from land overgrown with deeply embedded, unwanted roots, so choked with weeds that it took two weeks to make even the least bit of progress.

"Ah! *Mugunghwa!* Helen, come see!" Eunhee clapped in glee.

Helen pushed back her sun hat and pulled the garden gloves off her sweaty hands. She wiped them on her trousers and headed toward Eunhee, who enthusiastically wielded her shovel.

Her friend waved to her to hurry. "This is a wonderful sign," she said. "Do you know *mugunghwa*?"

Helen looked at the plant, just barely greening and sprouting papery pods of leaves folded in on one another. "I don't think so." It was a little embarrassing not to know the plants on her own property. That would change. She would know them and, like friends, know their names.

"Rose of Sharon," Eunhee said. "I'll show you a picture in one of my books when we go inside. It's the most beautiful flower. You will like them. Their name means 'eternal blossom which does not fade.'" She bent and began plucking tiny plants from the ground. "Their buds open in summer, and then the next spring, they try to make many more plants with seeds that fell to the ground. One plant, one seed, can make many more seeds and plants!"

Eunhee took off her hat and wiped her forehead with her sleeve. "Your friends the hummingbirds love *mugunghwa*. Korean people love *mugunghwa*. It's our most famous flower, very important, very respected. The national flower of Korea."

Helen's interest piqued. "Really?"

"Oh yes. As you see—" Eunhee stretched her arm toward the sprawling bushes—"they have many buds. But did you take care of them?"

Helen blushed. "No—I'm sorry they won't bloom for you this year."

"Ah, but that is the surprise! Even when you don't take care of them or there is little rain or not much food, or no one plucks small plants from the base or a terrible wind blows, they still flower. They bloom and are beautiful. This is why Koreans treasure them. We have had many difficulties—the Japanese occupation, war, more war, little food. And yet when no one takes care of us, we take care of ourselves and live to bloom again and again."

Eunhee looked so happy that Helen overcame her weariness for a moment and the sense that she would not get anything accomplished in the big mess of a garden. "That is lovely," she said. "Shall we plant your other seeds from home nearby the rose of Sharon?"

Eunhee smiled. "Yes, this is the perfect place. I have some starts in the greenhouse. Come, let me show you."

They walked from the back of the large, fenced garden—the first acre of fifteen to eventually be conquered—toward the house and where the pretty pottery shack stood, right in front of the pine grove Helen treasured.

Helen hadn't seen the little grow house for some time as the charge nurse had her working extra shifts to cover for a corpsman who'd switched duty stations. "The windows are so clean!" she exclaimed.

"To let sunlight in for things to grow, the windows must be clean."

"And look at these!" Tiny plants grew in clay pots, including the lettuce plants Helen cherished, the nasturtium seeds they'd found—pretty as well as edible, Eunhee had promised—and Eunhee's mother's seeds.

"Right now, they are safe and warm in here, being protected, like the baby." Eunhee patted her belly. "In a month, we will gently put them into the ground."

"If it's cleared," Helen said. So far, they did not have a very big patch of ground available for use.

"What would you like to plant first?" Eunhee asked.

Helen shrugged. "I love those lettuces. I'd like to grow herbs, as you teach me about spices. I can't wait to try to grow tomatoes—maybe cherry tomatoes."

"Do you have a favorite flower?"

"No," Helen said. "Nothing like *mugunghwa* is to you. Not yet!"

"Not yet," Eunhee promised. Then her face changed. She held her belly.

"Are you okay?" The nurse in Helen kicked in.

Eunhee nodded. "I felt her," she whispered. "She moved!"

"You felt . . . the baby?"

Eunhee nodded again, her face brightening. "Here. Give me your hand!"

She took Helen's hand in her own and placed it on her belly. "Do you feel that?"

A tiny flutter pushed against Helen's hand. Then nothing. Then a little push. "I do! I feel the baby!" As a nurse, she'd felt many babies, pressing against their warm womb, and had regrets and envy each time. But this time, Helen felt nothing but pleasure and anticipation. If she could not be a mother, she could be an auntie!

"It's the *mugunghwa*!" Eunhee said triumphantly. "As soon as I found it, the baby made herself known. It will be my emblem for her."

"Her?" Helen asked.

"Her," Eunhee said firmly. "It's my daughter." Eunhee reaffirmed that while boys were much favored in Korea, she wanted a daughter for herself first. "Then I can have boys." Eunhee intended to remarry someday. Practical. Practicality was something Helen appreciated about Eunhee and something they had in common.

Helen looked at her wristwatch. "The baby might have moved in response to the rose of Sharon—or at least her *umma*'s response to it—but she might also have made herself known ahead of the doctor's appointment."

"Time to go?" Eunhee looked at her watch and answered herself. "Time to go."

They rushed into the Buick and drove into Oak Harbor for Eunhee's prenatal appointment. Although Helen was no longer unduly worried about the fraternization issue, she'd made the appointment for a Saturday when she was less likely to run into Captain Adams. It was not just that, though. His presence and attention of late had made her uncomfortable. Some of the others had even noticed, and she'd heard one nurse whisper that Helen was his new "favorite."

He had instructed the charge nurse to give her the coveted weekday shifts. So maybe it was true.

Once at the hospital, they made their way to the second floor, where Eunhee would visit her doctor. They stopped in front of the reception desk.

"Has she had any worrying symptoms?" The pretty receptionist directed her question to Helen, clearly assuming that Eunhee did not speak English.

"I have not," Eunhee answered for herself. "Only good ones. I felt the baby quicken today."

The receptionist forced an awkward smile, and Helen held back a grin of her own. She sat in the reception area while Eunhee had her appointment, paging through a *Better Homes and Gardens* magazine. A little boy was on the cover, playing in a field of flowers. What were they? She knew once. Oh yes—irises!

Pleased that she knew the name of the flower, she opened the issue and began browsing.

A few pages in was the sweetest picture of a young blonde mother, about Helen's age, cradling a baby near her skin. *Fragile . . . handle with Johnson's*, it implored. *Skin so delicate, you stroke it in wonder.*

They must buy Johnson's products for Eunhee's daughter.

Helen looked longingly at the page before turning it. She flipped past the new flooring ads and considered a Mirro waterless cookpot before turning the page once more. Ah—a cartoon of things to avoid when building a garden.

A hand rested on her shoulder. "Don't plant trouble?" A man's voice read the article's caption from behind her. "I have a hard time thinking you'd ever plant trouble. Can be remedied, I'm sure."

Helen folded the magazine and stood. "Captain Adams. I didn't expect you'd be here on Saturday."

"Just checking in," he said. "High-ranking officer admitted last night, and I needed to follow through. Why are you here today?"

"Oh, I drove a friend for a visit. She's in with the doctor."

He smiled and looked up. Helen glanced toward the desk, where the receptionist kept her head down.

"Ah, well, I'm sure she'll need a ride home then. Another time, perhaps."

Another time for what? Helen nodded. "Good day, sir."

"Good day." He left and Helen thought she heard the receptionist sigh with relief.

Helen picked up the magazine but had a hard time focusing on the content. Thankfully she did not have to wait long until Eunhee joined her.

Once in the car, Eunhee said, "Are you okay? You do not look well."

Helen glanced in the rearview mirror. Her lipstick, bold as ever, only served to make her face seem paler. The white-and yellow-striped dress was cheerful. But her face was not.

"I'm fine. How was your visit?"

"Good and bad. He said . . ." Eunhee continued, but her voice was muffled.

Helen pulled up to a red light and loosened the scarf around her bouffant. It was so tight she could barely hear her. "What did he say?"

"Baby seems good. But he said I should do no heavy lifting and no heavy gardening."

Helen kept her face calm. Of course. She scolded herself. She should never have let Eunhee do any lifting anyway.

"I wanted to do the gardening." Eunhee seemed to read her mind or at least her face. "I can water and weed."

"We will just have your small patch this year," Helen said. "That is a good start."

"I feel bad. This was how I was to help you, to pay you back for your kindness and hospitality. Now I cannot do very much."

"You don't need to pay me back! I am so thankful for your company. And," Helen continued, "you must rest more. When Bob died, I spent months sitting around thinking and mourning."

"Did that help?" Eunhee asked.

Helen shook her head. "No. I didn't start to get better until I started doing things. When I went back to school."

"Exactly," Eunhee said as they pulled into the drive and Helen parked the car. "We can plant your baby lettuces next to my peppers, cabbage, and perilla. We cleared that. That will keep us moving. I already spend too many hours thinking about my husband and what might have been. I do not need more hours to do that, and I will rest when I feel tired."

Helen thought through the pots leaning against the greenhouse. "The other new flowers will die if they're not planted, but there's nowhere cleared to plant them."

"I know." Eunhee's tone reflected the mourning swaddling Helen. There would be no beautiful flower garden this year, and because Eunhee would return to Korea in the fall, they would never garden together again.

They had their little patch, though. And that day, the day of the baby's quickening, was not to be spoiled. "I will put up many bird feeders instead, and the hummingbirds will have the rose of Sharon. Now we must celebrate," Helen said. "What special food would you like to celebrate with?"

They got out of the car and made their way into the kitchen, and Eunhee took some ingredients from the shelf she used for the food they had purchased in Seattle's International District. "I will make *Yakgwa*."

Helen, more tired than her friend for once, plopped down in a kitchen chair. "What is that?"

"Famous Korean pastry," Eunhee said, tying Johanna's apron around her middle. "My mother likes to use rice syrup, but I like honey. That is *son-mat*, the taste of *my* hands."

Helen tilted her head questioningly.

"*Son-mat* means 'taste of hands.'" Eunhee worked the dough while allowing the oil to become hot. "Sometimes it means just how you spice things, to your taste. But sometimes it means more. For example, Umma makes things one way. I like it, but not completely. So I decide I will give this dish the taste of *my* hands. I will use honey and not rice syrup. Like Umma, but also like Eunhee."

Helen stood. "So wise. Keep what is handed down to you, but then make it your own—the taste of your hands."

Eunhee smiled and began adding the pastries to the oil. "Exactly right. That is perhaps the most important cooking lesson I can give to you."

Helen pointed at Eunhee's belly. "Perhaps this little one will also do *son-mat*. A little of Eunhee, but also some of her . . . Do you have a name for her yet?"

Eunhee shook her head. "Not yet."

Helen's mind went back to the Johnson's advertisement she'd seen in the magazine. "I have a name for my daughter," she blurted.

Eunhee dropped the rolling pin. "You are having a baby?"

Helen smiled at the shock still on Eunhee's face. "Not now. Probably not ever. But if I do, I will name her Lauri." *I have hope. For the first time in a long time, I will allow myself to hope that I may, someday, have a child.*

"A beautiful name."

"Lauri was my last name before I married Bob." It had been some time since she'd written to the current Mrs. Lauri, her mother. She hadn't yet responded. Helen pressed past the disappointment and continued. "Most American women would never dream of keeping their last names when they get married like you were able to. But I don't want to lose my name completely. I'll name her Lauri."

"And she will have *son-mat* too," Eunhee said, lifting the pastries out of the oil.

"If there are any recipes for her to inherit from me," Helen teased.

Eunhee untied her apron and then went to the cupboard, lifting down the platter that Johanna had left with her Cinn Rolls. "Let's bring some *Yakgwa* to Johanna."

Hmm. It was a terrific thought and all, but Helen was a bit protective of Eunhee's feelings. Could this, possibly, taste anything like the seaweed soup? If so, would Johanna respond bluntly? She did not want anything to tarnish this day. "Should I taste one?" Helen asked. "You know, closest friend first."

"You may try one and make sure you think it will be to her tastes," Eunhee replied.

"You knew what I was thinking." She needn't have worried. The pastries were flaky and filled with honey and ginger. Delicious!

Eunhee draped a clean dish towel over Johanna's platter, now heaped with treats.

"I'll bring some of the unplanted flower pots to her."

They filled the Buick and drove over. Once they arrived at the tidy yellow farmhouse, Eunhee got out with the platter, and Helen opened the trunk of her car. She lifted a potted plant out.

"Here, let me help you." A young man of about seventeen years ran over and took the pot from Helen's hands.

"Thank you!"

They went to the front porch, and Helen knocked. "Knock, and it shall be opened!" she said.

Johanna opened the door, wiped her hands on her apron, and hugged each of them. Two young boys and a dog tussled in the background. After delivering the treats and explaining what they were, to the boys' great enthusiasm, Helen asked, "Would you like some plants, too?"

"Plants?" Johanna asked.

"Yeah, Ma, like the big one I lifted out of her trunk. Plenty others in there, too."

Johanna shooed her son away.

"We won't be able to clear the land of debris, dead plants, and matter or hammer together the raised beds and such this growing season," Helen explained.

Eunhee looked downcast. Helen wished she wouldn't feel shame about it. No shame in caring for your baby!

"I see," Johanna said. "Is it just the clearing and hauling that is the concern?"

"We need to soften the soil and fix the beds," Helen added. "Heavy stuff. My boss has already noticed that I'm tired at work, and I dare not risk losing my position."

"I would like to offer the brawn of my sons. We are set for butter for several weeks," Johanna teased, "and they are as squirrely as ever. Maybe they could come clear and haul your acre?"

Helen sat down on the couch. "Come clear and haul?"

"Yes. So you can garden."

"That would be wonderful," Helen said. "I'm a bit embarrassed. That was not my intention when I came to visit."

"I know that," Johanna replied. "But I'm happy to keep them out of trouble after school and on the weekends for a few weeks."

Helen looked at the glum young men standing in the background. "I accept—on the condition that I can pay them."

Johanna looked as if she was about to refuse when Helen held up her hand. "I insist."

"All right then," their mother agreed.

"One dollar per hour," Helen said. At that, the boys whooped.

On the drive home, Helen said excitedly, "Did you see those flowers in the vase on Johanna's dining room table? They looked like the most beautiful Chanel gowns made of ruffled tulle."

Eunhee nodded. "Peonies. You mean you have found a flower you like?"

"Yes! Can we plant some of those? After the boys clear the way?"

Eunhee grinned. "You have some already. They are on the far portion of the garden, by the fence, bent over like men with bellyaches. Their heads are heavy, so they need hoops or stakes to hold them up."

Helen's heart raced. "I have peonies?"

Eunhee smiled. "You do. They can live as long as a grandmother, ninety to one hundred years. Go look."

"Let's look together tomorrow, and you can teach me how to care for them."

Eunhee went to bed, and Helen pulled out her uniforms to starch. The phone rang. Three short, one long.

Three short and one long again. It was the Adamses' ring. Helen set down the iron and walked toward the phone. It had stopped ringing, but she very carefully picked up the receiver and did something she had never done before. She eavesdropped.

"I'm sorry I missed your call earlier, dearest," a woman spoke. "And now Melvin has just gone to bed, and I should join him soon. But you call so rarely, I knew something must be amiss."

Sniffling. A whispered voice. "It's happening again," came Mrs. Adams's voice. "Not again!"

Then Mr. Beeksma—apparently unable to contain himself—revealed his presence by yelling, "'Not again,' what?"

"Who is that?" Mrs. Adams's friend demanded.

Helen quickly and quietly slipped the phone back onto the receiver.

She lay in bed that night haunted by one sinking thought. *Why had Mrs. Adams been crying? Not again, what?*

*　*　*

"Go take a break," one of the corpsmen who worked in the hospital with Helen urged her. They'd just finished redressing the leg of a man with an infected wound, and it was an hour past the time she'd typically have left, but she'd need to check on him once more to make sure he was pain free. Eunhee would be left cooking dinner for them alone, again, which was perhaps just as well. She'd run out of American recipes to teach Helen.

"Okay, I will do that," Helen said. "Let me grab a cup of joe, and then I'll be right back." She made her way down the hall to the empty break room and poured mud from the coffeepot, which had likely been left untended for hours. She sat down in one of the chairs and wriggled her feet out of her shoes. It would be a chore to put them back on, she knew.

Even as slender as she was, her feet swelled after standing on them for hours.

Helen pushed the cup of coffee to the side and tilted her head back, closing her eyes. Rest came quickly . . .

A hand on her shoulder. Even in twilight sleep, Helen recognized the weight and feel of the hand. After all, it had only been a couple of weeks since it had rested in the same place.

"Captain Adams." She shook herself awake.

"Helen . . . it's been thirty minutes past your break, or so the corpsman told me when I came looking for you."

"Oh, I'm so sorry, sir." Helen began to stand but he indicated she should remain seated.

"Let me refill your coffee for you."

The hospital CO was refilling her coffee?

He returned with it shortly and sat next to her. He drew his chair a little closer and looked a little too long at her stocking feet. "Making yourself comfortable?"

She nodded. "It's been a long month."

"You're here late quite often. Are the hours too much for you?"

"I don't think so, sir," she said. "I have a lot going on in my life right now."

"Perhaps you'd like a short leave of absence? A month or so?"

She could not do without income for a month or two—nor did she wish to! "It's probably just that I've been doing quite a bit of gardening. I've never done much on our plot of land, but this year I wanted to start. The hard part is over, and I'll be rested soon." She was hardly going to tell him that she didn't sleep well.

"*Our* plot of land?" He drew himself up a bit and glanced at her left hand, which still had a ring on it. "Oh. You're married?"

"My, uh, husband has been deceased a little less than two years," she said. "You recall? Lieutenant Robert Devries? I thought you'd mentioned him when you and the charge nurse interviewed me for this position. You'd met each other. Served together maybe, in Okinawa."

"Of course." Relief smoothed his face. "I'm just surprised to find you with a ring on your finger nearly two years later. I am glad you are taking steps to move forward with your life. Two years is certainly long enough to mourn, Nurse. It's long past time to move on. . . . Say. My wife says you are our neighbor. Perhaps I might drop by and visit. We could have a drink together, just the two of us."

How should she tiptoe through this increasingly threatening minefield? Helen sipped coffee and then gambled. "Yes, we're neighbors. Perhaps when the garden is in full bloom, you and your wife might visit my houseguest and me. My houseguest, too, is working in the gardens as she lives with me full-time, day and night."

He drew back. "Mrs. Adams is not fond of gardens, but I will most certainly stop by and see it sometime." He reached over and took her left hand in his own for a moment.

Her impulse was to jerk it away, but she knew she could not. It felt wrong. It was wrong. But it was not the kind of wrong that could be easily explained, and she couldn't afford to offend him.

"It's time for you to move on with your life, Helen," he said. "Take your ring off. Make new friends and interests and form new relationships. Don't you agree?"

Helen held his gaze. His blue eyes appeared both warm and cold simultaneously, like the sea, shifting, deep, and she could not fully sense what was beneath them though she could guess. If she agreed with the idea that it was time to move on, he might misunderstand that to be an invitation. If she disagreed, it would invite further conversation, and all she wanted at that moment was to stand up and get back to duty.

"Thank you for your concern, sir. I will see that I get more sleep so you won't find me nodding off on my break again, I promise. I take my position and call very seriously."

"I have heard that from others," he replied. "And observed it for myself. You are an excellent nurse. Move forward with your life. You are much too young and attractive to mourn any longer. How old are you, anyway? Twenty-six?"

"Twenty-seven," she answered.

"The perfect age. Not too young and certainly not old. I look forward to an invitation to see your garden and a rosy blush on your pretty face."

CHAPTER EIGHT

Although Captain Adams had offered unwelcome companionship, his advice, while ill-intended, was good. Secretly, though she hated to admit it, in the past few months, Helen had thought of Bob less and less often. Since Eunhee had come to live with her, memories of him had faded and become less painful. She now more often remembered the best parts of their past—their elopement, their card parties, learning how to dance together—without casting guilt on any future she might have without him. Together, she and her friend had decided to live forward, not in the past.

Bob, who had always had her best interests at heart, would want it that way.

One Saturday morning in late June—her wedding anniversary—when the strawberries were fat and so ripe they already smelled like jam and the blackberry brambles fizzed with buttery blossoms, Helen grabbed a tiny pail and headed out to the Buick. On the way out the door, she snapped a head from the unruly tangle of roses climbing up over the arbor on the path leading to the front door. Bob had loved roses. He would have filled the garden with them. She'd planted a few, sure, but she and Eunhee, who was teaching her to appreciate flowers, had also planted fancy-faced daisies, nigella the color of early dusk with otherworldly tendrils, virginal sweet peas, and sunflowers, whose seeds would birth blooms always turning their faces to the sun.

On impulse, Helen cut a head from her favorite peony bush, too, so she could take it to the co-op store and learn more. Fifteen minutes later, she was in Oak Harbor and at the farmers' co-op. "Here!" she presented the tin pail like a proud mother. "My first berries!"

The lady who had sold the runners to her two months earlier took a bite of one. "Juicy and sweet," she said. "How are the flowers coming along?"

"Perfectly."

"Good, good. I heard the Jansen boys cleared your land."

There were no secrets on this island. "They did." Helen fished the two blooms out of her bag. "Can you tell me the names of these?"

"This one, now, she's a beaut. 'Better Times.'"

Better times! "And this?" Helen held one of the rose blossoms out.

"Continuous bloomer. Name's 'Peace.' Every time you walk under an arbor or past a trellis thick with these climbers, you remember, peace. You know, if you'd buy that *Better Homes and Gardens* book I told you about, you wouldn't have to ask me."

Helen smiled. "But if I didn't have to ask you, I couldn't bring by berries." She reached over and selected a new peony plant, potted but blooming with luscious, lush raspberry flowers. "I think 'Better Times' needs a friend."

"I told you you'd be back for more." She nodded knowingly and lifted the purchase selection. "Cut this back late fall. Don't take it out of the pot and put it in the ground until December!"

"Aye, aye, ma'am!" Helen saluted her.

Once home, Helen put on her straw hat and then got her clippers and the ladder from the barn. Roses first. She trimmed carefully, like a mother cutting her baby's hair for the first time. A little here, a little there. Leaves with brown spots, dead twigs, disorderly branches, spent blooms all fell to the ground. When the plant was clean, she took the training twine and fastened the healthy bits to the arbor and trellis. She swept up, stepped back, and looked up.

"You liked this plant, Bob, remember? It blooms continuously, always fresh." She plucked another blossom, pale yellow dipped in pink, the color of sunrise, his favorite time to fly. She rubbed one of the petals between her fingers. So soft, tender like a baby's skin.

"I'm sorry we didn't have a baby." In the distance, she heard the cheerful hum and wheedle of Eunhee sewing. Her belly had grown to the point where she had put the chair farther back from the machine. "Although my life will go on, I will not forget you. As long as I am in this house—and I hope it is forever—these roses will climb toward the sky, like you."

She climbed the stairs to her bedroom and then pulled down the small set that led to the attic. The room was barely five feet in height and smelled of warm wood as the day was hot and there was little ventilation. To one side of the tiny room sat the few boxes with Bob's remaining items. She had shipped some things to his parents, but she'd kept his books and his uniform and insignia. On the right-hand side were suitcases, her grandmother's tea set, her hope chest, and the bassinet.

Helen turned toward the small case holding Bob's uniform, knelt, and lifted the lid.

Bob's dress blues were perfectly pressed, as always. Helen had rested one of his aviator's badges atop it after his death and she stroked it. She lifted his cap.

"I have my own cap—a nurse's cap. You'd be proud of me. You'd always said you wanted me to be a nurse, felt bad that you'd taken me from school, and so I finished." She drew her finger along his gold cap band. "I have a cap band of my own, too. Black. Shows I'm an RN."

She reached under his gold cap band and unbuttoned it

so it hung loose. She slipped her wedding ring off her finger and then slid it through the gold cap band before fastening it once more. Then she settled the rose on top of the uniform. "Be at peace, my love. Rest in peace."

She closed the lid, finally at peace herself.

Before turning the light out, she lifted the white wicker bassinet, blew the dust off, and headed down the stairs.

The sewing machine had quieted. She knocked on the door to the teal bedroom. "Eunhee?"

"Yes, I'll be right out," Eunhee replied and then came out. "How was your trip to town?"

"Good," Helen said, noticing Eunhee glancing at the bassinet. "I'd hoped to use this myself someday, but I'd be honored if you would use it for your baby."

"The honor would be all mine. My baby will warm it up for Lauri."

Maybe there could be a Lauri someday. Helen dared not hope, but she smiled and Eunhee took her hand. She looked up at Helen, recognizing, she was sure, that the wedding ring was gone. "This is okay?" she asked.

Helen nodded. "It's time." She let a moment elapse. "When I went to town today, the nursery lady told me we should buy a copy of the *Better Homes and Gardens, Garden Book*. I was thinking . . . too . . . maybe we should buy a cookbook? If I were ever to marry again, I would like to be a good cook for my family."

"Yes, of course," Eunhee said. A strange look crossed her face.

"What's bothering you?" Helen asked.

"I feel like there has been some squeezing around the baby. Just a little. It went away, but it is too soon for that, right?"

Yes, indeed, it was much too soon for a contraction. "Have they stopped? Can I feel?"

Eunhee nodded, and Helen put her hand over Eunhee's dress in several places. All felt quiet and still. "I don't feel anything now," Helen said. "But if you feel that again, come and tell me. We'll go right to the hospital. Tell your doctor at your next visit, too."

"And I will pray," Eunhee said.

Helen almost said, *"I will, too."* But she wouldn't. Didn't know how, even if she wanted to. Helen ran some ideas through her mind, things that might bring cheer. "How about this week we start driving lessons, nice and slow? I can move the bench seat back to fit your belly. Or do you want to wait until later?"

"Let's do it this week," Eunhee said. "I do not want to wait. I am very excited to come screaming down the street!"

Helen laughed at the reference they'd heard on *American Bandstand*. "Excellent. We'll go to the beauty salon, too, and get glam. I told Mr. Christophe all about you and he's excited to have a new client. He's from Paris by way of Seattle! Then, with my new cookbook, I'll make the best meal ever for us. You'll see."

Eunhee pursed her lips, holding back a smile, but said nothing. If Helen were to guess what was going through her mind, she'd have guessed *egg balls*.

That night, Helen harvested her first baby lettuces and shook up a blend of olive oil, French mustard, red wine vinegar, and salt and pepper. She set the dish before Eunhee. "Well?"

"Delicious!" Eunhee exclaimed. "I've never had better. A cookbook is still a good idea, though. It will give us many ideas."

* * *

"Men like meat, dear." A saleswoman came alongside Helen as she flipped through the salads and salad dressings section of the red- and white-checkered *Better Homes and Gardens New Cook Book*.

"Beet Relish Cups, Chili-Cheese Gelatine Cups, Kris Kringle Salad," Helen mused aloud. "These don't sound good? They sound delicious to me."

The woman, who looked about Helen's mother's age, glanced at Helen's bare left finger and said, "It's this section you'll want." She turned to the meats, poultry, and fish section.

"Cubes in Sour Cream? Spareribs and Kraut?" The book was a veritable treasure trove of deliciousness, and she couldn't wait to begin.

"Better." The woman tapped the top of the printed pink page divider. At the top, a pleasant man wearing a tie held knife and fork in hand. A young boy licked his lips, and a girl looked at her mother with anticipation. Mother was pretty in a pixie cut with a broad white apron cinched around her, delivering what looked like a crosscut ham. Full aprons were much more useful, though.

"Ham?" Helen said.

"Yes. And pot roast. Pork chops. Hearty fare."

Helen nodded. She would master the meals a man would love—starting that very evening. The gelatine salads looked terrific, as did the party loaf. She snapped the book shut. Plenty of time to make all of them.

"You can glue in newspaper clippings and recipe cards from friends," the saleswoman continued. "And write yours in your hand, for future generations. A daughter would surely treasure this."

Helen stroked the cover. *Lauri?* "Yes," she said. "I'll take it."

The woman smiled her agreement. "You won't regret it."

Helen also picked up a copy of the *Better Homes and Gardens, Garden Book* that the woman at the farmers' co-op had recommended and then wandered to the aisle where the pots and pans rested and found a sculpted Bundt pan. Could she? Would she be able to make a Bundt cake? She'd seen advertisements for them in her ladies' magazines. She selected a pan and a scalloped copper gelatine mold and went to find Eunhee, who was, of course, in the sewing aisle.

"Find anything?"

Eunhee held up a few maternity patterns for her final months and then some darling pattern packets with baby gowns and dresses with ruffles on the edge. One package had a pink baby's jacket on the front of it, with a knit cap and mittens to match.

"Gorgeous. Do you want to buy some boy things, too?" Helen asked.

Eunhee shook her head. "I do not think I am wrong, but if I am, then I will quickly sew some boy's clothing! I want to get started so I have all the clothes ready, in many sizes, to take back to Korea. That way, I will not have to worry about her having enough clothing."

They walked together to the diaper section, and she took a small package and a set of pins.

"Surely you'll want more than that!" Helen said.

Eunhee said matter-of-factly, "I can wash these every day."

Helen showed her the cookbook and opened it to the pages she'd been reviewing. "What do you think? I want to start with pork chops with gravy and snow pudding with custard sauce."

"Gravy is ambitious." Eunhee glanced over the recipes. She looked up with reserve at Helen, who held her breath. "But you can do it!"

"I can!" Helen exhaled. "Starting tonight! We will stop at the grocery store after we have our hair done."

"Do not forget: you promised my first driving lesson."

Helen nodded. She expected that her face held about as much hesitation at the prospect as Eunhee's had held when Helen had mentioned pork chops and gravy. They paid for their purchases, placed their shopping bags in the trunk of the car, and then continued their day out.

On the way to Mr. Christophe's, they stopped at the bank.

Eunhee approached the wire clerk. "I am wiring money to Korea again. Are you certain that my other wire transfers have gone through?"

The clerk looked at her over his thick glasses' frames. "Yes, ma'am. I have no indication at all that the money has not been received. You sure you want to send more—that is, if you're concerned?"

Eunhee showed her bank passbook to him. "No, please send the usual amount."

As they walked out of the bank, Eunhee said, "I hope Umma and Appa are well. It is not like her to go so long between letters."

Helen said nothing but recalled that Eunhee's mother had allowed a gap in their letters the last time she was forestalling a difficult discussion. At least her mother had responded.

A little bell chimed as they pushed open the door to Mr. Christophe's salon.

"Madame!" Mr. Christophe himself, wearing a crisp tuxedo and black bow tie, greeted them. He kissed both of Helen's cheeks in his oh-so-French fashion. "It has been very, very long since I have seen you. Maybe you don't like Mr. Christophe any longer? You are cheating on me with another hairstylist instead?"

Helen laughed. "It has been one week since my last wash-out, and you know very well there is no one else on the island who can do my hair. Please meet my friend, Mrs. Choi Eunhee."

Eunhee bowed and he bowed back. "How is it that I am so lucky that two beautiful women walk into my salon at once? I must have the—" he looked around the salon, seeming to count the clients—"eight most beautiful women on Whidbey Island in here right now. Do you want to be extra fashionable today?"

"Yes," Eunhee answered. "It has been a long time since I have had my hair done."

"Very well, then." He indicated that she should sit in one of the chrome and black styling chairs. "*Voilà!* For madame and her friend, I introduce hair flashes." He motioned for the woman who, Helen knew, was the senior stylist to come over. She wheeled a cart toward them, and Mr. Christophe opened the drawer to reveal swatches of brightly colored hair.

"Oh!" Helen said. "I saw those in a ladies' magazine."

"After your wash, dry, and set, I will personally affix the flash to your hair with a little glue, *n'est-ce pas?* It will last until next week's session. So beautiful. It will drive all the men mad."

"Whatever men that may be," Eunhee whispered to Helen. "But even so—I will take red."

"And I, teal," Helen said.

"*Bon!*" Mr. Christophe said. "Evelyn will do your hair," he said to Helen, "and Maxine, yours."

He left them. Fifteen minutes later, they sat side by side in comfortable chairs. Their hairdressers lowered huge, heavy metal hair dryers over their heads.

"The UFOs have been found," Helen said drily.

"Mr. Christophe, he does not look like an alien."

"Don't let him fool you." Helen winked and opened her magazine.

After they were dry, Evelyn teased, back-combed, and styled Helen's hair into her usual bouffant, but Maxine twirled Eunhee's long black hair into a shiny French twist. When Mr. Christophe glued the red swirl through it, every woman in the shop stared—in envy, Helen knew. Mr. Christophe clapped, and soon those envious looks turned to ones of support as one by one the women applauded.

Eunhee blushed. "Thank you." She bowed slightly, as was her custom, to each of them. The applause didn't die down.

Mr. Christophe took a picture of them with Helen's camera, which she had tucked into her oversize handbag.

They stopped by the grocery store, and then, on the way home, Helen pulled over on a country road, stopped the car, turned it off, and got out.

"Here we go. Your turn," she said as she came around to the passenger side.

"Really?" Eunhee's voice rose with excitement and she got out of the car, too.

"Really."

Eunhee settled herself into the driver's side, sweat beading on her forehead by her new red hair flash. Helen showed her how to put the key into the ignition, walked her through the brake and accelerator basics, and showed her how to shift into gear.

"Remember, I'll be right beside you," she promised. "The whole time."

Eunhee nodded, pale. She turned the car on and looked at Helen triumphantly. "I turned it on!"

"You did it!"

Eunhee shifted the car into reverse and slowly started backing up without looking in the rearview mirror. "Why are we going backward? More pedal?"

She pressed into the accelerator, and Helen had a passing fear of her backing them right into the irrigation ditch from which they would need to be towed. "No, no, take your foot *off* the pedal!"

Eunhee did, and the car slowed down.

"D for drive, to go forward."

"I see." She shifted confidently into drive and then pressed the pedal again, navigating onto the country road at about ten miles per hour.

"Look ahead most of the time, and only occasionally glance into the rearview and side-view mirrors," Helen said.

"Good advice," Eunhee said. "And not just for driving."

"Ha!" Helen agreed. "You're so wise!" They practiced on that road for about ten minutes, with varying results. Sometimes Eunhee did well. Sometimes she jerked the wheel so hard Helen feared for the cattle to either side or that she, not the car, might scream down the street as they rolled on.

"We'd better get the groceries home but will practice every day until you are ready to take your driver's license test."

"Do you think I should?" Eunhee asked.

"Definitely."

Eunhee looked doubtful. "I do not think I can pass."

* * *

Once home and the groceries put away, Helen cinched her apron around her waist, just like the woman in the cookbook, and set to work.

About an hour later, the pork chops looked done. Well, more than done. Done to death and perhaps into the great beyond. Helen might have dredged them a little too much and let the oil get maybe too hot. The chops' exterior had gone from brown and crispy to hard as peanut brittle in a flash. Still, that was what gravy was for, was it not?

Helen put the pork chops into the oven to keep warm and started the gravy. She left the drippings in the pan, as instructed, with the crusty bits. No shortage of crusty bits, that was for sure. She poured in the stock and some water. A little milk. When it was good and hot, she measured in the flour.

What? What was happening? The flour wasn't spreading out as it should, thickening the sauce into a gravy. Instead, it clumped into pebbles and marbles.

She stirred them further, with a fork, and then mashed them. Still, there were dozens of pebbles—too many to mash.

"Dinnertime?" Eunhee came into the kitchen.

Helen shrugged. "At least my hair looks good." She pulled the chops out of the oven.

"It's okay. We have knives," Eunhee said as she looked at the meat, which had, if possible, grown even firmer in the warm oven.

Helen then lifted the lid on the gravy. Eunhee's eyebrows rose and stayed there.

"I know," Helen said. "Gravy balls."

Laugh. Cry. Laugh. Cry. Which was going to win?

Eunhee laughed. "It's okay. You need to put the flour in cold water first and then add that to the warm liquid. Then—no balls. You will make this every night—with me at your elbow—until it's perfect."

Helen joined the laughter. "I do not think I can pass the test." She jotted a note next to the recipes. *Add the flour to the cold water first and then add to the warm liquid.*

Eunhee left the room, heading toward the living room. "I am calling Johanna."

Helen followed her, taking off her apron as she walked.

"Hello, may I please speak with Johanna? Thank you. . . . Yes, hello, Johanna. This is Eunhee. Helen and I would like to invite you and your family for dinner. Would sometime in early July work for you? Yes? We'll call soon to settle the time. I will pick your family up, and Helen will make dinner. We will see you then."

As her friend set the phone down, Helen smiled. "No turning back for either of us. Either you'll kill them in the car, I'll kill them in the dining room, or it will be a smashing success."

CHAPTER NINE

Helen surveilled her garden. Yes, *her* garden! The beautiful peonies were spent, but she'd see them next year. Perhaps they would become the emblem for her daughter—if she ever had one. Meanwhile, the white-petaled daisies and their cousins, fainting gerberas, competed in the midsummer beauty pageant for the nearby bachelor's buttons' affections. The finches flittered anxiously around the burgeoning sunflowers like a handful of tossed golden glitter. Greedy little fellows. It wasn't as though she didn't provide seed for them while they waited.

She cut some of each of the ready flowers, making a bouquet for Johanna. Although she knew Johanna loved her sons, she had once shared that she'd longed for a daughter, too, to bring the softer touches to her life. This day was to be a perfect celebration of friendship and mothers and their children.

The lettuces in their boxes still thrived, even though they'd been planted months earlier, due to crop rotation. Red was represented with a few ripe cherry tomatoes, caged for support. Helen twisted some off of their branches and plopped them into her white colander, closed her eyes, and breathed in the smell of their greens. Then she popped one in her mouth, and when she bit down, a firecracker of flavor exploded in her mouth. It tasted like no other tomato she'd ever eaten.

The taste of my hands!

Somehow the greens smelled like the ripe tomatoes she hoped for. Her gardening book said that if she watered them less, she'd force them to mature quickly, so she'd given them only the briefest drink. What good was a batch of green tomatoes? The heat was good for them too. She'd dragged the barrels in which they grew to a sunny spot against a concrete wall. Backs against the wall, they'd have no choice but to ripen. She'd tuck away some seeds in those brown paper envelopes tied with twine, for next year and the next. She'd have some for her daughter as Eunhee had taken those seeds from her mother.

She passed the barn and found Eunhee sitting in the car. "Praying?" she asked with a smile.

"Yes," Eunhee said. "This is the first time I will drive other people, except you."

"So my life is disposable," Helen teased.

"You know that is not true," Eunhee said. "It's just that I am most comfortable with you. Come with me. I want to show you something before you begin making dinner."

Helen followed her into the house and took a seat on the couch. It had a new slipcover, thanks to Eunhee.

Eunhee went into her bedroom, and when she emerged, she had something wrapped in tissue paper.

"You know I have been sewing so much," she said. "Embroidering, too."

Helen looked up at the new drapes in the living room. "My house is so much prettier for it. Your maternity dresses are gorgeous, too."

"Thank you," Eunhee said. "I am also making things for the baby."

"From the patterns?"

"Yes, but that is not the most important thing." She sat next to Helen. "The most important thing is the baby's *hanbok* for her *Baek-il*, the celebration to be held when she is one hundred days old."

"Like a birthday?" Helen asked.

"Kind of," Eunhee said. "More like a life day. Korea can be a difficult place to live sometimes. The winters are unbearably cold, and the summers sweaty. We have had years of prosperity, but many more of hard times when there was no money for a doctor or even a doctor nearby if you could pay one. A mother would not be certain that her baby would live, not until the baby reached one hundred days old. When the baby was one hundred days old, she could exhale and relax a little, because she knew her baby was likely to have a long and hopefully meaningful life." She began to unwrap the layers of tissue paper. "We celebrate with seaweed soup."

"Ah, now I understand why you dried so much seaweed!" Eunhee nodded. "I could not risk you collecting more." Helen grinned.

"Also, we serve special rice cakes. If you share those rice cakes with one hundred people, the baby will have a long and successful life. Anyone who eats a rice cake will bring a gift of thread in return. If the thread is long, then the baby will have a long life."

Eunhee opened the last layer of tissue and pulled out a beautiful gown of silk. The skirt was pink and so stiff it looked starched. The bodice was white, and so were the arms. All down the front and to the sides, Eunhee had embroidered *mugunghwa*, roses of Sharon. Butterflies fluttered around the blossoms, and a pretty tassel sat high above the waist.

"See here?" She pointed at an open spot on the sleeve. "I will embroider her name once I decide what it is to be."

"It's so beautiful," Helen said. "Kind of like a baptismal gown. Is this a Christian tradition?"

Eunhee shook her head. "No. I am indeed a Christian, and so is my family. But we have been Korean much longer than we have been Christians. Do you understand? I am coming to love America, but the fibers of my heart are still Korean."

She set the *hanbok* down. Helen reached out to touch it and then withdrew her hand. She wouldn't risk staining it.

"I think that is why," Eunhee continued, "when I marry again, it will be to a Korean man. I very much loved James and wish he could have lived. But next time I think it will be to a man who understands my heart's fibers because they are his heart's fibers."

"I want that for you," Helen said.

"And I for you." Eunhee wrapped up the *hanbok* and took it to her room. When she emerged, she wore her new apron. "Let's get to work!"

First, Helen set the table with beautiful dishes Bob's mother had gifted them at their wedding. She placed the huge bouquet she'd gathered in a crystal vase in the center of the table.

She made her salad dressing, using good olive oil and vinegar and herbs she'd picked from her garden. "It's the first recipe I've come up with and then clipped into the cookbook."

"A worthy offering," Eunhee said. "Delicious."

Helen headed toward the kitchen and pulled out the ham. "Look. I made the 'flowers' out of orange peels as the cookbook said. 'Baked Ham with Candied Daisies,'" she read off the page. "I also brought daisies in for the table. The lady at the variety store said men like meat, and as we will be feeding eight of them, I thought this best."

"If I don't drive two or three of them into the ditch on the way," Eunhee teased.

"More for us, then!" Helen replied. "No irrigation ditches, no tractors, and you can go nice and slow. I'll hide the bodies if you make a mistake."

Helen finished up the stuffing and checked the pantry, where her Bundt cake cooled. It smelled—and looked—perfect. No one needed to know that she'd had to throw three away before getting to this point. She carefully cut off the woody stalks from their first harvest of asparagus with starts she'd bought at the farmers' co-op. Hers had come in later than most asparagus crops, but they'd planted late, and she was thrilled to serve a vegetable from her garden. She'd cream them and serve them on the side.

An hour later, Eunhee smoothly drove out of the barn and, a few minutes later, back up the driveway with her first load of the Jansen family, Johanna and her husband, Eric, and their two youngest. The next trip found five boys in the car, top down, whooping and hollering as they came.

"Your house looks—and smells—divine," Johanna said. "I had no idea you could cook."

"I'm working on it. I'd like to try making your Cinn Rolls sometime," Helen said. "I could come and watch as you do it, marking down the measurements as you go."

"I'd be honored."

"Will you go to church tomorrow morning?"

"Oh yes," Johanna said. "We never miss."

Helen took a deep breath and let down her guard. She had

not grown up in a religious family and had never wished to be religious herself. But these two women, her friends—they had something she did not. A hole she needed to be filled. A closeness with God she had had no idea could be possible. "Maybe . . . maybe sometime I could come with you."

Johanna smiled softly. "I would welcome you anywhere, at any time. But many people at a Dutch church would not welcome a non-Dutch person. I would not want you to think that our Lord, who is a friend to all, was as unwelcoming as some of them would surely be. Perhaps I can suggest another church."

"I understand," Helen said and put her guard right back up. If a person was known by their friends, Helen wasn't sure what these church people's attitude said about their God. All for the better. She was happy to spend her Sundays at home preparing for the workweek. And yet she still longed to have a faith like they had, an intimacy with a God Eunhee and Johanna clearly knew.

The hours passed quickly, and by the time Eunhee was ready to return the Jansens to their farmhouse, all that was left of the ham were a few orange-candied daisies and glaze sticky on the platter.

"I'll stay here and start the dishes," Helen said. "Why don't you stop by the mailbox on your way back? We haven't checked it for a while."

Eunhee yawned and stretched, her belly pushing out as she did. "I will." Her voice did not sound hopeful.

Helen cleared the table and then headed toward the

kitchen sink, which overlooked the long drive into the farm. She filled the sink with hot water and Joy, which promised that dishes would go from grease to shine in half the time. Soon after she started washing, the Buick came screaming up the driveway. Helen dried her hands on her apron and slid on her shoes before heading to the car.

"Are you okay?" she called out.

"Oh yes." Eunhee handed the stack of mail to Helen but waved her thin airmail envelope in the air. "It's from Umma. There's one here for you, too!"

Helen looked through the small stack of mail. Bills, notifications, and . . . a letter from her own mother! She put it on top to read after Eunhee shared her news.

Eunhee pulled a bobby pin out of her updo and slit the side of the envelope. They walked into the kitchen together, and by the time they reached the table, Eunhee's face had fallen.

"What is it? Are they okay?" Helen sat down at the kitchen table, setting her own mother's letter in front of her.

"They are okay, but I am not. My parents do not want me to come back to Korea," Eunhee whispered.

"What?"

She pulled a handkerchief out of her dress pocket and wiped her eyes.

Helen looked at the neat, thin characters on the letter. "Does she actually say to you, don't come back? Or that she doesn't want you to come back?"

Eunhee shook her head. "No, she is not so direct. She says that things are still poor, but also she reminds me that Korea is not a place right now where . . . well, where babies who don't have both a Korean mother and a Korean father might be welcome. She wants us to be happy and safe and not shamed."

"But you have done nothing shameful," Helen said.

Eunhee's skepticism showed on her face. "This is true, but is it very much different here if a baby is born of a mother who is white and a father who is not?"

"No," Helen said. "It is not. It's the same. What will you do?"

"I will think about this. In my culture, we do not first think of 'me.' We think of 'we.' What is best for the family. I need to consider what is best not only for me and for my daughter, but my mother and father. I must do what is best for all and trust that God will do what is best for me."

She put her hand on her belly and winced.

"Another contraction?" Helen asked. "Have you had them again?"

"A little," Eunhee said. "Perhaps it's the worry for my parents and my baby."

"Enough worrying about 'we' and more worrying about 'me,'" Helen said. "From now on, we focus on you. Are you certain that you couldn't have gotten pregnant earlier? That it's not time for the baby soon?"

"No. I remember my last monthly. The doctor agrees with this time, though he is not very kind."

Helen knew the doctor well. "No, he is not. Nonetheless, if you feel these through the night or in the morning, we must go to the hospital. Do you promise you will tell me?"

Eunhee nodded. "Let's finish the dishes."

"Oh no," Helen said. "I will finish the dishes. You go to bed. Nurse's orders!" She slid an Elvis record out of its album case and turned the record player on low, both so she had something to listen to and to provide cover for Eunhee, who was weeping quietly in her bedroom.

Elvis crooned about his blue moon and how he hoped it would turn gold again. Could their blue moon turn gold? Eunhee could live with Helen as long as she liked, of course, but there was not much work on the island for women, apart from domestic jobs and the Navy. Where would Eunhee find this Korean knight in shining armor she deserved, if not in Korea? She'd shared with Helen that she'd missed attending church. There was no Korean church for her here on the island.

The immediate concern, though, was the early contractions. Many women had false contractions, so Helen wasn't genuinely alarmed. The most important thing she could do was to make sure that the baby was born safely. Everything else would fall in line after that.

Once the dishes were done, Helen sat in a kitchen chair, used her own bobby pin, and slit the envelope from her mother. Perhaps her mother would come, and they could be a "we" again. She began reading.

Thank you for your hospitable invitation. Unfortunately, we are in the midst of a very busy social calendar, and I cannot foresee a time that I might make a visit.

I do wish you the very best. You have chosen a life as a workingwoman, one without children.

I'm glad you reminded me of my mother's tea set. I had forgotten about that. I miss it. As you and I will not be able to share an afternoon's tea, I would like to request that you send it back. I'm sure you understand how valuable such an heirloom is to me.

Sincerely, Mother

Helen ran her fingertip over the letters, tracing the ink, touching the paper her mother's hand had touched. Why had her mother never shown love? Why did she need to reply with coolness and malice? Helen began to cry, and as she did, her tears splashed the pages. She pulled her apron over her face, hoping the fabric and Elvis would muffle the sounds from Eunhee.

Once quieted, she slipped her shoes on and walked to the evergreen forest at the back of her land. The trees ushered and held the silence, embraced her with peace, and she recalled something John Muir had written and whispered it aloud before returning to the house. "Come to the woods, for here is rest."

* * *

Maybe it was the way the twilight fell across the garden or the fact that though the plot was rich with spiky, proud dahlias in every bright color, but there was something of autumn in the mid-August air. Everything but the tomatoes and Eunhee's peppers were starting to wind down. The peppers were going great guns. Helen could smell them cooking in the kitchen through the open windows.

"Helen!" Eunhee's voice came pressed tight and weak, like the final gasp of the accordion on *The Lawrence Welk Show*, through the window.

"I'll be right there!" Helen yanked off her gardening gloves and then let them drop inside out onto the damp soil, nests of green rubber worms.

In the kitchen, Eunhee bent over, panting.

"Let me help. Oh!" A puddle slicked the linoleum, and Helen instinctively leaped back. "Your water?"

"I'm so sorry. The baby is coming early. Now!"

Helen hugged Eunhee to offer her comfort but also so she could unknot the ruby-trimmed apron, which barely fit her now, from the back. "Don't be sorry. We will go to the hospital where you and the baby will be well cared for. Let me help you change."

"No. I can do it." Eunhee's voice wavered and softened. "You'll stay close at hand?" She was a determined woman but afraid, as Helen had seen that nearly all mothers were, of the task ahead.

"Always. I promise."

While Eunhee gathered her small valise, packed in preparation, Helen tied a scarf around Mr. Christophe's hairdo and then turned the stove off, leaving the bubbling cauldron of pepper paste Eunhee had been tending in place.

They hurried into the Skylark. Helen glanced at her silent friend, ready to birth her first baby with no husband, no mother, no sister, no one but Helen. "They won't let me in the room while you're delivering, but I won't leave the hospital until you and the baby are safe."

Eunhee nodded and grimaced, resting her head against the window as they screamed out of the driveway, birds scattering from their path.

Once they parked at the hospital, they hustled into admitting. The receptionist turned to Helen. "Hello, Nurse Devries. What is this patient's name?"

"Choi Eunhee," Eunhee answered for herself.

"Come this way, please." The receptionist turned back to Helen. "*You* can wait over there, as you are not on duty." She pointed to the waiting room filled with plastic chairs the color and texture of Velveeta and tables heaped with crinkled newspapers and silver trays mounded with soft, spent ash.

Helen tolerated lukewarm, musky coffee and read through every article, every ad. Time passed much more slowly waiting for a patient than caring for one. She walked to distract herself. She checked in on her ward, told the staff why she was there, and then hurried back to the waiting room. They didn't want her on their floors during their shifts any more than she'd welcome oversight while she was on hers.

Two hours ticked by.

Six. Ten. Fourteen, as the day rolled over to Thursday, August 14. If there were only some way other than airmail to reach Eunhee's mother, in case. *Stop it, Helen. You're a nurse. You can't catastrophize typical medical situations.*

It was just that the baby was early, weeks early . . .

After sixteen hours, a doctor came and shook Helen by the shoulder, awakening her. "Nurse? Mrs. Devries?" At least it wasn't Captain Adams.

"Yes," she said. "May I see her?"

"Momentarily." He pulled a pack of cigarettes out of the pocket of his white lab coat, shook one out, then another, offering it to Helen. She shook her head.

"Take it," he pressed.

Her core clenched with anxiety as she accepted it and his light. Breathing the smoke into her lungs soothed her.

"I should tell you she is quite upset. We tried to give her some medication to calm her."

"Why is she upset?"

He exhaled a curl of smoke. "Her child. I suspect that her daughter is . . . her daughter is a mongoloid. I can hear a significant heart murmur, and she has the typical flat facial features. A thick neck. The baby is in the nursery with the other newborns, but we don't expect her to live long. It would, in fact, be better if the baby died."

"Better if she died?" What a heinous sentiment. Helen steadied herself on the back of one of the orange chairs.

"The child is damaged, you know. Down syndrome. I understand there is no father?"

Down syndrome? Helen knew so little about that. Had they even covered it in nursing school? She couldn't remember. No one aired shameful subjects. How could she protect Eunhee and the baby from the trauma that surely lay ahead for them? "The baby's father died serving his country," she responded curtly. "What do you mean it would be better if the baby died? How long could the child live?"

"Certainly, as a nurse, you'll know that it is better for the baby, who has no hope of a meaningful life. Better, too, for the mother who brought such a child into the world that this baby die so she can find another husband. Mrs. Roy made quite a bit of noise giving birth." He shrugged as though that were a character flaw. "The baby could live months. She could live a few years, but in my opinion, not longer than two or three with that heart murmur."

"May I see her now?" Helen asked, disgusted and not trusting herself to hold her tongue with this doctor, to keep from saying something that would cause her to lose her job.

"As you wish." He nodded to direct a nurse to escort Helen to Eunhee.

Helen entered the room, and as she did, her dearest friend turned toward her, thick black hair stuck to the side of her face, wrists and ankles raw and weeping from the birth straps. The iron smell of blood and the briny tang of sweat permeated the room.

They held hands. "Her name is Mi-Ja. Beautiful child. My beautiful daughter." Eunhee's voice was steady, strong.

"It's a lovely name, Eunhee. I'm sure she's a beautiful girl. You know she has some . . . difficulties."

"Yes." A moment passed. "I love her. It is sorrow and joy in one. But we will carry on."

"Han," Helen said.

Eunhee nodded. *"Han."*

Han, Eunhee had once explained, was the particular sense of both sorrow and hope, which grew from the many years of oppression felt by the Korean people. It had been especially strong after the war. The land had not been rebuilt. The Japanese had taken everything of worth during their occupation. There was little food. And yet, like the *mugunghwa*, the rose of Sharon, which thrived despite neglect, the Korean people dug in and worked and believed in a better future. It was strength and sorrow and hope, in one.

"I promised I would look after you, no matter what. Together we will care for Mi-Ja," Helen whispered. "Now sleep."

The new mama closed her eyes, and a tear rolled from each of them, sloping over her cheeks, still flushed with exertion. A phone rang in the ward outside, its strident voice becoming louder as a nurse opened the door and entered the room. The nurse pulled closed the thin curtain between two new mothers and then wheeled in a baby to the other side of that great, great divide. The mother and father exclaimed with joy as their baby cried with vigor and health.

Eunhee hummed a song Helen did not recognize, but the mournful melody she understood as reflecting *han*.

It sounded like a lullaby, though Mi-Ja was nowhere nearby.

Cassidy

CHAPTER TEN

"Because you're her sole heir," Grace had explained, "you just file the will and a probate deed, which will transfer the property to you. Then you've got a couple of months to sort out anything else, bank accounts and such, in probate."

So in early May I drove to the courthouse with both sorrow that Gran was gone and hope that I could do right by all of us. Within an hour, the land was mine. Vested title? Cassidy L. Quinn. Responsible party? Cassidy L. Quinn.

Owner? Boss? Cassidy L. Quinn!

On the way home I passed the Beeksma property. Mr. Beeksma stood outside the barn, and a young woman fed the chickens. Maybe that was Annika, the young woman he'd said might be interested in helping with the garden chores? I pulled into his drive and got out of the car. "Hey, Mr. Beeksma. I've got some things lined up for the ag tax."

"Good. I knew you could do it," he said.

"I wondered if you knew anyone who might want a part-time job?" I asked, hoping that would remind him of our conversation. Even though I was home, I was waitressing, so I still needed help. In addition to planting the vegetables necessary for my tax-saving little CSA startup, I'd taken *all* the plants Brenda had sourced. I might never have the opportunity again. I could afford to hire one strong young person. That was it.

He hit his forehead with his palm. "By golly, I forgot to ask Annika. Follow me."

I followed him to a large coop and run enclosure where the young woman was feeding chickens.

"Young lady, I would like you to meet someone."

The young woman set down her bucket and walked toward me. Her gloves reached up past her elbows, and her boots came above her knees. Her brown hair was pulled back into a ponytail. Sensibly dressed for outdoor work. I liked her from the start.

"I'm Cassidy." I held out my hand, but she didn't take it.

"Cassidy, like the old Helen Cassidy?"

"Yep. Helen was my grandmother. I'm Cassidy Quinn."

She nodded, not wanting to shake my hand with her dirty gloves on, I guessed. "I liked your grandmother," she said. "I'm sorry about her passing."

"Thank you," I said. "Me too. Mr. Beeksma says you're looking for work this summer. I'm looking for someone to come and harvest strawberries, weed, water, and do some general plant care. Maybe for about ten to twelve hours a week?"

She paused before answering. "Okay. I'm saving for photography stuff. I'm going to the community college in September to study photography. I need more hours, and I work hard."

"Perfect." Mindful of Brenda's admonition that summer help was hard to come by, I asked, "Could you come by soon and we'll figure out some hours together? I think Saturdays would be fine, with maybe an afternoon or two in the middle of the week. If that's not taking you away from Mr. Beeksma."

He shook his head. "No, no, I only have a few hours' worth of work each week for her and DJ."

"Great," I said. "Could you stop by tomorrow afternoon? I can jot down my address."

"Tomorrow is fine," Annika said. "I know where you live. I started working for your grandmother last year. It didn't work out."

She turned around and returned to the chicken runs and coops, feeding them from a scrap bucket and then heading to refill the feeders with poultry ration.

"What did she mean?" I asked Mr. Beeksma.

He shrugged. "First time I heard of it." He turned to return to work and then turned back to me. "Keep an eye on your septic. Helen replaced the pipes to the house a year or two ago, expensive business, but as I recall, the septic was acting up too. Gurgling noises. Slow flushes and the like." He pulled on his cap and headed back to his field.

That stinks, I thought with a wry smile, and then I drove the few short blocks home, pulled the car into the garage, and walked up the path to the house. After I'd trimmed back the dead leaves and black spot, the blushing yellow Peace roses revived nicely and would bloom soon. I left the wilting greenery on the winter bulbs so they could store up nutrients before I trimmed them back. Sometimes what seems dead is really quietly rebuilding a new life.

In the kitchen, Grace had set out everything we needed to make iced lattes. "The house is yours?"

"It's mine!"

"Let's celebrate!" We took our lattes outside and sat in two creaky garden chairs in the middle of the bed where I'd planted dozens of dahlia bulbs. I pointed at the forsythia branches arcing in long delicate curves lush with popping yellow blossoms. "Those make beautiful branch bouquets too. You want to take some to your mom when you go for dinner tonight?"

"She'd love that," Grace said. "Thank you!"

I found my snippers in the greenhouse and a bucket to carry the branches in, and we walked to the bush to cut some. "It's by the *mugunghwa*." I used the Korean name for rose of Sharon because Grace's grandmother always had.

Grace looked across the garden. "Your gran and mine, they were such good friends. My *halmoni* driving out here all the time after she no longer worked at the Naval base to spend time with your gran." Grace wiped away a tear. "I miss her. I was her favorite, you know, though she'd never have said so. Honestly, she was kind of perfect. My grandfather thinks so, for sure. If he didn't think it was idolatry, I'd say he worshiped the ground she walked on. That's why, well, you know." She looked down. "I can't really devastate him."

We hadn't said much about the *hanbok*. "You want to talk about it?"

She shook her head. "Not now."

She went to get ready for dinner with her family and I wandered out to the acres of evergreens, pines, and Douglas firs Gran loved so much. She'd walked her acreage almost every day, rain or shine, sometimes with me or a friend, but often alone. A few yards inside those woods, the temperature changed. The air grew cool, and as I stepped on the fallen needles, the scent of pine rose, perfuming the air I breathed.

Aromatherapy, Gran used to say. More like therapy, I'd tease, because Gran was of the generation that did not believe in therapists. Whenever she was tired or afraid or overwrought, she would leave the house and ramble among her trees. When she came back, all was right in her world.

I headed out of the woods and then back toward the house. As I approached the fruit orchard, I saw someone. Someone taking pictures with her phone. I headed over. "Annika?"

She didn't turn at the sound of my voice, even when I spoke right behind her. I touched her shoulder and she flinched as though I'd burned her. "I'm sorry—I didn't mean to startle you," I said. "I called out a few times."

She shrugged off my touch and then smiled lightly. "Can you believe the angles of the trees and how the blossoms are just perfect right now?" She showed me her screen. "The moss on the branches adds great texture. Don't ever remove it."

Her pictures were actually very good. She had an artistic eye. She couldn't have edited the photos because she'd just taken them.

"We should have lots of fruit this year," I said. "The bees did a great job pollinating them."

She stepped back from me and the tree. "Bees?" Her voice rose half an octave.

"Yeah, you know, to pollinate the plants. We can't grow apples without them. Do you have apples on your farm?" I asked.

"Nope. We pretty much stick to cattle," she said as she scrolled through her camera roll. "But this tree was named for my grandpa." She pointed to a picture of the biggest, best tree on our property. Right in front of it was the wooden sign, now truly weather-beaten, with a name burned into the wood. Mickey.

"Mickey was your grandfather?" I asked.

She nodded.

"Johanna Jansen's son Mickey?"

She nodded again. "She was my great-grandma."

Well, that was cool. "Johanna was one of Gran's very best friends." Maybe that had been one reason Gran had hired Annika. What had gone wrong? "I love knowing that your grandpa is 'in' the apple orchard," I said. "My gramps and I used to pick apples every year, just the two of us, and Gran and I would make and freeze pies for the neighbors." I glanced at my watch. "I know we said tomorrow, but should we walk to the garden, and I can show you some of the things I'd like you to do?"

"Sure," she said.

We made our way back to where the lettuce, tomatoes, and salad onions for the CSA boxes ripened. "Once a week, they'll need to be weeded. I'll show you how next week, as I've already done it this week. I might need you to do some planting for me, some hauling, watering if I haven't gotten to it—basic garden chores. Amending the soil and working with all of the flowers I've just settled in. I can show you how to do that, too. Cleaning the tools with the hose." I indicated the hoses and the tools. "Do those sound like things you can do?"

She nodded and then knelt to take a picture of the Korean perilla on the edge of the vegetable section. "This is the most amazing plant I have ever seen. Purple on the backside, super-sharp veins."

She stood up and showed me the picture. It was great and tightly focused. She was having a little bit of trouble focusing on what I was saying, though, and I wasn't sure what to make of it. "Last, I'll need help harvesting the strawberries so I can sell them. They'll start coming in early to mid-June."

She stared at me. "That's what I had problems with before.

The berries. Your grandmother needed help with them, but I just couldn't do it. I felt overwhelmed, so I had to quit. I'm autistic," she said matter-of-factly.

I admired her forthright approach. "Okay."

She continued, "Touching things with unusual textures, to me, is almost painful. I just can't deal with it. This year—" she wiggled her hands in front of me—"I bought long gloves. With touch screen fingertips so I can still use my phone."

"Smart," I said. "You sure you're good with it?" I could barely afford to pay her already, but I definitely couldn't afford to pay her for work she couldn't do.

"Yeah," she said. "I was sorry to hear your grandma died because I wanted to prove myself to her with the gloves this year."

"She'd be proud of you, and I think the gloves are an ingenious solution."

Annika looked around. "You've got a lot of work to do here. It doesn't even look like a garden. Just a lot of mud and half-grown plants."

"Well, I'm just getting started." I pulled out my phone and scrolled through my camera roll. "Here's the garden in California—the culinary garden—where I used to work." Picture after picture of lavender fields and herb gardens, raised boxes filled with lettuce, spilling with nasturtiums, hoops of tomato plants, backs bent with plump fruit. "My dream is to be a master gardener."

"Did you start all of that—" she indicated the ground before us with her hand—"from this?"

I shook my head. "No, I pretty much helped the master gardener, who was in charge, and she took over from someone else." Botanical manicurist.

Annika stared frankly. "Isn't that boring? Like editing someone else's pictures instead of taking your own?"

Taken aback, I stepped away by a foot. She continued to stare at me, but not rudely, with genuine interest. The thing was, she was right. "Yes, that's a good way to put it. I'm going to start with my own garden here."

"With those?" She indicated my vegetable boxes.

"Yes," I said. "Partly. My dream? Earning a living by growing acres of flowers. They feed the soul—mine and others'. From this." I tapped my toe into the ground near flowers I had carefully plotted and planted, but which looked nothing like the Insta-ready pictures I'd just shown her.

"Master of your own garden," she said with a smile. "Starting from scratch with what you want to do sounds more fulfilling."

I grinned. "You're right. It may be muddy, but hey. 'Do not despise small beginnings.'"

She didn't acknowledge that but instead glanced around at various points in the garden, her gaze stopping here and there along the way.

"Are you looking for something?" I asked.

She nodded. "You need more help. My friend DJ, who's twenty, works with me at Mr. Beeksma's. He needs about five more hours per week of work. I'll ask him."

I shook my head. "I wish I could, but after I pay you, I'll pretty much be tapped out."

"He'll be great here. You'll see. I'll work his hours for free if you need me to, if you take him on with me on Saturdays."

Was DJ her boyfriend? I didn't know how I felt about that. Sometimes it worked out, but sometimes one partner was just really not suited to the work. Intrigued by her willingness to forgo pay, though, I said, "You can bring him by, and we'll talk. That's all I can promise."

She nodded. "See you next week."

* * *

Both Grace and I were up early the next Saturday, she deep in her law journals, me deep in mulch, spreading some over my plant roots so they'd stay cool in the summer's heat. I visited my baby sunflowers at the garden's margin. Hard to believe they'd tower over me at six feet by the end of the summer.

Annika would arrive soon. I was just on the wire, financially, and no matter how I'd worked my bank account numbers over the past few days, I couldn't swing another person. I'd think of a good way to let her friend DJ down with grace and hope Annika wasn't hurt by it or quit. Despite my natural inclinations, all the practical people in my life reminded me that in the real world, business decisions need to be made by the head and not the heart.

About thirty minutes before they were supposed to arrive,

Annika texted, **I'll be there soon, and DJ is coming with his mom so she can check things out.**

His mom was going to check things out?

Okay . . . just a little confused, I responded. **Why is his mom coming?**

I think it's better to let him speak for himself.

All righty, then. I headed in to refill my coffee and met Grace in the kitchen. She seemed a bit more like herself in the days after we found the *hanbok* but still a little preoccupied.

"So apparently that guy coming to apply for a job is bringing his mom," I said.

"His mom? How old is he?"

"Twenty, I think." I poured a glass of iced coffee from the fridge and mixed in half-and-half, no sugar. "I wonder if it's her boyfriend. It's weird that she was trying to get him a job when she barely had one herself. I know they work together at Mr. Beeksma's."

"You'll have to let me know how it goes." Her voice sounded stressed. "Still coming home with me for dinner tonight?"

I put the coffee back in the fridge. "Yep. I'd love to show your mom my cookbook because she loves to cook, too, and I think there's a recipe from your *halmoni* in there. It's in Korean."

At 10:00 sharp, two cars pulled up the drive and parked at the barn. Annika got out of one car and then a woman about the age my mom would have been got out of the driver's side of the second car. She opened the passenger door and a young man emerged. There was something unusual about his gait—I could see it even at a distance. He was short—much shorter than Annika—and wore a baseball cap. As he walked, up on his tiptoes, tilting forward a bit, his cap slipped sideways.

As they came closer, I knew right away that he had Down syndrome.

"Hello." I held out my hand to the woman and then to the young man. "I'm Cassidy Quinn. Nice to meet you both."

"It's a pleasure," the woman said. "Marcia Peterson."

"Nice . . . to . . . meet you," the young man said. He lifted his head to meet my gaze. "My . . . name is . . . Derrick James. My friends . . . call me . . . DJ."

I glanced up at his sideways hat and smiled. "I see why."

He smiled too. "I . . . have Down syndrome. I . . . like to work."

"I remembered how much your gran loved birds," Annika spoke up. "So does DJ. When I was here last time, I noticed that all your bird feeders were empty, and all the birds I saw here when your grandmother was alive were gone. Once I met you, I thought maybe this would be a safe place for him and a good thing for you too. DJ and I know each other from a support group we both attend."

I nodded and said softly, "You're right. I haven't tended to the bird feeders. And . . . this, my real home, has always been my safe place. I want it to be like that for others too." I turned back to DJ. "What kind of work do you like to do?"

"I like . . . animals," he said. "I don't . . . like mean people."

"I don't either." Pamela flashed through my mind. "Where have you worked?"

"At a . . . restaurant." He hung his head and looked at his shoes.

"He worked for a local fast-food company," Marcia filled in. "His job was to greet people and take out the trash."

"I fed . . . birds. More birds came. They told me to . . . stop."

A minute ticked by, perhaps more than a minute. Annika, Marcia, and I waited. The wind blew a bit and kids riding bicycles chimed their bike bells, punctuating their chatter.

"I did not stop," DJ finally spoke. "The birds . . . were hungry."

"They felt his giving fries to the crows brought too many birds around the trash areas," Marcia said. "It just wasn't a good fit."

My heart softened. "What kinds of things do you like to do at work?"

"Feed birds."

I laughed and then he did, too, and Annika and Marcia joined in. "What else?" I asked.

Another long silence elapsed. "Feed . . . chickens."

"He feeds the chickens with me at the Beeksmas'," Annika said.

"I don't have chickens. At least for now. Do you like flowers?"

He quickly continued his thought. "I like . . . flowers. And . . ."

We waited.

"I don't like digging."

"I don't either," I said. "We'll leave that to Annika, and this year's plants are mostly in, anyway. Next year, we'll have many more and hopefully many more hands to help us!" After I figured out how to solve the immediate crisis, the tax exemption problem, I hoped to expand the flowers by an acre every year if I had "seed" money and the time and crew to do it, eventually building flower farming into a way to make a good living—and a good life.

"Okay," Annika agreed. And then in a flash, she whipped out her camera and walked toward the row of newly planted lettuces.

Well, I guessed it was a good time to talk with DJ and his mom.

I looked at him and then at one of the bird feeders, which had not been stocked since I'd been back. Gran had maybe twenty bird feeders all over our cleared property. Maybe more.

Gran loved birds. I loved birds. When I'd packed up Gran's room, I'd found an old-school metal box marked *Rainy Day Fund* with fifty ten-dollar bills inside. Gran hated banks. *Necessary evils,* she called them.

There wasn't a cloud in sight, but this was undoubtedly a "rainy day," and since Nick had put up my CSA website for free, I'd put that fund to good use. My safe place could be Annika's safe place and DJ's safe place, and then maybe one day, a safe place for an even bigger community. "Feeding the birds is a very important job," I said. "It's so important that God says he, too, feeds the birds. I would like you to fill those bird feeders for me every week. Would you like that job?"

DJ nodded, and from behind him, his mother nodded, too. He held up his hand for a high five.

I high-fived him.

"You might need to use a stepladder because some of the bird feeders are high. I have one with rails on the side and enclosed steps that my gran used when she felt a little unsteady."

DJ looked up and grinned. "I laugh in the face of danger."

I looked at his mom. "*The Lion King*," she mouthed. "Why don't you see what Annika is doing?" Marcia said. "Then we'll come and find you in a few minutes."

"Okay." DJ headed over to his friend.

Marcia turned toward me. "You didn't fill in his sentences when he spoke slowly."

I nodded. "Every summer, when I came to stay with my grandmother, we volunteered with the Special Olympics. Just like any team, I learned from the athletes, and they learned from me, but most importantly, we grew into a crew of friends and family. It's always been in my heart to return to that, and I hadn't had time to. Maybe this summer I am, but I'm building a team in a different way."

Marcia's eyes filled with tears, which she blinked away. "Yes. That's right." She'd been sizing me up, and the farm, to see if it would be a safe place for DJ as much as I'd been figuring out if he would fit here. "He's a hard worker," she told me. "I'm only ten minutes away if something comes up."

"Saturdays? Starting with a few hours today?"

She nodded. "Thank you. DJ likes to play *The Lion King* soundtrack while he's working. It's soothing. It's on his iPad. Is that okay?"

"Hakuna matata!" I replied.

She grinned and I motioned for DJ and Annika to rejoin us. "Let me show you where all of the bird feeders are," I said. "I'll go around and do each one with you today."

"Okay. This is . . . great!" DJ said.

"It's helpful if there is a whiteboard or something that shows the tasks," Marcia said.

I knew just what to do. I looked at Annika and her camera. "Annika, could you take a picture of each kind of feeder and then the food that goes in each? We could send them to his iPad, and he could scroll through to match them. Would that work?"

"Sure," Annika agreed.

I looked at Marcia and DJ for confirmation and they both nodded. We walked through the garden, the orchard, and the barn, pointing out each bird feeder to DJ. "You can come and ask me anytime if something gets confusing."

He nodded and then looked a little nervous. "Remember who you are," he said, seemingly to remind himself.

We headed into the little lean-to next to the barn and across from the honesty stand, where I'd begin selling flowers in a month or so. "We can set up a table here for you to fill the feeders, and I'll bring all of the food in here for you." I dragged a stand from the corner. "You can set up your iPad here."

He took his backpack off and unzipped it. He pulled his iPad out, but as he did, a large aluminum sign fell out.

"What is that?" Annika picked it up for him.

I recognized it. Signs like it hung on the docks to board the ferry to and from the island. It was a huge white sign with seagulls on it. It said, *Do NOT feed the birds!*

"DJ, what is that?" his mom asked.

"They . . . put it in here."

"'They' from your last job?"

He nodded.

A flush of anger rolled through me. Mean people indeed. "DJ, can I change this sign into something that I think is better for you?" I asked.

He nodded again.

"I'll be right back." I headed into the greenhouse, where I had drawers of supplies, and grabbed a Sharpie and a piece of twine, and then I headed back to the lean-to. I marked out the *NOT* so that it was completely covered. "There. Now it's your office sign. DO feed the birds!" He clapped with joy, and we joined him. I hung it on the building wall before we left so I could show him where the hoses were. "You can start today," I said. "If you like."

He nodded, and his mother said she'd be back in a couple of hours. It would be just enough time to show him how to fill the feeders with Nyjer seeds, sunflower seeds, or hummingbird syrup. Annika took pictures, and we sent them to DJ's iPad, *Lion King* soundtrack playing in the background.

"Can you start by weeding the lettuce and other greens and then the beds with the herbs?" I pulled the weed wagon over and showed Annika what I meant. "We only have a few CSA subscriptions now, but I'd like to keep these thriving in hopes that we'll get a few more buy-ins soon."

"Sure." She pulled her gloves up over her elbows and got right to work.

"It's only a better home and garden if it's used to nurture others," Gran always said. I looked out over the muddy promise and saw hope. As DJ filled the feeders, birds excitedly flocked around him. Annika methodically worked with the greens. In the distance, through the window to the yellow room, Grace studied.

I was nurturing others. But also, they were nurturing me.

An hour later, I glanced up at Annika. She stood far away from the raised box that held flowering thyme. "I can't do those," she said matter-of-factly. In her hands was an object that looked like a Rubik's Cube but with pretty pastel colors instead. She twisted it, making the patterns align.

"That's okay but——" I started.

She didn't wait for me to finish. Instead, she tucked the cube back into her pocket and beelined to the lettuce and tomatoes and the perennials, which were not yet in bloom.

Well, they needed weeding, too. I could do the herbs.

I rounded out the day by checking on the strawberries,

SANDRA BYRD

which were coming along nicely. We should earn a couple hundred dollars selling them in the honesty stand. I had every confidence that, along with a healthy CSA commitment, we'd make enough money to pay the tax deferment by the end of the year.

After seeing my new crew off, I hopped into the shower. Grace was sitting on the couch, all ready to head to Federal Way and her family home, before I'd even blow-dried my hair. "Am I late?"

She shook her head. "Let's just finish getting ready and get going before I lose my nerve."

CHAPTER ELEVEN

Grace drove, and I was in charge of the music. "I can't wait to see your parents again," I said. "They're not going to do anything crazy. Even if they know something, it will all be okay."

She looked at me over the rim of her glasses. "Yeah. I'm just going to float the name Mi-Ja tonight and see if anyone reacts. We are carefully balanced between love and honor, expectations and respect. A baby out of wedlock is nothing anyone in my family would expect from my *halmoni*, and I'm not in a hurry to figure out if anyone's going to kill the messenger if it's true. I just want to get out of here without raising any suspicions if they don't know and head back to my regularly scheduled life."

"Why say anything, then?" I asked.

"It bothers me," she said. "Your gran left it for me to find. Why? My lawyer's mind wants to know. Maybe they do know, and it was a long time ago, so no one said anything. Best possible solution."

"I get that. I'm worried you're talking yourself into believing there's an easy fix, but I admire you for doing the right thing, even when it's hard."

She nodded. "Thanks. What happened with that man who came to apply today? Did you hire his mom too?"

I laughed. "No, it wasn't like that." I explained about his situation and his Down syndrome and how he loved birds and that I'd reassured his mom with my own happy experiences with the Special Olympics. "He's going to make a great team member. The birds were already flocking to him."

"You always enjoyed working with the athletes when our grandmothers took us to volunteer. Me? I was just trying to figure out how to exactly mark the spaces where the athletes were to run so no one got hurt."

"You and I made a good team," I said.

"Still do," she answered.

Forty-five minutes and half a playlist later, Grace drove off the ferry and then onto the highway to her hometown. Shortly after, we walked to the front door, stepped inside, kicked off our shoes, and slipped on some soft house socks from a basket near the door. "Umma? Appa?" Grace called into the house.

"Here we are!" her mother sang as she came to greet us. I gave a little bow to her, and she bowed back and then kissed Grace, and then she kissed me. "How are you doing, Cassidy? I worry about you. But when I think that Grace is with you, helping you and keeping you company, I feel better. I just hope she's able to focus on her studies too."

Mrs. Kim smiled, but with a particular maternal smile that revealed that the bar exam was never far from her mind.

Grace's dad came into the room and greeted us. I bowed, as was their custom. "Hello, Mr. Kim."

"Hello, Cassidy," he said, bowing back. "I'm so glad you are joining us for dinner." He then pulled Grace into a hug, which I had never seen him do with his sons. "My favorite lawyer," he boasted. "I tell that to everyone. They know you, so they believe it."

Grace kept her head down. "Not yet, Appa," she said.

"Soon. Very soon." He let go of her and we wandered into the kitchen.

Grace took plates of *banchan* out of the refrigerator. *Banchan* was my favorite part of any Korean meal, and Grace's mom always had a big selection on hand for her family. A dozen or so platters filled with all kinds of tastiness—sour, soft, firm, plump, fried, fresh, greens, protein, pickled vegetables and eggs, *kimchi*, glazed lotus root, radishes, bean sprouts, various preparations of tofu, and . . .

"Oh, hooray!" Grace turned to me. "She hardly ever makes *pajeon*. Umma likes you better than she likes me. That's why she's made them for tonight."

"True, true," her mother teased with a glint in her eye. "Cassidy is my favorite."

Pajeon were thin, savory green onion pancakes. I loved them. "Thank you for remembering. I'll bring green onions and Korean chives next time I come." I was so happy I'd grown them, and the perilla, in my little veg patch.

"Thank you, Cassidy. That is very kind."

"Ooh—*doraji namul*," Grace said. Sauteed bellflower roots.

"Your grandmother grew that especially for Mrs. Kim," Grace's mother said to me. I'd never heard her refer to her mother-in-law as anything other than Mrs. Kim.

"Yep. We still do—grow bellflowers. I'll bring some roots for you next time too."

"Thank you, Cassidy."

Grace rolled her eyes. "Umma, Cassidy's gran and mom made notes in their cookbook for her, and she thinks there's a recipe from Halmoni too."

"Oh?"

I took it out of my bag. "I cooked some with Gran in the summers, but after that, I was just too busy and had no one to cook for anyway. I think Gran was too sad to look at the book again after my mom died."

Grace's mom wiped her hands on her apron, set down the jar of *kimchi* she'd been holding, and put on her reading glasses. "Your mom was my dear friend." She opened the cover. "This is a lovely treasure, Cassidy, and shouldn't be hidden any longer. Yes, yes, here is seaweed soup in Mrs.

Kim's hand. And all of your grandmother's best and most delicious recipes are in here. Look—I remember eating these chicken croquettes she's made notes on soon after I was married. Mr. Kim was doubtful that he would enjoy them but ended up eating seconds. I soon made them often for my family."

Mrs. Kim flipped through the pages and murmured, "Oh yes, yes, I remember your mother making this creamy chicken dish for your father and then for you when you were a little girl. It was wonderful."

I remembered her making it too. My dad loved it, so she made it for us often. Did he remember Mom making it? Did he remember Mom at all?

Mrs. Kim continued, "And this dressing, I still use it. With a few changes." She winked at me. "I see here that your mother made a note on one of your grandmother's recipes, saying she should add avocado, and your grandmother crossed it out and wrote, 'No!'"

"Gran hated avocados," I said.

Mrs. Kim turned to the final section. "Will you add recipes of your own here?"

"I will," I said. "I think it made Gran sad to read these, but for me, it brings hope. I'm starting with my sourdough bread and then maybe my hand pies. I always made hand pies for Gran, and I hope to make them for my own family someday, too."

"I would like to try one," she said in a kind voice. She browsed backward. "I don't think I have seen anything like this before—grandmother, mother, daughter. Mrs. Kim learned to cook at her mother's elbow. In Korea. She had no daughters, of course, but when her other daughters-in-law and I married into the family, she taught us."

"Didn't you know how to cook already?" Grace asked.

"Yes. I had learned at *my* mother's elbow. But your *halmoni* wanted to make sure I prepared food in the way her son was used to."

"Oof," I said. "Mothers-in-law."

Mrs. Kim's smile was a little cheeky, and I knew that while she'd never say it aloud, she agreed.

"So you didn't change anything at all?" Grace asked.

"Oh yes, some," her mother replied as she set the table. "Because of *son-mat*."

"Hand taste?" Grace set the long steel chopsticks by each place. I blinked away my anxiety. I wasn't a pro with them.

"So! You did learn something in Korean school," her mom teased. "Yes. Hand taste. Or the taste of the hand. It means that each woman takes a recipe or a way of making food, and then if she feels it should be different, if she's confident she can make changes that will be an enhancement for her time and family, she changes it, maybe just a little, maybe a lot to make it her own. To make it better. I think the root of the concept is in *kimchi*, where each woman blends her spices and then massages them in by hand, which stains them if she's not wearing gloves. Therefore, anything she touches afterward tastes of 'her' hands. But it's bigger than that now.

It can mean each cook, each woman, may change things to her tastes. Her life to her own tastes."

Mrs. Kim sat down at the table and patted the chair next to her for me. I sat next to her, blinking back tears, and she pulled a soft dish towel from a nearby drawer and handed it to me with gentleness and love. "Thank you," I said. "I wish I could have learned to cook at my mom's elbow."

"But you can." She tapped the cookbook. "It's all here." She handed the book back to me. "Here you have one of your family heirlooms—like a necklace, for example. You keep the jewels but have them reset to your tastes and the era in which you live. In this case—" she glanced at the book—"you take their recipes and their instructions. You follow some, and then you take your own path sometimes, too."

I nodded. Yes. Sourdough was much like that. It took on not only the taste of the land, which gave its wild yeast, but the hands of those who kneaded the dough.

Mine.

We chatted happily, and half an hour later, the meat was grilled on their indoor grill, and we all sat down to eat. Mr. Kim led the prayer of thanksgiving for the meal and also asked for the healing of his father, Grace's grandfather, who normally lived with and ate with them. The plates were passed. After a few minutes, Grace casually asked her mother, "Do we know anyone named Mi-Ja?"

Her mother finished placing food into her mouth deftly with the chopsticks and then said, "No." She looked at her husband. "Do we?"

He looked toward the ceiling and then back down. "Maybe some distant cousin of my father. I'm not sure. I don't think so. I can't be certain." He turned to Grace, and his gaze grew firm and wary. "Why?" It was a tone that expected an answer.

"Oh, just wondering. I heard the name and wondered if it was familiar or whatever."

The room grew silent. I could tell he was going to press her with a follow-up question, so I jumped in. "How is school going?" I asked Grace's youngest brother.

"Fine, fantastic," he answered.

"Except when he's playing on his Switch for too many hours." His older brother poked him.

The youngest brother looked at his parents before quickly starting a long discussion about the success of his current robotics project. Grace gave me a look I knew meant *thank you.*

On the way home some hours later, I said, "I've been thinking about dinners. I wish I had a family like yours. When I worked in California, Chef would always make family dinner for the team before service. Maybe some Saturdays I could make family dinners for all of us—anyone working at the farm, visiting, living at the house. You, me, Annika, DJ, Nick, whoever happens to be around? Justin could come someday. If I add more crew next year, they can come too. Our own family dinners. The thought of cooking for my friends and building a little community family really excites me."

Grace smiled. "This the happiest I've seen you since Gran died, so yes, it's a fantastic idea."

We chatted about Justin and then about Nick. "How are things going with him?"

"He's been traveling," I said. "And working a lot. But we text or talk every day. I mean, it almost feels to me like we never broke up."

"Are you thinking about getting back together?" she asked.

I shook my head. "No . . . not yet, anyway. I'm really loving connecting as deep friends, but I haven't forgotten why we broke up. He moved abruptly to chase success. He didn't want to commit. He stayed incommunicado."

"And you didn't want to do long-distance," Grace said.

"True," I said. "He's been really helpful with the CSAs, though, reaching out to friends and such to see if we can sign up more subscribers."

"How is that going?" Grace asked.

I shook my head. "Not well. Nick was right. CSAs have really come into their own on the island. Anyone who wants one has pretty much signed up. I started late in the game. I might see if I can add some additional vegetables, or maybe some of the pickled stuff in the cellar to jazz up our offerings, until next year, when I can make more on the flowers . . . somehow." I turned toward her. "You okay with how things went tonight?"

She nodded. "I think it's pretty clear now that no one had any idea about that baby, and I'm not even sure it has anything to do with my family. Maybe Mi-Ja isn't even some-one's name. I mean, it's just a beautiful child. I'd like to just let this go now if it's okay. I have a lot to concentrate on to make sure I pass, and honestly, I'm still having a hard time studying. I must pass the test."

But then who was the baby her *halmoni* was kissing in the picture? And why had Gran insisted we look together? Grace looked straight forward, neck taut. I needed to focus on work, too. Now that Annika had taken a lot of the gar-dening tasks, I'd have time to build more into the CSAs—or come up with an alternative. "Okay," I agreed. "Consider it closed."

* * *

A couple of weeks after we'd had dinner with the Kims, I was almost finished sorting through Gran's paperwork. A few more hours should finish it off. I opened the second-to-last file from her creaky, faded, pre–World War II filing cabinet.

There was a hanging file labeled *Home Equity Loan.* A red sticky tape said, *Mention to C. at Easter.*

C. Must be me. And Gran hadn't made it to my planned Easter visit.

I opened the file and pulled out a contract for a home equity loan taken out against the land. The line of credit was for $100,000, but only $75,000 of it had been used. Clipped to the loan contract were receipts for repiping the house inside and out, upgrading the electrical system to code, new siding, and water damage repair. A checking account statement was next to it with a password and log-in.

I pulled up the account and saw a balance. I had not realized that there was an additional bank account because Gran had always kept everything at the Navy credit union. This account was with the local bank that had made the loan.

Each month there had been a withdrawal for the home equity payment, and I quickly calculated the payments against the remaining bank balance. There was enough in there for two years' worth of payments. So *that's* what she'd meant when she said she'd given me a head start. Which was great, because even after the two years, I'd be okay; this payment was less than rent would be.

I walked downstairs and knocked on Grace's office door. "Found something. Can you take a look?" I showed her the documents.

"Wow. Gran hated debt, right?"

"Right," I said. "But how else was she going to upgrade a hundred-year-old house when she was in her mideighties?"

She put her hands up. "I wasn't calling her out for it. No worries."

I sat on the chair next to her. "Sorry. I'm a little defensive. Am I good with this?"

"Seems like it." She quickly scanned the paperwork. "I can look more closely later if you want me to. The payments are being made from her account. In a couple of years, when the account looks like it's going to be tapped out, you can just add some more. Sometime in the next month or two, head over to the bank and get the accounts put in your name too."

"Okay." I sighed with relief.

"I'm heading into Seattle tonight for a study break," she said. "Justin bought concert tickets. I'll stay at home afterward and be back tomorrow night."

"Okay! Have fun!" I headed out to the garden, brushing my hands against the silky rose heads as I did. I'd begun snipping some for bouquets in the honesty stand when I heard a car pull up. "Brenda!" I started to walk toward her.

"Don't come to me. I'll come to you, Mary, Mary," she called out. "I want to see how your garden grows." She walked by the herb boxes. "These are coming along nicely. The thyme is blooming, and everything else will shoot up with another couple of months of heat. Freesias are gorgeous, and I do hope you're going to sell some of the lilac branches. They go at a premium since no one thinks to cut them."

"I'm big into bouquets of branches," I said. "I've already sold a few." Very few. There wasn't much money coming in, and I didn't tell her how much I'd already composted. "You were right about a low level of traffic out here."

"I'm sorry." She handed an empty basket to me. To thank her for her help in organizing the plant drive, I'd made a huge picnic basket filled with things from our garden, cellar, and freezer. "In better news, this was delicious. Marv said he might leave me if you're still single. He especially loved the hand pies and wondered if he could put in an order. I'm not much of a baker. You could throw in some of that sourdough and unusual—delicious—butter too."

I laughed. "Thank you. I'm glad you both appreciated them. I don't sell the hand pies or the sourdough, because they are a signature labor of love I gift to those I care for, but I'd be happy to make more for a friend. Thank you for everything you've done for me. The blue poppies are coming up nicely." I waved my arm to show her. "Let me pick some for you before you go."

"You are so welcome, honey. And I'd love a bouquet of those rare beauties. They make me so happy." Her eyes twinkled. "Anyway, I'm sure we'd pay for another basket like that if you ever felt bored." She scanned the huge acreage. "Not likely. Proud of all of these flowers, though. Everyone who returned them would be too. In fact, a few of them have driven by to surveil and reported back, happy."

I set the picnic basket on the table in the middle of the garden, where we ate lunch, drank lemonade, tea, or coffee, and where, soon, I'd start holding our family dinners. As Brenda left, DJ and Annika arrived. I got DJ set up in the little lean-to with his iPad and showed him where I'd refilled the bird foods.

Annika had fallen behind at the weeding. She'd been doing great for a while, and then all of a sudden, the weeds went untended. There were other tasks in a late May garden—watering, feeding, making sure each plant had enough space to grow and had been placed near companion plants to help each other along. But I was going to have to talk with her and make sure she stayed on task. She was taking a lot of pictures, too, which was great. But I couldn't pay her for those. What kind of a boss and mentor would I be if I just let her slack?

I went to meet her. She stood among the peonies and roses, twisting her fidget cube.

"These beds are the ones that need to be weeded," I said, hoping to remind her.

She balked and looked miserable. "I can't weed them," she said. "I'm sorry. I don't want to fail you and your family another year. But I just can't bend into the flower beds. I tried." She tucked the small cube back into her pocket before looking at me.

Well, the flower to veg ratio was like five to one already and growing, so this might be a problem I needed to solve. "Hey, let's go have a seat at the picnic table and talk about it," I said. "We can keep an eye on DJ from there." We headed over and sat down.

"I'm deathly afraid of bees," she said. "I keep telling myself they aren't going to hurt me. But they do sting. Have you ever been stung?"

I had to be honest. "Yeah. Not often, but yeah. Once I knelt on one, and it stung me through my pant leg."

Her eyes grew wide.

I rushed to reassure her. "It was a long time ago!"

She pulled out her phone and opened her camera roll. "Look. Didn't get close. But look at their bee faces."

"Cute?"

She shook her head and zoomed in. "Beady eyes, and those stingers are like a medical syringe filled with poison. I can avoid other sharp things with the gloves and the boots but not the bees."

"They're pollinators," I said quietly. "They need to be there for the plants to grow. No bees, no fruit. No bees, no blossoms."

"I know." Misery swelled her voice. She scrolled through the photos.

I looked over her shoulder while she did. "Wait!"

She looked at me.

"Go back to the ones in the greenhouse."

She scrolled back to some close-ups of the glass flask I used for the salad dressing I'd nestled in Brenda's basket, right up against a wooden bowl with tongs, and the lettuce softly settled at the base. "This is gorgeous! Like, magazine-worthy!"

She blushed. "Thank you. I see everything in the world as a photograph. I just see the right lines and the right light."

"Do you have more pictures like this?"

Nodding, she opened the album called *Cassidy*, and there were hundreds, maybe more, photos of flowers, of the wagon, of the orchards in bloom and then with their tiny apples and pears hanging like dangle earrings from each branch. "This one's my favorite," she said. It was the sign that said *Mickey*, hooked like a crooked smile on her grandfather's tree. "I'm sorry about the bees like I was sorry about the strawberries. I'm sure you'll have to fire me," she said.

What to do? I mean, hadn't I said a business decision had

to be a business decision? And yet here she was, doing what she loved even though it was inconvenient. Like me with flowers.

I could tell her that I was sorry, but I couldn't keep her on because I needed help with the weeding and up-close plant care, and there were sure to be bees. Or I could do more of it myself. "I may have other things for you to do," I said. "Those orchard signs need to be painted."

"I could paint them and take before and after photos," she said. "The weathered look is cool."

She was a woman in love. With her camera. I smiled. "You're right; it is. Let me think about what else you might be able to do, and maybe DJ can do a little of the weeding, too, if he's willing to come alongside me. Do you mind sweeping out and straightening the honesty stand? Packing stuff to sell there once it's picked?"

"Not at all. I can dig in new plants, too. Weed anything but blossoming flowers."

"Let me think on it," I said.

I was back to clipping a few peonies for bouquets and organizing the summer bulbs for planting when Nick walked up with four iced lattes in a carrier.

"Hey. All hail the queen of spades." He glanced at my shovel and grinned.

I looked at the coffees. "This is most welcome."

"Me or the coffee?"

"Both. It was sweet of you to think of everyone."

"I remembered from your last order that DJ likes decaf with caramel and Annika prefers low-fat milk." He handed a wrapped package to me, too. "So since we know you have all the actual flowers you'll ever want . . . ," he said, looking at the acre outside the greenhouse, vibrant with new plant life.

"A book?" I pulled the ribbon, undoing it, and then unwrapped the package. *The Fully Illustrated Guide to Victorian Flower Language, Updated for the Modern Woman.* "Oh! Perfect!"

He grinned. "I thought you might like this, after talking about the apple blossom meanings and all." Warm pink flushed his face.

I reached out to hug him. "Thank you for this. It means so much." I paged through a few, stopping at poppies, their meaning listed by color. Blue, the ones I'd just snipped for Brenda, represented spiritual faith. *I'm not despising this small beginning, Lord. Thank you.* I took the book over to the picnic table, and Nick sat down next to me.

"So," he said, "I've got bad news."

I looked up from the book. "What?"

"I've been monitoring the website responses . . ."

I knew where he was going. "Me too."

"So you realize we probably can't rustle up enough interest in CSAs. I know I said produce was the way forward, and I still think it is. But there are so many CSAs on the island now that without something to stand out, we're not going to make it."

"I'm not selling enough flowers, either," I told him. "I'm not going to make enough money in time. I need to think about what to do, and I know I don't have much time."

He glanced at the picnic basket. "What's this?"

"Brenda came by and told me how much they loved the basket I sent over, especially my sourdough and hand pies, and could I please sell another one to her. I'm so happy that they liked my little thank-you."

Annika and DJ made their way over to sit down.

"Thank you . . . Nick," DJ said as the two of them sat down and took their coffees.

"Perfect!" Annika said. "Thanks for remembering!"

"You're welcome." Nick looked at the basket again. "So . . . ," he started again and then snapped his fingers. "What about a picnic basket subscription box? With salad, that fantastic sourdough, herbal dressing, and your hand pies? A small bouquet of your rustic-wrapped flowers? We could add up all the parts that come from the property and put it toward that $1,500. It's different. It's not just the typical CSA. Exactly what we're looking for!"

"A picnic basket subscription? With my bread and hand pies?" My heart sank, but I wasn't sure why. "I mean, I guess we could consider it."

"But will people on the island want salads week after week?" Annika said.

"You're right," I said, relieved without understanding why. "I don't think it will work."

"Hold on, sunshine," Nick said. "What about people who come to the island for weekly summer rentals? I can reach out to a couple of landlords. I can also add that to your website. It won't take long at all. Maybe a day or two tops."

Something inside me recoiled. "Maybe we need to slow down a little here? Let me think about this?"

"You just said you were running out of time, right? Time is money—tax money—so no slowing down. I can look for some royalty-free pictures of general farm and flower stuff. I'm sure I can find a picnic basket and some salad photos."

"Wait!" Annika stood up. "I have hundreds of pictures, and I can take hundreds more."

Skepticism crossed Nick's face, just a slight upturn of the lip, but I knew it well. He was a perfectionist where marketing graphics were concerned.

Annika opened up her photo roll and thumbed through the pictures. "Look at these flasks!" she said. "And I took some of Cassidy's hand pies as she was pulling them out of the oven."

He low whistled. "These are great. I'd need to pay you."

Annika shook her head. "I'm already being paid. You guys can tell me what you want shots of, and I'll do them during my regular work hours when I'm not painting or whatever."

She looked so happy to have solved the problem of keeping her job by doing what she loved. It did seem like a good solution, and I was happy that she was happy. "Thank you," I said, clinking my coffee cup with hers in a kind of toast. But why wasn't *I* happy?

"What should we call the business?" Nick looked at the fence by the rose garden. "White Picket Picnics?"

"Picnics!" DJ said. "We . . . pick . . . Nick."

We all laughed at his joke. "Okay," I said. "White Picket Picnics it is!"

Nick gave Annika his email address to send photos to him, and then Annika and DJ went back to work.

* * *

Later that evening I headed up to the attic, clicked on the light, and moved to the far, still-dry corner where I'd found a small stash of picnic baskets. Frugal Gran rarely threw away anything she thought might still be useful. On my way to grab a few more, I saw a bit of my mom's wedding veil sticking out of the hope chest. I didn't want it to get crimped, so I opened the trunk to rearrange it so everything fit in neatly. I lifted out the photos and the *hanbok*, which were now on top, and set them to the side. Then I took out my baby blanket and put that on the floor. As I did, I knocked over a small wooden thread box inside the hope chest, one I had not noticed when we'd sorted this the first time. As I picked up the box, spools and spools of thread fell to the side, including one of shimmering gold, which reminded me of Rumpelstiltskin. Flat inside the box, under spools of thread, were two onionskin airmail letters, addressed in English to Choi Eunhee, Grace's *halmoni*—opened once but now taped shut.

Ohhhh.

Maybe these letters weren't anything to cause a problem.

But then why had they been tucked into the previously locked hope chest?

I shook my head. Nope. I'd promised Grace the matter was settled. A promise was a promise.

Helen

CHAPTER TWELVE

September 1958

"You'll have to care for her at home now," the doctor told Helen. "It's been two weeks. We simply can't let her take that bed any longer. I've given her the birth certificate."

"Has her bleeding slowed?" Helen asked.

"It's slowing. Keep an eye on her. She's lucky to have you. Does she have a mother nearby who can help? I know you have shifts and patients of your own."

"I can take care of both Mrs. Roy and my patients," Helen assured him. "I can take care of quite a lot of people at once."

"Good. That is what I told Captain Adams."

They'd discussed her? The hospital had more drama and complications than *As the World Turns*. She and Eunhee had enjoyed watching soap operas while Eunhee was in the hospital and Helen visited her room.

"Is the baby well?" Helen asked. "She was premature."

"She's as stable as she'll ever be. There is little anyone can do for her. You've heard her heart . . ."

Helen nodded. The thumping murmur signaled a heart condition that Helen had been told was common among babies born with Down syndrome. Not only did the heart not work correctly, but Mi-Ja's lungs also had trouble due to the heart defect.

"Your best bet is to investigate institutions. I understand that the Buckthorn Institution is the place that would take the child. They have medical personnel and a nursery. People suited to care for the baby. It is best," he said, "for Mrs. Roy to forget she ever had this child. The child will die soon enough, and the mother is a young woman. Maybe she will go back to her country, find a husband from there, and start over. However, she should just be on her guard. She may have another damaged baby."

"Damaged?" Helen allowed outrage to color her voice. "You mean Mi-Ja's heart complications . . . correct?"

The doctor shrugged. "Something the mother did may have led to this, or she has a defect of her own that her child ended up this way. I don't plan to discuss this again, and I suggest you do not, either, unless you want blame attaching to you for your care while she lived in your home."

"Hello?" Eunhee spoke from the door of the restroom. How long had she been there?

Minutes later, Helen helped Eunhee to the car, and then another nurse placed the baby in Eunhee's arms. "Ready to go home?"

Eunhee nodded. "Yes, please. Let's go home."

"I'll fix some nourishing seaweed soup for you." Helen smiled.

Eunhee bent down and kissed little Mi-Ja on her cheeks. "I think I will make the soup."

Helen drove very slowly, taking an extra ten minutes to arrive at the house. Normally she would check for a letter from Eunhee's mother, but as there had not been one since she'd indicated Eunhee should not come home, she whizzed past the mailbox.

Once home, Helen turned the car off and came around to lift and hold the baby while Eunhee got out of the car. As she did, they could both see that she'd already bled through her dress and onto the car's bench.

"I'm so sorry," Eunhee said.

"Nonsense. I am a nurse. Do you think blood troubles me? Let's head into the house and get you changed and the baby fed and put down."

As she settled the two of them into their room—bassinet by the side of Eunhee's bed—Helen said, "May I take the clothes you've bled through and soak them in cold salt water so they won't stain?"

"Oh, thank you," Eunhee said. Helen stepped out of the room so Eunhee could change, and after she did, she handed the clothing over to Helen. Helen took them to the washtub and examined them. Dark clots, no red blood. Okay, nothing to panic over but merely to keep a close eye on.

Next, she took her clippers out to the garden and snipped an unruly bunch of rose of Sharon branches. The branches were lush with blooms of five white petals that felt like rough silk when rubbed between finger and thumb. At the base of each flower was a blot of color, and together they supported a yellow stamen, which looked like a hooked owl's beak, ready to nurture birds and bees. Helen gathered them into a bouquet and placed it in an enameled farm pitcher.

"I have some *mugunghwa*!" she called cheerfully into the teal bedroom. Eunhee, however, slept, as did Mi-Ja. Helen quietly set the flowers on the top of the closed sewing machine and then went into the living room to read her *Ladies' Home Journal*. Eunhee was still asleep thirty minutes later. Maybe the smell of soup would rouse her. Helen pulled a chicken carcass and some leftovers from the refrigerator.

Was that the baby? Helen didn't want to rush into the bedroom, but when the baby cried for a few more minutes, Helen turned the soup off and went in.

Eunhee did not wake.

Helen gently took Mi-Ja in her arms and paced circles in the living room, looking down on her tiny, beautiful face, her eyes open and bright, just like the rose of Sharon blooms. "Hello, sweet girl. I am Auntie Helen."

The baby quieted at the sound of Helen's voice, which melted her. The baby felt so good in her arms, a little warm bundle of love. It was true; to her practiced nurse's eye,

Mi-Ja's face was flatter, her ears smaller, and her neck thicker than a typical baby's. But perhaps there was another answer, not Down syndrome.

That heart murmur, though. The baby seemed to tire herself out, more than other babies, simply by crying, which was unusual and concerning. Mi-Ja stuttered a cry out just then. She wanted Umma.

Helen walked into the bedroom, bent, and gently shook Eunhee by the shoulder. "Eunhee. The baby needs you. She is hungry."

At that, her friend blearily opened her eyes. "Oh yes, of course. I did not sleep well in the hospital. The bleeding, too—I think it makes me weaker."

Without a doubt. "I have made some soup for you. One minute." Helen quickly brought a cup into the bedroom. "It's not seaweed, but it's chicken noodle. I roasted the chicken myself, and the rosemary, tarragon, and thyme are from the garden. I thought my teacher might be proud." She winked.

"Very delicious," Eunhee said after she finished the cup to the last drop. "I have never tasted this soup with those herbs, and now I think I will prefer it your way." She looked toward the other side of the room. "In my top drawer—" she pointed toward her bureau—"is a small bag with what looks like barley seed. Can you get it out for me?"

Helen opened the drawer and, among the clean bleached diapers, yellow-headed pins, and little pink caps and socks, found the burlap bag Eunhee mentioned.

"Would you please brew it into a tea for me?"

Helen looked at the bag, but the directions and title were stamped in Korean.

"It is a Korean tea called Job's tears." Eunhee answered Helen's unspoken question. "One tablespoon in a cup of water for two minutes. It may help my bleeding stop."

"Job's tears," Helen said. "What a funny name."

"They are named after Job, who was a good man that loved God," Eunhee said. "Satan was jealous and told God that Job only loved him because he gave him everything. God said no, that was not true, and that it could be proved. The devil took away everything that mattered to Job. His health, his home, his wife, his children. He cried a lot. These—" she pointed at the grains—"look like tears. Koreans drink this tea very often. It is said to help reduce the swelling for new mothers. I hope it will help my bleeding."

Helen brewed a cup and then blew over the tea, cooling it, on the way to Eunhee's bedroom. It did smell like barley, comforting, like the scent of morning oatmeal. She held it while Eunhee finished feeding Mi-Ja. The baby struggled to breathe as she fed. Her mouth was slacker than normal, and the muscles worked hard to clasp the nipple. The smallest exertion caused her to tire and her skin to take on a purple tint. Finally Mi-Ja's head lolled in contentment as she finished feeding. Eunhee kissed her baby once, twice, ten times, and then Helen rested the cup of tea on the dresser top before setting the baby in the bassinet.

For the first time, Helen prayed. *God, if you exist and are a friend to Eunhee and Mi-Ja, please let them sleep. Stop that bleeding. My friend needs to be well for herself and her baby.*

She could pray from that day until the next, but that wouldn't solve the immediate problem. The two of them needed someone here full-time. Eunhee did not yet have the strength to lift the baby, and if something happened during Helen's shift, who would care for them? She had taken the "Florence Nightingale Pledge" when she'd graduated. *I solemnly pledge myself before God and in the presence of this assembly, to pass my life in purity and to practice my profession faithfully.*

She could hire someone but did not yet trust anyone to give Mi-Ja the care she deserved, not given the attitude she'd encountered at the hospital. Sometimes the most important nursing happened at home.

While the two of them slept, Helen dressed in her pressed uniform, fastened her pin and hat on securely, cinched her belt with the songbird buckle she'd specially chosen, and drove to the hospital.

"Captain Adams?" she said as she knocked on his office door.

"Yes?" His voice was gruff. "Enter."

She opened the door and then stepped in. "May I have a word?"

He softened. "Always. Anything for you. Close the door behind you."

Helen did as she was told. Reluctantly.

"Sit here." He moved a chair from the front of his desk to beside him, out of the line of sight of the small window in the door. "You've been so busy. I've missed seeing you in the hallways and break room."

Helen perched on the edge of the chair. "I have been so busy with my friend and her baby. She is still having residual effects from childbirth. I wondered if I might have that month's leave of absence you'd mentioned earlier to care for her. She is, after all, a Navy widow."

He drew near to her. "I'll give this due consideration. Maybe I, too, can help take care of a Navy widow." He placed his hand on her thigh and looked down at her feet. "I liked seeing you with your shoes off."

Helen lifted his hand from her thigh. The skin burned as if he had branded her. "Sir, I am confused. You are a married man—and my superior."

"Helen, Helen," he said. "My wife and I are married, but not together in the most important ways. She has the children to raise. It's convenient for me to have a wife, of course, to tend to my household and needs. But we don't choose to spend time together, you see. We have so little in common. She doesn't understand hospital work like you and I do."

Helen nodded uncomfortably. What could she possibly say?

He continued, "We have an . . . arrangement of sorts. All sorts of arrangements can be made when you open your mind to them. If you and I had one, it would be our secret."

Helen catapulted off her chair. "I'm sorry, sir. I am not open to arrangements."

His face hardened. The blue eyes grew cold. "I see." A moment went by, and Helen walked toward the door.

"I do not recall mentioning any kind of leave of absence to you earlier."

Helen opened her mouth and then closed it again. No one else had been in the break room when he'd brought that up.

"I don't hire nurses to have them abandon their posts. I hire them to be . . . of use to me. Why do you think I hired you?"

"Because I offer excellent care for the sick; I am a trained, degreed RN; and because my husband died a hero's death." She looked him in the eye. "And lived a hero's life."

He flinched. It was not, perhaps, a good idea to fling your boss's vulgarity in his face after asking for a favor.

"Well, it seems you must choose your job or your friend. I need coverage, and I will have to hire a replacement nurse. When I do, I'll recommend that your position be permanently converted into a Navy position, not a civilian position, so we need not be concerned about covering our patients."

There would be no job waiting for her. It would be assigned to a Navy nurse.

"I will not leave a good recommendation or review in the personnel file of anyone abandoning their post. I am sure you understand."

"I understand perfectly, sir."

Just then a corpsman knocked on the door. "Sir, may I have a word?"

"Mrs. Devries, if you'll step outside for a moment."

Heaviness hit Helen's heart. How badly she'd misjudged Mrs. Adams. She was not a pleasant person but was carrying an awful burden being married to a man who would not reserve himself for his wife alone. Helen would undoubtedly be more introspective and gracious in the future. She now clearly understood Mrs. Adams's warning about fraternization. It had not been a warning against Eunhee . . . but the woman's husband.

She walked over to the nurses' station, where she had a small cubby for her things. Her coffee mug, the pens she preferred to use, an extra nurse's pin. Her Florence Nightingale book.

If she decided to care for Eunhee, she'd lose her job. She had no intention of officially joining the Navy and traveling for the rest of her life. She had little savings because she'd spent so much of Bob's life insurance finishing her education. Enough for a few months, and she'd find another job doing something—anything—if need be.

Stomach clenched, Helen paged through the book about Florence Nightingale, the nurse who had served on bloody battlefields and in desperate hospitals. She'd had no assurance of her security nor safety.

Helen knew just the quote she was looking for. There. Page 16. *"How very little can be done under the spirit of fear."* She snapped the book closed, startling the shift nurse charting nearby. She'd once so bravely offered a pledge and promise to Eunhee that slipped to the front of her mind.

"I'd like to live a hero's life," Helen had said.

"I'd like to live a hero's life, too," Eunhee had agreed. "I am not sure what two women like us could do to be heroes, though."

Helen had nodded. "Someday that opportunity may come to us. Will we be ready and willing, like our husbands were?"

Thirty minutes later, Helen said goodbye to her colleagues, emptied her cubby, and drove home.

Don't cry. Don't cry. Eunhee will see that you've been crying, and she doesn't need any more grief right now. Tonight, you can cry into your pillow when she's asleep.

She would tell Eunhee that it was a leave of absence. Unlike the one Captain Adams had suggested. Some secrets were kept for the good of others, not to do them harm. In a way, it was the truth, anyway. This was a leave of absence from her job, but not from her calling.

*　*　*

A few weeks later, Eunhee sat at the kitchen table rolling and shaping the dough for the rice cakes they would eat the next day, September 27, to celebrate *Chuseok*. Bowls of honeyed sesame paste she and Helen had pounded together sat nearby so Eunhee could stuff the cakes as soon as they were ready to be folded into pretty half-moon dumplings.

"So is this like the American Thanksgiving?" Helen asked, rocking the bassinet slightly to quiet Mi-Ja.

"Not so much. *Chuseok* means 'on the eve of autumn.' It's a time when Koreans give thanks to their ancestors for a good harvest."

"Not to God?"

"God, for me," Eunhee said. "I do not worship my ancestors, but I am grateful to them for the sacrifices they made for me. I will sacrifice for my family too. The one I have in Korea and the one I will have here."

She eyed Helen carefully, noting, it seemed, her starched nurse's uniform—which she'd purchased as a civilian and then kept. It hadn't been worn for three weeks. "Are you going to check in at your job before you go to the mainland?"

"Not today." Instead, Helen hoped the uniform would add to the sense of authority when she showed up to check out the facilities available for Mi-Ja. She wanted the truth if this was a good place or not, and she hoped to learn that by pretending to be on a professional mission.

Eunhee turned her hand back to the ingredient-laden table. "Our traditions say that if a woman can make a pretty *songpyeon*—" she touched one of the green rice cakes—"she will have beautiful children too."

Helen leaned down and wrapped her finger around Mi-Ja's small finger. "You make beautiful *songpyeon* and beautiful babies."

"I will teach you to make *songpyeon*. So Lauri, too, will be very pretty. Tonight, when you return home." A waver in her voice betrayed her anxiety about Helen's fact-finding mission. "We need to collect the pine needles so we can steam the cakes over them."

Helen nodded. "Don't worry. At the institution today,

I will see if I find the help we need. Then I will come straight home and not be late. Call Johanna if there is a hint of trouble for you or for Mi-Ja."

Helen steered the Buick, top up, northward, and then across the Deception Pass Bridge to the mainland, where the institution was located. The bridge represented how she felt spanning two worlds, one where care was available for all, or so she'd thought, and one where there seemed to be little available for the neediest among them. Two hours later, she arrived at the long, shrub-lined drive leading to low-slung, single-story buildings, arranged in a star pattern, very much like a military base.

She parked in visitor parking and headed toward the main door. The building was clean enough but certainly seemed like a hospital or base, not a home. *That's why it's called an institution, Helen.* Visitors were not usually allowed, but she hoped her credentials would get her in so she could make an honest assessment on behalf of Eunhee.

"May I help you?"

"Walk and talk with authority, move with a purpose, and people will follow you anywhere," Bob used to say. "I'm here to review the infant facilities for a possible placement." Helen flashed her Navy badge, hoping they would not call the base and ask about her expired credentials. Using them would be a crime, but she needed to see firsthand if this was a safe place for Mi-Ja. Somewhere the baby could get the help and care she needed and deserved.

The woman at the desk glanced at the badge and then

at Helen before nodding. "It's atypical, but yes, I will find someone to escort you."

Soon a young orderly arrived, and Helen followed him through corridors, past meeting and examination rooms, which seemed organized but cold. She peered into two rooms peopled with adults, some sitting in chairs staring into space, a few painting what appeared to be paint-by-number sheets with trays of watercolors. Glasses of water with inky swirls rested precariously on the tables.

"Adults live here too?" Somehow she'd thought this was just for children.

"Most of the insane are adults, miss."

Insane? Surely the children with disabilities were not housed with adults who were insane. Was this an insane asylum? Helen could not believe she knew so little about these places, but perhaps that was by design. No one in polite society spoke of them nor of the people they housed.

A few children played in a nearby room while their minder watched a soap opera. One child fell and started crying. She was eventually comforted—not by her minder but by another child instead.

"This way, miss." The orderly led her across the greens and into another building. He opened a door into a room where there were ten cribs all lined up in a row. The drapes were pulled tight against the day's sunlight, which struggled to enter the room through the window's edges.

He must have noticed her gaze. "Drapes are closed so they sleep."

"The babies, you mean?" she asked.

He nodded.

"All day?"

"If we're lucky," he said. "They don't know any different."

"Why wouldn't they?" She squinted so her eyes would adjust to the daytime darkness.

"They're . . . well, you know. Abnormal. Don't have feelings and such. I've heard they don't feel pain like normal babies."

Helen flinched but said nothing more so she could complete her investigation without being asked to leave. Some of the babies did, in fact, sleep. Others moaned, and a few outright cried.

"Will someone come and tend to those who cry?" she asked. "Is there a nurse for their care?"

"The nurse is in the other room, with other babies. She'll come by soon," he said. "There are thousands of people here. We can't be in all places at the same time."

The room smelled of ammonia, urine, and dirty diapers. It took everything within Helen not to rush over and pick up one of the crying babies or insist on a diaper change.

"Say. Where did you say you were from?" The orderly looked at her, face pinched and peering.

"Whidbey Island Naval Air Base."

He took out a notebook and a broken pencil from his breast pocket and wrote that down.

"I must be going now." Helen was thankful that she had tucked away her name badge. "Can you please lead me out?"

He pushed the notebook back into his shirt pocket. A sullen silence had replaced his open demeanor. On the way down the hall, they passed a nurse—Helen recognized her by her cap and locked eyes with her. Perhaps because she knew these were appalling conditions and against every standard of care they had learned in nursing school, the woman turned away in embarrassment. Had she attended the same nursing school as Helen? What could she be thinking, and how had she buried her heart?

And yet would those children be better off without her? Was this all a civilized world had to offer their fellow citizens and those most in need of compassionate care?

Helen walked briskly to her car before she could be asked, again, for her credentials. She drove back down the long drive and then, once out of view, pulled the car over and cried for the babies left behind, for the people who had been forgotten, and for the mothers who had been urged to forget them, knowing there was no possible way that could ever happen. Had the doctors recommending institutionalization ever visited one?

Mi-Ja must not be left there under any circumstance. She would die of neglect.

Mi-Ja still needed medical care, though, medical care which was not available on the island—if it was available anywhere. Helen drove up the highway and past the university, where she'd proudly studied. It had a world-class medical system.

It had a world-class medical system!

She exited at the next ramp, drove toward the nursing school, and parked. It was still early afternoon. Certainly Mrs. Pattison would be at her desk or in the lab. If it was the latter, Helen would wait.

Her heels clicked across the polished stone floor. She walked toward the department and instantly felt at ease. The familiar hallways embraced and reassured her, and the intent faces in each classroom she peered into brought her back to her school days. She'd hoped to bury the pain of her widowhood in books and clinicals.

"Helen!" Mrs. Pattison nodded for her to come in. "Don't you look smart in your uniform. My, how proud we are of you, the only civilian nurse on the base."

Helen kept her face impassive. She did not want to let down her mentor—who was like a mother, a supervisor, and a hero all in one—by admitting she'd lost her job. Yes, it was for a good cause. But a better woman might have been able to figure a way to negotiate out of that. "I have a nursing question I hoped you might be able to answer."

She explained Mi-Ja's situation, how they were looking for caretaking resources and medical assistance with people who might be experienced in such matters.

"That is unfortunate," Mrs. Pattison said. "Has your friend considered institutionalization for the child? That's where most of those children are cared for. I am not aware of individual caretakers, though one could perhaps be found, likely at a high cost."

Where *those children* were cared for. Even her beloved

Mrs. Pattison spoke as though Mi-Ja were not a baby like any other. And yet before she'd known the baby and fallen in love with her, would Helen's reaction have been so different? "Have you ever visited one of the institutions?" Helen asked.

"No, I haven't. I've not been involved in many cases. There is very little we can do for young children, especially where the heart is involved, and when we do, of course, resources are scarce. Decisions must be made about who is worthy of those limited resources. However, as to your query about medical assistance, I will make some inquiries and phone you with what I learn." She smiled warmly.

"Thank you." Helen reached over and embraced her mentor, but perhaps not as affectionately as she might have before. "I await your call."

Dusk and rain fell as one as Helen headed north toward the bridge to home. She'd promised they'd forage the pine needles over which they'd steam the cakes for tomorrow's celebration.

She pulled into the driveway and then went into the house.

Eunhee looked at her with anxiety.

"Do you still want to go into the forest and get the pine needles for the *songpyeon*?"

"Oh yes," Eunhee said. "This is the most important part. Their name means pine cake. We must have pine." Eunhee bundled Mi-Ja up and strapped her to her chest with the long cloth she used for just that purpose. The baby's skin looked pink, but not healthy pink. Working-hard-to-breathe pink. It was raining harder now.

Helen quickly changed, and then the two of them slipped on loafers and headed toward the back property. Helen had brought two flashlights, and they walked slowly so they didn't trip on the way to the wooded area at the back of the acreage. She knew the way well, having traveled it many times while Bob was away and then after he was gone. The peace and quiet of the mixed evergreen-, pine-, and fir-forested acres were her favorite place on all her land. Her life-giving place of safety.

A barred owl cried, *"Who?"*

Eunhee and me. Helen glimpsed the majestic creature, wrapped in barred shades of mink and beige drawn tight around its head and down the body, like a Russian noble-woman dressed protectively against the coming winter. A few minutes later, under the canopy of the tree boughs where they sheltered from the rain, Helen spoke. "I'm afraid I have bad news."

Eunhee stopped still, bracing herself.

"The institution is not a place for Mi-Ja. There was not good care there, nothing that could help us, I'm afraid. I do not think you would be comfortable leaving her there for any amount of time. They don't truly have medical facilities, and the babies seemed overlooked." *Left to die,* she thought but did not say aloud.

"Although I want her to have the very best care, I am thankful she will not have to leave me," Eunhee said.

Helen exhaled. "She still needs medical help."

Eunhee nodded and then bent and picked up some dry needles from the forest floor. "I know."

"I've asked a friend to help us," Helen cautiously offered. "She was my mentor at the nursing school. She'll ask the doctors if there is someone who might know what to do next." Helen picked up some needles too. "I'm hopeful that we can find a doctor to tell us what you must do next to help Mi-Ja. But—"

"I am hopeful, too," Eunhee interrupted, something Helen had never known her to do. "Let us go make the food for the festival and celebrate."

That night, the house smelled freshly of pine and soft sweets as the pretty rice cakes in green, white, and purple steamed over the branches, ready for a celebration.

CHAPTER THIRTEEN

Spent, the garden yawned, ready for hibernation. In mid-October, most plants had withered and decayed, slumping toward the ground to complete their transformation into mulch, except for the places Helen had cleared and composted. A few of the roses of Sharon held on—to please Eunhee, Helen thought. The two of them had harvested everything and collected seeds from the Korean plants and folded them into brown paper envelopes. Eunhee wrote on one, in English, *To plant next year and all the years after. I will make my new home my true home.* Then they tucked the seeds into the drawers in the potting shed. "We'll plant them together here next year?" Helen asked.

"Perhaps," Eunhee answered.

It had taken a month for Mrs. Pattison to find the right pediatrician and for an appointment to have come available. Finally the day arrived, and Eunhee and Helen bundled Mi-Ja for the trip.

"Do you want to drive?" Helen asked. "You're so good now and did fine the last time you drove over the bridge when we went to buy your ingredients."

Eunhee fixed a hat to her hair, then took it off and fixed it again. "No. I am too nervous. I will hold Mi-Ja."

Helen was nervous, too, but someone had to drive. She'd made a hearty breakfast for them of creamed eggs on buttered toast and hot tea and coffee. The eggs were delicious! She jotted a note next to the recipe. *Much better when cheese is added to the white sauce. Also, grind pepper on top, or it will seem like baby food.*

Eunhee picked at the toast and had two cups of tea at Helen's insistence.

"You not eating isn't a vote for my cooking skills," she teased.

Eunhee smiled wanly, and they bundled up themselves and the baby and drove to Seattle.

The doctor's waiting room was filled with low-slung chairs, piles of alphabet blocks scattered like the rubble of demolished brick buildings, and worn copies of *Highlights for Children*. Mothers shushed crying children. If only Mi-Ja could cry powerfully without choking herself blue.

Soon the nurse came to show them to the examining

room. The doctor's demeanor upon entering the room was warm and welcoming. He sat down in a chair across from Eunhee and spoke to her directly. "What a lovely baby girl." He rubbed his hands together to warm them and then asked, "May I hold her?"

Eunhee struggled to hold her face impassive, and Helen knew why. It was the first time a doctor had noted Mi-Ja's loveliness as the first reference to her. "Of course." She handed the baby to him, and he unswaddled and undressed her, leaving on her little undershirt and diaper. He examined her body, listening to her heart and taking her toes—which were slightly more rounded than those of typically developed babies—in his hand. He looked at her skin tone. "Does she always have this purple cast to her skin?"

Eunhee nodded. "More so lately. When she is tired." The baby had been doing nothing but resting, so it went without saying that there had been nothing that should have unduly tired her.

He opened the baby's fist. "Do you see that?" He gently traced the line across Mi-Ja's palm. "Most palms have lines which are diagonal in some sense. Not like this single transverse crease. It's very commonly found in people who have Down syndrome. I would say that due to all of the elements she presents, she most certainly has Down syndrome."

Eunhee nodded. "The other doctor—the doctor at the hospital where she was born—he said maybe it was my fault somehow, that Mi-Ja is different. That I have done something wrong, something shameful, or something is wrong with me, and that's why Mi-Ja is unwell. That the best thing is to let her die and forget about her."

Oh, she'd heard that. Helen wanted to weep.

The doctor's voice was gentle. "We are not quite sure what makes a child susceptible to Down syndrome. My own belief is that it has nothing to do with the mother."

"I believe God made my child," Eunhee said. "The Bible tells us that he made her in his image." Her tears flowed, and Helen drew near to her.

The doctor looked a bit surprised. "Are you a Christian?"

She nodded. "I am. As was her father."

He thought for a moment before speaking again. "That doctor was wrong. I often see children who are sick and parents who worry they have harmed those children somehow. When they share my faith as you do, I remind them of what Jesus said about a man who was born blind. He said the man's blindness was not due to the parents' sin but rather to show the work of God in his life. It is hard to understand that, but I believe it to be true."

"Not everyone believes that," Eunhee said. "Some definitely blame the parents."

"I'm sorry to agree with you. In fact, few believe that. Even people of faith. That is something for you to consider wisely and speak about her and of her with discretion."

"What will happen to her?" Eunhee asked.

The room grew quiet. Helen pulled a handkerchief out of her pocket and handed it to Eunhee.

"Her heart is in very bad shape, and it's getting worse. She cannot live without heart surgery, and we cannot offer that to her. In my best medical opinion, I believe she is too weak to survive surgery even if we had it to offer. In a few years, yes, we maybe could. The field is growing. But we simply don't have the ability now for a baby this small."

Eunhee took the baby from his arm and drew her close to her heart. "If you had the ability, would you do it? Would you, yourself, do this surgery for a baby with Down syndrome? Right now?"

The doctor looked at her frankly. "Before you came to speak with me today, I am not sure. Common medical wisdom is that such children are not worthy of scarce resources because of their intellectual difficulties and likelihood to die young."

Helen could barely keep herself from crying out in anger, but for Eunhee's sake—the mother who showed such great dignity—she remained quiet.

The doctor continued, "But after today, yes. Yes, I would see that it would be done for her as for any other child. I will see to that when it's readily available."

Eunhee swaddled Mi-Ja and stood up. "Please remember that vow, and this child, when the time comes for you to make those decisions." She tenderly kissed the baby's head before pulling the cap back on Mi-Ja's head. "She is seventy-seven days old. Will she live to one hundred days?"

He stood, too. "I am not certain. Her breathing . . ." He looked up and his face betrayed doubt. "Are you attending church?"

"There is no Korean church on Whidbey Island. I do not even know if there is another Korean person on Whidbey Island."

The doctor pulled a card out of his pocket and scribbled on the back of it. "I have a Korean colleague here in Seattle who is also a Christian. He and some other Korean people meet for services in another church during open hours. This may be a time when you would like to attend a church and draw strength. He can tell you where they meet."

Eunhee tucked the card into her purse. "Thank you, I will consider it. I appreciate your time, Doctor."

As she turned to leave, the doctor caught Helen's arm. "Take care of her while she takes care of the baby, and maybe the little one can make it twenty-three more days."

* * *

Later that evening, Helen prepared a meal of dried beef on fried noodles. *Not as good as creamed chipped beef,* she wrote on the recipe, clipped from the newspaper and then glued onto a piece of paper and snapped into her cookbook. *Also, add some fresh tarragon from the garden.* When she stood straight after writing, she looked out the kitchen window and saw Eunhee bend down in the garden. She did not come back up again. Had she fallen? Was the baby on the ground, too?

Helen wiped her hands on her apron, ran toward the garden in her stocking feet, and pushed open the gate. Eunhee knelt by the *mugunghwa,* the shrub that represented beauty prevailing through difficulty and neglect. Helen went to her and knelt, too, the wet soil seeping through both of their dresses.

Eunhee sobbed, the baby wrapped to her chest with the long strip of fabric.

"Will he take everything from me?" she choked out between anguished cries. "My home, my country, my brother, my mother and father, my husband, my child? Is it not enough that I must relinquish one or two of those things while others enjoy them? He must demand them all?"

Helen held her close while she cried, Mi-Ja protectively sandwiched between them. Helen did not need to ask who "he" was.

Eunhee continued to sob, the rain and tears coursing down her face.

Helen cried, too. "I do not know. I do not understand."

When Eunhee started to shiver, Helen helped her to her feet, and arms around one another, they made their way to the kitchen. Helen made some tea as Eunhee fed Mi-Ja, who had barely woken during her mother's crisis.

"I think I would like to visit that meeting of people for a Korean church on Sunday," Eunhee finally said, calm having returned to her voice. Her eyes brimmed with fatigue and hurt.

"Really? I thought you were angry with God."

"Oh yes." Eunhee looked into her cup. "I am. Remember Job? From the tea I drank after Mi-Ja's birth? Job was a good man, and God took everything away from him. When he did, Job spoke to him in pain. In despair. In honesty. Love and honest talk make for friends. I am not happy with God. But I still believe in him and his goodness. Will you stay with the baby and let me borrow your car?"

"Of course, of course," Helen said. "I will stay with the baby every Sunday, as many as you want to go." She held her handkerchief out. "I will finish dinner while you tell me all about the *Baek-il*, the one hundred days celebration."

Eunhee's voice was tinted with anxiety. "Will Mi-Ja live until then? It will be on November 22. One hundred days, that is."

"Yes," Helen said. "She will wear her beautiful *hanbok*."

"We can have a small celebration," Eunhee said. "Just the three of us."

* * *

The next Sunday, as soon as Eunhee drove out of the driveway, Helen cleaned the house, looking at her watch. The Dutch church got out at 11:00 a.m., and she figured Johanna would be home thirty minutes after that. At 11:30 promptly, Helen picked up the phone.

"Hello, Johanna? It's Helen. Listen . . . you know that Eunhee's baby, Mi-Ja, is very ill and is likely to die within the month."

Gasps came across the line—not from Johanna—but Helen did not care at that point. "The baby must have her one hundred days celebration before she dies. Will you help me?"

"Anything," Johanna replied.

"It's important to Eunhee that one hundred people are given gifts of rice cakes. In her tradition, that means the child will live a long and happy life."

"But didn't you just say the baby was dying? Oh . . . ," came a voice Helen did not recognize. Was there a new party on this line?

Helen answered anyway, for all who listened, "Yes, but she is a Christian and believes her child will go to heaven. Doesn't your Bible say that heaven lasts forever? Isn't that a long and happy life?"

"It certainly is," Johanna agreed.

"Today, Eunhee is in Seattle attending the Korean church. If you can come and pick up some of the food by say—" she calculated how long it would take Eunhee to return—"three o'clock? And store it in your freezer? I'll make a few more things next week and the next, and that should have us set for November 22, which is Mi-Ja's hundredth day. Please bring some special food of your own to share if you can, and also, each person must bring a long piece of thread."

"For her sewing?"

Helen looked at the baby in her bassinet nearby. She had started to wiggle a little bit, and Helen knew she'd need to eat soon, a tiring task for both of them as it was hard for Mi-Ja to clasp her mouth firmly enough around a bottle nipple to suck.

Helen turned back to her conversation. "Tradition says that long threads indicate a long life. We know—and she knows—that the baby won't live long. But could we come together and encourage her that Mi-Ja's life will mean something to all of us, and to people we don't yet know, for a long time?"

"Amen," Johanna said. "I will bring Cinn Rolls. I'm sure others, ahem, will contribute as well."

The lines clicked off.

Helen rolled rice cakes the way Eunhee had shown her and then stuffed them with the red bean paste they'd bought in Seattle and the sesame-and-honey concoction they'd made in September. There was plenty of seaweed, and Helen could make clam broth with clams dug right on the island. She'd buy disposable paper cups so that if, hopefully, one hundred people came to take a rice cake, they could also sip a little soup.

How would she keep such a huge batch from Eunhee, though? She wanted the size of the party to be a surprise.

The afternoon weather cleared, so she dressed Mi-Ja warmly and went out into the cold garden. All the plants had been cut back and the debris hauled away, yet some birds had not flown south for the winter. They pecked here and there on the ground, looking for nonexistent insects, and at the thin evergreen huckleberries. Helen entered the barn and filled a large jar with the Nyjer seed her bird friends preferred in their mesh feeders.

Orange-crowned warblers stood out as a slash of brightness against the early dusk. The yellow-throated warblers joined them, rising like little sunrays, and the black-throated ones flew up to feed too.

Nearby, a small clan of European starlings waited their turn, tan and teal, cool and regal. For certain, day in and day out, her beloved goldfinches would visit. Who would feed them this winter if she did not? If she did not find employment on the island, she must move to Seattle.

Who would care for the sparrows?

When Helen filled the last feeder, Mi-Ja stirred. As she looked down at her, a thrill of love rushed through her.

Mi-Ja had smiled at Helen for the very first time.

"Do not worry, little sparrow," Helen said. "I have you close to my heart."

* * *

"It's the big day!" Helen sang as she came into the kitchen. Eunhee was already at the table, and the baby was sleeping in her bassinet. She hadn't been awake much the past few days, and her skin had begun to shrivel and wrinkle as she lost weight. Helen had despaired that Mi-Ja would even make it until Saturday. But she had.

Helen set out a big stack of paper cups.

"What are those for?" Eunhee asked. "This will be a small party."

"Soup. Seaweed soup." Helen lifted the big pot she'd found in the canning shed onto the stovetop. "We need to make a big, big pot."

"For us?" Eunhee looked around. "Two of us?"

"Oh no," Helen said. "There will be many more."

"Really? Johanna and her family?"

"Go get changed! Dress Mi-Ja in her pretty *hanbok*. This is to be a large celebration."

Eunhee picked up the baby and went to change, her face brighter than Helen had seen it for a while. Helen slipped into the mud porch, where Johanna had sneakily dropped off the rice cakes earlier in the morning—the cold weather kept them at just the right temperature. She brought them inside and placed them on the table on her prettiest platters, next to dainty napkins she had purchased at the five-and-dime.

Soon Eunhee came from her room, her eyes widening. "Rice cakes! You already made them!"

Helen grinned. "You taught me."

"So many! So pretty!" Tears welled in Eunhee's eyes, and she brushed them away quickly. She reached out and bowed to Helen. "Thank you."

Helen bowed back and then went to change her dress. When she came back downstairs, Eunhee held Mi-Ja in her arms, enveloped in her beautiful pink *hanbok*. "She is a perfect little blossom," Helen said. "And now—I do believe your first guests are here!"

The Jansens arrived first, Johanna with a large platter of rolls, the boys with neatly combed hair and wearing ties. One by one, they came into the house, and Eunhee bowed to each of them. They looked at the baby, resting quietly with her eyes closed in her mother's arms. They each took a rice cake.

"We snuck some when they were stored at our house," the youngest boy, Mickey, whispered. "My brothers didn't care for them, but I love them. I ate theirs too."

Eunhee grinned and put a few into a napkin and handed it to him.

More cars were coming up the drive, guests with food in hand. After sipping some soup, Johanna said they would leave. "But first—a gift," she said. She held out a spool to Eunhee.

"What is this?"

Johanna looked at Helen for reassurance. "Thread. It is your custom, right, to give thread at the one hundred days celebration?"

"Yes, yes," Eunhee assured her. "A long piece."

"This is the longest piece," Johanna said. "A spool of pink thread from my sewing drawer."

"A spool is a very long thread," Eunhee agreed.

"For a very long life, with her earthly father, who awaits her, and her heavenly Father, who does too, both of whom love her." Johanna spoke softly. "When you hold her in your arms for the last time, you remember that. You are placing her into his arms. She will go from loving hands to loving hands with no space in between."

Eunhee nodded and fought the tears. "Thank you."

The Jansens left, and all of the neighbors came, one by one, to the house. Helen completely forgave any of them who had not shown up when Bob died. Celebrations were for the living, after all. She knew many of them; some she did not know at all, but had been invited by those on the party line. Even Mr. Beeksma, the chicken man, showed up with his grandson, Dirk. Only one neighboring family did not drop by, thankfully. Captain Adams and his wife.

Some people looked at Mi-Ja adoringly, but some, Helen knew, stared at what they thought was "wrong." Despite that, family after family came to bring a dish to share, try the soup, eat a rice cake, and hand over a spool of thread. Helen finally fetched a little wooden box from one drawer of the sewing machine so that Eunhee had someplace to keep the rainbow of spools.

After the last family left, Helen began cleaning up. "Please tell me that there are no more holidays with seaweed soup," she teased. "Unless you are going to buy some seaweed."

"I promise not to send you to the beach again," Eunhee said with a tired but satisfied smile. She began to put away the leftover rice cakes. "Did I tell you why we make them into the shape of a half-moon?"

"No, you didn't."

"A full moon can only get smaller, but a half-moon can grow into something bigger and more beautiful. A full moon."

Helen nodded. "That's lovely."

"I wish this day could last forever. I wish my mother and father and James were here to celebrate with us—Lieutenant Bob, too. I wish Mi-Ja could grow up and be with me, here. That she could grow from a half-moon into a full moon."

"I wish that, too," Helen said. She reached into her dress

pocket and withdrew a spool. "I asked the variety store to order some gold silk thread."

"Thank you." Eunhee took it from her hand. "You said you wanted a family . . ." She held her precious baby in her little *hanbok* close to her heart. "Here we are."

CHAPTER FOURTEEN

I prayed for a week about the letters I'd found in the attic because Grace had told me she didn't want to look into the baby stuff anymore, and I had agreed. But that was before I found the letters. I'd tucked them back into the hope chest with the thread box holding the beautiful spool of gold silk thread, the *hanbok*, and all the other treasures that Gran, sometimes reluctant to hope for herself, must have thought would bring hope to Grace. Otherwise, why would she have kept them? And insisted we look at them "soon"?

They belonged to Grace, and maybe they were nothing but cool letters that would lift her spirits and help her learn more about her grandmother and great-grandmother, which would be rewarding. They were probably nothing at all to do with Mi-Ja.

But why would they have been at Gran's, then?

Finally, one evening, I knew I had to do it. I knocked on Grace's door. "Hey. Can I come in for a minute?"

"Sure! I'm getting ready to do a face mask. Want to do one with me? It's herbal," she teased. "Gardening. You'll love it."

"Maybe." I sat next to her on the bed. "I found something last week." I handed the packet to her, and she opened it.

"Korean letters?" She shuffled through them. "My Korean isn't good enough to read these completely, especially as they're *hanja*, but yeah, they're addressed to my *halmoni*, and it looks like they came from her mother. Okay." She shifted her weight uncomfortably and set the letters down next to her.

I left, glad that I'd done the right thing, and went into the kitchen to keep working on my plan for the picnic baskets.

Five minutes later, Grace shrieked. I ran to her room, where she sat on the bed with her head in her hands.

"What?" She held a piece of paper out to me. I took it into my hands. A certificate of live birth. Father? James Roy. Mother? Choi Eunhee. Baby girl.

"I'm sorry," I whispered. "I had no idea it was in there."

"Your grandmother did," she said. "It was inside one of the envelopes."

"Maybe," I replied. "The letters were taped shut. I don't think Gran was the type to read someone else's mail. Maybe your *halmoni* put it in there."

"Yeah." Her face looked confused, not angry. "You're right, I guess, because she would have had it. But finding out that my *halmoni* was married to another man, a non-Korean man, and had a baby that no one knows about would devastate my grandfather. He's super sick, and I don't want to be the foot that pushes him into the grave. Is this baby—now, woman—somewhere out there, alive? Could she show up, and that's why your gran wanted me to be warned?"

"I don't know," I said. "I do know that Gran loved your *halmoni* and considered her to be her best friend. She would never hurt her. She would never do wrong by her. She must have known that your *halmoni* would want you to know about the *hanbok* and kept the letters for you. I mean, it's not like she could read them."

"My grandmother could have told me herself if she wanted to."

"You weren't even twenty when she died. Maybe she thought you weren't ready, and she went downhill quickly, like Gran."

Grace stood up. "I'm just stressed," she said. "I didn't mean anything bad."

"I know you didn't."

"I need to talk about this with Justin and look into having my friend who can read *hanja* translate the letters so I can decide what to do next. Just have to think this through."

"I get it. Maybe family dinner tonight will be fun and take your mind off of things? I've already invited Nick, and Annika and DJ are staying, too."

She remained silent for a moment. "I'm not sure."

"If you want to eat dinner with us?"

"It's nothing about you, Cass. I just—I mean, this is really distracting. I feel like I'd be faking cheerfulness and adding a weird vibe. Do you mind if I pass until the next one?"

It wouldn't be a family dinner without her, the most important member of my family. But I got what she needed. "That's fine," I said. "Let me know what I can do."

"Nothing."

You've done enough, I could see her thinking, distress written across her face.

"It might take some time before my friend can read this. I think I'll head to Seattle and visit her in person. I'll be back soon."

"Okay," I said, wishing it weren't awkward, that I hadn't made it awkward. But it was.

She left. I hoped she'd come back soon, as she'd said.

* * *

When Nick arrived a bit later, I caught him up. "You did the right thing," he said, and he reached out, enveloping me in a bear hug, one of the places I felt safe again and like life was going to be okay.

For our first family meal, I'd prepared a test run for the picnic baskets. Buttermilk-brined fried chicken I'd made from organic-fed, humanely raised chickens raised on the island, fresh greens from my farm tossed with my herbs, pickled farm vegetables I'd pulled from the canning cellar, but all grown in our garden, sourdough biscuits, and of course, hand pies.

I'd set the picnic table, and Annika took pictures of everything. We staged the photos with things from the farm and the kitchen and then called the guys to the table.

We set about getting everything ready to eat. When I looked up, DJ's head was down, and he was tearing his napkin into tiny bits, methodically, piece by piece. Why?

"Instead of a blessing," I said, "when I was growing up, my mom and dad and I would hold hands and sing the 'Johnny Appleseed Song.'" When I'd had a family. I wanted a family. Except for missing Grace, here they were. "Would that be okay?"

Everyone nodded and took one another's hands, and I led off. "'Oh, the Lord is good to me, and so I thank the Lord, for giving me the things I need, the sun and the rain and the apple seed. The Lord is good to me.'"

Then we all dug in. Well, almost all of us.

"DJ, aren't you hungry?" I asked. He still tore his napkin. He looked at the chicken. "I don't . . . eat . . . birds."

Oh no. What had I been thinking? "Of course. You bring up a great thought. Next week I'll make a vegetarian menu because our clients might like that too. Extra pie instead?"

"Yeah!" The bits of napkins blew off the table and Nick chased them down, laughing, his body lean and fit. I looked at him longer than I maybe should have, and he caught me and winked.

* * *

June somersaulted in with the same tumble and joy currently infusing my life. Could it last? Even though I felt strangely unsettled, we'd moved full speed ahead on the White Picket Picnic Basket idea as the busy tourist season bore down. I figured I could handle ten baskets per week. If I did that many through the summer months, it would be enough to make sure we hit that all-important $1,500 mark. The taxes would be covered.

After setting aside a batch of Cinn Rolls to cool for Annika and DJ to eat on their break, I whipped up some vinaigrette and poured it into tiny flasks before going back into the garden to cut just a few bouquets of peonies and put them into the honesty stand. I set one big bouquet of whites, reds, and pinks into a pretty enameled pail in the lean-to so they'd be close at hand for Mr. Nordgren's tour. He owned a set of rental properties on the island and was very interested in the White Picket Picnic Baskets for the summer season. He was the only person who'd contacted me, but if he owned enough properties, the taxes could be paid.

Midmorning, just as I'd finished tearing the greens, packing them in Baggies, and assembling two picnic baskets, a car pulled into the drive. I went to meet it and the driver. "Mr. Nordgren? I've been expecting you."

"Yes," he said. "And you must be Cassidy Quinn." We shook hands and talked as we walked. "You have an excellent website," he said, "and the idea of subscription picnic baskets is fresh and new."

Score one, Nick.

He continued, "My summer guests come mostly from Seattle. Because they can't check in to their rental until 4 p.m., many will be relieved to have no need to shop their first night here. They have high expectations, though."

"I hope to meet those expectations. Would you like to see the farm?"

"Sure. I'm always interested in source and provenance."

I showed him the rows of green gem lettuce, from which the salad came, and the aromatic herbs that seasoned the quiches. "As you can see by the menu, I offer both a vegetarian option and one with fried chicken. The chicken is local, and almost everything else will be made from the farm."

"Bread?"

I nodded. "Handmade sourdough biscuits."

"Dessert?" he asked.

I swallowed hard. "Homemade fruit hand pies. My own recipe."

"Impressive," he said.

"Hey, DJ," I said as he walked by us on his way to fill a bird feeder.

"Hey . . . Cassidy." He glanced at the man next to me.

"How ya doing, kid?" Mr. Nordgren asked.

DJ looked at him for a long time.

"Can't speak?" Mr. Nordgren asked me.

"Yes, of course he can," I said. "You just heard him."

It looked like Mr. Nordgren wanted to move on, but DJ hadn't yet answered. I stood firm. Finally DJ said, "I'm . . . not a kid. I'm . . . a man."

Mr. Nordgren looked at me with surprise. I smiled sweetly and said nothing.

"That's good to know," he answered DJ, but they both seemed flustered.

DJ headed back toward the lean-to to refill the seed pail before heading to the next feeders.

I took a few more minutes to finish the tour and then we went into the house to grab the sample picnic basket I'd prepared for him. Then I remembered his flowers. "Oh, let's go grab the bouquet I made for your wife," I said. "In the language of flowers, peonies represent a happy marriage."

He laughed aloud. "If this is the kind of forethought you bring to your business, I can see you'll do very well."

Once we reached the lean-to, though, there was no whole bouquet in the pretty enameled pail. Instead, each flower had been plucked bare—like a chicken—leaving only the stems and leaves. Red, white, and pink petals littered the ground.

I looked up. DJ stood stock-still, shame on his face. I remembered the napkin he'd shredded at family dinner.

"I'm sorry," DJ said. "The birdseed . . . too high." He pointed to a shelf.

"That's my fault," I said. "I forgot to return the stepladder."

"It looks like you're having a party in here, ki—young man," Mr. Nordgren said. "Look at all of this confetti!"

At that, DJ's face broke out into a grin. "A party!"

"Maybe I can take this confetti back to my wife," Mr. Nordgren said. "Sprinkle it over the table when I serve the food."

"I don't mind running to get another bouquet for you," I said.

As I turned to leave, Mr. Nordgren said to DJ, "Would you like me to lift down that bag for you? It's pretty heavy."

"I'm . . . a man," DJ said.

"I am too," Mr. Nordgren replied. "Two men working together should get this job done. I'll lift it down, and you grab it."

A few minutes later I returned with the flowers. "I hope your wife enjoys these, and thank you for your understanding."

"My pleasure," Mr. Nordgren replied. "I think you can count on us for, perhaps, three baskets each week? Maybe more next year?"

Three baskets. I'd become really good at keeping a fixed smile. "Sure." I held out my hand to him. "Please let me know if there are any adjustments you'd need to be made."

He drove away, and I sat at the picnic table, thinking. At this rate, it didn't seem as though the picnic baskets were going to save me, but after all, I didn't want to build that business forever, did I? I had choices too, just like I'd told Grace she did, after Gran's funeral. Maybe just not ones I wanted to make. But I had to. In the far distance, the evergreens waved gently in the wind. They'd waved goodbye to Gran, as she left.

I texted Nick. **Mr. Nordgren came over.**

Did he like the picnic baskets?

Loved them. Wants three each week for the summer.

Oh.

Yeah, that's not going to do it, I typed back. **I need to consider some options.**

I'll be right over, he texted back.

Anxiety flooded me. I appreciated his help, but I'd been
hoping to have a little quiet space to consider my options
first. I was going to text him to not bother, but he'd been
really helpful, and I didn't want to be rude to him.

Once Nick arrived, he joined me at the picnic table, and
he took my hand. "It's simple. We just need to find a way to
sell more baskets. We can work this problem." His face was
lit with joy and energy. My heart was not.

"What's wrong?" he asked. "You don't look happy. I know
the three were a disappointment."

I set my coffee down. "He's a really nice guy and I said yes
to him when he was here because, well, I wanted to deliver on
what I'd advertised. But since he left, I just feel really certain
that I don't want to do the picnic basket subscription."

He leaned toward me. "Really? Why don't you want to
do them?"

"I made the baskets as thank-yous, as gifts out of my
heart, and now I'm monetizing them."

"Right?" he said. "That was the plan. Make money."

I nodded. "True." The sun shone on my bare head, and
the warmth strengthened me. "It was so fun to do the family

dinner—to cook for people I love. It was rewarding and meaningful to make the hand pies for people who mean a lot to me. But when I take what is nearest to my heart, things I can do on a small scale for my friends and family, to share with them, not to make money, it's like taking the little bits of Cassidy, the hopes I had for what my own family would look like once my childhood family dissolved, and selling them."

"Yes," he said. "But I thought we were doing this to save the most important part for your family—the land."

"I am," I said, softly correcting his *we* to *me*. "I just need to find another way to do it. To keep the land and keep the personal treasures for those who are close to my heart so there's something left of me. Going forward, after the taxes are covered, I want to make a living with flowers. Even though I'm not making any money on them at the moment, I can figure out a path to make them work. Grace said I had good ideas." I smiled. "I just need time to figure the way out."

"I know that flowers are what you want to do, and you do have good ideas, but maybe that's a dream. I don't see anyone making money on the island with flowers alone."

My face flushed. "More space for me to do that, then. That's why they call it a dream job."

"Dreams aren't going to pay your property taxes," he said. "Vegetables are. Picnic baskets are. They're a great idea. A practical idea."

I looked over his shoulder. Annika and DJ were busy in

the distance. I kept my voice down so they couldn't hear me. "But picnic baskets *aren't* working."

"We just need to lean into it. More marketing."

"I *am* being practical—I waitress at Tony's five days a week. But I believe I can find a practical solution that works for what I need for the taxes, and for a living, doing something I'm good at and that doesn't steal my joy. Gran did, in nursing. No reason the heart and the brain can't work well together. In fact, they were designed to do so."

"I get that," he said. "It's just that the picnic baskets were your idea, so I thought that was working for you."

"Picnic baskets for *cash* was your idea, not mine."

"I heard this quote: 'You can have anything you want, but you can't have everything you want.' You want to keep the land. So far, to me, it seems that food sells, even if slowly, and flowers don't. The clock is ticking and at least the vegetables have potential."

I knew the clock was ticking. It hadn't ticked half an hour between when I told him about Mr. Nordgren and when he arrived at my house, so I hadn't had time to process this. "The vegetables do have potential for sure, and if I have to circle back to them, I will. Mr. Nordgren backed you up. You always have good ideas. Great ideas. But they're your ideas. Not my ideas. It's not like I'm telling you how to run your digital marketing business."

"Yeah," he said. "It's honestly not even like you ask me about it even though there's lots to tell."

My face fell. Ouch. True.

"Why are you so touchy?" he asked. "You asked me for help, help saving the property. I thought that is what I was doing here. What else can I do?"

I cooled my voice, though my head and heart ran hot. "Nothing." *You've done enough.*

He stood. "All right then, I understand. The email is in your website in-box, and all of the pictures and contact forms are up so you can log in and run it without help. Call me if you need anything." He grabbed his keys from the table and walked toward his car.

So much for my not wanting to be rude to him. I wanted to run after him, but I stopped myself. Instead, I watched him drive away and then joined Annika and DJ. I put on a cheery face though I was gutted. I'd gutted myself. Why had I just set off a bomb?

"You guys did a great job painting the apple tree signs!" I met them in the barn where they were putting the paint away. "But you're both a mess."

DJ laughed. "My . . . hands."

Annika held hers up, painty, though gloved. "Mine, too."

"Come on! Make your mark!" I showed him what to do, and then DJ placed his painty hands on the barn wall, leaving his handprints. Annika painted enough on her gloves to make an impression and put her prints next to DJ's. Then she stripped her gloves off.

"I'll buy new ones for you," I promised. "Ruined in the line of duty."

She smiled. "Nah. I've got more."

They left and I headed toward the house. As I exited, I looked at Nick's tire prints, which had flattened the grass next to the barn as he drove away.

CHAPTER FIFTEEN

The next afternoon, when I got home from my brunch shift at Tony's, Grace sat at the kitchen table looking soft but sad, parked in front of the batch of Cinn Rolls. "You want one?"

I nodded. "Yeah." She unwrapped a bit of the roll and put a pat of butter inside before handing it over. "You okay?" I asked.

She nodded, and after she finished her whole roll, she tapped a little stack of papers on the table. "I found the death certificate online—so we know the baby isn't alive anymore. She was my *halmoni*'s daughter with a man named James Roy, a Caucasian American man who died, too, just a few months before their baby, Mi-Ja. I saw his picture in an online Navy archive." Anxiety tightened her face. "I can't tell my grandfather. That's why these things were left hidden with your gran at her house. To be kept secret."

As soon as she'd said *death certificate*, I immediately remembered where I'd seen the Korean characters on Mi-Ja's *hanbok*. "I know where the baby and her father are. Sunnyside Cemetery."

She looked up and held my gaze. "How do you know?"

"I've seen it before, wandering around when visiting my mom's grave. I just didn't recognize it until I saw the character on the *hanbok*. I can take you there."

"Not now," she said softly. "I'm not ready. There's no rush because I'm not going to do anything with this right away, now that I know an unexpected aunt isn't going to pop up from anywhere. I need to study. My test is less than two months away. My friend who translated Mi-Ja for us read the letters that were with the birth certificate. They were from my *halmoni*'s mother. They were filled with love, but it was also clear she didn't want my grandma to go back to Korea. I know everyone was so poor in the years after the war and long after. My mom told me that much. I'm sure my *halmoni*'s mother just wanted her to have a better life, but I can't imagine my mom telling me not to come home. My grandmother had lost her only daughter and then couldn't tell anyone about it. What a horrible secret to bear."

"Come with me." I led her out to the garden. "Gran loved peonies more than any other flower. Truthfully, she liked vegetables and herbs better than flowers because she was a child of the Depression, and they were more practical. Except for peonies, which are frilly, fluffy, a pain in the neck to care for—divas, really. She grew early season to late season varieties."

I led her deep into the field of beautiful peonies. "'Petticoat Junction' I called it, after a show Gran used to watch, because the flowers looked like layers of silky tufts and swirls of petticoats. Your *halmoni* knew how much Gran loved them." I rested a tight bud from one of the late-blooming plants onto my open palm. "When my mom died, your *halmoni* came over and cut down every tight-fisted bud, every almost blossom, and put them in vases that filled the house. It looked odd. I remember thinking that Gran was going to be so angry that they'd been cut down before they could bloom."

"I remember that!" Grace said. "By the time of the funeral, when everyone came over for coffee and rolls, every flower was blooming, like posh little powder puffs."

"Exactly. Gran told me later that because your *halmoni* was a good gardener, she knew that cutting them down and feeding them would force the blossoms after they were disconnected from the plant. It was her way of showing Gran what your *halmoni* believed in her heart—and now we know why. Even though it seems as if someone is taken too soon, they will continue to bloom long after their 'death.' Perhaps even more strongly. Those blossoms looked so beautiful and lifted Gran's hope after the funeral. It's why I take so much time and care with the peonies. Even though it hurts me. Because they are my mom, in a way."

I walked her back to the roses of Sharon. "Remember the roses of Sharon on the baby's *hanbok*? Now we know why Gran took such good care of these, too. It was her way of showing your *halmoni* the same thing as with my mom and the peonies. Their daughters were gone too soon and yet . . ."

"They live," Grace said.

"They live. And the flowers are a remembrance of them. No one but your *halmoni* could tell Gran she understood. Now we know Gran stood by her when Mi-Ja died, and your *halmoni* stood by her week by week, month by month after my mom died, till Gran began to heal. They shared that secret, and your grandmother comforted Gran with the comfort she had received. They were widows together. They lost daughters together. They understood. They were strong. We won't ever really know, because we weren't there, but I'm sure they were better for being together."

Grace looked up. "I've been feeling sorry for her, but really, I admire her. I have no idea what it's like to live in a devastated world and have to make those kinds of crazy tough choices for myself and my family."

I nodded. "They both had challenges. Lived through wars. Were widowed young. That hasn't happened to us—not yet, anyway. But we have our own heartaches and hardships. It kind of reminds me of Queen Esther. She was born for her time and for her challenges. So were our grandmothers. We are born for our time, for our challenges."

Grace nodded and tenderly touched a rose of Sharon blossom.

"This is why flowers matter so much to me," I said. "To celebrate, enjoy, and spread love. In the end, our very practical grandmothers each chose a flower to represent their daughters, the rose of Sharon and the peony. Flowers are present at weddings and funerals and pressed between Bible pages to remember something or someone important. Mothers get them every Mother's Day. Sweethearts send them to convey affection. Sometimes sentimentality is more important than practicality—at least to the heart."

"You are right, Cass. I see that now." She plucked the blossom she'd caressed, representing her *halmoni*'s baby. "But do I have to tell my father, his brothers, and all of my family about Mi-Ja? Maybe my *halmoni* just wanted me alone to know."

"For sure, Gran felt your *halmoni* would want you to know, or she wouldn't have left these for us to find together. What you do with it is your call."

Grace paused. "Maybe everyone would think poorly of my *halmoni*. Is that why she kept the secret?"

"I don't know. We might never know. But maybe in this day and age, they'd admire her strength and sacrifice, like we do. You always say you don't have any agency in your own life. But you have a lot more agency than your grandmother did. She gave that to you."

That evening, after the gardening work was done, Grace and I made dinner together. I set the table, and a few minutes later, Grace set the farmhouse pitcher filled with peony buds on the table and then sat next to me.

"Here you were today, comforting me about my *halmoni* and the loss of her baby, but the whole time, the *whole time*, we were talking about your mom and her death."

My eyes filled with tears. I nodded, not trusting myself to say anything.

"I see you," she said softly. "I see what you do. You do good for everyone. You are good."

I blinked fast. Should I tell her? Bring it up on this day, which had already been heavy for her? "I'm not as good as you think I am. I drove Nick off yesterday."

She reached across the table and took my hand. "Let's eat dinner, and then you can tell me all about it."

Half an hour later, we took our wine and some marshmallows outside to the firepit. I recounted everything that had happened and all that had been said.

"Why did you go off on him?" she asked.

I sipped my wine. "I'm not totally sure. Probably a lot of reasons. First, because I needed some time and space to think, and he was in such a hurry to solve my problems for me, to know what was best for me when I hadn't decided that for myself, that I didn't get that space."

"Did you ask him for some time to think about things when he said he'd be right over?"

I grimaced and sighed. "No. Should have. I didn't want to be rude to him, but if I would have just honestly asked for some space, I would have avoided the super rude way I approached it. Should have told him even sooner than today, honestly. But until I made the family dinner and then Brenda asked me to sell her another basket, and then it all came clear in the blowup, I didn't fully see why it bothered me. I didn't want to hurt Nick's feelings because he'd worked so hard on the picnic basket idea. And earlier the CSA idea, which I also didn't love."

She twirled her marshmallow. "If you didn't like the CSA idea, why didn't you speak up then?"

I twirled my own marshmallow. "It took some time for me to figure it all out." I took a bite before answering. "It's like when I was a little girl and did jigsaw puzzles with my gramps. He'd hide a few of the pieces around the house, and I'd have to find them—in the silverware drawer or the towel cabinet or under the TV. Until I found them all and snapped them in, the picture wasn't complete. So when Brenda brought the flowers back and I saw my own hand in them, that was a piece. Finding the cookbook and the heirloom recipes shared only with family and friends was a piece. Seeing the recipes your mom made for her family, and the ones from my family, was another piece. Not wanting to sell hand pies to Brenda—who I love—was a piece. The relief I felt not having to do the baskets was another. When they weren't working, I felt off the hook, not panicked."

I sipped my wine. "Remember when you said you weren't sure you wanted to be a lawyer, or that kind of lawyer, but you didn't want to upset your family? Well, you and Nick both thought that food ideas were good." I closed my eyes and thought about how angry Pamela had been when I hadn't fallen in with her plans. "I wanted you and Nick to be happy and didn't want to let you guys down when I didn't have an alternative idea anyway."

Reassured, I looked up from the fire and offered my next honest thought. "I appreciate that CSAs and picnic baskets are what you guys think is best for me. They're just not what I think is best for me. I didn't see it before, but now with the missing pieces snapped in, I have a clear picture. Maybe I wasn't strong enough to push back then. But I need to if I'm going to own my own life. Does that make sense?"

"It does," she said. "You're right."

"Maybe. You and Nick are both so successful."

She laughed. "Yeah. I failed the bar exam, and he made a call to join a firm that went bankrupt a year after he uprooted his life to take it."

"You went to law school, though, and he is doing great with his big client and his start-up."

"Pamela desperately wanted you back. And you have your own start-up now."

"Which isn't doing so well." I sat back in the squeaky lawn chair. "One time Annika told me that working on someone else's already-perfect garden is like editing someone else's pictures. I can make it better, but it will never be mine, at the heart of it."

"She's wise for her age," Grace said.

"I wonder if I wasn't blooming in California because it was someone else's vision. Kind of like you not wanting to practice DUI law."

She nodded.

"I don't know if there is an official definition of a master gardener. For me, though, I guess I'm coming to see that it isn't someone who tends to what has been done for her. That's a caretaker gardener, for a perfectly manicured Napa tour garden. This one here? I'm building it on my own. Win or lose. But—" I looked at the starts Gran had begun—"it's not like I'm starting from scratch exactly."

"No one starts from scratch, Cassidy." She seemed to look beyond me, deep in thought. "Take what is here and give it the taste of your hands."

"Yes," I said. "That's exactly what I want to do with the flowers. Nick's ideas just seemed to work, and he knew it, so he kept pushing them and I kept caving and then I was resentful and blew up."

"Did he listen?"

"Kind of. But I didn't make it easy, either."

She sat back in her chair. "Maybe you guys really aren't supposed to be together."

"I'm coming to the same miserable conclusion. But if it's the right conclusion, why am I miserable?"

She poked another marshmallow onto a stick. "Why were you so upset the first time you broke up?"

"He wanted to do long-distance and made no commitment to me. I wasn't going to be a silent second-best and follow along after him for a job, like I had to with my dad, swallowing my own plans and discomfort because I had nowhere else to go. I have choices. And now Nick's raced off again rather than deal with it, like my dad, too."

She stared at me. I stared back. "Wow. I didn't see it. My dad."

Grace nodded. "Nick is not your dad. You are not a kid. Maybe Nick didn't ask you to marry him then because you guys weren't ready. Maybe he didn't want you to have to make a choice between Whidbey and him. But he didn't do a great job communicating, either."

She handed the gooey marshmallow to me, and after I blew on it, I took a bite. The crunchy shell yielded to a soft heart. "I think you're right," I said. "I didn't see him; I saw my dad in him."

"And maybe, in being afraid to lose him and me, you see your dad and Mary Alice in us too. I'm not them, Cass. I'm not leaving, just like you didn't leave me when I drove off in a huff the other day."

"Never."

She smiled and licked a white thread off her lips. "Didn't you just tell me I have a lot more agency than my grandmother did? You do too."

"You're boomeranging the things I said to you!" I teased.

"Yep. You have choices."

I nodded. "We have choices."

"We do," she said. "Maybe we should both get to work. I have to study . . ."

"Excited about law again, then?"

She shrugged. "Not sure yet. Not this way. No stopping now, though. Have to think about that agency thing, and maybe like you've discovered for yourself, about owning my own life. As for you, if not picnic baskets, then what?"

I shrugged and looked at the pine forest behind her. "I have some ideas I need to think through."

She didn't press, and I noticed. "Thanks for giving me some space."

"Remember what you told me when we found the *hanbok*? I'm here to support you with whatever you want to do. I should have said that the first time instead of pressing."

"And I should have spoken up the first time."

"Better together, right?"

"Better together," I agreed.

"I need some sleep," she said as she stood. "See you in the morning?"

"Of course." I stood to hug her before she made her way into the house. I stayed a few more minutes, though, pulling up my Notes app on my phone.

Nick's note of ideas that he'd shared with Grace and me was still there. I reviewed them, thankful for his friendship and eagerness even though I hadn't made a go of the ideas. I should have spoken up with him too.

Yes, but I didn't understand. Now I do. I'll speak up next time. If there is a next time.

I opened a fresh note.

Ideas
1. Flowers. Sure, but how?
2. Graze cattle. Too late.

3. Nick was right. Vegetables are it—necessities, not luxuries. Ask Tony if he'd be willing to buy vegetables for the restaurant this year.

4.

My hand hovered. I wavered, looking at the cool forest encircling me in peace. I left number four blank, not willing to fill that in yet. Last ditch, if I must. But maybe I wouldn't have to.

I dumped a pail of sand over the embers of the past, quenching them, I hoped, for good, before heading to bed.

* * *

I showed up early for work and grabbed Tony's arm as he walked by. "Hey, can I talk to you for a sec?"

"Sure, kiddo," he said. "What's up?"

"I'm just wondering—I've got quite a bit of lettuce coming up, good tomatoes and such. You know our cukes are famous. Any chance you can use some in the restaurant?"

He smiled. "I'd do almost anything for you, but I've got a produce contract. Everything is corporate now so I can price accordingly, and the quality is consistent from day to day. You know how some guests are. They want everything the same yesterday, today, and tomorrow."

I could tell him about the tax issue, but he'd been so good to me, I didn't want to put him in a bad spot. Besides, it was an uncertain way forward, and I'd had enough of those. I needed to act decisively so all would be settled for me and my land, too, yesterday, today, and tomorrow. "Okay, thank you."

He grinned. "You got it."

* * *

In the near background, DJ's *Lion King* loop boomed out, *"Remember who you are!"* Annika and DJ sprayed silver streaks of water streams over each other with the garden hoses. Their laughter carried on the wind, filling my heart and soul. My garden was beginning to bloom, and due to DJ's diligence, the birds were back sitting on the phone line, watching us benignly like Mr. Beeksma's mother hens.

It was time to visit Mr. Beeksma. *Remember who you are.*

DJ and Annika left in the early afternoon, and I drove to the old man's chicken farm. He teetered on a step stool, painting the side of his barn. "Well, hullo, young lady. How is life treating you?"

"I'm doing okay," I said. "I've come to ask if you can recommend a company to log my acres of evergreens."

He almost fell—I quickly reached out and took his arm to steady him. He stepped down and pulled a bandanna out of his pocket, then wiped his head. "Helen wouldn't do that. She most definitely would not approve."

"I'm not Helen," I said softly. "The taxes, as you know, must be paid. I need someone who will log and pay me fairly for the timber. I know I won't profit much from that, as I'll have to pay them to take down the trees and stump the land.

But I've done some research. If I clear-cut the five acres, I can lease those acres to corporate farmers for—" I swallowed hard—"vegetables. Cabbage likely. Maybe broccoli. If I do that, the ag tax requirements will be covered, and I will be free to do what I want to do with the other acres."

"Helen loved those trees." He looked doubtful.

She did. Please don't make this harder than it needs to be. "She might not approve of cutting down the trees, but she'd approve of my saving the property." The memory of DJ and Annika having a water fight flashed through my mind, as did my dream of developing further acreage for flowers. I could invite more and more people—those who needed additional support and those who did not—to build a community with me on that land. That was my vision. My hope. The taste of my hands. And it *was* in my hands now.

"I'll be right back," he said. A few minutes later, he returned with a slip of paper. "They will treat you fairly, and if you tell them I sent you, they'll get the job done quickly."

"Thank you, Mr. Beeksma. For everything." I turned to go, but this time he took my arm and held me back.

"One time, when I was a boy, Helen told me in this very barn that sometimes a limb must be cut off when it's necessary to save the body."

My eyes filled with tears at what I knew was his blessing. "Thank you, sir." I returned to my car and sat there for a moment, praying. *"Be strong and courageous,"* my gramps had quoted from the Bible, arms around me, as I faced the first weeks without my mom. And I was. Because I had to be. Before I could lose my nerve, I called the logging company. Timber was at a premium, they said. They could come within days.

I headed home and knocked on the door to the yellow bedroom, where Grace was studying.

"Come in," she said. I did and sat on the wooden dining chair across from the makeshift desk she'd worked up.

"You might want to plan to be in Seattle Wednesday through Friday. I'm clear-cutting the evergreens. It's going to be noisy, and I don't think you'll get much done."

"Clear-cutting the evergreens? All of them?"

I explained the plan. "So you and Nick were right—vegetables win after all. But so do flowers. And people. And dreams. Hope. I won't ever have to worry about that $1,500 again, and while the logging company won't pay me a ton this year, it will cover what I'll need to have the land plowed and prepared, not only the part I'm leasing out, but the part I want to expand on next year. I'll have money to expand into more flower fields year after year, building a community and making a viable career."

"Okay," she said. "Want to come to Seattle with me? Girls' getaway? Spa visit?"

I shook my head. "I need to be here to manage it, to see it, to own it. Can't run away. I couldn't have done it without you," I said. "Better together. Nor could I have understood what was going on in my head about Nick without your insight. After the trees are down, I'm going to make an apology picnic basket for him, head over to his house, and see if he'll talk with me."

"Not before? Not now?"

"I need to do this on my own first."

"I'll pray," she said gently and then turned back to her work.

*　*　*

Wednesday morning, I got dressed before DJ's birds began warbling and walked down the well-trod path into the ever-greens, going in far enough to be completely enveloped in the forest's arms. *"Come to the woods, for here is rest,"* Gran used to say. She'd always found rest there. But she was truly at rest now, and I needed the land for other important things. Important people. If only I could remain in the cool, dark shade of towering timbers. Sheltering in their shadow felt safe.

"I need to open up the land to sun, Gran. Other stuff has to grow. It's the practical decision, right?" I spoke as if she were right beside me. Maybe the Lord would relay my thoughts to her. Maybe I spoke to make myself feel better. "Remember when we transplanted the sunflowers to the margins of the garden because they towered over everything? They—unintentionally—blocked the sun from everything around them. I can't thrive under the shadow of what was anymore. Nor can the people I'm growing to love. I've got to plant myself, stake myself, feed myself, water myself where I can grow too."

It occurred to me that, in some ways, Grace and I lived in the shadow of our grandmothers, too—strong women, but women who had lived their full lives in the times and with the challenges they'd been given. It was time for us to take their legacy in hand and live ours, too, with the challenges we'd been given. It was what Gran would want, for me to take the baton—trowel—she'd given me and run it further down the line. Out of her shadow and into my own light, as she had done for herself. My legacy was not in the trees. It was with the little community, the family, I was building.

I took off my straw hat as a sign of respect and the wind rustled through my hair. If I wanted to, I could interpret that as Gran saying, *"Hi ho, sunshine. Go. It's yours now."*

This land was your land, Gran. But this land is my land now. I will never forget how and by whom it came to me.

Two hours later, I stood on the edge of the forest as the crew began their work. The delimbers, feller bunchers, grinders, and mulchers had arrived and screamed to life. I watched the first tree fall. Like a man kicked behind the knees, it fell forward and then was caught by a cable. "Make snug houses for people to live in," I spoke to it softly. "Make good books for kids to read." I wiped a tear and turned away.

It was done.

* * *

On Saturday, I pulled into Nick's driveway and then walked to the front door, where I rang the bell. His dad answered.

"Hi, Mr. Harper."

"Well, Cassidy. How wonderful to see you here." He turned and shouted behind him. "Calista! Cassidy is here!"

Nick's mom hurried to the door. She had the same dark hair and eyes as Nick, warm, like his. "Oh, how lovely to see you!" She pulled me into an embrace, one that pushed the picnic basket against her. She stepped back. "What is this?"

"Is Nick here?" I held out the basket, filled with all good things to make things right. "I brought this for him."

The Harpers looked at each other. "Oh. No. Nick is in Boston. The final interview and all," his dad said. I didn't respond. How could I? I'd had no idea. He spoke again, hoping, I thought, to prompt my memory. "The manager's position he's been offered. In Boston proper—not remote. It starts in September, I think. They're building a new site."

I shook my head and watched their faces fall.

"You didn't know," his mother said.

"I didn't," I said.

They looked as crestfallen as I felt inside.

"Please don't tell him we told you," Mr. Harper said. "I'm sure he's waiting for the right time to tell you himself." He glanced at the picnic basket.

"Have you planned dinner?" I asked. "I'd like to leave this for you." His mom took the basket. "Maybe you should empty it, though, and let me take the basket back," I said. "If we don't want Nick to know I was here."

She took the basket to the kitchen and then returned with

it, but it wasn't empty. "Greek walnut cake. You'll love it. I only make it for family." Her eyes watered and so did mine.

I startled myself by realizing that I wouldn't have minded her teaching me how to make it, to make it the way Nick liked, as Mrs. Kim had once taught Grace's mother.

"I hope we see you again soon," she said, pecking my cheek. "I'm sure Nick will call when he's back."

"I'm sure he will. I'll wait for it." But I wasn't sure at all. Nick had mentioned, before our fight, that he had something to share with me about his work but wanted to discuss my job first. He'd been right. I hadn't paid any attention at all to his job.

As I started my car and drove home, I thought, *He won't call.*

CHAPTER SIXTEEN

I took my phone out of my pocket. Then I put it away. At shift break, I held it out once more and then set it down while I drank a glass of iced tea in the break room at Tony's. Where we'd met.

Tony looked up from his paperwork. "How's Nick doing?"

"Great," I said. "Lots of good job things on his horizon."

"Better move quick then," he teased. "Before he heads to parts unknown!"

Tony knew our history. But he was right that it was okay for me to move, if I wanted to, and I did because it had been more than a week. As soon as I was in the car, I clicked on Nick's contact. He wasn't going to call me because I'd made it clear he wasn't welcome. I didn't think he'd accept my invitation, nor my apology, and who could blame him? I didn't even think he would answer, but he did.

"Hello?"

Not *"Hey, Cassidy."* He surely knew it was me unless he'd removed my contact, but that didn't seem like his style.

"Hey, it's, um, Cassidy," I said. "You said to call if I needed anything?"

His voice remained firm. "Do you need something?"

I spoke gently. "I don't need anything. I need someone. Would you be willing to come over and talk?"

"Sure." His voice was softer. "When?"

"Tomorrow night?" I asked. "For dinner at—I don't know—six? I'd just . . . well, I'd like to thank you for all your help, hear about what's going on with you and your job, and catch you up on what's gone on here."

"I can do that." His voice was definitely friendlier but guarded. "I'll see you then."

* * *

The next night, Grace helped me string Edison lights in the greenhouse. I brought the portable speakers out, set the table, and placed a centerpiece of lilies in the middle.

At six, Nick pulled up and greeted me with a smile, but not a hug. It was okay. I'd be at peace no matter which way things went. Gran had told me it was better to part as friends, if we must part at all, and I'd botched that the last time.

He caught a glimpse of the naked acres where the evergreens had once stood. "Whoa! What happened there?"

"I'll tell you over dinner," I said.

"Steaks?" He looked at the grill. "Or pizza?"

"Steaks," I said. "Do you want to grab them off the grill and bring them to the greenhouse? There's a big plate on the sideboard."

"Sure." A few minutes later, he delivered the steaks from the grill and poured our wine. I served the caprese and bread. "I bought more of that salt from Penn Cove and added herbs I'd frozen last year to Irish butter to make some compound butter for the sourdough. One hundred percent Whidbey terroir. What do you think?"

He put some on his sourdough. "Amazing. I mean it. Maybe you should go into the butter business. But . . ." He looked down. "I'm sorry. I'm back on the food ideas again."

I set down my fork. "Listen, that's why I wanted you to come for dinner. First—I've put your book to good use." I pointed at the calla lilies in the center of the table. "They mean humility and devotion. I'm really sorry for the way I handled our last conversation. It was immature and reactionary. You asked what you could do, and hurtfully, I said nothing. What I really meant, but hadn't been able to articulate, was that I had to do something on my own first. I had to own this decision. These choices and all of their consequences."

"It's okay," he said.

I shook my head. "No, it's not. But I understand it now." I explained about his ideas and Grace's, and that I had felt overshadowed and worried about speaking up because I didn't want to alienate them. They were the only family I had left, with Annika and DJ coming close too. "So—the trees." I explained why I'd had them cut. "You were right—vegetables win. But in a different way. I get to keep my cooking for friends and family. But I'm sharing the land with others, through cauliflower—" I winked—"and flowers."

"You win," he said. "Well done. You just needed some time to think it through. I was in such a hurry to help, I steamrolled."

"I could have done it differently too." Encouraged by his kindness, I pressed on. "I think I know what happened last time too. I mean, last time we broke up."

"Yeah, I know what happened. I insisted on hustling to grab the job I wanted without thinking about you," he said. "And I didn't communicate really well. I wasn't sure about a marriage commitment, but I didn't talk it through, either."

"As we now know, I also was not the best at speaking up rather than expecting everyone to be mind readers. Going to change that." I smiled. "But I've also just realized that I thought you were going to run to what you wanted, like my dad, and once I was out of sight, I'd be out of mind. He was in such a hurry to get over my mom's death he didn't stop to think about my needs. Just his own. He chose Mary Alice over me. I felt like you were choosing your job over me. Left behind again."

"That's not what I was thinking," Nick said.

"I know. I know that now. And I'm really sorry for thinking you did. I didn't see it till it surfaced." I thought back to his apology at Tony's during our first dinner after Gran's funeral. "I had some growing up to do too. I could have handled a long-distance relationship." Even though he hadn't mentioned Boston, I was just going to put it out there. "I could now too."

He nodded thoughtfully but said nothing about Boston. He said nothing at all.

"Do you forgive me?" I rushed to fill the silence. "I'd like us to part as friends."

"Yes—and no," he said.

I took a deep breath. Well, I'd tried.

He came around to my side of the table. "Yes, I forgive you. And you know what? I could have reached out earlier in friendship, or even to apologize, instead of being embarrassed or hesitant. I held back too long. And then when it was time for me to hold back a little, like with your businesses, I pushed my ideas again instead of giving you the space to think before running. I apologize. I'm learning to pace too."

I smiled. "Sounds good."

He leaned toward me. "Just friends, though? Or maybe more?"

I gave him a friendly side-eye. "Maybe more." Then I faced him full on. We held each another's gaze for a few moments, and then he backed away but didn't return to his side of the table. Instead, he reached across and grabbed his plate so we could finish our meals next to one another. "Your tomatoes?" He looked at the caprese.

"Yeah," I said. "The tomatoes and the basil grow side by side. They're companion plants. There's a saying in gardening: what grows together goes together. Seems like we're growing and maybe growing together." I risked it. "Do we go together?"

"I need your thoughtfulness," he said.

"I need your hustle," I responded. "After thinking things through!"

"I've recently understood that I need your sense of dream and wonder," he volleyed.

"And I need your practicality. I mean, people do need to eat, and bills need to be paid, after all."

He smiled. "We go together. No doubt."

"We've got this." I raised my hand for a high five.

He clapped it back. "We've got this."

I nodded. And as if by divine cue, in the background, the song "Build It Better" played. The lyrics reminded the listeners that we always build it better the second time around. Nick laughed. I blushed. "I know, I'm obvious."

"Want to give it one more try? To see if we build it better?" he asked. "We weren't, maybe, mature enough to do it last time. But I think we are this time if you do."

"Yeah," I said. "I do."

After dinner, we built a fire in the firepit and roasted marshmallows and drank wine. *"Coffee is a cup of morning confidence; wine, a glass of evening calm,"* my mom used to say. Just past the first day of summer, dusk came late. The setting sun cast a pink glow over the garden. *Is it right to say a man is beautiful?* His thick, dark hair invited my fingers to run through it. His new beard was masculine and flirted with his jawline. Mostly, though, his eyes drew me and held me. They allowed glimpses into his tender heart. "How is work going?" I asked.

"Good," he said. "Progressing in a lot of ways. But let's not talk about that tonight."

His job. His lead. We talked for hours about nearly everything else, including what kind of career in flowers I wanted to build. "It's important to me to make a good living and at the same time make a good life, now that the taxes are covered." The fire had burned to glowing embers, hotter than the fire that first produced them. A late sunset honeyed the garden, but the company made it sweet, and I let my mind be called away toward ideas.

"Hey, sunshine by starlight. Where are you? What are you thinking about?"

I grinned. "Flowers."

He grinned back and then stood and said, "I'd better go. I'll be around this week, this month, if I can help in any way."

"You can. I'd like your help. But I can handle my challenge now."

He looked out at the field that used to be filled with trees. "Clearly."

I groaned at his pun.

He laughed and pulled me into a hug, wrapping his arms tightly around me, enfolding me in himself. In the back acreage, crickets rubbed their rough wings together. It sounded like a field of violins tuning.

"You can definitely handle your challenges. Always could—you just didn't know it. Now you do. Confidence is very attractive in a woman," he said.

"Is it? Can I kiss you, then? Or is that an overconfident request?"

He bent down so I could put my lips on his, a soft kiss, one that didn't last too long but was just right for the first kiss of a second chance. His finger traced my jaw. "One hundred percent Whidbey terroir right here. So sweet. A little salty."

He left for home, and I hummed "Build It Better" as I headed into the house.

Grace was waiting for me in the living room. "How'd it go? No, no, I don't have to ask. I can see it on your face."

I laughed. "Yeah. We're going to give it one more try."

"Did he tell you what was going on in Boston?" she asked.

I shook my head. "Nope. But I did let it drop that I was okay with long-distance dating now. Maybe he's waiting to see how things go and—"

"Justin told me he loves me," she blurted. "Oh, my goodness, I just interrupted you!"

"That is a worthy interruption," I said. "How can he love you when I haven't even met him? I have not given my consent. Hey, I know. Let's have a double-date dinner for the Fourth of July. I've been dying to use Gran's Bundt pan, maybe her old-fashioned blue-and-white Corelle dishes.

Wait. Let's make it a menu that our grandmothers would have cooked in the fifties—but maybe with a little twist."

"I've wanted to try adding cola to *galbi*," Grace replied. "I'm going to try to learn to cook a few things. Not just Korean food, but I might start there. Taste of my hands!"

"Since when do you want to cook?"

Her eyes were rimmed with fatigue, but she smiled. "Maybe . . . since Justin."

* * *

The sun, my faithful friend, clocked in regularly in late June, making my garden pop and filling my heart. Grace focused on books—the bar exam was just a bit more than a month away. Annika and I focused on my new business, Flowery Language. It was exactly what I needed to make the flower farm work.

"My idea is to make money selling bouquets to brides on the island, especially as we're getting to be a destination wedding location. I have a huge variety of flowers to choose from and could plant even more next year."

"You do have a lot to choose from," Annika agreed. She moved the bouquet I'd just finished in front of the green-house window so as the natural light fell across it through the pane, it cast the shadow of a cross over the bouquet.

"Genius!" I said as she snapped some photos. "Perfect for a church wedding."

"Thank you. But . . . aren't there a lot of other florists in town?" she asked. "I mean, look at all the flowers you'd have to sell."

"Having that many flowers is going to work for me because here's my plan to set me apart from other florists." I held up the book on flower language Nick had given me. "Every bouquet I make will be custom-selected by the bride to convey a message through the meaning of the blossoms in her bouquets. The bouquets are called tussy-mussies, and they're old-fashioned in the loveliest way. You wrap the bouquets and slip them into these little silver holders—" I tapped the fluted silver hand vase—"for the bride or bridesmaids or flower girls or mother of the bride or whomever to carry." I pointed at the bouquet I'd just wrapped and slipped into a silver tussy-mussy holder. "So for example, this one has lavender for elegance, sweet marjoram for joy and happiness, roses for unity and love, and honeysuckle for devotion. Or a bride could choose nigella." I pointed to the beautiful blue blossoms of which Gran had been justly proud. "They mean 'kiss me twice,' setting apart that bride's wedding from those poor fools who only get one kiss."

"Genius!" she echoed.

"We make a good team!" I fist-bumped her—with our gloves on—then lifted a few stems I was preparing to wrap next. "I'll also make bridesmaids' bouquets that speak personally of the strengths of each friend. Lamb's ears for a gentle friend, blue salvia for one who is wise, baby's breath for a friend who is always happy."

Thyme for bravery, courage, and strength went into a

sample boutonniere along with a bleeding heart for fidelity. Annika snapped the pictures. After editing them, she emailed them to Nick. Although I was going to continue making picnic baskets for Mr. Nordgren because I'd promised I would, I was not taking more orders. Nick had replaced the picnic basket page with a new one for Flowery Language and had switched my business email to that address.

I gathered up all the samples, put them in a cooler, and closed the lid.

"Is that it for today?" Annika asked.

"Almost." I wrapped flowers. "Angelica for inspiration." I pointed to the long green branches tipped with starry white, pinprick flowers. "And oregano from my herb garden, for creativity. Pink dianthus for talent, and dried magnolia for perseverance." I handed it to her. "This one is for you."

She blushed. I had never seen her blush. "Thank you, Cassidy. No one has ever given me flowers before. I'll keep this always."

A neighbor boy stopped by to see if I had any summer work—he liked hard work, heavy work, because he was preparing for the military in a few years and wanted to be fit. I told him to come back next year—and to bring a few friends! I'd have more to tend to then. Soon after, Nick arrived, and I popped into his Camry and drove to some of the most popular wedding venues on the island so I could present the flowers in person.

I read the first address into the nav. "So I looked up venues on The Knot and contacted a few. Some said just to send the web link and follow up with them. But a couple said I could bring samples by."

Nick grinned. "You're gunned up, aren't you?"

I grinned back. "I am. I was even thinking . . . I mean, it would be a year or two away, but why couldn't my barn and garden be wedding venues of their own?"

"It would make the very best wedding venue," he said.

I didn't look at him and he said nothing more, but we let the warm idea hang shyly in the space between us for a while.

We pulled up to the first venue, a gorgeous winery. Nick waited in the car while I took my bouquets inside. A few people perched happily at the tasting bar, but it looked like a crew outside was gearing up for a wedding. "I'm looking for Ashlyn?"

A woman in her fifties smiled. "That's me!"

She led me to a table in the vineyard, and I presented my thoughts and bouquets to her. I looked at one of the grape-vines. "We could twirl some of your vines in here, and a leaf if you'd like, too, so it would be unique to your venue."

She clapped. "I love it. I'm in! I'll present the idea to every bride who books with us."

"Thank you! I put together a bouquet that might repre-sent some portion of our new business venture. Laurel for success, peonies for happy marriages, lavender for loyalty, clover for luck." I showed her the little hand-lettered tag with the flowers' names and their meanings that I'd bring with each order, then handed it and the posy to her. "Please keep this as a gift from me."

I kept my cool until we'd pulled out of the driveway, and then I pumped my fist. "One down!"

We delivered other samples throughout Coupeville, Greenbank, Freeland, and up toward Oak Harbor and the Naval base. After I hit the last venue, we headed home for lunch and made sure we were back before DJ arrived.

As DJ and Annika worked around us that afternoon, Nick and I reviewed the morning. "All of this is great, but . . . ," he said. Then he stopped.

"What? Don't worry," I reassured him. "I want your thoughts and ideas."

"Well, even if you get a bunch of brides to sign up—and you will, for sure—what are you going to do the six months of the year when no flowers are blooming?"

"I've been thinking about that, and I'm not sure yet. You've done a great job with the website, so maybe something I can sell online? Weddings are year-round, after all, even if flowers aren't fresh."

Nick smiled. "I didn't want to pop your bubble. But it's something to think about."

"It is," I said. "Let me give that a little more time. I can always keep waitressing until I figure it out. Meanwhile, let's check to make sure DJ has enough birdseed because I know it upsets him when we run out."

We walked toward the mini barn, where DJ worked, passing the greenhouse. On the shelves were the bouquets Annika and I had staged that morning for photos but hadn't taken to show.

"They're looking pretty sad," Nick said. Through the window, we could see that they'd begun to dry and slightly curl.

"Yeah . . ." As the afternoon sun blazed through the windows, the petals dried even more quickly. We walked toward DJ's zone. His brother and sister had come to work with him because he wanted to show off his "office," including his *Feed the Birds* sign.

"Hey, everything going okay?" I checked in with him.

He gave me a thumbs-up. I looked at where the dried peony petals from Mr. Nordgren's first bouquet still decorated the ground. I started to leave and then turned around. Wait. *Wait.* "DJ. If I wanted more petals, would you do this again? Pluck the petals? And put them in a basket?"

He nodded. "Yes."

His brother grinned. "You've got this, man!"

Nick and I started walking back to the flower beds as I flushed with joy. Why not dry everything I didn't sell fresh? There would be . . .

"Earth to Cassidy!" a voice whispered in my ear, interrupting my thought, the breath on my skin sending a shiver through me as an arm wrapped around my shoulder. "Where are you now?"

"I have the seed of an idea that may just 'blossom.'"

Nick groaned at the pun as we headed out into the field of flowers.

"I was thinking about when DJ took all the petals off of the flowers. And Mr. Nordgren called it confetti. So why not? People use floral confetti for weddings now instead of throwing rice or birdseed or whatever like back in the day. Flowery Language, just like the bouquets, except year-round, nationwide, in dried petals."

"Okay," Nick said. "This is a very creative idea. Not surprised."

"Then—" I plucked a palette of petals and placed them on my palm—"a bride can choose the colors and meanings of the petals to toss as they leave their wedding venue. For example, tulip petals for spring weddings, meaning consuming love, happy years, good memories. Champagne rose petals on the champagne table, for festivity and sparkle. The flowers I don't sell fresh, I will dry for tossing." I looked at the greenhouse. Sun and air-dry. Best way to preserve petals.

"I could also set up an Etsy shop for you," Nick said. "And a way for people to order through your website."

I tossed the confetti in my palm. "Why stop with weddings? I can do petals for baby showers. Daisies are for newborns, and wisteria is for sweet daughters. I know there's one for sons, too . . ." I racked my brain. "I can look it up. I could offer it for graduations and for birthdays, for anniversaries and gender reveals. The opportunities are endless . . . and year-round."

"You're a genius."

"I know." I laughed. "Just kidding. Annika and I were telling that to each other earlier. *You* are the genius. Without your Internet marketing capabilities, this would never be possible. Without DJ's petal plucking, I would never have had the idea. Without Grace's encouragement, I wouldn't have figured out what was holding me back. But I do believe . . . this is going to work! We are a team. Of. Geniuses!"

* * *

Our team of geniuses was about to gain an important addition. "Why do I feel so nervous?" I jiggled the Under the Sea Gelatin Salad in the fridge to make sure it was set. It was. But if I kept jiggling, it was going to have stretch marks. "I just want it to be a 100 percent easy-living, stress-free night for both of us."

"Yes, please. No stress, just glam!" Grace patted the red swish she'd painted in her hair with temporary color and then touched the teal one she'd swished in mine. She wore her grandmother's apron, the pretty cream one with garnet-and-pink flowers on it, trimmed in ruby. I wore Gran's, the beautiful blue one, dotted with peach and baby-blue flowers.

"Justin and I both love you," I said. "So we will like each other for sure. Also, I put together a Captain Obvious oldies playlist."

She laughed. "What did you put on it?"

"'Nevertheless, I'm in Love with You,' 'Can't Help Falling in Love,' and 'Love You Madly.' Cloaked among other songs, of course. Hopefully, Justin will pick up on it."

"Subtle, subtle. I like your style."

"So I've got this great wedding flower business underway, and I think you would make an awesome client."

She laughed. It was wonderful to see her so happy.

Right on time, at 7 p.m., both men arrived, which was something of a stroke of luck given that Justin came via the ferry. We watched as they shook hands and walked up the drive together.

I squealed. Grace squealed. "Are we teenagers again?" I asked.

"Yes!"

We headed out the door to meet them partway and steer them to the outside barbecue area, which we'd decked out for the night with lights and flowers and a large flower bin filled with ice.

Grace hugged Justin and then brought him to me. "Cassidy? This is Justin. Justin, Cassidy. I've wanted you guys to meet each other for so long."

"So good to meet you," I said. Justin's dark-brown hair was stylish, but what really made him handsome was the way he treated Grace—with love and with respect. His dark jeans and white shirt matched hers. I side-eyed her. Couple's clothing? She grinned.

We sat down and Justin put a couple bottles of rosé in the ice-filled planter. I put the music on, and Elvis came on first, singing that he couldn't help falling in love. Nick looked at me and winked. Good grief. I'd thought I had put that in the middle of the playlist, but when I'd hit random play, it chose that one first!

But maybe it was okay. I winked back and then headed into the kitchen to get the food. Grace came with me.

"I like Justin already," I said.

"You hardly know him!"

"I see how he looks at you. I know you said he's the right man. I remember your *halmoni* saying that your *halaboji* shared her heart's fiber, and I see that with you and Justin."

We'd set up a long sideboard, and I brought out the gelatin salad, the chicken croquettes that Mrs. Kim assured me had been a big hit, and a 7UP Bundt cake. Grace brought the *galbi*, *kimchi*, and *banchan*. The sun went down as we talked and talked and laughed.

"What do you do?" Justin asked Nick.

"I'm in Internet marketing. Big tech."

"Aren't all firms in Seattle tech firms?" Justin teased.

Nick looked up and laughed. "Seems that way, but not really. Lots of tech in Seattle. And biotech, which is what I'm working for, on the East Coast."

Boston. I wished I'd never promised his dad that I wouldn't bring it up until Nick did!

"What do you do?" Nick asked him.

"I'm a resident at Virginia Mason hospital," he answered.

"Ah. You're a doctor like Grace's grandfather." I turned toward Grace and then back to Justin. "Her *halaboji* must love you."

"I hope he will," Justin said. "I haven't met him yet."

"I haven't been to visit him for a while . . . ," Grace started and then stopped. "I don't want to startle him," she finally finished.

"Maybe time to visit him," Justin said. "You don't have to say anything startling." I knew just by the tone of his voice that he knew everything about Mi-Ja, which made me very happy. If he was advocating for her, he was a good man.

She shook her head. "No way. He'll ask about the bar exam, and there's no way I would, or could, lie to him."

"He might not have much time left," Justin said softly. "I'm thinking, after what you've told me, maybe not."

Grace nodded. "Yeah. There's that."

I cut a piece of Bundt cake for everyone, and as I did, I felt Nick's hand on my shoulder. He spoke softly. "You okay?"

"I'm okay but thank you for asking." I missed Gran. I missed the wrap-up chats we might have had if I'd only come home sooner.

When the sun went down, we started a fire and stayed up late talking and laughing until there was no way Justin was going to make the last ferry home.

"You got a place to stay?" Nick asked him.

"I can drive up and across the bridge," Justin said.

"Nah, the bridge is an hour out of the way. You can crash at my place," Nick offered. Justin looked pleased.

I didn't look at Grace, nor she at me, but I knew we were both thrilled that they liked each other. They helped us bring everything indoors and load the dishwasher before leaving.

"I'm exhausted," Grace said. "See you in the morning?"

I couldn't share a thought that had been on my mind since dinner, after Justin had commented about Grace's *halaboji*. Should I speak to her about it now? Or later?

Later. "For sure. Couldn't have gone better."

She went into the bathroom to take off her makeup, and

I went upstairs to sit in the rocking chair in my bedroom and think about what to do.

I met the next day from the rocking chair, by the open window. Birdsong underwrote the earliest hour, trilling, *"It's time, it's time, it's time."* Goldfinches fluttered to and fro, chiding my inaction before flitting off to a new adventure.

After getting dressed, I headed downstairs. Grace was studying, of course. Fewer than four weeks until her test. "Knock, knock," I said. "Want to get coffee?"

"I don't think I can leave," she said. "Even though I want to. My mind keeps wandering, and I'm still unmotivated." She glanced up at me and didn't glance away. "Uh-oh. I know that look."

"What look?" She'd caught me.

She sighed.

"Coffee first." I padded to the kitchen and made espresso in the Bialetti. I sucked down two bitter shots followed by a soothing half-and-half chaser and then returned to the living room. The flowers in front of the window played peekaboo in the wind. *Now you see us*—a puff of wind—*now you don't.*

I'd been going to leave all decisions up to Grace—her life, her lead—but then I thought about my last minutes with Gran. I took a breath and dove in. "I think you need to visit your *halaboji* as soon as possible. You don't want to leave it late, like I did," I said. "I didn't mean to. But what I wouldn't give to have come back a week earlier and talked with Gran at length."

"I know," she said. "You're right. I don't want that regret.

But if he asks about the bar exam, like if I already took it or if I'm studying hard, well, I can't lie to him. He'll know if I'm holding something back. And I don't want to face his disappointment."

"You could tell him about Justin," I suggested. "That would make him happy and could be a diversion. You don't have to mention law school or anything having to do with Mi-Ja."

"Trust me, I'm not going to. He's very traditional. I'll visit because you and Justin are right, but I won't upset him at the end of his life. I'm not discussing law school or my grandmother and the *hanbok*."

"The secret can remain a secret forever." I held out my fifth finger and she hooked it with hers. "Pinkie promise."

Helen

CHAPTER SEVENTEEN

It was Thanksgiving Day, but Helen's first thought was not about the holiday. Her first thought was the same one she had every morning. *Please let Mi-Ja live.*

Although they did not talk of it openly, death moved toward them like a slow train in the distance. It could be heard and seen and felt, and it was louder and faster and shook the ground more clearly day by day as the baby weakened.

It would soon arrive.

They spent the morning watching the Macy's parade on the television set. There were the usual festivities of floating balloons. The Rockettes danced their way down the open street, beautiful in their glittery costumes, long legs kicking upward, feet encased in silver shoes. Later, Elvis appeared on a midday news program.

"Look, he got a promotion." Helen pointed to the new private first-class insignia on Elvis's uniform.

"Very nice, Mr. Elvis," Eunhee said, smiling a bit. Mi-Ja rested on the sofa between them. She had barely woken all day, and Helen's nurse's eye noticed that her skin grew more slack and dry, likely from dehydration. Helen and Eunhee cooked the meal together, some Korean food and Helen's first hand at a Thanksgiving dinner. She'd made little mounds of cottage cheese and snipped chives to sprinkle across the top and set the little dish alongside a long tray of Sunshine Hi Ho crackers, her favorites.

The turkey was small enough that there had been room in the oven for the Delmonico potatoes. *Use cheddar next time,* she wrote on the recipe card. *The Swiss makes them taste a bit sour. Crush up crackers for the top, too. Mmm.*

There was cranberry sauce and pumpkin pie—*Don't use nutmeg; it gives me heartburn*—but when they sat down at the table, candles lit, both of them picked at their food.

"The potatoes are delicious," Eunhee said, trying to bring cheer.

I should be cheering her! "Maybe we're not used to eating this early in the afternoon. Thanksgiving leftovers are always better than the meal itself, anyway."

After they packed up the food and stored it in the fridge for later, Eunhee said, "I think I'll take a little nap. You should too. That was a big meal to prepare."

Helen nodded and then made her way upstairs. She sat at her dressing table and took off her pearl earrings and necklace. She picked up the soft-bristled brush, the silver one she'd received as a wedding present, and ran it through her hair. She took off her ruby-red holiday dress and then put on a day dress before reaching for the dressing table's light.

That lamp. She'd brought it from Virginia, one of the few things she'd kept from a turbulent girlhood. When they had to move regularly because her father inevitably irritated or offended his superiors, she had been allowed one box to take treasures. The lamp always took up half of it. Its base was a porcelain woman from the bust up, her nose pert, lips red, golden locks dripping down onto her shoulders. Atop her head was a pretty white hat, and atop that, the light bulb and its shade. The chip in the shade made the lamp even more lovable. It had lived long enough to be chipped and yet still shone.

Someday, maybe, Helen would have a daughter to pass it along to. Lauri. A girl with golden locks, like Helen's and like the lamp girl lighting the way. That would be something for which to give thanks indeed. She turned the light off.

When Helen woke, the room was black. Darkness fell early as the tail end of autumn whipped them toward winter. She pulled on a sweater, slipped into her satin house slippers, and went downstairs. Eunhee must not be up yet. The house was dark.

Helen walked into the living room and flicked on the

corner lamp. It illuminated the room, and she saw Eunhee on the couch, Mi-Ja in her arms.

"She's gone," Eunhee said quietly. "She slept next to me on the bed, and when I woke up, she had passed from my hands into the hands of her Father."

Helen quickly walked over and placed her hand on Eunhee's arm. "Are you certain?"

"Yes. But you may check."

Helen took the baby into her arms. Although the little girl had always been a bit more flaccid than other babies due to her Down syndrome, her muscles were completely relaxed now. Helen felt for a pulse, but there was none. She checked for breath, but there was no breath, either.

She hugged the little girl tightly, squeezing her grief into a small place inside for the moment, and then handed Mi-Ja back to her mother. "She's gone." She readied herself for Eunhee's tears, but they did not come. Perhaps she was in shock. "Are you all right?"

Eunhee nodded. "My heart is broken, but I know hers is not anymore. I will never be the same, but I am all right. I was prepared. I know she is safe and well now in heaven and not tired when she breathes." She tenderly stroked her cheek, as she did when she'd encouraged the baby to nurse, as if locking in that memory. Then she pulled Mi-Ja tightly to her before gently brushing back her hair. "I would like to bathe her one last time. Would you help me?"

They walked into the bathroom, and Helen drew warm water into the tub. Eunhee unswaddled Mi-Ja, and together they washed her little body and her hair. After they'd bathed her, Helen said, "What would you like to do next?"

Eunhee sat with the baby on her lap. "I will bury her next to her father. I will have a stone made for the top of her grave with her name on it and the beautiful *mugunghwa* and a line of thread connecting with a little box full of spools, but no dates. This way, we will always remember that her life has no end and will be very long indeed."

"I can drive to the mainland and telegraph your mother," Helen said. "If you want her to know right away."

"I will mail her," Eunhee said. "I have other things to tell her."

Helen didn't press. "Do you want Mi-Ja to be buried in her *hanbok*, the one for her *Baek-il*?"

"No. I may have another daughter—I hope I will have another daughter—and if I do, she can wear her sister's garment so that they may know one another in that way. They will share it. It will be for them both. It's my fondest wish."

Eunhee made a few phone calls to get the arrangements underway. The burial was arranged for Saturday. "I will drive you," Helen said.

Eunhee shook her head. "If it is all right with you, I would just like to be there as the three of us, one time. Mother, father, and baby."

"Take these to scatter." Helen held out several small muslin bags. It was too cold, of course, for fresh flowers. But she had collected petals from the rose of Sharon over the past months and dried them, in preparation for her friend.

Eunhee reached out her hand. "Thank you," she said. "These will always remind me of Mi-Ja."

* * *

On Saturday morning, Helen helped Eunhee into the car. "I wish there was something else I could do for you." She knew from experience that there was nothing anyone could do to help.

"You can," Eunhee said. "I have looked at Mi-Ja's things one last time. To go on, I must not cry into them any longer. Could you wash and pack them and then perhaps ask Johanna to put them into the barrel of clothes that their church sends to missionaries?"

"Yes, of course," Helen said. She would do whatever it took to make Eunhee comfortable, no matter what she asked. "And the *hanbok* and thread box?"

"Save them someplace," Eunhee said. "I will give that to my next beautiful daughter."

As Eunhee drove down the driveway, toward Sunnyside Cemetery, a flock of sparrows took to the air, flying higher and higher, until they were entirely out of sight.

Fly freely. Helen blew a kiss skyward. *Be well, sweet baby.*

Helen went into the teal bedroom. Drawer by drawer she opened the bureau and took out the baby's items. She carefully wrapped the *hanbok* in tissue paper and then walked to the attic. "You are living a joyous life now, little Mi-Ja, our rose of Sharon. Your *umma*'s strong faith in heaven makes me believe in it too. Your eternal blossom will not fade." She glanced at Bob's case. "All my hopes," she said. "So many have been crushed. And yet somehow, because of this child and her mother, I believe that many more good things will come my way."

She nestled the *hanbok* and the one hundred day threads in the hope chest, closed it, flicked the light out, and walked down the attic stairs.

Once in the kitchen, Helen prepared the spicy crab bisque she knew Eunhee enjoyed. *Make sure to add the cooking sherry, or else it's too thick,* she jotted to the side of the recipe. Then she set it in the refrigerator until dinner.

As morning broke into the afternoon, the sun broke through the clouds. The Skylark pulled into the driveway, but instead of coming into the house, Eunhee walked across the orchard in the front of the house and sat on the swing the Jansen boys had fixed. It was right in the middle of the apple trees.

Helen slipped on a soft cardigan and went to join her friend. "How did it go?"

"Sad, quiet. But I felt togetherness. She is whole and happy, and I will see her again. God helped me to bear the pain."

"Not angry with him anymore?" Helen dug her foot into the soft ground and gave the swing a little push, hoping that the rocking motion would soothe.

"A little," she said. "But I did not tell you how Job's story ended."

"You did not."

"We all experience loss, but God will make good of it somehow, even if I cannot see it yet. God blessed Job more in the second half of his life than he did in the first. I choose to believe that he will do that for me too."

Helen did not cause the swing to rock any longer. "You do?"

"I do."

"I would like faith like yours," Helen said. "You said all I had to do was ask."

"Ask," Eunhee said.

Helen closed her eyes. *Jesus, I'm not sure if this is how I'm supposed to start. But I want what she has,* she whispered in her heart. *That faith. You.*

When she opened her eyes, she was lighter, freer, and the sparrows on the apple tree lifted to the sky. Life was possible again.

"You look beautiful," Eunhee said. "I see him in you."

"Only because I saw him in you," Helen said. "Am I a Christian now?"

"You are a Christian now, my sister and my friend. Now I must write to my mother. I will tell her that Mi-Ja died. She does not know that Mi-Ja had Down syndrome."

Helen tilted her head. "Will you tell her?"

Eunhee shook her head. "It is for her best if she does not know. She will worry about later babies. She will feel shame if her friends ask her. They may not think well of me. They already don't think well of me because I married a non-Korean. But they honor my mother because I am living the

American dream. I don't want to bring shame to her. I will tell her that we will never speak of this again, which will be easy, as I won't return to Korea. America is now my home."

Helen started the swing rocking again. "I'm happy to have you stay here with me as long as you like. Forever."

Eunhee smiled, a gleam in her eye for the first time in a long while. "I do not think that Lauri's father will be happy if I am living with you forever."

"If there is ever a Lauri's father." Helen loosed her anxiety. Would she ever have a family of her own? "We can look together to help you find a job here."

Eunhee spoke carefully. "I may have a job. In Seattle."

"You have a job?" Helen's surprise lifted her voice, and a little rabbit nibbling grass nearby stood on his hind legs and then scrambled under the blackberry brambles. "How . . . ? Where? With whom?"

"Someone at the Korean church in Seattle knew that I was looking for a job. I told them I had worked as a translator for the Navy."

Just not here.

"And they said the Boeing Airplane Company, where they work, contacted the Korean department at the University of Washington because they are always interested in people who can read and speak Asian languages for translation purposes. I speak and read both Korean and Japanese, of course. I did not know what to say because of Mi-Ja. But now that she is no longer with me, I could consider this job."

Helen shivered. Months ago, she thought she'd be kind

to allow Eunhee to stay with her for a while. Now she grew desolate at the thought of losing her companionship.

"You are cold," Eunhee said. "Let's go in."

As they walked under the quiet arbor of roses, Helen felt it, truly felt it. Peace.

That night, over a bowl of spicy crab bisque, Helen asked, "If you move to Seattle, when would you go? Where would you live?"

"I understand that the translation position starts after the beginning of the New Year. I will still have to interview, of course. I could live with a Korean family from the small church gathering. They would make room for me in their home."

Helen nodded. "And someday you will remarry?"

Eunhee shrugged. "I want a family to love, and to love and respect me in return. I thought I would return to Korea and marry a man there, but I now realize that is not what my life is to be. I could not leave America and leave Mi-Ja here alone, even in her grave."

Helen set her spoon down. "Do your friends at this church know about her?"

Eunhee shook her head.

"Do they know about James Roy?"

Eunhee shook her head again. "There is no reason to tell them."

Helen nibbled on a Hi Ho cracker. "If you decide to marry again, will you tell him? I mean, your husband?"

"I . . . I hope so. If it is possible." She looked at Helen.

"In my culture, mothers-in-law do not like it if a new wife has already been married, or even if she has had a boyfriend, much less a child. I would not want to shame my husband before his parents. Korean men are very traditional. But I also want to be truthful. I will know if I can ever tell him and why I should. Sometimes secrets are kept out of love and not a wish to deceive. But then they may be shared when the time is right."

Eunhee looked intently at Helen. "I am strong, but I do not think I am strong enough to lose anything more in my life—not now, perhaps not ever." She sighed as if to underscore her weariness and fragility. "It's been a long day. Let's clean the dishes and go to bed."

"Yes, let's." As they worked, Helen made jokes and cheerful talk to help lighten the day's burden. "I hope Johanna will come soon and teach us how to make the Cinn Rolls. They'd be particularly welcome now on cool mornings." She talked about the plants she'd like to have the next year, and they planned together to replant the Korean corner with seeds from Eunhee's old home, giving them the taste of her new land, her practiced hands. "Like you!" Helen chirped. She spoke of anything that would blunt the sadness she knew Eunhee would feel when she went to sleep in the room without the baby.

As they parted, Eunhee to the teal bedroom and Helen to head upstairs to her room, Eunhee said with a smile, "It makes me very happy to think that now you can return to your job at the hospital. You are an excellent nurse."

Helen swallowed hard. "Good night. I will see you in the morning!"

"Sometimes secrets are kept out of love and not a wish to deceive."

Cassidy

CHAPTER EIGHTEEN

After pinkie-promising Grace her secret was safe forever, I headed off to the greenhouse to get some shelves set up to dry petals. I'd barely spread a few petals across the top row of wood when she came flying out of the house.

"Can you come with me to see my *halaboji*?"

"Sure," I said. "You want me there?"

"He does! I mean, I do too, but I think he feels he hasn't been able to offer his condolences since your gran died. Tomorrow?"

I shook my head. "Annika and DJ are hosting their support group friends here tomorrow—they lined it up with the others in their group and the staff. I gotta be here all day."

"Sunday, my family visits him." Grace ran her hand over some of the roses. "Today?"

I blinked. "Today? Okay. I have to work the dinner shift. Will we be back?"

"For sure," she said. "I know it's fast. I'm sorry."

I wanted to make sure to see Dr. Kim while he was still alive, too. "I'll go shower. You bring the leftover *galbi*. Remember—men like meat!"

We were out of the house in under an hour, and as it was a Friday and midday, we were able to make the next ferry. Not long after, we pulled into the large skilled nursing center in Des Moines, just north of Federal Way. As a doctor, Grace's grandfather had surely known where he could get the best care. The campus was beautiful and overlooked the sound. I parked and we checked in with the front desk before making our way down the hall to his room.

We stood outside for a minute. "Want me to wait in the hall?" I whispered.

She shook her head. "He specifically said you were to come in." She knocked on the door. "Halaboji? It's Grace."

"Come in, come in," a frail man's voice called out. We walked in. Dr. Kim sat in a recliner in the corner of the room, looking out the window. He turned when we walked in, and I was shocked at how thin he'd grown. No doubt, this was why he was still here—not ready for hospice but needing care.

Grace's stricken face showed she, too, realized how ill he was.

I bowed. "Hello, Dr. Kim. I hope you are well. Have you eaten?"

He grinned. "So you remember how to greet someone properly?"

I grinned back. "I've been well taught."

Grace held out the containers she brought. *"Galbi?"*

He nodded. She warmed it in the microwave down the hallway, placed it all on a little plate, and brought it back into the room for him. "The perilla is from Cassidy's garden."

He wrapped some meat and rice in a leaf and then daubed it with a bit of spicy red pepper sauce from a clay pot on the table next to him. "This is different. What's different?"

"Do you like it?" Grace asked.

"Ah, what a lawyer! She's deflecting the questions and asking some of her own," he teased. "I do like it. Better than your mother's." He bent down a bit and lowered his voice. "But don't tell her."

"How have you been?" she asked.

"Let an old man eat, and then I'll answer your questions, Esquire."

Grace could not yet be addressed as esquire. She'd have to pass the bar, and that, of course, hadn't happened. Misery had crossed her face at the mention of her being a lawyer. She so wanted him to be proud of her.

Her grandfather finished eating, drank some water, wiped his lips, and then said, "You found the *hanbok*, of course."

Grace drew a deep breath. I sat down, a bit dizzy.

"Yes, we . . . we found a *hanbok*," she said. "The name embroidered on it is Mi-Ja. Do you know of anyone named Mi-Ja?"

He nodded. "I do. Mi-Ja was Choi Eunhee's first child."

Grace gasped. "So you knew!"

"Yes," he said. "I've always known—but no one else does. No one except Helen, of course." He looked at me and then back to his granddaughter. "Choi Eunhee was nervous to tell me, but she was an honest woman, and despite her fear of losing our future life together, she would not keep that from me."

Grace sat down in the chair next to me.

"When I met your grandmother, we both attended a small church meeting of other Korean people in Seattle. Another Korean doctor had invited her, and I met her there. About a year or so later, I asked her if I might pick her up at the home where she stayed and take her to a play. She said yes, and we soon found out we had much in common and were . . . actually . . . affectionate in our sentiments toward each other."

"You mean in love," Grace finished, purposely poking the bear. He blushed just a little, and I saw her smile. She'd needed to regain her confidence too.

"Well." He cleared his throat. "In time, I asked her to marry me. She said yes, but that she needed to tell me about her past before we went forward. She'd married an American sailor in Korea. They came to the US, and he died of the flu in 1958. She had nowhere to go and called the wife of her husband's former Naval superior." He turned toward me. "Her name was Helen Devries. Choi Eunhee moved into her home."

Then I gasped. "You mean—Mrs. Kim lived at Gran's? They didn't just meet at the base and become luncheon friends?" So that's why he wanted me here. Maybe to support Grace, as Gran had wanted, but also to learn about my own grandmother.

"I'm quite certain they were luncheon friends. But Mrs. Kim lived with your grandmother for the best part of a year, in the room in your home that has the sewing machine. She stayed there until the baby died."

Grace shook her head. "But . . . why? Why did the baby die?"

He leaned forward again, and his voice grew quiet and perhaps shook a bit. "The baby, she had what we now call Down syndrome. In those days, there were few ways to treat children who had Down syndrome. Most mothers were told to institutionalize the child and forget the child ever existed. Many children died young due to physical complications. Their mothers were shamed into thinking that they somehow were to blame for their child's diagnosis. Mi-Ja had a significant heart defect, as many people with Down syndrome do. The baby died . . ."

"At three months," Grace said. "Just past her hundred days celebration."

"You found the death certificate," he said. "You are a good legal researcher."

Voices percolated in the hallway, and a nurse leaned in. "You doing okay, Dr. Kim?"

"Of course," he said. "My only granddaughter finally made time to come and visit me."

She smiled. "Okay. I'll be back in an hour."

Grace looked at her grandfather, reminded again, I thought, of the gravity of his situation.

"Is that why Halmoni kept it a secret? The shame?"

"Yes. I found no shame in her, and I found no shame in her child. But this was many years ago. I had arranged for my mother to move to the United States, and she would never have approved of your grandmother having been married before marrying me. Society then did not look favorably upon mothers who had given birth to children with Down syndrome. We kept it a secret, and then later, we'd kept the secret so long it just never seemed possible to say differently, nor did we have a reason to bring up this shocking news. Your *halmoni* had lost so much. In fact, she had lost everything. Although she was a strong woman, she could not lose anything more—the adoration of her family, the respect of her community—by revealing that she'd kept a secret for so long. I would have seen to it that she never suffered loss again if I could."

"But she kept the *hanbok*," Grace said.

"She loved Mi-Ja like she loved all of her children. Like she loved her grandchildren. Like she loved you. I am not certain why she kept the *hanbok* because I did not know about it until a few months ago when Helen called me and asked what she should do with it, once she knew she was dying. She told me, 'This is the time, now and soon, for Grace to understand the full strength of her grandmother.'"

He sipped his water before continuing. "Helen said, 'Once, Eunhee told me that she would share this information with the right man at the right time, and she told me when she'd shared the information with you. She said that sometimes secrets are kept out of love and not a wish to deceive. But then they are shared when the time is right. The time is right to share the *hanbok* with Grace.'"

"What did you answer?" Grace asked.

"I said, well, the *hanbok* was left in Helen's care, so if she felt the time was right, it was right. And now you should decide what to do with it, Grace, as it's been left in your care. You are the only girl left now. And you know you were her favorite." His eyes glistened with a tear and a twinkle.

Grace drew closer to him.

"You are her 'Mi-Ja.' The only girl in the family. This is your legacy from your grandmother. This *hanbok*, this knowledge, and the understanding of her hard work and sacrifice. You do what you like with them."

Grace put her head in her hands. "No one else knows about the first husband and the baby? How will they react if they learn of it?"

"I do not think anyone else knows, but of course, I cannot be sure. I do not know how my sons will react."

"I can guess how my father will react," Grace said. "Poorly."

"Maybe," he agreed. "It's your decision. With choice comes responsibility. But whatever you decide to do, I will support you." He coughed repeatedly, and a bit of blood flecked the handkerchief he brought away from his mouth. "For as long as I'm here."

"You're not that sick, are you?" Grace's concern turned from herself to her grandfather.

He patted her hand. "No."

I didn't believe him, and I was pretty sure she didn't, either. I spoke up quietly, asking the question I knew Grace wanted an answer to but couldn't ask. "Why did Gran say this was the time and send us to find it quickly?"

"She did not tell me. Perhaps because she was dying and did not want to leave it unremarked. Possibly so I could be here to confirm the truth if Grace asked. She told me she thought Grace had a special reason to learn of this soon, and I trusted her. I am sorry for your loss." He looked at me.

"Thank you," I said.

Now he turned back to Grace. "I'm glad you know. I think my wife would be glad that you know now too. What will you do with this knowledge, hmm? What are you doing today that fulfills the hopes and prayers of someone yesterday?" He smiled. "And now, if you'll indulge an old man, I would like some more of that delicious *galbi*."

Half an hour later, we got into the car. Grace seemed shell-shocked. A hard, unexpected rain sluiced over the windshield as we waited for the ferry. "I'm surprised—happy, but surprised by how he reacted about the baby," Grace said.

"Love changes things," I answered. "No one really knows what goes on between a husband and a wife."

She nodded. "Eunhee means *grace*," she said softly. "I was named to honor her, and your gran felt that my *halmoni* would want me to decide how to do just that. What can I do today that answers her hopes and prayers?"

I remained quiet. I knew she was musing and not asking me for an answer.

"I wish I knew," she said distantly and to herself.

*   *   *

Later that night, I returned from my shift flush with tips. Grace was hunched over her laptop in the living room. "Studying hard?" I asked.

"Mmm-hmm. But not for the bar." She looked up. "Thinking about my *halmoni* and what her hopes for her daughter might have been. I've been researching. I looked into the history of children with Down syndrome and their moms and how they were treated then and now." Her voice was the no-nonsense, almost-lawyer, did-my-research Grace that I knew and loved. "One state had long tunnels leading into the institutions where the children were cared for, underground tunnels, so anyone visiting wouldn't have to risk being seen coming out. Shame could attach just from a simple visit."

My heart sank. "Barbaric."

She pressed on. "Among Hitler's first victims were

intellectually and physically disabled people. They were called 'unfit to live,' and at least 275,000 of them were gassed to death."

I sat straight up, adrenaline and revulsion coursing through me.

"Intelligence level is still sometimes used in the United States to determine who gets rationed medical treatment. Parents often have to apply to be guardians of their own children to ensure treatment after adulthood. Sometimes other guardians take advantage and fleece those they are supposed to protect instead."

I shook my head. "Why don't we hear more about this?"

"I don't know. There's a firm in Seattle, a part of a larger, national firm that advocates for and represents clients with developmental or intellectual disabilities. I already emailed them to see if I could come and talk about the kind of work they do."

I didn't hide my surprise. "You mean . . . as a profession?"

"I don't know. I've been thinking and praying. Turns out, maybe I do want to help people get out of trouble. The kind they got into through no action of their own, but for which they need help to get out." She looked up. "I think that was why your gran said to hurry. So I'd see the strength my *halmoni* had and draw from it as I faced the next bar exam. Take her legacy and run with it."

"Take your heirloom and give it the taste of your hands." I scooted next to her and hugged her. "And maybe so your *halaboji* would have your back."

"For sure." She shook her head slowly. "All those years volunteering at Special Olympics. Now we know why," she said. "Our grandmothers were serving in honor of Mi-Ja. I wish I would have paid closer attention."

"What are you going to do now?"

"I'm not sure. I have only a few weeks more to study for that test. I have to focus on that first and then decide what comes next." She looked up with a firm, determined look on her face. "I care about passing the exam now. I really, really care about passing so I can honor her legacy. I mean, she could have returned to Korea, but she chose to stay and build a new life. For herself. For us. For me."

I nodded. "This is your inheritance. I know your *halmoni* would be proud of you. And your *halaboji*. I am."

"I'm running with it, but not telling my dad. If I pass the bar, everything will work out for me. And—" she smiled—"now you get to keep your house and your land, as you promised your gran!"

We sat together in the quiet.

"Did you hear that?" she asked.

"Hear what?"

She put her fingers to her lips and pointed at the attic.

Drip. Drip. Drip.

CHAPTER NINETEEN

When the last set of roofers came to quote, they pointed out that it wouldn't be long before the garage and barn needed roofs, too. The pleasure and pain of a property rounding in on one hundred years. A jealous mistress, wanting my time and money—money I didn't have—to keep her afloat. However, I was prepared to fight. "Do you have a payment plan?" I asked. Yes, they'd said. But the rates were extraordinarily high. Was there another way? There was. That home equity loan.

"I need at least ten thousand dollars, but there's more available on that loan," I told Grace. "With the money I'll have coming in from leasing the acreage next year, I should be more than able to cover the additional payment."

"Did you get your name on the account as a signer?"

I shook my head. "Not yet."

"Go get your name as a signer on the account," she said. "Then you can write the check to the roofers. Just bring the probate document, the new title, and the will to the bank, and you'll be set. It's been almost four months since Gran's death, so it's a good time to resolve that detail, too."

So on a beautiful, mid-July Friday morning, I headed a few miles south to Coupeville, whistling cheerfully, knowing that soon my home would be snug and dry.

My brakes squealed as I pulled in and parked. Maybe there'd be a bit left over for them to be replaced.

I walked into the reception area. "Hello, I need to see the personal banker." I read the name on the business card that Gran had clipped to the documents.

"Oh, I'm sorry. He retired late last year. Alain DuBois has taken his place. Would you like to see him instead?"

"Sure." I took a seat in the waiting area, and shortly after that, a middle-aged man with an oily slick of black hair and a perfectly tailored suit came to meet me. Wow. Dressy for Coupeville.

"Miss Quinn?"

I nodded.

"Follow me."

He led me into an office with glass walls. "How can I help you?"

I explained the situation and handed over the paperwork. "I'll need to be added to the account."

He took a minute, then five, to read the paperwork. Surely he was familiar with his own company's documents, right? What was taking so long?

He finally pushed the papers back toward me. "You'll see here, on this line, that assignation of the loan to a new party is not automatic when the property transfers to a new owner, even an inheritrix. You'll need to qualify."

"Qualify?"

"Yes. It's *possible* for the loan to continue—to follow the property, as it were—but that's the bank's call. Just fill this out—" he rummaged in his drawer for a clipboard and then fixed a document to it—"with your employment information, your Social Security number, debts, etc. We'll run your credit and check on your employment."

My credit? The student loans. And I'd had to use a few credit cards to live in superexpensive California. My job was at Tony's and my tips hadn't even built up yet.

I filled the paperwork out and handed it to him and he left the room. I waited and waited and waited. A bead of sweat trickled from my forehead and made its way to the corner of my eye, where it stung. I wiped it away just as Mr. DuBois returned.

He saw me wipe the corner of my eye. "Yes, yes, you must have known it would be bad news," he said, assuming, I thought, I'd wiped away a tear.

"I'm afraid, as you know, your credit is less than stellar, Miss Quinn. Your employment is new and not at the level to support an additional debt burden. Frankly, it won't even support your current debt burden. Like so many of your generation—" he waved his hand condescendingly—"more debt than you can handle. I'm sure you have the latest phone release, though."

I refused to acknowledge his gibe. I stood. "Thank you for your time."

"Miss Quinn? You may want to have a seat again."

I remained standing.

"I'm not simply saying that you can't sign for more debt. I'm calling this loan in. The contract allows me to do so, after property transfer, within sixty days, at my discretion."

"But . . . the land is worth much more than the amount due. There's a lot of equity."

"It is true that the land is valuable. However, we are not in the real estate sales business, Miss Quinn. We are bankers, interested in safe, reliable investments."

"I haven't missed a payment, and you can see that there's money in the attached checking account to cover another eighteen months. Seems reliable to me."

"Nevertheless. It's in the binding contract. I'm going to be gracious and give you sixty days from today to bring in the money, instead of sixty days from the death of the original debtor."

The hackles on the back of my neck rose. "How am I going to get the money in sixty days?"

"A sale, Miss Quinn. I looked up the property while awaiting your reports and found that it has rare, beautiful water and mountain views."

Had that played into his decision? Seemed possible. But why?

He reached back into his desk and withdrew a business card, which he handed to me. "Here. Trustworthy developers. We work with them as often as possible."

"Developers?"

"Networking, Miss Quinn. It's the way business is done in the real world. A good deal helps everyone involved. If you sell it to them outright, you won't pay the legal fees and other charges that come with foreclosure. If we need to foreclose, these same developers will certainly be on hand as the highest bidder. Land like yours is hard to come by."

I folded the card into my purse and left after nodding a curt goodbye. After I was halfway out of the lobby, I turned back. He was already on the phone. Perhaps he was calling the developers at this moment so they could sharpen their parcel-dividing knives and continue to do business with them as he handed a plum property to them—literally.

I headed to the Coupeville dock, parked, and walked to the ice cream store. I took my chocolate cone to a bench on the pier. *There must be someplace else to get the loan.* After securing the ag tax, after following my dream for flowers and a community of people supporting one another, after promising Gran I would keep the land, I couldn't give up. I finished the cone and opened the app for my bank on my phone, clicking through to apply for a loan. I entered the information. Within a minute, I received an email notification reporting that my application had been declined. I would receive a letter in the mail within thirty days explaining the factors behind their decision.

I didn't need to wait for the letter. I knew the factors that had gone into it. The truth was, I wasn't a crazy debtor. I didn't take vacations. I drove an old car. I worked hard. No, my generation hadn't faced widespread war; instead, we were crushed with debt, and if we wanted opportunities, we had, for the most part, to make them.

I guess I could have taught school. But it wouldn't have been fair to the kids to have a teacher who didn't want to be there.

Should I have said yes to Pamela? I couldn't have known. Was I going to lose everything after all for standing up for myself? Insisting on being treated with dignity?

Lord, I need your help. I've done all I know how to do. I blinked back tears as I drove home. Once there, I walked to the swings under the apple trees, already yielding their fruit. I looked out at the fallow field where Gran's beloved evergreens had grown. I'd cut off the limb, but it hadn't saved the body after all.

I texted Nick. **Does your mom know a good Realtor?**

?

Yeah. Time to sell.

I'll be right there.

He arrived in about twenty minutes, and as he pulled in, I texted Grace, inside studying, and asked her to come and meet us in the orchard. She sat in a wooden Adirondack chair across from us.

SANDRA BYRD

I handed the paperwork to her. "There's a clause in here that says when the house transfers title, they have the right to call in the loan. He's calling it in."

Grace flipped through the pages rapidly; then she slowed down and carefully read one paragraph, underlining it with her finger as she went. She snapped the page back and looked up at me. "That's right. They can. But the bills are being paid, right?"

"Yeah. Because I have so much debt and no job security, I'm a default risk. He handed me the card of a developer he knew would be interested. I have sixty days to pay the loan in full, or they will foreclose. Taking the amount owed . . ."

"And interest and penalties and attorney's fees," Grace said. "With you having no say over to whom it's sold because it will go to auction, and he's already told you that his 'friends' will be the high bidder. How thankful they'll be to him for providing this property, and I'm sure they'll find some way to reward him. Is there another way?"

I laughed, but it was laced with pain. "Either of you have seventy-five thousand dollars lying around? And even if we did, I still need a roof and operating expenses."

"How about your dad?" Nick asked. "Can he help?"

I shook my head. "They are definitely in no financial place to do that—I know that for sure. Even if he wanted to." Which I doubted.

Nick looked beyond the front of my property to the water and mountains. "You could sell this for a lot."

"Yeah. I'll be house poor and cash rich, I suppose," I said.

341

"I have control over only one more thing. To whom it is sold. I do not want this to be sold to a developer. I just want another kid to sit on this swing, watching the deer eat the apples that fall to the ground, reaching up and picking one for themselves. I don't want the Mickey tree bulldozed. I don't want the roses of Sharon ripped up or the peonies shopped out like orphans. They hardly ever grow when they're transplanted. More likely, if I move them in the summer, they'll die."

A heart death.

Nick understood what I was saying and squeezed my hand.

"I want a family to live here. Private party sale, not corporate."

"You need to make sure that is in the listing contract," Grace said. "I'll look it over . . . as a friend, not as a lawyer, since I can't yet." She met my gaze. "I'm sorry I didn't see that clause in the loan docs earlier."

"It's a dozen pages of tiny print." I reached out with my open hand and took hers. "I can hang on to the house until you hear back on the exam, long enough for Annika to finish earning her money and for us to sell bridal bouquets this summer."

"Then what?" Grace asked.

"Then I'll do what your *halmoni* did. I hold my head up and do what I love, with people I love, but on new land."

Grace squeezed my hand and went back inside to study. She had only days before the exam.

"What do you need from me?" Nick asked. "Anything."

"Help me enjoy the rest of my time here. This land, this house—this was always my happy summer place. When Labor Day came, I knew I'd have to head back to school and Dad and Mary Alice. I want to savor one more summer. And help me find a good Realtor."

"You got it. My mom says you can trust this Realtor." He pulled out his phone and shared a contact with me. "I know this is hard. But this beautiful woman I'm seeing, Cassidy Quinn?" He smiled and I smiled back. "She's really wise. She told me that there is a reason the heart and the brain work well together. They were designed to do so." He touched my bicep. "You are strong." He gently tapped my heart. "You are courageous." He touched my temple. "You are smart." Then he touched my hands, one after the other. "You can take what you know and what you love and build this again. Build it better."

I smiled. "Build it better."

He looked at his watch. "I'm sorry I've got to run. I have a corporate Zoom meeting this afternoon."

"Oh, that's right. How's work going?"

"It's all good." He pulled me into a bear hug. "Don't worry so much about making sure you're asking about me right now. Sometimes *me* takes precedence over *we* for a little while. You have a lot to balance. We'll talk about me once you get the sale underway. Okay? One thing at a time."

I nodded. "Thank you. One thing at a time."

He tilted my face upward and gently kissed me. "One thing at a time."

After he left, I reached up and grabbed a small apple, bit into it, and then sang the song Gran had loved best. "'The Lord is good to me, and so I thank the Lord, for giving me the things I need, the sun and the rain and the apple seed. The Lord is good to me.'"

Like anyone, I'd had many losses but so many blessings, too. What other kid got to spend every summer on a property like this? Maybe, if I couldn't keep it, it would be about another kid who could eat apples from the Mickey tree, like me. I was not going to rehearse a litany of my losses. Instead, I'd recall the bounty of my blessings.

I called the Realtor. "I want a family to buy my property," I told her. "I'm willing to be accommodating on the price for the right family—but keep that between us. I'm sorry, but because time is so short, I've got to limit this to a thirty-day listing." She needed to be able to sell it quickly, or I needed to give it to someone who could.

"Of course," she said. "On all counts." We'd spend a few days preparing the property and then she'd list it. "Bring some things to a storage unit," she said. "Neat and sparse before listing. That way, the buyers can imagine their own things in the house, not yours."

In principle, I agreed. Practically, that was going to be tough.

I headed up to the attic. That was the most jumbled space in the house. Almost everything up there should be brought to storage eventually.

I pushed the uniform box to the center of the room. I'd

move those. I'd leave the hope chest because it was vintage and looked attic-y. Plus, I wanted all the hopeful things nearby to give me courage and cheer. Kneeling down, I opened the lid to the tea set again. Grace and I should have a little tea in the garden. Or maybe Annika and me. Better, the three of us!

I raised one of the delicate bone cups to the light and could see right through it. Beautiful roses vined up the sides. Why hadn't Gran used these with me and Mom, instead of her heavy coffee mugs?

An envelope tucked to the side of the cups caught my eye. It had been awkwardly resealed. On the outside, in Gran's handwriting, was scrawled *Moving On*.

Should I read it? I opened it, feeling slightly guilty. It was from her mother. The delicate stationery looked like it had been splashed with water . . . or tears.

Thank you for your hospitable invitation. Unfortunately, we are in the midst of a very busy social calendar, and I cannot foresee a time that I might make a visit. I do wish you the very best. You have chosen a life as a workingwoman, one without children.

I'm glad you reminded me of my mother's tea set. I had forgotten about that. I miss it. As you and I will not be able to share an afternoon's tea, I would like to request that you send it back. I'm sure you understand how valuable such an heirloom is to me.

Sincerely, Mother

Oh, Gran. I'm sorry. And apparently, despite the bold scrawl, Gran hadn't moved on. She didn't return this tea set. But she hadn't used it, either. Pain contained. Had Gran meant for me to find it? She hadn't said so all these years. Knowing her, she'd been ashamed that her own mother wanted nothing to do with her. But she hadn't given it away, either, and she'd clearly not sent it back as had been demanded.

Had she meant for me to find this?

I carried it downstairs carefully and set it on my dresser.

* * *

All my beauties bathed in the August sun. The tomatoes were saucy and fresh, and I ate them breakfast, lunch, and dinner. The dahlias had opened their wide faces, and while I still didn't have many buyers at the honesty stand, I continued to put out bouquets. I sold them cheap for the pleasure they'd give others.

Gina, my Realtor, had a couple of showings on the house, but with fifteen acres, the price was more than a lot of young families could afford. I still held out hope, and sure enough, one day she called me, adrenaline surging through her voice. "Operation Greenhouse! I have a family on the island looking for a property. They were ready to give up and head back to Seattle after a long weekend when their Realtor saw your listing. I know it's Sunday evening, but we'll be there in twenty minutes!"

That's all I wanted. For my home to be a family home.

I'd just pulled Gran's William Tell's Never-Miss Apple Cake out of the oven. I left the cake to cool on the counter. It'd give a homey feel to the kitchen! The sourdough biscuits I'd made had cooled, too, washing the kitchen atmosphere with their tang.

I headed out to the greenhouse—where I'd taken refuge for all the showings—just ahead of the prospective buyers' arrival. On the way, I plucked a dandelion and blew the fluff, sending the seeds into the air as I had in childhood. Older and wiser, I prayed rather than wished. Those seeds—prayers— would land and take root. Even if I never saw what blossomed, I had set them in motion.

Please let a loving family make this their home.

Gina pulled in first, and then a Range Rover pulled in behind her. If that was the potential buyer, they must have enough money for this house.

Lord, this is a family home. This is my family home. It's always been a safe and warm place for everyone I know and love. If I can't keep the house, give it to someone who will love and honor our legacy.

I texted Nick. **Kids! This family has two kids. Maybe they have a dog. And the barn could do with another kitten.**

Praying, sunshine, he wrote back. **Let me know.**

They came into the garden. I waved to Gina from the greenhouse and then sat on the floor so that they couldn't see me when she walked them by. I tugged at one of the oldest drawers, almost sealed shut with rust. Gran had never used the old section once she'd built the new greenhouse around it. The drawer finally opened. Old plant name stakes. I took one out. Gran's handwriting. *Peas, please.*

I tugged another drawer. Empty. A third drawer. What were these? I reached in and pulled out some brown paper envelopes tied in twine. Written across one was *To plant next year and all the years after. I will make my new home my true home.* It was definitely not Gran's handwriting. It looked like Grace's *halmoni*'s handwriting.

I opened one of the packets and shook some of the tiny, dry kernels into my hand. When a plant dies, it leaves a seed that waits to be activated. If not planted and watered soon enough, they died and all that they were in the past, and everything they promised for the future, died with them. If planted, tended, weeded, and watered, they grew, carrying forward their past into the future to nurture others in a new season.

I needed to sell the house. The land. The grounds. I needed to move forward and plant a new life, not let my hope die. I'd follow Eunhee's courageous lead. She'd made a new home. I would too.

Within the hour, the prospective buyers took off, and Gina called me inside. "I have an offer!"

"Oh. Wow. Incredible."

Silence filled the space between us. "I know this isn't easy for you," she said. "But they can close on time if we hurry. Their mortgage company will send someone for the inspection within the week, and we're pushing for a quick closing before your lien complicates things."

"Whatever you need to do," I said.

She said she'd run over with the paperwork later that night, and things would be underway.

* * *

Three days later, as I packed the jewelry in Gran's dressing table, a car pulled into the driveway. Gina? Why was she here? Why hadn't she called first?

Grace came out of her room when the car pulled up. "Want me to get out of the way?"

"No, stay."

I met Gina at the door. "This is a surprise. I've got to leave to work my shift in about an hour." I invited her into the living room, and we all sat down.

"I wanted to tell you in person and right away. The house failed the inspection."

I sank into the couch. "The roof?"

"Yes, and we knew that might be a possibility. But because that leak had been going on much longer than anyone probably realized, there is also dry rot in the attic. It's nothing that's going to collapse the house immediately, of course. But a lender won't lend on the property without having that fixed. And the buyer then worried about mold."

"Anything else?" Grace asked on my behalf.

"The septic seemed a little slow . . . nothing immediate, again, but noted. When the buyers were told about all of this, they pulled out of the deal."

"Understandable," I said. "Can we find another buyer?"

"I don't think so—not a family, not in time. A lender is not going to approve the property without those fixes being made first. You could, of course, ask that those fixes be made out of the proceeds of your sale, but you don't have time to get that done before your other note is called in. Your current lender has a reputation for not being afraid to call in loans because they make so much in penalties and interest and will keep lots of fees for themselves. However, it's still hard to understand why they are doing this because foreclosure is costly. Anyway, you need a cash buyer who is willing to overlook those complications."

"A unicorn?" I asked.

"A developer," she answered. "It's the only way I see. They have the ready cash, and you'll make the most profit."

Why does it always come down to rich people having money on hand for what they want?

"You okay?" Grace asked.

"Not really," I said. I turned back to Gina. "Can a developer close quickly?"

"Yes," she said. "Once you had a contract, they could even write a check within a day or two to pay off the lien, and then if closing took a few weeks or more, there would be time. You need to have that lien paid off by mid-September. Because your listing contract with me specified a family buyer, we can terminate that now. I can locate some developers for you if you're ready."

I stood and walked to the old phone table and opened

the drawer. I withdrew the card the banker had given me and handed it to Gina. "These guys?"

Her face soured. "Where did you get this card?"

"The banker. I thought it was weird that he gave it to me, but he said it was only networking. The way business gets done in the real world."

"Huh. Yeah. Well, your land is really valuable, and if it goes to auction, I'm pretty sure that they'd win the bid. They'll put tiny little boxes on the property with no space between them." She looked up at me. "I'm sure the banker let his friends here—" she tapped the card—"know this would be coming on the market soon. Which is why they're willing to foreclose. 'You scratch my back, and I'll scratch yours.'"

"What can I do?"

"There are other developers, better ones, who parcel with the land in mind. I'll line up a few others for you. If you decide to go with one of them, we'll sign a contract then. You can save the fees and choose the developer you want."

I nodded. I needed to help Annika and DJ finish the summer well. I wanted one final harvest. Grace needed to hang out until her test results were in.

"Can it wait until the day after Labor Day?" I asked.

"Yes," she said. "Or even a few days later because they'll have the cash on hand. But no longer. Let me know."

After she left, I sat quietly for a long time.

"Cass?" Grace asked. "You're starting to scare me. What's going on in your head?"

"Packing." I told her about the seed packets that had been

her grandmother's. "I guess I'll go get them. You should take them."

She shook her head. "Nope. In the same way that Gran knew what I needed to go forward, you are in so many ways like my *halmoni*. Take them to encourage you to do as you said. Plant a new life."

"Okay. I'll be back in a bit." I headed back to the greenhouse. I took the seed envelopes and tucked them into my purse, then grabbed a bag of dried peony petals from the shelf, got into my car, and headed to the cemetery to think.

I hadn't visited since we'd buried Gran. I hadn't been ready to. Now I drove up the drive and parked and then walked through the peaceful, shady grounds. Cognizant of whose seeds were in my purse, I walked toward the back of the cemetery first. I knew where to find it.

The large grave marker read *Chief James Roy, 1930–1958. Rest in Peace.*

Right next to it was a tiny marker with characters that I now knew spelled Mi-Ja, a beautiful child—her daughter. There were rose of Sharon blossoms on it, but where there would be dates for birth and death, a small box with spools of thread had been carved instead. I recognized the thread spools from the hope chest. What did they mean? Why had Grace's *halmoni* had those carved onto the headstone?

I walked to where my family rested. "Hey, Mom. I miss you. I'm having a good time cooking through your recipes. I'm adding to them too."

I turned toward Gran's grave. It was so new the grass hadn't completely grown over the wound inflicted on the land when the grave was dug. The edges were still dirt, but with time, like with Mom's and Gramps', the edges would blend seamlessly with the grass around it, healed. "Well, Gran, here you are. You said you wanted to be buried at Sunnyside so you'd always have a sunny disposition."

The wind caressed me; the view of Ebey's Landing in the distance soothed me. I prayed and thought at the same time, blending both in my head. The problem was, sometimes when I did that and an answer came, I didn't know if it was my voice or God's.

Maybe that was how it was supposed to be, wills and hearts folded together into one. I walked back and stood in front of the markers for my beloveds. "I'm sorry we can't keep our home," I whispered. "I will find a way to save our legacy, though."

What was next? And what to do with the one heirloom I hadn't sorted?

I pulled out the bag of dried peony petals and lifted a handful of them high into the air. When I released them, they whirled through the air and landed, like the prettiest pink confetti, on each of the graves.

Confetti meant a celebration. So what was next?

A party.

Helen

CHAPTER TWENTY

December 1958

"A job is a job." Helen snapped her bankbook closed—after having closed her eyes when confronted with the balance. She put on her beloved nurse's uniform, straightening her cap, buffing her pin. "And you need to find one if you want to keep your home." She retrieved a handkerchief from her top drawer, moving aside a linen bag of dried rosemary, lavender, and peony petals, and tucked it into her handbag before heading downstairs.

Eunhee munched on a piece of toast. "Oh, you look wonderful. I'm so glad that you're back to work again. How long will your shift be today?"

How to answer? "I'm not sure," Helen said. "Do you need anything from town?"

Eunhee shook her head. "No. I'll start packing things up while you are gone and make dinner for us. You are certain it is okay if the boxes remain here for a while?" She held her hand out toward where her things had been stored since she moved in. "I don't want to inconvenience you, but my room in Seattle is tiny. I may want you to keep a few other things here, too. That is, until I am ready to share them."

"Of course," Helen said. "Be back . . . later today." She'd considered wearing her uniform out of the house and then changing somewhere before seeking employment. Soon she'd tell Eunhee the truth, but she didn't want to burden her with the idea that she'd contributed to Helen's current difficulty. Besides, perhaps her experience and suitability would carry more weight if she showed up in uniform to apply for a new nursing position. Finding a job might be her first "test of faith," as Eunhee had called them.

Her first stop was at the Haskins Maternity Home in Oak Harbor, not far from the hospital where she'd worked. She'd heard of mothers who had gone there to give birth, the first "hospital" on the island. Rumors said that no mothers or babies had ever died under the watchful eye of the proprietress.

Before Eunhee and Mi-Ja, Helen would not have considered working as a mother-and-baby nurse, as that situation had always evoked sadness over her childlessness. But helping Eunhee and Mi-Ja allowed her to see how useful she could be to them and how she could come to love babies that were not her own, feeling a pang of desire for her own daughter still, without drowning in sorrow as she helped others.

Thank you, Mi-Ja. You have healed me of that.

Helen parked in the driveway of a small, neat house and walked smartly to the front door. She opened it into the reception room, which had been the hallway into a family home.

"Hello, may I help you?" The woman looked her up and down, noticing, no doubt, that Helen's slender build hid no baby. But also, perhaps, she noted Helen's uniform?

"I'm looking for Mother Haskins. My name is Mrs. Helen Devries, and I'm looking for a position as a nurse."

The older woman held out her hand. "I am Mother Haskins. Welcome."

She led Helen to a side room, an intake room of sorts, where the living room would have been if the house were still used as a family home.

"I am an RN," Helen said. "Lately, I'd been working as a civilian nurse at the Navy hospital." Mother Haskins nodded, and Helen continued. "I have experience delivering babies and caring for newborns, but also in all sorts of other kinds of medicine."

"But you desire to focus on helping mothers deliver babies, and that's why you're here."

Helen could lie and agree, but that would be a disservice to herself and this woman, as well as the mothers served here.

She steadied herself. "I enjoyed serving Naval personnel

and their dependents with a variety of medical needs, but . . . that position has been made permanently into a Navy position."

A long minute passed in silence. "Thank you for your honesty," Mother Haskins said. "In truth, even if it were your desire, there simply isn't enough work—or money—here to support two of us. I could offer you a job washing the linens or helping with the cooking, but it would not pay a nurse's salary or provide an opportunity for you to practice nursing."

Helen worked hard not to show her disappointment. "I understand."

"Have you tried any of the other maternity hospitals?" Mother Haskins asked.

She was no-nonsense but kind. Just the type of woman Helen might like to have in attendance if she were to deliver a baby. "No. You were my first."

Mother Haskins opened a squeaky desk drawer, removed a piece of paper, and then wrote for a minute. "You may want to try some of these, though I suspect you will find the same response at all of them." Suddenly she put down her pencil and said, "Well, there is also Goss Lake Home. They offer much more care than your typical maternity hospital will. The only other one on the island to do so. Down in Freeland." She glanced at the black stripe on Helen's cap. "Run by Doria Jones, who is also an RN." She looked Helen firmly in the eye. "She's sharp. She will check your credentials."

A slight blush crept up Helen's neck. Had she somehow given something away? If anyone were to call the hospital and ask for a review of the notes in her personnel file, she knew what Captain Adams would say about her.

Wailing came from upstairs. "I'm sorry. I must go attend to my patient." Mother Haskins handed over the paper upon which she'd put some names. "Good luck, Nurse."

"Thank you. I do appreciate this," Helen said.

She got back into her car. Undoubtedly one of the other maternity homes could use her services. She yearned for more diverse work, but Goss Lake Home was likely to check her references.

She drove all the way south to Langley, never thinking she'd go that far for work, but at least it was not off-island. Soon she pulled up in front of the maternity hospital of Mrs. J. J. Rigby. Mother Haskins had jotted, *Unwed mothers from Seattle often seek shelter and privacy here* on the note she'd given. The circumstances did not matter to Helen, but the place had the feel of despair and rejection. These women would have their children removed from them for adoption and be forbidden in polite society from ever mentioning their existence.

A different terrible secret so many mothers were asked to carry and hide.

When Helen spoke with Mrs. Rigby, she was given the same story anyway. There was no money to pay for a nurse, and the woman added that she was not interested in the competition Helen might present as an RN.

Helen had a bite of lunch at a diner and then got back into the Skylark. It was time to drive to Freeland. She turned on the radio to cheer her. First, Elvis came on singing about a hardheaded woman. Well, she could indeed be called that if it meant she was going to do the right thing. She didn't mind being a thorn in the side of Captain Adams.

He had likely forgotten about her by now anyway, happy in the security of his rank and position, knowing he could not be accused of wrongdoing, even when he did. And yet here she was. Needing a job.

Connie Francis came on next. *"Who's sorry now?"* she sang. Helen snapped off the radio. "Not me."

She pulled into the driveway of the address Mother Haskins had scribbled down. She had not been to Freeland often, but there was not much there, and therefore it was not too hard to find her destination. "'White Acres Convalescent Home,'" Helen read aloud.

The building was quite large, and it looked as if construction was underway to make it even bigger. Helen got out of the car, put her keys into her handbag, straightened her cap, and went in.

A receptionist greeted her. "Hello. Do you have an appointment?"

Helen shook her head. "No, I'm here to apply for a job with Mrs. Jones."

The receptionist smiled. "Is she expecting you?"

"No," Helen said. "I don't mind waiting."

The lady indicated an armchair where she could sit. Helen admired the professional, clean, and yet homey environment. On the wall was a newspaper clipping that had been matted and framed. Mrs. Jones had been named by the South Whidbey Business and Professional Women's Club as their "Woman of Achievement." A worthy employer, indeed. About thirty minutes later, a woman came to greet her. She, too, had an RN's cap on, her chestnut hair tucked neatly beneath it. She wore no-nonsense, black-framed glasses and wide-heeled shoes. Helen liked her immediately.

"Hello." She held her hand out to Helen. "Please, follow me to my office."

Once there, Mrs. Jones explained that she had set out, when she bought the facility just a few years earlier, to provide more complete medical care on the island. "I do believe, other than the Navy's medical facilities, ours is the only one offering anything beyond maternity or basic care."

Helen kept an impassive look at the mention of the Navy hospital.

"We care for the young and the old," Mrs. Jones continued, "and I have physician coverage available at all times for our patients."

Impressive!

"I'm adding on a sixteen-bed wing, which will have hoists and electronic call buttons. That wing will be ready sometime next year."

Helen explained that she had had excellent training and faced a wide range of medical conditions in her few months working as an RN. That she was looking for a full-time nursing job on Whidbey Island, and that she was a Navy widow.

"Where was your actual nursing experience?" Mrs. Jones asked.

"At the Navy hospital in Oak Harbor."

"But work at the Naval hospital is not to your taste?" she asked.

How to answer? *Honestly.* "It was very much to my taste, but unfortunately my supervisor was interested in, uh, extending our affiliation beyond work hours."

There. She'd said it, it was on the table, and Mrs. Jones could do with it what she liked.

"I'm sorry," she said. "That's rather more common than we wish it were. I assume I may be in touch with your academic advisers, were such a position to open."

"Oh yes," Helen said. "They would endorse me, personally and professionally, I am sure of it."

"Fine," Mrs. Jones said. "I appreciate your honesty, and I will be honest in return. I will not have room for another RN until my new ward is complete, in perhaps six months. Maybe longer."

Helen's heart sank, and it must have shown because Mrs. Jones rushed in to complete her thought. "I could offer a domestic position to you until then. Something to tide you over. You would work under our housekeeper."

Laundry and cooking. Well. She knew how to do both now. It would cover the bills for the time, and she could stay in her house and in her newly beloved garden.

"May I have some time to think about it?" Helen asked.

"It's a big decision, and I want to do the right thing for both of us."

"Of course. Please let me know within a week, as I will have to fill that housekeeping position if it's not suitable for you," Mrs. Jones said. Helen thanked her for her time and then went to her car.

On the drive home, she prayed but still felt no peace. Instead, she felt grief. She was so thankful for the possibility of any job, especially one that could lead to an RN position in time. It was just that she'd felt her calling, her nurse's purpose, was with the military. She had been a proud military wife and had enjoyed serving Navy families. She was proud to help every sailor and their children. It had felt like, well, home.

Perhaps that had all been about being prepared to care for Eunhee. Wouldn't that make sense?

No, if that were the case, she'd have been working in a maternity hospital.

She shook her head. She could make no sense of the matter, but she had a job offer, and that was enough. She would choose to be happy. It might be nice to work for a woman, in an environment where she didn't have to worry about unwelcome propositions.

It would allow Helen to remain in her own home, on her land, and cultivate it so that she might perhaps hand it down to her children and their children someday. What had Eunhee said? *"I do not worship my ancestors, but I am grateful to them for the sacrifices they made for me. I will sacrifice for my family too."*

After parking the car, she headed toward the house, cold rain spattering her jacket and shoes. She kicked them off at the mud porch.

"You are home!" Eunhee said. "How was your day at work?"

"Satisfying," Helen said truthfully. She'd tell Eunhee the truth about her employment as soon as she'd accepted Mrs. Jones's offer.

"Look." Eunhee held a wrapped gift out. "I bought something for you in Seattle, last time I was there talking with the family I will live with."

Helen took the thin, square package in her hands. "What is it?"

"Open it, and you will find out!"

Helen unwrapped the ribbon and neatly slit the tape with one of her fingernails. She'd have preferred to rip the paper right off but wanted to show care to Eunhee's wrapping. She lifted out a record and turned it over. "It's an album, with some of our favorites on it!" Helen said.

Eunhee tapped her finger on one song. "See? It's the one you always say you like. Look out over your garden. Even though it sleeps, it is clean and ready to be bigger next year and bigger the year after. This land is your land. And now, because of James and you and the new friends I have in Seattle, this land is my land, too."

It was true. The house and the garden were hers. This was

well and truly her land. Now she had a job, and she could keep it. "I'll put it right between Elvis and Connie Stevens," Helen said. "After we listen to it."

"So you will think of me even when I'm in Seattle. I will come over to visit you next year, and we will cook together. You will make seaweed soup," she said with a grin, "and I will make Tutti-Frutti Bars." She shivered with pretend revulsion. She liked nothing but sliced fruit for dessert.

"That sounds wonderful," Helen said. "Only I will miss you in between." She stepped into the kitchen and tied on her blue apron before making a salad. She'd cut out a recipe for 7-Up Pound Cake she could make in her Bundt pan. Maybe she'd try that tonight too.

The phone rang, but she did not pay much attention to it. It rang again. And again.

"Aren't you going to answer?" Eunhee asked. "It's your code."

"Oh! So it is." Helen walked over and picked up the receiver. "Hello? This is Helen Devries."

"This is Dirk Beeksma," came a boy's voice, breaking with panic and puberty. "Aren't you the nurse?"

"Yes," she said.

"Come quickly! It's my pawpaw!"

Helen grabbed her keys and her handbag once more and hopped into the car. It was a quick trip to the chicken man's farm. As she pulled up the long drive, she saw Dirk waving his hands to and fro in front of the barn.

"He's in here, miss," he cried out.

Helen shut off the car and headed into the barn. The light was on, and she took stock of the area. A tall ladder was akimbo on the ground, and next to it lay Mr. Beeksma, moaning like his chickens. She raced over.

"My leg." His voice was weak with pain.

She carefully lifted his left pant leg from the cuff upward, but she knew by the angle that the leg was broken even before it was exposed. Once the fabric was off, she saw the bone sticking out of his calf. Blood trickled but did not spill freely onto the hay. Good. No artery was involved, then.

"Dirk." She nodded toward a stack of wood slats for fencing stacked nearby. "Bring three of those to me. Then go into the kitchen and bring out some rags. Is anyone else home?"

Dirk shook his head. "My pa went to Mount Vernon, and he's not home yet."

Helen nodded, and Dirk flew into the house.

"The ladder board broke," Mr. Beeksma said. "More fool I for not checking before I got on it. My eyes," he said.

"Your eyes hurt?"

"No, just can't see as well as I need to. My ribs . . . I think a few are broken. Had that before, so I know. Can't breathe too well."

"Don't talk any longer, then," Helen said. "I'll get your leg set and then take you to the hospital in Oak Harbor. Former Navy, right?"

He nodded. "World War I."

Dirk ran out with the rags, and Helen placed them all around the wound so the leg would be cushioned when she put on the splints. She removed her apron and tore it into pieces. "You hold this board," she told Dirk, "while I start to tie around it."

"Are they going to have to cut off his leg?" Dirk asked.

Old Mr. Beeksma's eyes twinkled through his pain. "Might be, son, might be. Then I'd be a peg-legged sailor."

"Oh no!" Dirk cried.

"Now there," Helen reassured, "sometimes limbs must be cut off when it's necessary to save the body. But that is not the case here."

She made a donut-like shape around the open wound with the fabric to keep the broken end of the bone in place and then covered it to prevent further infection and movement. After using two boards—one on the inner portion of the leg and one on the outer—she tied it in four places, making a figure eight around the foot and ankle on either side of the break. After that, she wrapped her apron around the wound as it was cleaner than the rags.

To his credit, old Mr. Beeksma made very little noise while she wrapped him, just allowing the occasional groan to escape. His breathing was ragged and quick, though, and she knew she needed to get him to the hospital soon. "Can you help me with your pawpaw?"

"Yes, miss," Dirk said.

"Go grab the wheelbarrow."

Dirk ran for it, and when he'd returned with it, they rested the older man inside and then wheeled him to the car, where they gently set him on the passenger bench. Helen pushed the pedal and screamed up the street to get the old man to Oak Harbor.

Once they arrived, she flashed her expired credentials to save time and pulled up right in front. "We're going to brace him again," she told Dirk.

Once they got in the door, she signaled to a corpsman she knew. "Can we get a wheelchair? And can someone take this young man to the break room until his father can come and get him?" She turned to Dirk. "Tell this nice man how to reach your father by phone and then wait where he tells you until your pa or I come to get you."

"I will." His lip trembled. "Is PawPaw going to die?"

Helen ruffled his hair. "Nope. He'll be good as new in a few months. Maybe better."

He grinned and followed the young corpsman to the break room.

Helen waited until a doctor came to collect Mr. Beeksma and then briefed him on the situation. "Can you help me?" he asked. "Everyone else is occupied with patients."

"Certainly." Helen did not recognize the doctor but read his rank. Captain.

They gave Mr. Beeksma an injection to help with the pain and began to prepare him for surgery. After seeing him adequately cared for, Helen said, "I need to check and see that his grandson was taken care of."

The doctor looked up, bewildered. "Yes, please do so. Stop by my office before you leave for the evening." He pointed down the hall, to Captain Adams's office.

Was he sharing the office? Filling in?

When Helen arrived in the break room, she found Dirk putting on his jacket. "My pa is here," he said. "Is PawPaw okay?"

Helen smiled. "Yes. I'll show you to his room on the way out so that you can see for yourself."

As they walked down the hall, Dirk's father said, "Thank you for coming to take care of my father."

"I'm glad your son was smart enough to call for help!" Helen answered.

"Dad has a chart with everyone's ring code on it," he said. "Right next to the phone."

I'll bet he does, Helen thought.

"Yours says *Nurse,* so Dirk knew who to call."

She stopped outside the room where Mr. Beeksma was comfortably resting. "Here you go. He'll remain here as long as necessary to ensure he's well on the path to recovery. They'll call you when it's time to come and collect him. Keep him off the ladders."

"Will do, ma'am."

She left them and then shook her head in both amusement and sorrow. She was speaking as if she worked here still.

Helen sat in the coffee room, which had been decorated for Christmas, pouring a cup to wake a bit before looking for the doctor who had asked her to stop by his office. She took a sip and then closed her eyes.

"Mind if I sit here?"

Helen bolted up. Bad memories rose in her cloudy mind.

But when she opened her eyes, it was not Captain Adams. Instead, he was tall and perhaps five years older than Helen. His brown eyes crinkled as he smiled and took off his cap. "Name is Ben Cassidy. Nice to meet you."

"Helen Devries. Nice to meet you." Helen worked to keep her voice steady and professional though her heart pounded like a schoolgirl's.

He didn't break his gaze, either, and a slight blush colored his lightly bronzed face.

Their conversation blossomed from a polite discourse between strangers to laughing at military humor and young enlistee shenanigans. They talked about their lives, discussing movies they both loved and sharing their love of music. Ben was a widower, and his wife had died from diabetes before they could have children. He spoke of her with affection and respect, but it was clear that he was at peace about it now, as Helen was with Bob's passing. Ben's parents owned an apple orchard in eastern Washington, which was why he'd requested to be posted to Whidbey Island, to be near them, a request that had been accepted.

"Oh, my!" Helen looked at her watch and realized an hour had passed. "I need to stop by and check in with the doctor."

Ben stood and pulled back her chair. The moment hung awkwardly, as it seemed neither of them wanted to bring their time to a conclusion. "Do you like to dance?" Ben asked.

"I love to dance, but I haven't for quite a while," Helen answered.

"I'd like to change that if you'd be willing to give me a try."

"I'd love that." She told him her phone code. "It's a party line, so others are listening."

"I don't much care if they listen to me arrange to take a strong, pretty nurse to a dance," he said. "Might make me call twice."

Helen grinned as he headed back to duty. She got up and walked down the hall, peeking into the offices that still had their lights on. When she reached Captain Adams's office, she stopped.

A new captain sat at the desk. "Sir?" she called into the office.

"Come in," he said. He did not encourage her to close the door as Captain Adams would have. "Have a seat." He indicated the chair across from his desk. "Do you work here? I have not seen you before, but people seem to recognize you, and you're wearing a nurse's uniform."

She hadn't changed after her job search earlier that day, which seemed like weeks ago. "I used to work here, sir. Under Captain Adams. Is he . . . away?" She looked around the room. The decor seemed different.

"Captain Adams was . . ." The man struggled for a word. "Reassigned."

"Reassigned? I had no idea," Helen said. "Was this antici-pated?"

"He was reassigned," the man said, clearly unwilling to divulge more. "About a month ago." His eyebrows rose in an unasked question.

"I worked under him," she said. "Until September."

"That's why I haven't met you. Are you a Navy wife? Leaving for deployment with your husband?"

Helen inhaled. "I am—was a Navy wife, sir. My husband was Lieutenant Robert Devries, a pilot who died in a training accident a few years ago. I am very proud of my husband, but I no longer identify myself merely as someone's wife. I am a nurse. After Bob died, I returned to school and earned an RN. I very much enjoyed working here. Patient care was my highest priority."

His face looked puzzled. "Then why did you leave your position?"

This was her golden chance. Say it all! "I needed a month's leave of absence to care for another Navy widow and her newborn. The leave was offered to me at one time, but when I didn't . . . comply . . . with further personal, non-duty related requests outside the scope of my position, Captain Adams made it clear that I was to either choose my job or caring for a recent widow with no family."

He didn't look shocked. Had Captain Adams's philandering had something to do with his reassignment? Perhaps he had propositioned a woman with a husband or a girl with a father, someone who could come to her side.

"You didn't consider it a dereliction of duty to ask for leave?"

"No, sir. Not when that leave had been offered first." *Ask and it shall be given to you.*

She dove in again. "It was my understanding that my

position was to be designated Navy. If it hasn't, and you still need a nurse, would you consider rehiring me? I will serve with professionalism and compassion. When I became a nurse, I took a pledge to 'devote myself to the welfare of those committed to my care,' and I intend to continue doing that, here or elsewhere. Preferably here."

He held her gaze. "I am impressed with your work this evening. But as you are aware, it's a complicated situation. There is a nurse's position that was to be reassigned—it must have been yours—but I have been putting out fires and have not got around to doing that so far. I'm not sure I can pull the paperwork on it, how far it's gone."

Helen nodded, afraid to hope.

"I could look into it. I will need to review your person-nel file," the captain said. "I will certainly speak with those who worked with you and with your nursing supervisor at school."

What had Captain Adams written in her file? Were there enough corpsmen and nurses who still worked here who held a good opinion of Helen's work? "I understand, sir."

He stood. "I'll be in touch as the situation warrants."

She nodded. "Thank you, sir."

It was late when she got home. Eunhee was already in bed. Helen went up to her room, opened her purse, and took out Mrs. Jones's phone number. She'd need to let her know within a week.

CHAPTER TWENTY-ONE

Six days later, Eunhee called out to Helen. "Let me help you plant that last peony before we leave."

"Oh, please don't worry about that," Helen said. "I can do that without you. It's just the one."

"For old time's sake," Eunhee insisted.

"Okay." Helen put her trousers on, slipped her loafers on, and walked to the potting shed, where she grabbed the spade. Eunhee, strength fully restored, lugged the potted peony from the side of the greenhouse. Together, they went to the back of the garden, where most of the peonies had been cut back for the winter, perhaps for the first time in years.

Eunhee laughed and lifted the plant out of the pot. When

she did, the plant's name tag fell out. "Oh, look, this one with the beautiful raspberry blossoms is called Big Ben."

Big Ben, eh? Helen looked heavenward. *You do have a sense of humor.* "I'll put him right next to Better Times," she said, indicating her favorite peony bush. "Because I suspect they are just ahead." Once the plant was nestled in the ground, they went into the house and changed.

Their work done, they stood and looked at the sleeping garden, arm in arm. "Your kindness to me will never be forgotten. I do not know where I would be without you," Eunhee said.

Helen hugged her. "You are not just my dearest friend, but your steadfast faith led me to my own. I do not know where I would be without *you*. You brought joy back into my life and gave me hope, something that never comes easily to me. Let's just forget all about this crazy Seattle plan, and you can stay here with me."

Eunhee said nothing. They both knew that could not be.

An hour later, Eunhee came into the kitchen with her suitcase and a couple of envelopes. Helen recognized them. They were the letters from Eunhee's mother. "Will you also keep these for me?" She held them out to Helen.

"You're not taking them with you?"

Eunhee shook her head. "Not now. When the day comes that I retrieve the *hanbok* and spools of thread, I will take these with me too."

When the secret could be made known. "Of course. There will be a right time to share these." Helen reached out and took Eunhee's mother's letters, which had been neatly taped shut. Helen understood. She couldn't bring herself to throw away her mother's letter, either—nor the beautiful bone china set in the white box, an heirloom bequeathed by her grandmother and stained not by tea but rejection. Like Eunhee, she needed to move on.

After packing the few things Eunhee had yet to take to her new home, they got into the Skylark and headed toward the big city.

"You'll come back often," Helen said. "Right?"

"Of course," Eunhee said. "I'm a bit nervous about my job. It may be some time until I have days off. Will you pray for me?"

"I will pray for you, and because of you, I know how to pray and to whom."

Once in Federal Way, a city near Seattle where Eunhee's new hosts lived, Helen waved goodbye and got back into the car. Yes, she was sad. Yes, Eunhee was sad. But they were both former Navy wives and understood that time apart almost always made reunions more joyous.

They were friends forever.

Helen returned home, arriving just before noon, driving cautiously up her driveway. Why were the kitchen lights on? She had not left them on, she was sure.

She got out of the car and closed the door behind her, walking slowly toward the house. When she approached the kitchen, she looked in the window. *Johanna?*

After kicking off her shoes in the mud porch, she burst through the door. "Johanna. Is everything okay?"

Johanna turned toward her. "Yes. I knew you were taking Eunhee to Federal Way today and thought maybe you'd like to make Cinn Rolls when you returned."

Helen smiled. *She knew I'd be a bit lonely.* "I would love it. Let me put my apron on and get a recipe card so I can write down your instructions." She clicked the light on in the under-stairs pantry and took a new peach apron from the hook. Eunhee's cream, ruby, and pink apron still hung there, waiting for her next visit. A pang of loneliness passed through Helen, and then she opened her cookbook and withdrew a fresh card from the envelope in which she kept recipe cards.

Pencil in hand, she rejoined Johanna in the kitchen. "I'll stand right at your elbow," she said, "and learn properly."

They spent the next hours activating the yeast, mixing flour, and rolling dough. "These cinnamon rolls are moist, not dry as you often see in commercial bakeries," Johanna said. "The secret is a moist dough. Keep plenty of flour handy to be able to roll out the dough."

"Yes, ma'am," Helen said.

"Next, pour the melted butter over the rolled-out dough, spreading to cover evenly. Sprinkle lots of brown sugar over the dough and butter. Be liberal with the cinnamon for a good taste."

Be liberal with the cinnamon for a good taste, Helen jotted onto her card. "Can we add even a bit more cinnamon?"

"Yes," Johanna said. "Make them taste as you would like them." She showed her how to cut and roll them, and then they placed the pan of rolls in a warm area to rise. "You can add walnuts or raisins to them," she said, "to give them the 'taste of your hands.'" She smiled at Eunhee's lesson about *son-mat*. "Just never add—"

"Frosting!" Helen declared. "I promise. How about chopped apples?"

"Maybe . . . ," Johanna said.

"Come with me for a moment while they rise," Helen said. They slipped on their shoes from the back porch, and Helen led the way into the orchard. Although it was the end of December, the day was temperate, as much of Whidbey Island lolled in the rain shadow of western Washington. Helen stood in front of the small arc of apple trees. "I have seven apple trees," she said. "Planted before I owned the farm and house, of course. I've always been a big quote collector and love the one that said, 'A person plants a tree not for himself, but another generation.' Someone planted these trees, and I will benefit from them. I will pass this down to my children and their children and hopefully generations after that."

"True," Johanna said. She walked up next to one of the trees. "What is . . . ?" She turned toward Helen.

"Take a look at all of the trees," Helen told her.

She watched as Johanna looked at the wooden plaque hanging on every tree. Then she returned to Helen, who sat on the bench swing.

"Those are my sons' names," Johanna said, her voice bright with incredulity.

"I named every tree for one of your sons," Helen responded. "They will continue to bear good fruit year after year, decade after decade. It is something of me that I can give to you and your wonderful boys. Something everbearing."

Johanna leaned over and, though not a woman given to demonstration, hugged Helen. Then she returned to her no-nonsense ways. "I think the apples would do better in pies than in Cinn Rolls."

Helen laughed and agreed.

Later that afternoon, after Helen had eaten two Cinn Rolls, the phone rang.

She listened carefully, as she'd done all week, to the ring code. Yes! Two long, three short. She lifted the receiver. "This is Helen Devries."

"Hello. Captain Martinez. We spoke last week after setting your neighbor's broken bone?"

"Yes, yes, Captain." She held her breath.

"I was able to intercept the paperwork that would turn that nursing position into a permanent Navy post. You have all the qualities I wish to see on my nursing staff. The civilian nursing job is yours if you want it."

"Yes, yes, I most certainly want it. When do I start?"

"Next Monday," he said. "Please come to my office, and we will start the paperwork. I will see you then." He hung up the line.

But not everyone did. Cheers broke out, and hoots and whistles along with sentiments of congratulations.

"Thank you all!" Helen said.

She finally set the receiver down and looked out the window. "Thank you, Lord." One by one, a flock of Brewer blackbirds in midnight-blue cloaks alighted on the phone wire and cawed their applause while the nearby sparrows sang praise.

Cassidy

CHAPTER TWENTY-TWO

Where would the birds go when the property and plants were destroyed?

Annika and I spread petals over the greenhouse boards as I watched DJ fill the bird feeders. "Ready for school?" I hoped I'd injected cheerfulness into my voice.

"Yes. I enrolled in all my classes. A little nervous. Hey, do you think you might need help after I leave? I have a friend who loves flowers and gardening. She was so jealous when I told her where I worked."

"I would like to hire her, but I can't."

She took her fidget cube out of her pocket and twisted it for a minute before answering. "She's not afraid of bees."

I couldn't let her think that she'd done anything wrong. "Annika, I am extremely impressed at your courage to come back after last year. Your ingenuity in bringing gloves. Your amazing talent with photography. You are so gifted, and I'm going to be excited when you're famous, to say I knew you back when. I'm not thinking about bees anymore."

"So then what's the problem?" She scooped dried petals from another shelf into a small bag.

"I'm not saying anything publicly yet, but there won't be a next year. There were some financial issues, and I'm going to have to sell the property to a developer."

She looked out over the acres where the evergreens had once stood. "Is that why you cut down the trees?"

"Yeah," I said. "Kinda."

"I'm sorry," she said. Then she froze. "What about the Mickey apple tree?"

"It's too big to transplant. We'll take all the apples off it and bring big bushels to everyone in your family. We'll take some cuttings and graft them so we can both grow them wherever we end up."

"Okay," she said. "I don't want it to die out."

"Me neither."

"So what's next?" she asked.

"A party. A huge dinner party Labor Day evening. We're going to invite everyone and have a huge feast and celebration." I'd already decided that I could use a chunk of the money in the account that was paying the home equity loan for the party because soon there would be no need for

those funds. I'd have money to live on from the house's proceeds until I decided where I wanted to go next. Somewhere
close—smaller but close. Whidbey was home.

"That sounds fun!" she said. "Am I invited?"

"Of course you're invited. You are invited, and your
family and the group you and DJ meet with and his family
and everyone who brought plant starts or who knew Gran
and me. Grace is bringing her new boyfriend and a friend
from her new job. I'm going to send out an email to the
Flowery Language mailing list and invite anyone on it who
might want to come. Plus, text and call friends." I was sure
everyone would come.

Well, almost everyone.

"Cool!" Annika said. "Are you going to make the White
Picket Picnic foods?"

I shook my head. "No. I'll make the desserts ahead of
time—the hand pies maybe, with the berries and apples
from the garden. A guy who has a barbecue business in
Oak Harbor will come and smoke meats for everyone, so
I don't have to worry about that part. It'll then be a community potluck so everyone can bring something of him-
or herself and share. Nick's invited a disc jockey he knows
so we can enjoy that during dinner and maybe dancing
afterward."

She looked sad. I felt sad. "Hey—would you do me a
favor?" I asked.

"Sure."

"I want an official photographer. Pictures of everything,

all the tables, dancing, the property from every angle. Would you be willing to take those? I'll pay you for them, for sure."

"I'll do it. But for free, as a gift from me to you."

"Thank you!" I spent the rest of the day sorting seeds to take with me when I moved. I'd take starts from the plants after the party—maybe I'd make them available to others, just like they had sown them into my life. In the email announcing the farm's sale, after the party, I'd let people know what they could take after I'd removed what I needed. That way, my garden would continue to grow, with Gran's hands, too, after we were gone.

I sat in the middle of the garden, at the picnic table, and drank iced tea. I looked at my phone. *Call, Cassidy. Just call.*

As I was about to dial, Annika came and sat next to me, then pulled out her phone. She'd hung my Hello, Sunshine, hat on a row of the dahlias. "I thought maybe you'd want to use this when you send out your party invitation?"

"Perfect!" She texted it to me, and I got on a graphic image app and made it into an invitation. I emailed it from the business account and texted it to friends.

Within minutes, I got positive RSVPs. The first to say yes was Mrs. Kim, Grace's mother.

The whole family would love to come, she texted.

I'm so glad. I would love to give you some bellflower roots and I'll dig up some perilla for you. It'll self-sow next year. Would that be okay? A bit of my garden and life sown into hers.

Yes. Perhaps I could come next week for a visit, and bring lunch for you, Grace, and me?

Of course!

I looked over the peony field—a few blossoms, more leaves. I wished my mom were here to join us. To pick flowers with me. I at least felt her here. Would I feel her in the same way at the new place?

I went into the house, up to the attic, and continued packing. Gran's old nurse's uniform hung in a corner. I saluted the uniform, as I would the woman, and then took it down, folded it carefully. Then I sat down. I'd put it off long enough. I was going to reach out—again. I texted my dad.

Hey, Dad. It's Cassidy.

After sending it, I turned back to packing, not expecting to hear from him quickly, if at all.

Shockingly, my phone buzzed within minutes.

Hi, Cassidy. It's Dad. ☺ I know how to use the smiley faces now.

That was cheerful. I should just ask him if I could call. I should just call. No. I didn't really want to hear him say no in person. Better on a text.

So I'm selling the house and the land.

What? Why?

Lots of reasons and I can get into it later. But what I really wanted to ask is would you and Mary Alice like to come to a party I'm having on Labor Day evening? It'll be a huge send-off, my last big shindig on the property. I'd really like to have you here.

He didn't answer for a bit. Maybe he was asking her?

Please don't say no.

My phone buzzed. **Let me talk with Mary Alice,** Dad texted. **I'll let you know. I**

I?

Sorry, I hit Send too soon. I would like to see you. I miss you. Tears caught in my throat. **Me too, Dad.**

I didn't, however, believe that Mary Alice would let them fly out.

* * *

After Nick and I ate a beach picnic that night, we walked on the beach and started a fire, then snuggled on a wool blanket I'd brought and draped across the sand. He scooped up some sand in a shell and let it drop slowly to the ground. "If this were an hourglass, I'd be wishing for the days and weeks we let slip away when we broke up."

"There's a lot of sand out there that hasn't yet been counted."

"Let's count it together." He opened my palm and then stroked his thumb across it, and as he did, nerves tingled and twitched to every point of my being. Then he poured sand into my hand before closing his hand around mine. "Lots of days. Weeks. Years."

He pulled me closer. "You doing okay with all of this? The party? Moving?"

"Not really, but I will be." I told him about Grace's grandmother's seed packets and how she'd written, *To plant next year and all the years after. I will make my new home my true home.* "She wrote it in English," I said. "Not Korean. As if to underscore that she was here now and was going to make it work. I will too."

"So you're willing to try a new terroir? Pack your seeds and transplant?"

I nodded. "I'm ready to move."

He folded his hand over mine. "I'm proud of you."

* * *

Mrs. Kim started pulling things out of bags. First, three aprons. "Here. Put these on." She handed one to me and one to Grace and then tied one around herself.

"Oh, are we cooking?" Why else would she have us put on aprons?

She gave me a long-suffering look, as a mother would to a child. "Yes, of course."

Next, she pulled a crock of *kimchi* out of the bag. I loved her *kimchi*, the perfect blend of crunch, umami, heat, sweetness, and tang. "I do not have time to show you how to make this today. Perhaps you would like to set aside a day this fall for a *kimjang*?"

"I don't know what that is, but I'm sure I'd love it." I placed the jar into the refrigerator.

"It's a day when the women of a family get together to make *kimchi* and gossip." She smiled. "I would like for you and Grace to be there together. I can show you both how to make *kimchi*."

"I would like that, Umma," Grace said.

"I would, too!" Mrs. Kim opened another reusable shopping bag. "First, we put the meat in the freezer." Mrs. Kim gathered us to the island to watch as she made the marinade. "*Bulgogi* is a good cut of meat, so you want the marinade to enhance the flavor, but not overwhelm it. I mix a little *gochujang*—red pepper paste—with some brown sugar, sesame oil, minced garlic, ginger paste, and soy. Like this." She whisked it all together. "I don't put pear in mine because if you use good quality meat, the acids from the pear are not needed to tenderize it. Mrs. Kim always included pear but . . ." She shrugged.

"Taste of your hands," I said.

"Exactly."

"I wonder what would happen if you put cola in there?" I grinned at Grace.

Mrs. Kim dropped her wooden spoon. "Never!" She went to the freezer to take out the meat. "When it's almost frozen, you can slice it nice and thin. Then, when it's time to cook the meat, you can put it into the skillet for just a few minutes, and it will be done but not tough."

She deftly sliced the meat and then handed a knife to Grace and me, along with a piece of rib eye each.

We sliced our chunks of meat with varying levels of skill. I had a big piece at the end, and Mrs. Kim took the knife from me and showed me how to shape it into a thin strip. "See? Just like this."

I tried it myself. And got it! She was right in between

Grace and me. Grace to her left, me to her right. She was teaching both of us to cook at her elbows. "Thank you for including me," I said. "I've always loved *bulgogi*."

"You are most welcome." She drew us each close for a moment, one to either side. Two daughters, one mother. My mom would have approved. Mrs. Kim showed us how to place the meat into glass containers with the marinade. "Let this sit for a few hours, and then tonight, quickly stir-fry it, serve over rice with sesame seeds and chives."

She showed me how to quick-pickle the radish, chopped into chunks. "It will be ready in a few hours, and if you serve it on the side, the vinegar will bring out the best taste in the *bulgogi*. Now, for lunch."

She opened the third bag. She'd brought some fresh fruit and a salad made of *japchae*, glass noodles made from sweet potatoes, vegetables, and an Asian-inspired vinaigrette.

"Should we sit outside?" Although I'd had no idea we'd be cooking together, I yearned for our afternoon together to go on. Even grown women, it seemed, needed mother love. I thought about Gran and knew she'd yearned for that, too, but wouldn't risk reaching out again.

"Yes, certainly," Mrs. Kim said. We went out to the picnic table. I brought napkins and napkin holders and quickly snipped off three small branches from the rose of Sharon and slipped them into the holders with the napkins.

"This is beautiful," Mrs. Kim said.

"The meaning of rose of Sharon is perseverance," I said.

She set down the plates of *japchae*. "Necessary for success."

She maneuvered her noodles with the chopsticks. I savored the slippery noodles, bathed in vinegar.

Grace didn't eat. I looked at her, noticing, and Mrs. Kim looked up, too. "What is the matter, Grace? Don't you feel well?"

Grace grinned. "I feel wonderful. Umma—I have something to tell you. First—I took the bar exam last February, but I did not pass."

Her mother nodded. "Yes, I know."

Grace let her chopsticks slide between her fingers and clatter, akimbo, in her salad. "You knew?"

"Yes, of course." Her mother took another bite. "One day I went to get the mail and there was an envelope from the Washington State Bar Association registration in there. I left it in the mailbox for you to find."

Grace's mouth opened and she shut it again before opening it once more to speak. "I did get that and then changed all notification to electronic only. But I can't believe that you . . ." She stopped herself.

"Didn't open your mail?" Her mother smiled. "I have not taken the bar exam, but I can do difficult things."

We all laughed.

"But how did you know I didn't pass?" Grace asked.

Her mother took a bite and then answered. "The information about who passed the exam is published. When your name did not appear on there, I knew you did not pass. I had to look hard to find the publications."

"Does . . . does Appa know?"

Her mother shook her head. "No, he does not know."

"Would he be mad?"

"I don't know. But you might be surprised. Sometimes opening a secret to sunlight—" she glanced at the bright sky—"brings freedom and joy."

Grace took a drink of her tea. "I retook the test and passed this time. I just learned this morning." Her face brightened with pleasure and pride.

I stood up and clapped. "I knew you could do it!"

Her mother's face broke out in a big smile. "Grace. That is wonderful. Congratulations!" She handed the rose of Sharon stem to her, and I held out mine, too.

"Perseverance," I said. "Does . . . ?" I almost said, *Does Justin know?*

Her mother's hair was tucked behind her ears in her usual style. Her ears perked.

"Does anyone want more iced tea?" I asked. I poured some for Grace and me. Mrs. Kim did not prefer to eat and drink at the same time.

"Will your boss be pleased?" her mother asked.

"My new boss will be. I've taken a position with another firm. I'll be much happier there. I'll tell you and Appa all about it soon. You'd told Cassidy to take her life and add *son-mat*, the taste of her own hands. I hope it is okay if I do the same thing."

Her mother pulled her close for just a moment. "Of course it is. When I was telling that to Cassidy, I already knew you had not passed the first time. I knew you'd be listening in and understand that if I was telling her it was okay, I was telling you it was okay, too."

Joy blossomed on my friend's face.

Later that evening, while I was packing papers from the filing cabinet, my phone rang from where I'd set it on the old phone table. It was Grace's ringtone. "Hey, what's up?"

"So I just told my parents about my new job. I decided to tell them about Mi-Ja and Down syndrome and why I was motivated to move in this professional direction. I'd just concluded that I would not be able to represent folks with disabilities and their family members with integrity if it seemed like my own family had to hide this like it was something shameful. It's not shameful, and though I understand why she hid it, I want them all to know my *halmoni* for the strong woman she was—her whole life, in truth. And to know of Mi-Ja. That is the legacy I will carry forward. No more shame. I mean, after my mom knew about the bar exam and then all her talk about opening secrets to sunlight, I thought maybe she knew about Mi-Ja. My grandfather did. So I brought it up."

My heart fluttered. "Had your parents known?"

"Nope. Neither of them," she said. "They were shocked."

"Did you tell them your grandfather knew?"

"I did. I'm not sure that made my dad happy, either. He got on the phone with my grandfather, and they had a rapid conversation in Korean. I couldn't follow it all because he was in another room."

"You going to be okay?" I asked. "Can I help?"

"I am going to be okay. I don't regret my decision nor my career path or calling. I feel at peace about it, as far as my *halmoni* is concerned. It's what I am choosing to do with her legacy, and I am proud of the choices I've made. However . . . things are still in an uproar here," Grace said. "My dad wants to visit the room where my *halmoni* stayed before the house is bulldozed. Can we visit?"

"Anytime," I said. "Is . . . is he mad at me? At Gran? For keeping this secret?"

There was a long silence. "I don't know. Appa doesn't really share his emotions easily. Plus, well, it took me a little while to process all of this. So I have to cut him a break. It's startling news."

"That's true." How would I feel if I'd just learned my mom had another baby before she'd had me—and that she'd been married before she married my dad but had not told anyone? Surprised. Shocked! I'd definitely have to process it. "When should they come?"

"It's a big ask, I know, but it's hard for my grandfather to get out and about anymore. He wants to come to the party on Labor Day. Could we all just come a bit early?"

Oh. Hmm. What if Mr. Kim was upset before the party? I mean, he had a right to be. But I just wanted the party to be a happy sign-off with no surprises.

"Having my grandfather there will help," Grace reassured softly. Her grandpa had said he'd have Grace's back. He'd have mine, too.

"Of course."

* * *

The rental company had come the night before and set up all the tables and clipped tablecloths to them so they would not blow away. Still, their white corners fluttering in the gentle breeze looked like dove's wings straining to take flight. I'd placed vases, anchored with heavy stones, in the center of each table and arranged flowers in each one. We'd moved the picnic table into the center of the greenhouse and cleared the shelves so they could work as serving areas, places for everyone to set their offerings to share. Grace had arranged canning jars with solar rice lights inside each and put them on the tables. When the sun set, the lights would flicker like fireflies. The smoker belched and the barbecue crew flipped and basted brisket and ribs.

It was go time.

Also, it was "no" time.

I'd never heard back from my father. It was okay. I'd tried. For the moment, I'd help Grace and her father come to peace with one another and their family situation, and then, as far as things went with my dad, I'd do what Gran couldn't do with her parents. Her motto had been *move on*. Mine was, perhaps, *move forward*. Hers was *contain the pain*, and after all the pain she'd suffered, I understood. Like Grace's *halaboji* had said about his wife, I would have seen to it that she never suffered loss again if I could. Because of her lifelong unconditional love, I had the heart space to keep an open door and hope to mend things in a way she hadn't been able.

Mr. Kim's SUV pulled up the driveway two hours before the first guests were to arrive. Grace's parents helped her grandpa out of the car and into a wheelchair. He looked so frail. He must have been, what? Ninety? Plus, I knew men didn't do as well being widowed as women. I was so thankful that he'd lived long enough to tell Grace the truth, that he'd known about Mi-Ja and supported Grace.

Mr. Kim pushed the wheelchair up the drive, his wife and daughter following them. I met them at the door and bowed, first to the elder Dr. Kim, then to his son, then to Mrs. Kim. They bowed politely in return.

"No need to take off your shoes," I teased Grace's grandpa as I looked at the wheelchair. He smiled.

"Let me show you where your mother stayed," I said to Grace's dad. "I mean, I know you've been here before, but let me show you her room."

I headed into the teal bedroom. "This room is mostly how it was when Mrs. Kim lived here. I didn't know either that she'd lived here until recently. But now I understand so much more." Like why Gran had kept that sewing machine when no one in our family sewed.

I made way for Mr. Kim to wheel his father into the room. "This was her bed, and I brought down the bassinet that—" I looked at Grace's dad—"your sister may have slept in. It's been in our family for a long while. My mother and then I slept in it."

He blinked fast. I knew from my own grandpa that men of a certain age liked to remain stoic. My gramps, the military man, had not shown easy emotion except to my gran, my mom, and me. Even then, not in the company of others.

I rushed on. "I know your mother was a wonderful seamstress, and this is the machine she sewed at. She probably made the *hanbok* here."

Grace's dad winced. After a moment, he said, "May I see this *hanbok*?"

I went to the attic, fetched it and the box of threads, and brought them back down. "Here."

He took the *hanbok* in his hand like it was an actual baby, awkwardly but with tenderness. He stared at it, blinked rapidly again, and handed it to his wife.

"Her needlework is so beautiful," Mrs. Kim said. Grace drew near to her mother and looped an arm through hers for a moment. "And this is the box of threads where Grace said the birth certificate was found?"

"It is." I handed the wooden box to Dr. Kim.

"Those spools were gifts from the neighbors," he said. "My wife told me that when Helen held the *Baek-il* for the new baby, the neighbors all brought spools of thread."

Now that Gran's name had been raised, I needed to speak up. "My gran kept this secret not to harm anyone or to deceive. She loved Mrs. Kim—Choi Eunhee—very much. She was her best friend, and Gran would have done anything for her."

Grace's grandpa patted my hand. "We know this," he said. "We are honored. And now my sons will know that while they understood that their mother was strong and loving, she was stronger and more concerned for the happiness of their lives than they could ever have imagined. At an expense to herself. Keeping a secret for a long time is tiring."

Grace's dad nodded. "I cannot thank your grandmother in person. So I will thank you." He turned toward me and bowed deeply. I bowed deeply back.

"The *hanbok*, of course, is Grace's now," I said.

"I will dress my daughter in it for her *Baek-il*," Grace said.

Her mother lightened the tone. "First, you need a husband."

Poker face, Cassidy. She will know the truth very soon.

The doorbell rang. Guests? Already? "Please excuse me for a moment," I said. No one ever came to my front door, always the side door, by the mudroom.

I opened the door. "Dad? Dad! What are you doing here?"

He stood there, just outside the door. "I'm here for the party." He looked behind him, where the grounds had been set up. "It's today, right?"

I nodded. "Is Mary Alice . . . ?"

He shook his head. "I told you I'd be coming but she would not. May I come in?"

I stepped out of the doorway. "Of course!"

We went into the living room. Mr. and Mrs. Kim remembered him of course. "Hello, Mr. Quinn. How lovely to see you here," Mrs. Kim said. "I'm so glad you could come. We missed seeing you at Helen's funeral."

I pursed my lips to hold back a smile.

"We had no idea you'd be here," she continued, always on my team.

They relaxed into polite chatter for a moment and then headed out to the party.

"You can put your things in here, Dad." I nodded toward the teal bedroom. Thankfully I hadn't packed it up.

He lifted his small suitcase onto the dresser top. "I texted that I was coming." He pulled out his phone and showed it to me.

I smiled. "Dad, that's not a text. When you clicked on your contacts, you accidently sent it from your phone to an old email address I never check. It doesn't matter. I'm so glad you're here. How long can you stay?"

"Just until tomorrow night," he said. "I couldn't get much time off. But I wanted to be here for you. I'm sorry I wasn't there for the funeral."

I wished he had been. But I could nurse that grudge or let it go. He was here. I was moving forward. The door was open to let pain flow out and hope rush in.

In the background, the deejay started up the music. "Let's go outside, Dad," I said. "I want you to meet the rest of my family."

CHAPTER
TWENTY-THREE

Annika was already snapping photos. She waved to me, and I went to where she was and introduced my dad to her.

"Come and meet my family too," she said. A middle-aged woman, man, and two twentysomething men stood under the Mickey tree.

"Hey, you get in there too," I said to Annika. "I'll take a picture of all of you."

They smiled, I snapped. I handed the phone back to her.

Mr. Nordgren sat at one of the tables closest to the greenhouse and waved me over. "I'd like to introduce you to my wife," he said. "Renee, meet Cassidy."

His wife held out her hand. "So nice to meet you. We're

looking forward to continuing the picnic basket service next year. It's been such a boon for our guests. Would you consider a weekly bouquet subscription too? For placement in each of the properties?"

No sad feelings. I swallowed hard. "That is a wonderful idea! Thank you so much for your encouragement and support." I introduced them to my dad, and they told him how proud of me he must be.

"I am," he said. Was that a tear in his eye?

DJ and his family walked up behind us. "Marcia, it's so good to see you," I greeted his mother and introduced my dad to them. She introduced me to her husband, and of course I'd already met her other children when they came to visit DJ.

"Sit here," Mr. Nordgren said to DJ as he pointed at the empty chairs around the table. "It's nice to see a friend."

DJ smiled, and as his family took seats with the Nordgrens, I slipped away to give them time to get to know one another.

I headed toward the tables near the garden. Someone was in my garden. Two someones were in my garden. I headed over there to see them.

"Mr. Beeksma!" I hurried toward him. "I'm so glad you could come."

My mom's old friend Brenda stood nearby. "I was just telling Dirk what a fantastic job you'd done this year. This garden is as pretty as anything I've ever seen." She looked at my dad. "Mark?"

"Hello, Brenda. It's good to see you."

She teared up. "I haven't seen you on the island since . . ."

"Since Lauri passed," he finished for her. "It took me a long time to be able to come back to the places we shared. Too long."

He was loosening his contained pain too. *Mom would be happy.* "We'd better find a table before the slots fill in!" This was a night of hellos, but mostly it was a night of goodbyes. I wanted to make sure it was a great night before saying goodbye.

I looped my arm through each of theirs and walked back to the tables. I took a deep breath and walked toward one particular table. "Mr. and Mrs. Harper. I'm so glad you could come."

Nick's mom stood and embraced me, her dark hair twisted in a bun, a silver necklace gracing her neck. "Cassidy, it's so, so lovely to see you again. I've wanted to have you over for dinner all summer."

Mr. Harper stood up and hugged me next, the big, tight squeeze of a dad. "And no more 'Mr. Harper.' From now on, it's Gregory. I'm sure Nick was going to make sure you weren't going to slip away from him again before he risked bringing you over. I'm not sure Calista would forgive him if he let you go."

Mrs. Harper beamed at me, I beamed back, and we stood as a triangle of happiness for a moment. "I just love these little paper-doll chains you have decorating each table. We are all connected. Some more than others." She smiled knowingly at me, and her dimples, so like Nick's, made her face even more beautiful. "Should we save a seat for you?"

I nodded. "I would love that. I'd like to introduce you to my dad. Mark Quinn, please meet Gregory and Calista Harper. They are Nick's parents."

"Nick?" Dad asked.

"Yes, Nick." Nick stood and faced my dad. "Dad, please meet Nick Harper." I turned toward Nick. "Nick, this is my dad, Mark Quinn."

Nick stuck out his hand, and Dad shook it. "I don't have to ask what the relationship is here," Dad said. "I can tell by how you look at each other."

I hugged him. He'd gotten it right. "So glad you're here, Dad," I whispered in his ear. I glanced at where the Kim family took over a large table, but with two seats open. Grace's pretty face flushed with joy as Justin held her hand. Her mother and father both laughed at whatever story Justin had underway. Grandpa Kim basked in the adoration of his grandson, who was attentively refilling his water.

Other neighbors arrived, as well as friends of Gran. Many members from the support group Annika and DJ attended, who had fallen in love with the grounds when they'd visited, sat at tables with friends, new and old.

"When will we eat?" Gregory asked. "I have been looking forward to those wonderful hand pies you made. I hope you made more!"

Nick looked at me. Then he looked at his dad. "When did Cassidy make hand pies for you?"

I caught Gregory's eye. He had the proverbial deer-in-the-headlights look. "You're right!" I said. "Smelling that amazing barbecue smoke makes people restless. A few might make a break for the food if I don't get this party started."

I headed to the platform on the grass, took the mic, and then, after ensuring it was on, tapped it lightly. I looked out over the grounds. Apple and pear trees strung with lights illuminated the outer boundaries of the grounds. The firefly jars flickered just a bit at each table as the sun started to dip.

Gran, I thought, *this is it. Here we are. And our big community family all turned out. We had a good run, and although you had to take this place into your two hands after Bob died, look how many hands are here now. Hundreds. The garden is you. The hospitality is Mom. And now I'm wrapping up. But I have all of our seeds wrapped, too, and our cookbook and every other heirloom. I'll take them with me and start new, with my two hands, for all of us.*

Instead of bringing tears, my thoughts brought strength as I spoke. "Thank you, everyone, for coming out tonight. Each one of you in some way or many ways poured blessing over our property, with your hands, your plants, your work, your support, your prayers. Welcome to my home—my mother's home, my grandmother's home, the home of everyone we love—and know that you are appreciated."

A quiet hush came over the land.

"And now . . . it's time for food!"

The crowd whistled and clapped, and the disc jockey struck up the first few lines of "I Can't Wait" by Nu Shooz. People headed toward the greenhouse potluck area, the barn where the smoker was.

Summer party music bathed the grounds while everyone ate. I sat with Nick and his parents, Dad, a couple of neighbors I hadn't seen for a while, and one of Annika's friends. She knew all about the flowers in the tablescape. Was she the friend who'd hoped to work with me? I wished I could hire her.

When a song from *The Lion King* soundtrack started up, I looked at Nick. "Did you request that?"

"Yeah," he said with a smile. "I knew he'd get the dancing started."

Sure enough, DJ was dancing near his table, and others joined in as he did. Next came Elvis's "Can't Help Falling in Love." Nick took my hand and led me to the front of the green where others danced, too. "Hand pies?" he whispered in my ear.

I grinned. "All will be revealed. In time."

Grace and Justin were there. She drew close to me. "After this song, come to the table with me. I have someone I want you to meet."

"Sure," I said. "Friend from work?"

She nodded. "Remember. Networking. It's the way business gets done. Be you."

I had a hard time relaxing into Nick's arms then. *What did she mean?*

The song wrapped up. "I'll meet you in a few," I told Nick. "Grace wants to introduce me to someone."

He nodded and headed off to meet with some friends a few tables away.

Only Grace and her friend were at the table. I glanced up and saw Mr. and Mrs. Kim wheeling Grace's grandfather toward the greenhouse, maybe for seconds. Perhaps to give us some time alone.

"Cassidy? This is Paloma Garcia. She heads up the interface with foundations at my new firm. She connects foundations to organizations and activities geared toward folks who have additional physical needs or are neurodiverse and in need of a supportive setting. She was on the interview panel when I applied for my job. She was most interested in Mi-Ja as my historical motivation and you as the contemporary motivation for my work. When she asked more about it, I thought I'd invite her to come tonight and see for herself what's going down here."

I was Grace's contemporary motivation? I was honored! She held my gaze, telegraphing her thoughts. Sometimes when you've been friends with someone for a long time, you know what they are thinking, what they want, even if they don't say it aloud. *Go!*

Was there a chance? "I'm glad you could come." I looked at the seat next to Ms. Garcia. "May I?"

She nodded, and I sat down.

"Tell me what you do here," she said.

"I grow flowers. I nurture people. That's really what it all comes down to." I looked at the crowd, dancing, eating, talking, sitting. "My grandmother bought this farm when it was a run-down house and former victory garden, which had been neglected. Of course, World War II was won, but other victories needed to be worked toward. My mother died when I was young, and this property became the one place where I felt safe, to be me, and it was my goal to keep that going for other people."

"For people with developmental disabilities?" she asked.

"Yes. And for those without—together. We all have needs; we all have strengths; we each have something to offer; we each have challenges to overcome." I spread my hand out over the area. "Everyone here has different backgrounds, differing ages, financial statuses, abilities and need for support, temperaments. Isn't that what makes a community? When we all fit together?"

She nodded. "Grace told me a little about the work you do here. I could easily connect you with several corporate foundations who would be interested in underwriting your work. Foundations geared toward assisting those with disabilities—or differently abled, as we might say now—are most interested in community, not setting people apart from the world as a whole. There must be other grants, too, for women-owned businesses, things like that. We could get you set up in maybe six months." She looked so pleased.

Grace did not. My heart sank. I did not have six months.

"Thank you," I said. "I'm so glad you came tonight and that you are willing to share your resources."

I stopped talking. She waited out my silence.

Be strong and courageous and take the land.

"Do you know of any foundations that can work more

quickly?" I explained the lien situation to her. "I only have a few weeks."

She nodded thoughtfully. "Maybe. Maybe a family foundation. Corporate foundations have a lot of layers of questioning and sometimes red tape. Family foundations are basically just a group of family members, and maybe some friends, who pool resources to give to causes about which they care deeply. Kind of like when you write a check to support the library fundraiser or GoFundMe for someone you know."

"But, well, I'd need a huge amount of money. Not library fundraising money."

"How much?" she asked.

"Seventy-five thousand dollars to pay off the lien, plus maybe twenty-five thousand more to fix the roof and the grounds. To start with. I'd like to hire more people next year, work more acreage, build our inclusive community. It's a lot, I know. But it can do a lot of good."

She smiled. "This will seem difficult to believe, but for some people that kind of money is like us regular folks giving five dollars to the library. They understand that they've been given a treasure to steward, and they try to do it thoughtfully and well, in alignment with the things they care about. Rich or poor, we each have the opportunity to invest whatever we've been given."

"What would I need to do?"

"Write a letter, a note, anything I can give to them to show what you do and what your heart is."

I looked beyond her. In the distance, Annika snapped pictures. "How about a video of this event, which says it all, with me sharing my rationale?"

Paloma Garcia grinned. "Perfect. As time is of the essence, let's do it now. Repeat on the video everything you just told me."

I walked to Annika. I breathed slowly for a moment to tamp down the adrenaline coursing through me. "Hey. Can you take a video?"

"Sure," she said.

I explained about the foundation. "We're going to send them a video of everyone here enjoying themselves, and I'm going to talk a little bit about why I want to have an integrated community of people of all backgrounds and abilities."

"And . . ."

"And if they like it, they may give us enough to keep the land. Keep going. And give your friend a job next year." I grinned. "A little personal motivation."

Annika looked nervous but did not pull out her fidget cube. She flicked her camera to Pano and recorded the tables, the food, the neighbors, the friends, and her group. She and I walked into the gardens, and she took a video while I talked about the variety of things people did on the farm and repeated what I'd told Ms. Garcia. Annika videoed the bird feeders that DJ filled, the petals she photographed. I stood under a fruiting pear tree because they had lights and hoped a pear wouldn't drop on me while I made my final plea.

Ms. Garcia joined us. "I'd like to ask a few questions on camera," she said. "Things I know they'll be interested in hearing."

Annika turned the video on once more.

"Why do you want to continue to do the work you are doing here? Building a community of people who need varying levels of support?"

"I've worked for people who condescended to me, and I felt small. I didn't want to feel like that, nor did I want anyone working for and with me to feel like that." I paused. "It used to be that I wanted to be on the A-plus team, to do something great."

"Like what?" she asked.

"Oh, I don't know. Like, have a plant named after me or work at a big-name nursery with an impressive paycheck. I've come to realize that I don't need to *be* great. I want to *do* good. I'm not the sunflower that catches everyone's eye as soon as they arrive in the garden. I'm the gardener, working hard to make the garden healthy and beautiful, filled with companion plants supporting each other. Clearing trees so everyone gets sun. In turn, everyone here also supports me. We're a community. We're a family, where everyone fits. That's the real A-plus team."

Ms. Garcia nodded, and it looked like she was about to wrap it up when Annika turned the camera on herself, deeply blushing.

"Hi. I'm Annika. I'm a photographer and I'm autistic. Cassidy is a master gardener, placing plants and people where they'll do best and giving them what they need to blossom and bear fruit. That's all."

She took the camera off of herself and shut it off. "I can edit that out if you want."

Ms. Garcia shook her head. "No, leave it as it is." She told Annika to message the video to her. "I'll be in touch," she said to me. "I know your timeline. I just don't know how quickly the family foundation I have in mind might be willing to review. It's a holiday week."

"No matter what, thank you very much for reaching out for me. I can't express my appreciation enough."

She headed to the Kims' table.

"Thank you," I said to Annika.

"I hope it works," she said. "I'll edit the video and send it tonight."

As she walked away, I remembered my angry thought about the developers, now flipped on its head into a prayer. *Why does it always come down to rich people having money on hand for what they want?*

Please, let them want this.

A few hours later, after everyone had left and the grounds were packed up, Dad went to bed. With a long day's travel, then the time zone change and jet lag, he'd barely made it to the end of the evening. After we'd said good night, I headed to the kitchen. I opened the cookbook to my mom's section and found exactly what I was looking for. *Mark's Favorite Scottish Shortbread.*

Butter. Flour. Sugar. Every baker—including me—had

those on hand. Before I went to bed, I baked a batch and left them to cool for morning.

* * *

Dad was up early, of course, still on East Coast time. I glanced out the window and saw his rental car. "Time for breakfast and a chat before you head back to the airport?" I asked. He'd have to wait for and catch the ferry to the mainland, drive to the airport and return the car, and then wait to board. He didn't have much time.

"Yes, of course," he said. "I'm looking forward to it."

He went to shower and pack, and I went to my room and brought down the big box that held Gran's tea set. I washed two cups, two saucers, and two small plates. I brought them to the little wooden table in the living room and set a small posy of flowers in the center, then brewed the tea.

He smiled when he saw the setup and sat at the table across from me. He sipped his tea and ate one of the short-breads. "My favorite recipe," he said softly. "Tea for two. Just like when you were my little girl. Remember? You'd host tea parties for me and get upset when I ate all the cookies at once?"

"I do remember, Dad." In some way, our roles had reversed. It had been up to me to take the lead in reconciling, but when he came to Whidbey, knowing Mary Alice hadn't approved, and made himself face Mom's loss, I knew he was doing what he could do too. We each needed to be vulnerable and reach out a bit. I stretched my arm across the table and took one of his hands in mine. "I'm not little anymore. Am I still your girl?"

He squeezed my hand. "I'm sorry about things. About not being here for the funeral. About not being here when you left to go to California. Just about . . . not being here since your mom passed. When you needed me most. I'm still your dad. You are still my girl if you want to be."

"I want to be," I said. "Let's talk more often. Just maybe not . . . text."

He laughed. "I'd like that. I'd like to come and visit again." He looked around. "Here, if that's where you stay. Or wherever you are."

"I'd like that too," I said. "I'll keep the tea set just for us. You and me."

We caught up for a few hours, and then I sent him back on his way. I hadn't needed to move on from him. We moved forward together instead.

*　*　*

For the next few hours after Dad left, I supervised as the rental company came to haul the tables away.

Any word? Grace texted.

Nope. Have you seen her at work?

Big place. Plus, I spent all my capital to bring her and let you present. I don't think I can say anything else. I'm the new girl.

I know. Thank you. You have done so much!

Nick was next. I hadn't had the chance to tell him about Boston because the party had gone so late, but I would, in person.

How is your day? he texted midafternoon on Tuesday. **I'm praying for you.**

I knew he was really asking if I'd heard anything. **It's only been one day. But I need to call Gina within a day or two. She said right after Labor Day to get the cash in time.**

Hold on, sunshine. Ride it out another day or two. No matter if it's Gina or the bank, it's a developer either way, so it's worth the risk of waiting. Right?

I nodded, though he couldn't see me. **You're right. Thanks.**

* * *

Annika dropped by with photos from the party, and I took one she'd taken of me with her, Nick, DJ, and Grace into the pantry, pulled out the red- and white-checked cookbook, and slipped it into the envelope with my name on it.

I'm so happy, Mama. I wanted a happy picture because you and Gran have happy pictures. A thought came to me—there was another divider in the cookbook. I wrote *Quinn* on the tab right after mine. *Someday, Mom, my daughter will have a section here.* Goose bumps scrambled up my arm. *Maybe she won't like flowers. Maybe she'll prefer vegetables or animals or want to fill the whole place with fruiting trees and bushes. It won't matter, though, because I will tell her it's hers to do with as she sees fit. Dream, little girl, and then give it the taste of your hands.*

I headed upstairs to the attic. I clicked on the light and then knelt before the hope chest and lifted the lid. Yes, it was good to have hopes, fragile as they might be. I lifted out Mom's wedding veil and put it on to keep it out of the way. It was so light. I felt light now too. She'd have been glad Dad and I had our tea party. I set the heavier white box of the tea set inside. I'd reclaimed it as a family heirloom, one that had, indeed, delivered hope. It belonged inside the chest now.

I rearranged a few other things in the chest. The jigsaw puzzles I used to do with Grandpa Ben and Gran. Gramps always held back the last piece of the puzzle and slid it to me, his only grandchild, at the last moment, so I could win. *I hope we're going to win this time, Gramps.*

Under the puzzle boxes was my old Spirograph. I lifted the lid and then pieces of paper with spheres and swirls, loops and circles, a rainbow of rings and coils overlapping and entwining. You couldn't see where one pattern began and the others ended, as they all fed into and overlaid one another exquisitely. Eunhee, Grace, Gran, Dirk Beeksma, Annika and Johanna, her grandmother. Brenda. Mom. Mrs. Kim. Grace. Me. Through the years and generations, lives that circled and overlapped in ways that couldn't be separated.

My phone buzzed. An incoming . . . FaceTime call?

I didn't recognize the number. "Hello?"

"Hello, Miss Quinn? It's Paloma Garcia." She looked at the top of my head. "Did I catch you at a bad moment?"

I reached my hand up. The veil was still on! I carefully

lifted it off and set it on the floor. "No, no, this is a great time."

She smiled. "It's a great time, indeed. I have wonderful news. The family foundation that I had in mind for you has already responded—in the positive! They are eager to help support the expansion of the work you do and the community you're building. They are ready to write a check to pay off your lien and the additional twenty-five thousand dollars."

"They are? They *are*?" I stood up and nearly cracked my head on the sloping ceiling. "That is wonderful news!"

She laughed. "I wanted to see your reaction—hence the FaceTime call. There will be some paperwork to fill out, of course, and you can come into the office and do that soon. We'll talk a bit about the expectations, but they shouldn't be anything over which you need to have an undue concern. This family has a very personal reason for supporting people like you who support others, and I suspect they would be interested in helping you grow even further in your reach. You connected with them heart-to-heart. Keep up the good work. Take a look at your calendar and tell me when you might be available."

"I will," I said. "Thank you!"

We clicked off the call, and I picked up a picture of Gran and Eunhee. *We did it!* I found one in the chest of my mom and me. *We did it!*

I moved the veil next to the box of spooled thread and the *hanbok* I'd brought back up for safekeeping after the party.

Mi-Ja.

What had Mrs. Kim said at lunch? *"Sometimes opening a secret to sunlight brings freedom and joy."*

Without the *hanbok*, without the girl whose life it represented, Grace would not have found her calling nor her passion to help those who needed support and their families. She would not have met Ms. Garcia, which meant that without Mi-Ja, I could not have kept my land. I plucked a spool of bright-gold thread from the thread box and held it to the sunlight streaming in through the window. "Your life, little Mi-Ja, has stretched way into the future, to today, and through all who come to work here, to build a community, and it will continue to stretch way beyond. A very long life indeed." This land, then, this house, these flowers, the birds, the gardens, our friends and community, Grace's legal advocacy work, all were answers to the hopes and prayers of so many years before.

I closed the hope chest. Hope. Courage. Every one of us had taken hold of both, in our own way. I headed downstairs to share the good news.

They're funding us! I texted Nick first.

They're funding YOU, Cassidy. You did it!

Come over in an hour? Bring coffee and I'll have . . . hand pies? There had been some left over. I knew how to put them to good use.

Yes, he texted. **I've waited long enough for this big reveal. Meet me in the barn.**

* * *

I set two comfortable lawn chairs in the barn and placed a table in front of them with a stack of blackberry hand pies.

"Hey." Nick set the coffees on the table. "Still flying high?"

"Oh yeah. High as a barn swallow. Got lots of plans in here—" I tapped my head—"and this—" I tapped my heart—"is full too."

He bit into one of the pies. I had to give him credit. He hadn't mentioned his dad's comment at all. "Looks like you won't need to pack up the seeds and plants after all. No new terroir."

"So that's what I wanted to talk with you about. My roots are here and now my dream is coming true. I can't move to Boston with you, but I don't want to hold you back from *your* dream."

He looked off in the distance. "Ah. You must have stopped by when I was in Boston."

"Yeah, I dropped by. Your dad told me you were finalizing an on-site job there. I swapped him hand pies for the info." I grinned. "No, really, I'd brought by a picnic basket to you to say I was sorry." I took his hand. "I can't move to Boston, but I'm good with a long-distance relationship this time around, if you are."

He shook his head. "No." He set his coffee down. "This time it's me who isn't good with long distance."

"Okay," I said. "That's fair."

He leaned over and kissed me. "I'm not leaving. I turned the job down."

I pulled back a little. "When?"

"When I was there, of course. Which is why I'd never said anything. No need. Before our fight, you'd said it was okay for the brain and heart to work together. I had a long plane ride to think about that truth. The money was good, but it was not as exciting as my start-up, which is doing well. And . . ." He paused. "A good job may be hard to find, but a good woman, the right woman, the only woman for me, well, she would be impossible to replace."

"You mean you said no before I apologized? Before I explained what happened?"

He nodded. "I still wanted to try to make it work. These have been hard months for you, and I knew once you worked through them—well, I hoped once you worked through them, we could both make a living as well as make a life."

I shushed him with a kiss. "I'd like to help with your business, too, now that my head isn't so crowded and the property stuff is sorted."

"Absolutely. I can't wait to share some ideas and get your insight." He looked at the barn cats circling us—or circling the pies anyway. "So why are we in the barn?"

"Come with me." I took both of his hands in mine and lifted him from the chair. At the side of the barn was a hay bale, and on top of that, a bucket of paint. I used a nearby screwdriver and flipped the lid off. I dipped my hands in and then took both his in mine, slathering them with white paint.

"What?" He held out his palms like they were burning. He hated getting messy.

I led him to where Annika and DJ had made their marks. I slapped my hands on the barn wall. "You in?"

He slapped his hands on the wall right next to mine.

When I stepped back, I saw four sets of praise hands. "We'll add to this every year," I said. "New people. Bigger community. Lots of dreams. Me. You. We. Us."

With his sticky right hand, he took my sticky left one and we stepped outside the barn. A handful of tiny finches flew toward the feeder DJ kept faithfully filled; it hung from the cherry tree right outside the barn door. Neither of us moved so as not to startle the birds. One by one, they landed on the feeder ledge, nestling under the protective cover of early autumn leaves.

They were safe at home. We were safe at home. Forever and ever.

Amen.

A Note from the Author

I often write about family and friends because they are, for most of us, what brings the most pleasure—and sometimes the most pain—during the course of our lives. At the end of those lives, which comes faster than most of us imagine, we wonder, *Did my life count? Was I able to achieve my dreams, goals, and live in hope despite fluctuating circumstances?* Like Eunhee and Helen, I think many of us wish to live a hero's life, but the hero's life is mostly found in the day-to-day decisions we make to do good rather than be great. Some are able to pass along financial resources or material treasures to those who come after them. Mostly, though, our most valuable heirlooms are gifts of the heart, the soul, and the will, offered day by day throughout life rather than given after death. Helen and Eunhee lived heroes' lives and then passed the baton to their granddaughters, who did the same in their own time and with their own challenges.

Although my last ten novels were set in England, I am excited to return home in my writing, especially to Whidbey

Island, a place my family loves. Although *these United States* have our share of challenges, there is truly no place like home. I wanted to explore a little corner of the universal thrill and challenge of those immigrating to America. During my research, I read and watched many accounts of those voluntarily immigrating to the United States, with a foot in each culture, as it were. Most of those folks wanted their children to be Americans but yearned for them to retain something of the mother culture too. Most of their children and the generations that came after had both feet firmly planted in America, a source of both pride and pain for their forebears. My friend Joan Nienhuis recounted that her Dutch forebears spoke Dutch but did not want their children to do so, so they would become fully Americanized. And yet continuing their cultural heritage was very important to them. Whidbey Island, to this day, hosts a Holland Happening celebration each spring, though most of the Dutch immigration took place in the late nineteenth and early twentieth centuries.

Closer to home, each of my grandparents was in the first generation of their families born in the United States, their parents having immigrated here from Italy, Lebanon, and Scandinavia. My great-grandparents sacrificed to establish new lives in the US, leaving culture, friends, family—in some cases even children—behind forever. Happily American, I am so grateful to them. As with many voluntary adult immigrants, my forebears' motivations included increased financial well-being, a desire to escape a dangerous or hopeless situation in their homeland, and a goal to achieve a new, happier, more promising life—the American dream—for themselves and the generations who would follow. Although in *Heirlooms* these various paths are expressed through Dutch Americans to some extent and Korean Americans in a larger part, each with their own unique culture, I peek at the broader emotional intersection of immigration and the American dream.

The twentieth century had its fair share of wars, if any share is fair, but the Korean War somehow gets eclipsed by World War II and the Vietnam War. However, it was not an eclipsing experience for those who served in the armed forces, nor especially for the Korean people.

My affection and respect for Korean Americans and their culture sparked when I taught in a Korean American *Hagwon*, an after-school prep school of sorts. I taught English, essay, and preparation for the SAT. I grew in affection and admiration for my boss, my students, and their families as I knew them better and learned more about their culture. I not only came to love their delicious food, courteous manners, beautiful language, sense of humor, devotion to achievement, and customs, but my respect for the sacrifices made for the children made a huge impression.

Mothers sometimes lived in the US while their husbands remained in South Korea so the children could get the best possible educations. Fathers sometimes slept at their businesses so they didn't need to hire additional employees, instead saving money to educate their kids and bring relatives to live with them. Many well-educated people took jobs for which they were overqualified in order to be the proverbial foot in the door for their families. And yet I also witnessed that tug, felt by many children of immigrants to the US, from whatever their background. *Many have sacrificed to get me here, and I love and appreciate that, but can I shape my own life without disappointing my family?* My research took me beyond personal experience, of course, into in-depth interviews with Korean Americans and into many journals, letters, books, and firsthand reports.

As a whole, our country is getting better at educating ourselves about and including and respecting those with developmental disabilities and the experiences of neuro-diverse people. I researched both autism and Down syndrome to understand a bit about what it is like to be neurodiverse in a world built for neurotypical understanding or to have a family member who has developmental delays or disabilities or other physical and intellectual challenges. It was painful and horrifying to read about the treatment of the mothers of children—and those folks themselves—diagnosed not only in the fifties but also within my lifetime. I honor and admire the families, then and now, who have tirelessly fought for themselves and for loved ones who need additional support. I am thankful to all those who helped me better understand these challenges—they are listed in the book's acknowledgment section.

In the historical section of the book, I use the name *Down syndrome* to portray what was known at the time as *mongolism*. I do that for sensitivity's purpose and also because I hope many readers may not even have heard of *mongolism* being used in such a way.

There are varying positions on identifying autistic persons with either identity first (*autistic person*) or person first (*person with autism*). The language changes frequently, and under advisement, I chose to go with the identity-first position (see this article for a helpful explanation of this perspective: https://autisticadvocacy.org/about-asan/identity-first-language/) as the best way to convey respect and autonomy at the time of publication. Differing opinions are valid, of course.

When researching autism, I came across the phrase "When you know one autistic person, you know one autistic person." I have adopted and expanded that philosophy for each of the characters in my book regardless of their cultural background, neurotypical or neurodiverse, physical or intellectual challenges, or current life situation. Although I strove to honor and represent norms for each culture in the book, I worked hard to avoid stereotypes with each person portrayed.

In the end, this is a story about family ties and deep friendship, how we balance one another, fill the gaps for each other, and hopefully find our love and sacrifice for each other in a healthy combination of "me" and "we." The best family and friends stand in the gap for each other no matter the cost. Cassidy and Eunhee are very much alike—each, to some extent, lost her family and their support and so had to make a new life. Each was strong in her faith, ready to pack her seeds, as it were, and plant them anew. Grace and

Helen were very much alike, focused on their careers and then pulled out of them for a moment to find the real meaning in their callings. The older generation provided strength and love for their own grandchildren and examples and support for each other's.

I hope the book will strengthen you not only to dream but to set goals, to act for yourself and also for others, and to honor the heirlooms you've been gifted and plan for those you'll leave for those coming after you.

Cinn Rolls

By Joan Nienhuis

There are many aspects of my Dutch ancestry I greatly value. At the top is my Reformed faith. Close up there are my mother's cinnamon rolls. Food was a major way my mother showed love to her family, providing lavish Sunday dinners for decades. But her signature creation was her cinnamon rolls. I have many fond memories of my family gathered on Saturday mornings at her house for coffee, cinnamon rolls, and lively discussion. Her rolls were always the first to be grabbed up at church or extended family potlucks, everyone wanting one of Johanna's treasured treats.

I remember the first time I had a commercially made cinnamon roll at a coffee shop. I was shocked at the dry cardboard texture of the dough and the vain attempt to cover the inadequacy with a sugary frosting. I had only known my mother's moist rolls, turned upside down with caramelized brown sugar and butter dripping down the sides. I decided to get her recipe but when I asked for it, she chuckled. She had made hundreds of batches by then and created them from memory. If there had ever been a recipe, it was long gone. I convinced her to let me stand by her at the next baking session. I struggled to take adequate notes on her method. How could I interpret on paper adding enough flour until it "felt right"?

Why cinnamon rolls? Perhaps it goes back hundreds of years. I have a Dutch brother-in-law who was raised in Indonesia. While his father was a translator with the Netherlands' Bible Society, the Dutch presence in southern Asia was a remnant of the Dutch East India Company and the spice trade of the 1600s. The Dutch had a monopoly on the cinnamon trade for a hundred years. Is it any wonder that snickerdoodles and cinnamon rolls are Dutch favorites?

Cinnamon rolls are more than tasty treats to me. They are symbolic of my mother's giving nature, freely offering her rolls to relatives and guests as a sign of her loving heart. Family lore says she even brought rolls to soldiers from Fort Casey who were doing practice maneuvers in a field near our house during World War II.

My mom went to glory twenty-five years ago but her legacy of showing love through her rolls lives on.

Johanna Nienhuis's Cinn Rolls

Ingredients

½ cup warm water
2 packages of yeast

3 sticks butter
2 to 2½ cups hot water
¾ cup sugar
2 teaspoons salt
2 or 3 eggs
2 cups flour plus 5 additional cups
cinnamon
½ cup (or more) brown sugar, plus additional for
    melting in pan

Instructions

Mix warm water and two packages of yeast. Set aside. Set at least one stick of butter in a small pan over low heat to melt. Get two 9-by-12 baking pans (or one 12-by-18 baking pan) and place on a very low burner. Put at least a half stick of butter in each to melt.

In a very large mixing bowl combine two to two and a half cups of hot water, one stick of butter, three-quarters cup of sugar, two teaspoons of salt, two or three eggs, and two cups of flour.

Stir well. Add yeast mixture.

Add flour, stirring by hand, until not too stiff, about five or six cups in all.

Place dough on a large and well-floured surface and roll into a rectangle about a half-inch thick or less. This will not be a "dry" dough and you may have to flour the top of the dough and the rolling pin a few times. (These cinnamon rolls are moist, not dry as you often see in commercial bakeries. The secret is a moist dough. Keep plenty of flour handy to be able to roll out the dough.)

Pour the melted butter over the rolled-out dough, spreading to cover evenly. Sprinkle lots of brown sugar over the dough and butter. Sprinkle lots of cinnamon over the butter and sugar mixture. Be liberal for a good taste.

Carefully roll up the dough, starting at the long edge. Again, this will be a moist dough so you may need to dust your hands with flour several times. I have been known to use a pancake turner to pry up the moist dough that has stuck to the surface. When the dough is almost rolled up, take the far edge and slightly pull it over the roll, pinching it a bit to secure it.

Once the dough is rolled up, retrieve the pan(s) with the melted butter. Sprinkle a liberal amount of brown sugar in the pan as well. (Yes, these are sweet rolls.)

With a sharp knife, frequently dusted with flour, and a quick hand, cut the rolled dough into segments of about one to one and a quarter inch in length. Place the segments, cut side

down, in the pan so they are touching. The rolled dough segments will be dripping with melted butter and sugar so you
might have to be quick here. (This may take a bit of practice
to see how many rolls you will make, depending on how wide
you cut the segments and how large your baking pan is and
how closely you pack them together in the pan.)

Lightly cover and let rise until the dough is starting to go over
the edge of the pan.

Bake at 325 degrees for thirty minutes.

Serve warm. Have butter available. Eat by hand, unrolling
the baked roll, adding a bit of butter for each bite. Do not
put frosting on the rolls, ever.

Variations

If you want, you can place chopped walnuts or pecans in
the pan with the butter and brown sugar before adding the
cut dough segments. You can also sprinkle raisins on the
rolled-out dough. My mother generally made the rolls plain,
allowing us to savor the sweet bread experience without the
distracting flavors of nuts or raisins.

Miyeok Guk (Seaweed Soup)

By Tina Cho

One of the first Korean soups I experienced was *miyeok guk* or seaweed soup. *Miyeok* is a wrinkly, greenish seaweed, rich in calcium, iodine, and vitamin K. New mothers who just gave birth eat the soup to help their bodies as they nurse their babies. It's also a tradition for Koreans to eat a bowl of *miyeok guk* for their birthday breakfast to honor the mothers who gave birth to them. *Miyeok guk* is also a common soup served with rice during meals. My family likes to eat *miyeok guk*, and this recipe doesn't use meat and is quick to make. Traditional recipes use beef and even anchovies to flavor the broth. While eating this soup, I also like to think of the *haenyeo*, or diving women off the shores of Jeju Island. Without any breathing equipment, they dive, catch this seaweed, and harvest it.

Enjoy serving this nourishing soup and celebrating your loved one's life.

Ingredients

    2 chicken bouillon cubes

    4 cups water

    2 tablespoons dried *miyeok* seaweed soaked in water

    2 garlic cloves, minced

    1½ tablespoons soy sauce

    1 tablespoon sesame oil

Instructions

Soak the seaweed in a bowl of water until it turns soft and expands.

Boil bouillon cubes in the water in a soup pot on the stove.

Add in the seaweed, garlic, soy sauce, and sesame oil.

Continue to let it boil for about ten minutes.

Discussion Questions

1. Both Eunhee and Grace's mom, Mrs. Kim, discuss the concept of *son-mat*, the taste of your hands. In what ways do Cassidy and Grace apply the concept of *son-mat* to their lives? Are there items, attitudes, or ideas passed down to you from your family that you have changed or tweaked to make your own? Why? How would you feel if your child, grandchild, or another loved one changed something you gifted to them?

2. Helen and Eunhee agree that they would each like to live "a hero's life," ultimately finding that such a life is earned day by day, decision by simple decision. Can you trace the choices and sacrifices each of the women in this book makes to build their lives and carve a better path for others? What do you see in your own life, or the lives of those around you, that is genuinely heroic, though they might not find that to be so?

3. Cassidy struggles to reconcile her passion for flowers with her feeling that she must do something practical to make money and save her land. Is it selfish to want to make a life at the same time you make a living? Do you believe that the desires of our hearts are placed there by God? How do we balance the need to work, as outlined in Genesis, with Jesus' promise that he has come to bring us an abundant life (John 10:10)?

4. Eunhee tells Helen, "Sometimes secrets are kept out of love and not a wish to deceive." But Grace's mother offers, "Sometimes opening a secret to sunlight brings freedom and joy." Do you think Helen and Eunhee were right to keep such a significant secret from their families? How do you know when a secret should be kept and when it should be shared? Does it matter whether that secret is your own or someone else's?

5. Grace's *halaboji* asks her, "What are you doing today that fulfills the hopes and prayers of someone yesterday?" Can you see in your own life the fulfillment of someone else's hopes and prayers? Which of your own hopes and prayers would you fervently desire to see come to pass in another generation?

6. Do you cook, bake, or even just eat a favorite family recipe? Why do you treasure it? Have you written down your recipes to share with your friends, children, or grandchildren?

7. Helen and Cassidy both experience loneliness and a longing for family. How does each woman see that longing fulfilled in unexpected ways? How would you define *family*, and who fills that role in your own life?

8. We usually think of heirlooms as physical possessions, often of significant monetary value. But can sentimental possessions be just as valuable? What about attitudes, approaches, understanding, or care? What is the most treasured heirloom you have ever inherited, and why? What is the heirloom you most wish to bequeath to your loved ones?

Acknowledgments

Some people assume that writing is a solo sport—but nothing could be further from the truth. From the moment an idea comes to a novelist, others must be invited into the circle to brainstorm, critique, inform, correct, aid, edit, and encourage. I am so grateful that for each novel I am called to write, a circle of the above is always at hand, generous with their time and talents.

Heirlooms took me to familiar people and places but needed additional vetting to ensure proper portrayal. My dear friend Bonnie Christensen, who leads Exceptional Families Coaching, shared her life, wisdom, experience, and insight during the research portion of my work. She also read the completed manuscript to ensure that terminology regarding and portrayal of folks with Down syndrome and their families were represented respectfully, honestly, and sensitively. Bonnie and her husband are parents to AJ, their adult son with Down syndrome, as well as two adult sons who do not have developmental disabilities. As her organization's name alerts, she also coaches exceptional families.

Makiko Reslier, mother of a young son with Down syndrome, and Chris Newlon, family support and outreach coordinator for the National Association for Down Syndrome, generously offered their personal and professional insight on various aspects of Down syndrome.

A beautiful confluence of friends brought me to Erin Burnett, a talented autistic woman who has become a friend and who served as a resource for me from research through final manuscript sensitivity read. As a young professional, Erin modeled for and then helped me develop Annika as a young autistic woman with professional aspirations successfully navigating a neurotypical world as a neurodiverse person.

I mentioned in my author's note that I am familiar with and fond of the Korean American community through professional experience, but that does not, of course, provide the same insight as would be had by a member of the community. Much thanks to Andrea Soe and Connie Oh for informative and generous interviews as I researched the book. Along the way came the priceless assistance of Janelle Wee-Chung, who not only allowed me to interview and query about her and her family's experience as Korean Americans as well as that community at large during the development of the book but offered suggestions for clarity during the final manuscript's sensitivity read. I'm so thankful that Bradleigh Kim joined me from the beginning of the book, brainstorming plot ideas and offering insight into the Korean American culture into which she's married. She brought a unique outside-but-inside perspective that helped me convey cultural norms, I hope, with accuracy and esteem.

My friend and noted author Tina Cho brought her writer's eye to the final review of the manuscript and bolstered my confidence with her assurance that the Korean and Korean American cultures were accurately portrayed. I'm truly thankful for Kyung Yeon Chong, who offered her understanding and guidance in the proper rendering of the *hanja* characters and their translation. A special thank-you, too, to Grace Kang for her recording of proper Korean pronunciations ahead of the production of the audiobook.

Thank you, too, to experienced nurse Hayley Gudgin, who ensured that I kept Helen's nursing experience true to life with her careful, amusing, and detailed notes.

My husband is former military and so was able to help me with military background for the book. I was, for a while, a military wife too. I was also blessed to have two men speak freely and from personal involvement as Naval personnel stationed at Whidbey Naval Air Station during the years in which the historical portion of my book took place. James Ball generously granted several interviews to me and shared his Naval experience, especially as it relates to the late 1950s. Senior Chief Ball retired with twenty-six years of service, from 1955 to 1981. Not only was Senior Chief Ball on a plane with an officer like pilot Bob Devries, but his daughter was born at the Whidbey Naval hospital in September 1958, just when Mi-Ja would have been born. I'm so grateful for his wife, Lonnie, who graciously liaised our priceless interviews and correspondence.

William C. Smith, IC1 USN retired, was in the Navy for twenty years, including time spent posted at Whidbey Naval Air Station in the late fifties. His memories of the early 1958 flu epidemic and how it affected the base were invaluable, and his memory of life on and around base helped me accurately fill in details. The book would not be the same without his input.

Susan McConnell, executive director of the Wesley Community Foundation, generously offered her professional insight to explain to me how foundations work and helped me understand the difference between corporate and family foundations and how they might best work with my plot.

My friend attorney Scott Kalkwarf is an excellent source of legal information, dos and don'ts, brainstorming legally appropriate complications and background as far as inheritance, banking, and property laws. His son, Ethan Kalkwarf, is a digital marketing professional and offered valuable insight on the kinds of professional paths that might be available for Nick.

Whidbey Island is a place I absolutely adore, the place where my heart feels most at home. So it was with great joy that I chose to set this book there. Although we are there quite often, I am blessed with friends and new acquaintances who live on Whidbey and offered their insight, experience, history, and even homes!

Suzie Johnson, the daughter of William, mentioned

above, is an author friend to whom I first reached out. She shared books and resources with me, including the book *A Common Need*, a history of medical care on Whidbey Island, including those maternity hospitals. She generously answered many questions and arranged for necessary meetings, including liaising interviews with her mother, Barbara Smith, who also graciously shared her knowledge of base life in the late fifties. Then Suzie put me in touch with Joan Nienhuis.

As mentioned in the author's note, Joan's family has lived on Whidbey since the late nineteenth century. Dutch immigrants, like many of the early Whidbey settlers, their roots grow deeply into its soil, and Joan's heart is immovably Whidbey. Joan shared books with me and generously read the final manuscript to ensure I hadn't misrepresented my beloved Whidbey in any way. She drove me around during my research stage to show me how things are now and how things were then, and helped me brainstorm locations and so many other things. In the process, she shared about her mother's famous Cinn Rolls, and I just could not get them, nor a motherly prototype, out of my mind. Because this book is largely about grandmothers, I had thought to name one character after my husband's grandmother, Johanna. Serendipitously, Joan's mom was also named Johanna, and that was the frosting—or not—on the roll which has made its way into both the book and our family's recipe repertoire.

When I told Joan that I thought the perfect place to set the book was near Coupeville, on the site of the current Bell's Farm, she wholeheartedly agreed. Not only was the location right, but she, as a girl, had lived adjacent to the property and her mother had taken her there to pick strawberries. Bell's Farm, a family farm of many generations, is currently run by Paige Mueller and her husband, Kyle Flack. Paige made time in her busy schedule to show my husband and me around her family farm, answer my questions, and generously share her insight on Whidbey farm life.

Although the location of Helen and Cassidy's property was near Coupeville, I based the property itself on the 1907 Anderson Farm, located near Langley. Tamara, the only granddaughter of the original owners, lovingly restored the farmhouse to its early days but also filled it with modern conveniences. Tamara allowed me to sift through her family's papers and deeds and all manner of items from the 1950s and earlier. I even found a Whidbey phone book from the midfifties, which allowed me to accurately represent that wonderful, gossipy party line.

Although the house at Anderson Farm is beautiful, its glory is its garden. It bursts with fireworks of flowers, season to season, some vegetables, orchards, cows, lots of birds, and friendly farm cats. Loveliest of all are the dahlias, I think. Tamara plants seven hundred of them each year—a true labor of love. Our stays at her home while researching and writing were some of the happiest days I had all year.

I couldn't do everything required of me as an author day in, year out, without invaluable assistance from my most wonderful friend and longtime assistant, the multitalented Renee Chaw. She's also an early manuscript reader and offers insight and encouragement in a gently honest way. My critique buddy, Melanie Dobson, read an early draft and then made later suggestions to my great benefit. I'm so grateful for her expertise, her kind attention, and the time she spent brainstorming and reviewing editorial solutions.

The first reader of my manuscript—apart from my husband—is always my longtime friend and amazingly sharp editor Jenny Q of Historical Editorial. All authors have some readers and editors who are dead right in their critical assessment nearly all the time, and for me, that's Jenny. When I hand my first draft to her, I'm always reassured that she will be honest, find what needs to be fixed on the first pass, and reassure me that I'm doing what I am meant to do—write.

Editors Jan Stob and Sarah Rische graciously took on this book and its editing challenge, skillfully guiding me at each editorial stage to help the book be everything I hoped it would be. They are an answer to prayer, and I'm thankful for their gifts, their talents, and their faith in the novel.

I am blessed with a lovely circle of encouragers who hold up weary arms along the writing path, pray for me, share life and recipes with me, and do their best to spread the word when my books launch—Sandra's Readers Inner Circle. Thank you, ladies, for your constant support. In particular I want to thank Pat Caffrey Rzonca, who, for more than a decade, has taken time to personally support, uplift, and cheer me on. Pat, your reinforcement always arrives at just the right moment. I so appreciate your heart. My friend Jan

Potter, sister to my nearly lifelong friend and excellent manuscript reviewer Debbie Austin, made aprons using patterns from the 1950s, to share with my family, my editors, and my readers. I'm so grateful for her talents, generosity, and time.

My adult children, Samuel, Elizabeth, and Rocky, cheer me on, pray me on, love on me, and support me in every imaginable way while writing. Although they are busy professionals with full lives, they take time to brainstorm with me, read my work, make the recipes, and cheer me on. I'm so grateful for each of them. Now, of course, I have a precious little beauty to read with and to—my granddaughter, Mirabelle.

When people ask if I have a writing partner, the answer is yes: my husband. At the time of publication, we will have been married for thirty-five years—the best, as he says, thirty-five years of my life. And it's true! He is the ultimate researcher. He notes inconsistencies, travels with me, plots with me, lifts me up, picks up the slack when I'm writing, and mostly, loves me unconditionally. I love you unconditionally too, Michael. I could not write a book without you.

Finally, thank you to the Lord, who supernaturally provided all that I needed according to his riches in Christ Jesus as he does for every other need in my life.

About the Author

Bestselling author Sandra Byrd continues to earn both industry acclaim and high praise from readers everywhere. The author of more than fifty books, her work has received many awards, nominations, and accolades, including the Historical Novel Society's Editor's Choice award, two Christy Award nominations, two *Library Journal* Best Book selections, a *BookPage* Top Pick for Romance, and inclusion on *Booklist*'s Top Ten Inspirational Books of the Year list. In addition, as an editor and an in-demand writing coach, Sandra is passionate about helping writers develop their talents and has coached and mentored hundreds of writers at all stages of their writing careers.

A dedicated foodie from the age of sixteen, Sandra cooks through the topic and location of every book she writes. In her free time, she collects vintage glass and serve ware and loves long walks with her husband, Sunday Suppers with her growing family, and Mimi time with her precious granddaughter.

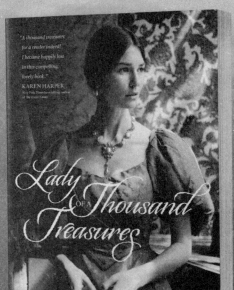